CARESSE

CARESSE

JOYCE WILSON

ST. MARTIN'S PRESS
NEW YORK

Library of Congress Cataloging-in-Publication Data

Wilson, Joyce.
    Caresse.

    I. Title.
PS3573.I4569677C37   1987   813'.54   87-26598
ISBN 0-312-01011-7

First published in Great Britain by Century Hutchinson Ltd.

First U.S. Edition

10 9 8 7 6 5 4 3 2 1

On the distant fields,
On the bird's wide wing,
On the whirlwind dark,
I write your name . . .

Eluard, poet of the
French Resistance, 1942

CHAPTER ONE

Once, in the dark ages whose long shadows still touched the quiet streets of the Paris suburb far below, the cell had been built to house two prisoners. Now the four women took turns in the hours after lights-out to sleep on the narrow beds that were fixed.to the longer walls. They had no means of telling the time, and it was pure instinct that told each of them when her turn had come. In the daytime, in a slow, deliberate routine, they folded one of the two beds flat to the scarred brickwork, to make room for exercise. They took turns – or those who could still walk took turns – to pace the length of their cell, from the barred square of pale light that was their window on a world that averted its gaze to the door with its one all-seeing eye.

It was important to keep to a fixed routine, they told each other. Otherwise inertia would creep up on them like some fifth prisoner and bring them all down. What remained unsaid was that it was important simply to stay alive.

After a few days the small, half-smothered cries of pain which the women gave as they eased their limbs from one oddly careful posture to another became almost companionable. A detached observer might have compared them to a group of caged animals seeking identity in rituals learned in captivity.

The night after her third beating Leonie made no sound. For several hours she wavered between consciousness and a kind of oblivion in which she was almost beyond pain. At a movement from one of the women, the girl whose turn it was

1

to take Leonie's place on the narrow bed spoke softly into the night. *'Laissez l'américaine. Elle a besoin de dormir.'*

Just before dawn she woke suddenly to total awareness, bile in her throat as sharp as fear. A noise from the heart of Fresnes prison had reached through the darkness and touched her.

'I killed a man.' It was always her waking thought. Her eyelids fluttered, seeking light, and for a moment she thought she was blind. She fought panic and a sense that she had been abandoned, until gradually the place in which she had spent the last four weeks edged into focus in the blurred dark.

She touched her eyelids, her fingers trailing on down the dry skin of her cheekbones to her throat. She swallowed nervously, remembering that the commandant had not let them touch her face. They had been ingenious, none the less.

As if to cut through the images of what had happened to her body in the hands of the Abwehr guards the night before, the grid in the door of the cell slid harshly open. One of the other women groaned as she put her feet to the floor and groped automatically for the chipped enamel mug that stood on the cell's only shelf above her bed. Still grumbling softly to herself, she shuffled in the direction of the panel of yellow light from the corridor that now gave the cell the aspect of a jaundiced, ageing engraving.

'I swear if I were one of Pavlov's dogs I'd have salivated when the bloody grey mouse was ten yards away,' the woman said. *'La souris grise'* was the nickname given throughout occupied France to the German women auxiliaries who had followed the Nazi troops in the summer of 1940 and settled down to what to them for the time being was a good war. They were even to be seen lunching at Maxim's in the drab grey uniform that gave them their name – much to the ill-concealed disgust of the maître d'hôtel.

From dark eyes sunk in a wasted face that had quite recently been beautiful the woman watched tepid liquid poured by an anonymous, grey-cuffed hand until it reached

2

the brim of her mug. A second woman joined her, waiting her turn for the morning ration of soup.

'Think yourself lucky we're not really part of some over-curious doctor's experiments – yet,' she whispered.

'It will come, ma chère. That is one thing you can be sure of in this uncertain world.'

The third voice came from the far corner, where a young girl with close-cropped hair crouched in the semblance of a foetus, knees hugged by stick-like arms to a matchstick frame.

'Silence!' the grey mouse spat in guttural French. 'Or your companion gets no soup today.'

'That's you, américaine,' the girl in the corner said.

Leonie sat up, too quickly. She lurched towards the white outline of the lavatory at the back of the cell. But moments later she had somehow rejoined the line of women at the door. In the last month she had learnt that if she was to survive she must take whatever food was offered. Today she was lucky. Her refusal to answer questions yet again on the previous night could have meant they would starve her. She drank greedily when her turn came, and had finished her portion of black bread before the grid of the cell door slid heavily into place.

Later she found the position in which her shoulders hurt the least, and lay on her side watching the morning slowly light up the wall above the opposite bed. A prisoner who was perhaps no longer alive had scratched a rough calendar on the worn brickwork, each day crossed through with a ragged line that became progressively weaker.

She lapsed into uneasy sleep again, wondering how many more days she herself would be there before she was moved on, or murdered, or grew too weak to care. And if she would ever see Tony again.

If anything worthwhile had come out of it all, it was the slim chance that Tony, who loved all things and could never bring himself to kill a fellow creature – as she had done – would be safe by now. Back in New York. Where it had all begun.

3

Leonie watched her mother through eyes narrowed against the sun as she picked her way along the copra matting catwalk, down the North Shore beach to the water's edge. A stiff breeze had come off the ocean that morning as they drove out of the city, but Zoe always insisted on her Sunday afternoon bathe. And an hour ago they had escaped the dreary formalities of a Long Island lunch party, leaving the other guests scattered post-prandial on an Italianate terrace amongst the surrealist sculptures that were the latest fad of their host.

With Leonie frowning at the nape of her mother's neck as if to convey to the world in general that the decision to leave had not come from her, Zoe of course made her usual stylish exit. She conveyed the impression that she had done them all a graceful favour by being there at all and knew she had been good value. Zoe always gave good value – as she did now to the appreciative males of the numerous families that had headed for the Island in the grip of what had become a stifling June day.

The faintly mechanical sway of her boyish hips was all that betrayed just how much Zoe's body owed to her masseur. Her tubular bathing dress – a fashion that had given most women that season the aspect of clowns – touched in all the right places; the bermuda-length drawers just cleared the delicate concave at the back of her knees.

She dropped a scarlet monogrammed towel at her feet and with a slender fan of finger nails painted in matching red tucked her dark bob into a bathing cap. Once in the water, she swam a dozen careful breast strokes parallel to the shore, touched bottom and swam back.

'Your sister sure has class,' a fat man in creased alpaca and a derby hat pushed to the summit of a sweating forehead called over to Leonie. He was perched a yard or two from where she sat, and dabbled a square hand in the shingle as he devoured Zoe's sauntering return.

Leonie closed her book with a snap. She did not need him

4

to touch her to know that his palms would be damp. The whole afternoon clung about her like an unwanted blanket, her thin, still childish body too heavy with indolence to shake it off. When she suggested that as she had her period she might just paddle in the shallows Zoe had told her sharply 'You're too old for such antics, baby', and she had flinched inwardly at the hated pet name.

It was one of the very few things that dated her mother. Zoe was a true daughter of the recently defunct Jazz Age, and it sometimes showed.

The fat man's mistaking them for sisters was nothing new. It had happened frequently since Leonie, against her mother's wishes, had bobbed her waist-length hair on her sixteenth birthday the previous summer. After the shouting match that followed they had stood side by side before the large gilt-edged mirror in the vestibule of the apartment off Gramercy Park and frowned ironic approval of the twin images that stared back.

They were much the same height, Zoe in her louis heels standing perhaps an inch taller than Leonie's five foot six. Mother stared quizzically at daughter from the same deep-set blue eyes under winged dark brows. Their skins were pale olive, stretched on high cheekbones. Both had identically small strong chins and straight noses. But there the likeness ended. Zoe's mouth was an artist's creation, a pouting bow of crimson concealing the thin line of the reality. Her daughter's lips were unpainted, the vulnerable curve an echo of the guarded look in the eyes. The truce was one of many, and would be short-lived.

At thirty-six Zoe Byron contrived, sustained, and paraded an image which with every step she took was a hymn to femininity and a bandbox advertisement for the beauty parlour she owned on West Forty-fourth. Her personalized range of treatments was the most expensive in New York, and she used them herself – to effect. It was also her frequent

5

claim that she had acquired her know-how in Paris, France. The claim was almost legitimate. On the euphoric wings that had borne the young in heart to Europe in 1919, Zoe had gone too.

In the flush of victory over the Kaiser in 1918, the Germans' sleeping resentment safely frozen in the mirrors of Versailles, Paris stretched graceful arms to all comers, and began a dance that was to last for twenty years.

Zoe liked dancing.

Everything Leonie knew about her mother started with that yellow-car exodus from a small mid-Western town which Zoe never saw again. And everything in their close-knit lives had been shaped by what followed, as sharply as Zoe's young wrist had been cut by the green rail ticket which she kept tucked in her glove all the way to New York.

Zoe arrived at Le Havre with the price of a month's stay in a modest Paris hotel, if she stuck to the frugality of the puritan inheritance she was about to discard. On board ship she avoided the bar and spent her evenings in an airless cabin with her Rosenthal, in a determined effort to improve on her schoolgirl French.

In the daytime she found herself adopted like some kind of mascot by a brace of young authors who favoured, respectively, E.M. Forster and James Joyce. Their much-thumbed copies of *Howards End* and *The Dubliners* were abandoned for long walks round C deck, while Zoe – a Princeton man on either side – regaled them with her plans for survival in France.

They were Zoe's first audience of any importance. They found her pert innocence and pretension to sophistication a delicious combination. She talked with them in sharp, witty little bursts of newly discovered – perhaps newly invented – philosophy that Forster would have appropriated on the spot for one of his forthright heroines. It was before her mouth narrowed into a careful line.

The Princeton men dropped her off at her Left Bank hotel, promising to return. In the privacy of her room she grimaced at the red flock wallpaper and unbuckled her valise. She hung the grey two-piece for which she had saved for months carefully in the ornate mahogany wardrobe. With instinctive flair she had gone for the one item in the mainstreet store in the mid-Western town that would pass for chic on the rue St Honoré.

At the bottom of the valise lay two pairs of strappy dance shoes wrapped in tissue paper to stop them from tarnishing – one pair silver, one gold. The beaded jacket rescued from Aunt Abbey's attic trunk would go over the blue silk with the handkerchief hem which Zoe had made herself – copied from a picture in a magazine she had found on the train on her trip east to stay with Aunt Abbey. It was thanks to her aunt that she had been able to make her escape to Europe unnoticed by the family back home.

'It's a vacation I just have to have,' Zoe told her aunt. 'I'll be back before anyone need be told a thing.'

As it was, by the time she did get back to the States Aunt Abbey had died and Zoe had added to her story many things that could not be told.

She was wearing the grey two-piece the afternoon she met Paul de Byron. The two Princeton men had called for her at her hotel and told her that they were invited to a literary tea party that would need some pepping up. Zoe, they assured her, would do just that.

The severity of the grey suit enhancing her particular brand of American prettiness, she was in fact the object of much attention. Enjoying the effect she created, Zoe was none the less subdued. She was aware of the hazel eyes of a young French officer who watched her for some time from across the room before he asked for an introduction. She accepted a cup of tea from a woman in a floating multi-coloured dress, pince-nez, and a pre-Raphaelite cloud of

7

auburn hair. The young officer stood back a pace, and she had time to notice that his blue uniform featured a great deal of gold braid and medals.

'Capitaine de Byron cannot stay long,' their hostess told Zoe. 'You must talk to him. He has the most ravishing *petit manoir* in the Pyrenees.'

At that moment Zoe was not exactly sure of the whereabouts of the Pyrenees, and something in her face must have given her away.

'The Pyrénées-atlantiques. Perhaps Biarritz is our most famous town.' He touched her white-gloved hand briefly and his hazel eyes smiled a little, belying the stiffly formal bearing of the St Cyr graduate. As they moved away together he took her cup and gestured towards a Louis Seize sofa that had somehow survived their hostess's obvious determination to turn the apartment into a mock-medieval treasure house. Zoe noticed then that Paul de Byron limped, quite badly.

'I am an escapee from the Military Hospital,' he told her in clipped, fluent English. 'Tonight is my last there, before I go home. I must see my doctor when he tours my ward – before he goes out for one of his enormous dinners.'

She suppressed a look of disappointment, and decided to try out her French.

'May I ask if you have many American friends in Paris, capitaine?'

Thanks to Rosenthal and a week listening avidly to everyone and everything about her, it was a success. Forty-eight hours later Paul de Byron was to confess to her that it had cost him all the discipline he had learnt at St Cyr not to lean forward and kiss this clever American child on her very straight nose.

'Perhaps only one – a new friend – that matters,' he answered in French. Then, as if to spare her any ambiguity, he went on in English for the rest of their conversation. 'If I am to get to know her before I go home I have to hurry. I am late already for *le grand travail* – I think your word is harvest.'

8

She looked at him with added interest. He did not have the appearance of a man who worked on the land. But then neither was he the sort of Frenchman she would have expected to meet in this ornate drawing-room over a cup of tea. The longer she spent in his company the more she believed that he was a man who belonged very much to himself.

'You have a farm?'

He shrugged. 'A small vineyard . . . which but for your country would not even exist. My grandparents faced ruin some years ago. The phylloxera. We lost everything, everything that had been ours for centuries. But we held on. Then we started again, in a small way, and the Bordeaux growers introduced an extraordinary idea. We grafted native vines on to good, imported American stock, which was immune.'

'I should like to try the wine that came from that,' Zoe said.

'Perhaps one day you shall. They made excellent companions,' Paul murmured, and then fell silent, leaving her to wonder if he had intended the metaphor.

Suddenly he stood up, leaning on the sofa's arm to get to his feet. Not for the first time she thought he was probably in some pain.

'It would give me infinite pleasure to dine with you in Paris before I leave, mademoiselle. For perhaps two or three nights after I am discharged from hospital I shall stay at a family apartment – it belongs to my father's sister – on the other side of the Seine. May I call for you at your hotel, perhaps tomorrow evening?'

Mentally she ran quickly through the contents of her valise. The beaded jacket was warm enough for mid-September – or so she hoped. Fall seemed to have come sooner here in Paris than back home. Only that morning she had stepped through a flurry of leaves on the sidewalk beneath the chestnut trees in the avenue Foch. She would blow her rainy-day savings on a silver hairband she had glimpsed in the window of an exclusive boutique in a side street off the Champs Élysées, and wear the silver shoes.

'Why, I'd like that very much, Capitaine de Byron,' she said, smiling, and she gave him the directions to her hotel.

'It's your birthday next Sunday,' Zoe told Leonie through a cloud of cigarette smoke. The windows of the living-room were wide open and the smells of New York in high summer were laced with Zoe's perfume. Sunday was their cook-general Maddie's day off, and they had come back from the beach to be greeted by a blast of oven-like heat from the closed rooms. Zoe had raced the length of the hallway to her bedroom and flung open the sash windows before she went into the bathroom beyond it and began to run a bath. 'We could go to the Penthouse if you want.' The restaurant, on Central Park South, was enjoying a vogue.

Leonie stared impassively at her mother.

'Antoine would make a cake for you.' Zoe tried again. 'You'd like that. And I saw Charles Boyer eating there last time.'

They sat facing each other on twin white sofas on either side of a low table made of tubular steel and glass. Leonie stifled the impulse to rise to this particular bait. She had lately become a film buff, rushing straight from school to the movies two or three times a week, and getting home just before Zoe's own return from the salon.

Now she thought how they themselves resembled two characters in some film about wealthy people who had forgotten what it was to love and be loved.

'Maddie always makes my cake.'

'OK. So Maddie can make the cake. But what shall we do after? Seventeen's a special age.'

'It would be nice to *do* nothing, Mother.' Leonie stretched her long legs on the sofa's plump cushions in a maddening gesture of pretended boredom.

Zoe tensed visibly. 'I've got your present. Got it weeks ago. It's all packed up.'

10

Leonie said nothing. The mother-daughter battles were getting more frequent, but she never actually intended to provoke them. Yet she found herself hating the thought of the perfect gifts in the perfect packing, the mute pleas for affection they embodied. And this sudden out-of-the-blue mention of her age annoyed her more than anything. Until now there had always been the studious avoidance of the subject of her age in front of the birthday guests who were always chosen by Zoe and always came. The delicate way in which they all moved around the subject of her ever-absent father made the occasion an annual ordeal. Ever since she had known the truth about her birth.

Since then Paul de Byron had seemed to stand each year at her shoulder, like a ghost, as she blew out the candles on the cakes Maddie always made.

'Anyone could guess you're late Gemini.' Zoe took refuge from the growing storm in a quasi-change of subject. 'I hardly know what you're thinking these days. Or how you're going to turn out, for that matter.' She got up and crossed the room to the cocktail bar and its gleaming battery of glass. 'Damn, there's no ice.' She spoke loudly, as if still seeking a safer subject.

'I dare say I'll turn out your way, Mother,' Leonie said with infuriating casualness as she got up and went into the kitchen to check the icebox. 'Like all of your clients. To the Zoe Byron image.'

Zoe took the ice without thanking her and mixed her cocktail. As she took her place on the sofa again she put her glass on the low table with a slight tap, concealing her mounting anger in the controlled gesture.

'It would be quite a cliché – hardly your style at all, Leonie – if you were to resort to judging me at this late date.'

'I'm not judging you, Mother. It's just that I'd like for once to do things my way. You have everything planned. Our Sundays, my birthdays. Our lives.'

'I was under the impression' – Zoe's tone was flat with control now – 'that I had just asked you what you would like to do next Sunday.'

11

'Oh, is that what you said? I thought it was what *we* should do.'

Zoe emptied her glass. 'When you have thought of something you have only to tell me. Now, let's eat.'

Zoe was at the kitchen door, her back to her daughter, when Leonie announced that on her seventeenth birthday she wanted neither to swim, nor to eat cake, nor to make polite talk with her mother's friends.

When Zoe turned to face her Leonie saw that the colour had drained from her mother's face.

'It just so happens,' Zoe said evenly, 'that if you're really set on making your own plans for next Sunday, that suits me. I wasn't going to be the one to spoil the day. But if that's the way you want to play it, then it lets me out. Erich Mannheim gets in on the *Normandie* on Friday night. He wants me to spend Sunday with him.'

At the mention of her mother's Swiss banker, Leonie bit her lip. Erich Mannheim had been a frequent visitor at the apartment on his last stay in New York, which was unusual. Zoe rarely mixed business with pleasure. Maddie had a habit, too, of freezing any male caller with one look that ensured he would not lightly call again.

What Zoe did on West Forty-fourth was her business. Gramercy Park was sacred.

But Erich Mannheim seemed immune to Maddie's disapproval, and on his last visit had taken to calling unannounced, always bringing flowers for Zoe and some small gift for Leonie. He knew better, it seemed, than to attempt to bribe Maddie herself.

A heavily built figure touching six foot, he had close-cropped fair hair and pale blue eyes that followed Zoe with what seemed to Leonie a mixture of admiration and concealed amusement. For her part, Zoe treated him with quiet friendliness in front of the Gramercy Park household, always thanking him for the flowers, and frowning at Leonie if she did not match her enthusiasm.

Leonie resented the gifts, as she resented the heavy

12

masculinity of his intrusion at the apartment. She hardly knew why, but the news of his impending arrival disconcerted her. She was not aware of any romantic relationship between her mother and Erich Mannheim, or for that matter between Zoe and any of the numerous men with whom she had business dealings. But the Swiss banker was the first to be asked to stay for an impromptu supper when he called (again uninvited) earlier that year – in spite of the waves of disapproval Maddie sent down the hall in his wake.

'Will Erich come to the apartment on Sunday?' Leonie hoped she sounded disinterested. 'I think I'll take in a movie with some of the girls from class if he does.'

'Of course he'll call for me here,' Zoe said casually. 'But it's Maddie's day off. I guess we'll eat out.'

Both of them sounded vaguely disappointed, as if each had won some Pyrrhic victory. An outright shouting match would have left a cleaner mood. For the next five days they met only at breakfast, and hardly spoke. Zoe was working late each night at the salon and Maddie prepared a supper tray for her after Leonie had gone to bed. On Friday night the phone rang, and through the half-open door of her room Leonie heard her mother welcome Erich Mannheim to New York in honeyed tones.

A few moments later Zoe walked in and sat on the rose-sprigged coverlet. 'Are you sure you won't join us, baby?' Her voice was conciliatory. 'He's remembered your birthday. I must have mentioned it way back some time. He has a very special gift for you, he says.'

'It's too late, Mother; I've made plans now with Sue and her brother . . . there's a Jean Harlow movie and I'm eating at their place.'

They avoided each other's eyes as Zoe smoothed the coverlet with a thin, careful hand. 'I suppose it had to come sooner or later.' The voice matched her touch. 'But I'd have liked to tell Maddie. Your cake has been all she's talked about every night this week. I hadn't the heart to stop her.'

'We could have it in the morning. With coffee,' Leonie said miserably.

13

'I have a better idea.' Zoe jumped up and went to the mirror, then turned dramatically, smiling at the girl who in the last few days had begun to assume the aura of a stranger. 'We'll have the cake mid-morning, as you say. Maddie can be there, before she goes to her sister's. But we'll not have coffee. We'll drink champagne!'

Mother and daughter stared at each other. The storm, they both knew, was safely weathered this time. But both knew also that they had reached a milestone in their relationship.

On Sunday, Maddie agreed to stay for the opening of Leonie's presents and the cutting of the cake. She had bought Leonie a thick handknitted sweater in tangerine. Maddie loved bright colours and expected her friends to share her taste. Zoe's gift was a silk dress, with a rosette at each shoulder. Delicate and frivolous as Zoe herself in a good mood.

Leonie was kissing her mother and Maddie had just opened the champagne when the doorbell rang. Erich Mannheim was early, very sure of his welcome. Moments later he sat on a sofa, his presence filling the room. Smiling up at Leonie from the pale blue eyes she now actively disliked, he held out a slim package tied with gold ribbon.

'Seventeen is a very special age, I always think,' he said in his slightly guttural but otherwise faultless English. Leonie frowned. It was the second time she had heard the remark in a week. She took the package and began to untie the ribbon. Zoe – for Maddie had flounced into the kitchen to fetch her Sunday hat – fluttered into action, pouring champagne into a fourth glass. She brought the drinks to the low table just as Leonie raised the lid of a white leather box and lifted a long rope of perfect milk-white pearls in a hand that suddenly trembled.

'My word, such pearls,' Zoe said.

'Do you like them? Why don't you put them on?' Erich

leant back, his eyes on Leonie's face.

'They're very beautiful. Thank you.' Leonie looked at her mother. 'I'll try them later today. Maybe with my new dress.'

'Show Erich the dress, honey,' Zoe suggested. Leonie caught what she took for a conspiratorial smile. Did they still see her as a child to be humoured, or worse still put on display? The gift of the pearls had been planned between them; she was suddenly certain of it. This large, alien man who seemed so close to her mother hoped to win her affection with so crude a ploy. She had grown used to such tactics from Zoe, and would have loved her had there been no gifts. Erich, complacent, knowing, already going to seed, she could never even bring herself to like.

The minutes that followed were like a charade. They drank champagne, and ate the cake under Maddie's approving eye.

'I'm so happy at this moment.' Zoe raised her glass.

'Sho' you's happy, honey,' Maddie grimaced behind Erich Mannheim's back, 'but don't you worry – you'll get over it.'

'You stole that line from the maid in *China Seas*,' Leonie grinned suddenly. Maddie loved acting the theatrical Black.

'No. That coloured girl who played Jean Harlow's maid stole it from all us who know it's real-life true.' Maddie patted her hat into place and made for the hall. 'See you tomorrow, birthday girl.' She was gone.

Erich looked at his watch and Leonie gathered up her presents and took them to her room. When she returned she had her purse with her, and kissed her mother on both cheeks. She held out her hand to Erich, who stood and bowed formally. Her hand lay heavily in his for a fraction of a second before she pulled away. Moments later she was walking rapidly through the sweltering streets, a long-legged colt of a girl unaware of the way men's eyes waited for her as she came towards them.

CHAPTER TWO

If Paul Byron had sent her pearls, Leonie told herself as she walked, she would have worn them. With the silk dress, with Maddie's tangerine knit, under her bodice at school. But he had never acknowledged her birthday, and she had thought she had grown used to the fact – until now. It was something she could not have mentioned to Zoe. They had not discussed her father for some years. Not, in fact, since the day she had learned the truth.

'You may be a bastard,' Zoe spoke in the cool drawl she had adopted years before on her return to New York, 'but you're a bastard out of the top drawer. Your father was too proud, not too ashamed, to face me. Don't ever forget that we have his name. And it's because he was from one of the best families in France that I spend every cent of my allowance from Paris on that snob school of yours. My work provides us with all the other goodies.'

The day after their conversation Leonie had sat at her desk in the 'snob school', dreading the moment when her name would be called on the register. Until then she had always believed that Zoe was a widow and that her father had died of wounds received in the war in France, not living long enough to know that his daughter had been born.

Now she felt that everyone at school, in her class, must have known the truth all along. Everyone except her. When she answered roll-call she felt sure that her voice would give her away, betraying her new knowledge that the name was not hers by right, and that her mother had fought for it as she had fought for everything since.

'Leonie Byron.' The words came from a great distance.

16

Her mouth dried. The name was repeated. She answered.

To her surprise the earth did not open to swallow her up. No one turned round to snigger. The deep blush that had spread from her throat to her hair had gone unnoticed. But from that moment the knowledge that she was illegitimate became a dull ache, sharper on the day, early each calendar month, when the allowance from the offices of the Parisian lawyers Charles Vincent et fils dropped unfailingly through the mailbox.

There was never a letter with the cheque. Leonie had sneaked a look more than once. The anonymous complimentary slip initialled in violet ink in a sloping, Gallic hand was the only sign that any human agency had been employed in the operation at all. In Zoe's frequent absences at the salon Leonie would study the lawyer's address for hours at a time. She knew it by heart. Boulevard de la Madeleine. Paris. France. It held no clues to the things she really wanted to know.

What Zoe had withheld from her was the most important detail of all. That Paul de Byron had never been told that Leonie, his daughter by the pretty American girl he had once loved, even existed.

Three days after Zoe's first meeting with Paul, his Tante Berthe had come home to her apartment in the tall, narrow house just off the rue de Rivoli to find a dark-haired, fine-boned American girl helping him to pack. Her nephew's bedroom was golden with the shadows of an afternoon in late fall. The bed was neatly made; perhaps too neatly. The heavy white lace coverlet was turned down in a fashion strange to her, to show matching pillows edged with the same heavy lace that was a de Byron heirloom.

Her tall aristocratic elegance framed against the dark hallway, Tante Berthe spoke quickly – in French – to her nephew. Zoe could not quite catch the words. But the tone, of dry humour tinged with disapproval, was unmistakable.

17

Afterwards they sipped aperitifs in the drawing-room, the curtains closed against the noise of the evening traffic. This was a *quartier* where the old families of Paris still maintained their town houses. The de Byrons, Tante Berthe told Zoe, had once owned the entire building, but had long since sold off the other floors to pay for the upkeep of their beloved ancestral home in the Pyrenees.

'My nephew must go home before the winter. To Briteau. His father needs him there. My brother is *un grand monsieur* in that region, mademoiselle. There is much for Paul to do.'

As Zoe put down her empty glass Tante Berthe said that she must be sure to call on her again while she stayed in Paris. It was the signal to leave.

'I would be enchanted to do so, madame,' Zoe answered in her best French – much improved by the three days with Paul. Her effort evoked no more than a look of veiled amusement. Irony, Zoe was to learn, was Berthe's hallmark.

'You are very pretty, mademoiselle.'

Zoe's chin went up a fraction of an inch. Being in love with Paul gave her the courage to weather this first encounter with his family. She had been sincere when she said she would like to call again at the apartment. With Paul at Briteau for the harvest there would be so few links with him. She intended, if she could find a job, to stay on in Paris until he could get back to her. She had not yet booked her passage home. In fact the way her money had gone in the last few days – on hairdressers, more shoes, a bottle of fine cognac she had bought for Paul as a farewell gift – she would have to find work to get home at all. As other expatriates she had met were already doing all over Paris.

She went to the bathroom while Paul waited with his aunt. As she crossed the hall on the way back to the drawing-room she was in time to see Tante Berthe through the half-open door fold the lace cloth on which she had served the drinks, an air of grim finality in the movements of her strong hands.

'Such a girl, of course, is not for you,' she said in crisp, aristocratic French which Zoe had no trouble at all in understanding. Paul did not reply, and she could not see his face.

She stood very still, counting to five. Her first lesson in survival surprised in her a talent for thinking fast when at bay. She walked back into the drawing-room the picture of transatlantic unconcern, blue eyes merely darkened by unshed tears. This stifling apartment and its intransigent owner were her only contact with Paul from now on, and she would not lightly throw them away.

In the teeth of Paul's silence she went through the goodbyes as if nothing had happened. Her eyes told Berthe: 'If you want to make me your enemy, then you must get to know me first.' She asked to call on her again, ignoring a slight gesture of contradiction from Paul, and suggesting a day the following week so prettily that his aunt dryly agreed. It was a deft move, and both women were aware of its significance. But when she made it Zoe had no idea how important it was to prove.

Within three weeks the calls at the de Byron apartment had become a habit. Zoe began to gain ground with this dark-eyed, ramrod Frenchwoman who had much of the American girl's spirit in her make-up. By the time she had guessed that Zoe was pregnant – almost as soon as Zoe herself was sure – they had established enough mutual respect for Berthe to face her with the truth.

'If you go to Briteau – and I hardly think you can afford the journey, nor the risk to your pride – then the family will ignore you, believe me. Paul is needed there. His father is dying; there is no money. It is you who will be seen as the guilty one. He would follow whatever line the family took, if it came to a confrontation. You are not for him.'

'Would he say so if he knew that I am to have his child? And that I love him?'

The Frenchwoman smiled, shaking her head. 'There are half a dozen girls of noble, wealthy families in the region – here in Paris, too – ready to give my nephew a child. Does that surprise you? You Americans who come to France and

19

talk and think and write of love. You lack the ancient virtues. Loyalty, for one. The de Byrons require Paul's loyalty. As a soldier he understands such things. They also need money . . . a great deal of money. Love will not come into it, when my nephew marries.'

Zoe knew it was true. True enough for Tante Berthe to become her ally in the conspiracy of silence that was to protect Paul from all knowledge of Zoe's condition. It was the price she had to pay if she was to be helped. Paul was not even to know she was still in Paris.

It was agreed that in return for her discretion Zoe would be granted an interview with the de Byron notary, Monsieur Charles Vincent. He and Paul's aunt would between them make all the arrangements. For the *accouchement*, the financial settlement, and the journey.

'The journey?' Zoe stared blankly across the white lace cloth and the remainder of their tea.

'Back to New York. Where you belong. How else could we hope to keep your secret for a lifetime? If we are to help you at all, then you will undertake never to return to this country. Neither you nor your child. If you did so, it would cost you everything I am prepared to pay.'

'If I go back to the States,' Zoe said after a short silence, 'I travel first class. And everything I need will match up to that. Is that understood?'

'I am glad you did not weep,' Tante Berthe replied. 'For that, you get your first class passage. I will see to it that Monsieur Vincent arranges these matters.'

At eleven next morning Zoe turned into the boulevard de la Madeleine, shivering in the wind that had taken Paris in its grip for the last few days. In the ancient iron lift that jerked its way to the *deuxième étage* she rubbed at her cheeks, knowing she looked too pale. Moments later a white-haired notary's clerk ushered her into a large panelled room overlooking the boulevard.

20

Charles Vincent stood behind a wide leather-topped desk, the picture of professional integrity, a single pearl in his grey silk cravat betraying something of vanity perhaps in an ageing, still handsome man.

He took his seat as Zoe settled in the high-backed chair facing him across the desk. She did not realize that the play he made of sorting the papers before him was because he needed time to absorb the shock of her appearance. The girl who had walked into his office was no more than a child to his eyes, and yet she carried herself with an elegance that would not shame a Parisienne. He knew she had no money, yet her innate style and the clever, pale face spoke of infinite potential. She was not beautiful, but to the lawyer Zoe's firm chin and the blue eyes now tinged with a dark, wild quality made her deeply attractive.

In carefully modulated tones Charles Vincent began his recital of the conditions on which the de Byron family would take the American girl under its wing.

Paul de Byron was never to know of the existence of this child. The birth would take place in New York. The mother would undertake never to return to France, and never to allow the child to travel to its father's native country. In return for these undertakings the mother would receive a settlement for life on herself and the child, to be paid by the offices of Vincent, notary of Paris. If the conditions were broken, the allowance would automatically cease.

Zoe heard him out, then as he looked down at his papers again fought inwardly for the self-control which she knew she was going to need if she was to survive on at least some of her own terms. This was not a man to be swayed by hysterics; Charles Vincent was merely a front for the steely woman who had arranged all this. Tante Berthe was as real a presence in the offices overlooking the boulevard de la Madeleine as she had been that afternoon almost ten weeks ago when she had stood framed in the doorway of her nephew's bedroom and assessed in one glance that Zoe was not for him.

When Zoe spoke at last it was in a low, fierce voice, very fast, and with such conviction that the notary listened without interruption, his eyes not leaving her face.

'These things are monstrous. I love Paul de Byron. I believe he loves me. Whether he knows of its existence or not, our child must have his name. I'll make no promises unless I get that promise from you first, Monsieur Vincent.'

Charles Vincent raised one eyebrow. 'The family name is a matter of much gravity. My client will be most reluctant in this matter; I can tell you that before I consult her. And if I am able to arrange anything at all, chère mademoiselle, it would not include the *particule*.'

Zoe looked puzzled.

'The "de" Byron is out of the question. For you to return to America with what amounts almost to an aristocratic title here in France would be to invite ridicule, you must believe me. But . . . perhaps a simple, single *nom de famille*? Tell me, does the name Byron in itself – I should say by itself – appeal to you?'

She sat quite still, her hands clasped tightly on the grey of her skirt, white-gloved fingers straining against a sudden, furious urge to scatter all the papers on the desk before sweeping out of the lawyer's office and telling him to go to hell.

'It will be quite acceptable, monsieur, so long as my own conditions are met. You know of them?'

He spread his hands. 'You will travel in the fashion suited to your condition. Rest assured that such details are in the hands of my most trusted assistant. There is no need for us to bargain with each other . . .'

Zoe nodded, thinking that if this was not bargaining then she would like to see him in the market place buying from the peasant farmers she had encountered on an early morning walk with Paul to Les Halles. 'Very well.'

'But remember.' The notary held up a warning hand. 'Just as I can do such things for you at the touch of a pen to paper, I can also undo them – and with equal facility. Is that understood?'

A fortnight later, her pregnancy confirmed in a discreet private clinic in the Paris *faubourgs*, and the examination paid for – in cash – by the clerk from the boulevard de la Madeleine who had accompanied her, Zoe sailed for New York.

The name on her papers was Zoe Byron. Her purse was filled with French bank notes of high denomination. She travelled A Deck.

She stood for a moment in her stateroom when she arrived, surveying the red flock wallpaper with some disdain, before she rang for the steward and demanded to see the purser. Ten minutes later her set of pigskin luggage was transferred to a luxury suite recently made over in art deco.

There she spent the voyage being sick and reading a dozen French beauty magazines she had brought from Paris. Occasionally she varied her occupation by making notes on how she would invest the allowance she would receive from the de Byrons, and make a living for herself and her child by her own wits.

More rarely, she looked in the mirror. If the image of Paul de Byron and their first meeting ever intruded, she developed a technique for blanking out her thoughts. For as long as she lived she never again wore grey. And in none of the homes she was to make for herself was there ever a drape or a cloth or a coverlet edged in white lace.

The first of Zoe Byron's homes on her return to New York and the news of Aunt Abbey's death was a cheap cold-water apartment down town. On the day she moved in she wrote to inform her family that Aunt Abbey's walk-up apartment had been taken by the owners of the block and that she herself was staying on elsewhere to find work. Her visit to France was not mentioned; her new address was not at the head of the letter. Within days she had disappeared into the city forest as if it were her natural habitat. There the law of survival – instilled in her blood as she sat in the second-floor offices overlooking the boulevard de la Madeleine – applied.

There was no false economy in the way Zoe handled her pregnancy. The cheap apartment released cash for the latest pre-natal treatment and the smartest back-street clinic in town was booked months ahead for the confinement. Maddie Smith, the young negress who lived across the hall, saw to it that Zoe ate for two.

Maddie, already plump, and a great cook, was recovering from a love affair and had vowed she would never go with another man. She too had run to New York from a Calvinistic background and could not run back. Zoe never did get to know how deep the hurt had gone for Maddie, but the vow stuck . . . all the way to Gramercy Park. And in that long summer of 1920 the two women licked their wounds, stayed close, and prepared to guard the unborn baby like the pair of young urban tigresses they had become.

Very early on a June morning, Leonie was born. Three hours later Zoe sat up against the feather pillows in the high clinical bed and dictated a cable to the offices of Charles Vincent, Paris, France. On the day she carried her baby home the first of the monthly envelopes containing the de Byron allowance was on the mat. Inside, nothing more personal than the initials CV in violet ink marked the meeting in Paris. Next morning Zoe came to a business arrangement with Maddie, moved the crib across the hall for the day, and went to look for work.

Six months give a week or so before Leonie's birth the 18th Amendment had finally run the whole country dry, and Prohibition had put a lot of small hoodlums into much bigger time. Among them was ex-cab driver Larry Fay, whose long-nurtured ambitions to carve for himself a niche in New York society now came into their own.

Zoe chose night work because it meant she could be at home during most of the baby's waking hours, and Maddie could then find a day job of her own. A day or two spent making the rounds of the agencies convinced Zoe that her best strategy was to tour the night spots on her own and not

24

be tied for good to some ten per cent arrangement and a bad scene.

She found a hostess job quite soon, in a dance hall favoured by a clientèle she thought she could bear to be touched by if the price were right – small out-of-town businessmen, guests of the newly booming ad-world two blocks away on Madison. They were good spenders, and went for her convincing act as a half-French war widow. She kept rigidly to house rules and never so much as left the building with a client to smoke a cigarette. She wore out the silver sandals, and then the gold, in two months flat.

The third month, when Zoe was breaking in a pair of new silver shoes, Larry Fay happened to call in to discuss a takeover with the club's owner. He was looking for a class joint, as he characteristically put it. His years in the front seat of a cab had made Larry a snob, but he was an informed snob, and had the inside knowledge he needed when he decided to go places. None of them knew it that night, but buying the club where Zoe worked was his first step towards founding the legendary Beaux Arts on Fortieth.

One glimpse of Zoe as she took the floor with a client told Larry that her presence would lend any place that certain something which brought people – and their money – back again. Once he knew she went with the deal, he wrote her a long-term contract.

Right from the start Larry knew that Zoe was not the material for an affair. They saw each other as useful commodities. Once Larry knew about the baby he saw that Zoe got home by cab every night, fast and safe as he put it. This routine had a double purpose, being also designed to reassure Larry's steady girl, Mary Louise.

There was only one thing Larry was scared of . . . and that was Mary Louise. 'Make love or else' the other girls called her, in tribute to the constant gleam in her eyes and the size of her biceps. She had been a regular winner on the beauty queen circuit when she and Larry got together, and she considered him to be her very own property. She was not so

25

dumb that she could not see in Zoe the symbol of what Larry wanted for himself. Mary Louise lacked the style that was to be the imprint of his biggest club, El Fay's.

When El Fay's was in its early stages Mary Louise began to drop hints to Larry that Zoe would not be moving on there with them. The night Larry found the nerve to pass on the information to Zoe herself, she shrugged her thin, square shoulders and walked away . . . making for the group of richest-looking men in that night and breaking the rules by staying at their table the whole session.

She had picked well; a party of out-of-town bankers passing the hours after a gloom and doom-laden convention in a desperate last fling before the high jump.

'If your bank really is going to have to close,' Zoe fixed blue eyes on the youngest, best-looking – and least drunk – man at the table, 'what do you have to lose? Why not unload fast, into something that will pay off? We should talk. I have ideas. I also have some savings, believe it or not.'

Next day a demurely elegant Zoe called at the banker's hotel. The top-notch quality of her clothes, her hairstyle, and her manners did not escape him in the sobering light of morning. The deeds for the premises of her first beauty parlour were in her handbag, and she signed them next day. Only she and her backer knew that the salon – although the treatments and the products were to be genuine – was a front.

The Byron beauty parlour was a long, narrow establishment with an intimate reception in the front of the shop, treatment rooms behind, and finally a back room with an exit in another street. In the back room was a speakeasy . . . with a difference: the clientèle was limited to ladies only.

Prohibition lasted long enough for Zoe to make herself and her friend from the bank a small fortune. When the repeal came in she was able to send Leonie to the best high school in the city without asking Charles Vincent for a cent more. On her thirteenth birthday Leonie was a guest at the opening of her mother's first wholly genuine beauty salon, on West Forty-fourth.

Zoe's clientèle was ready-made. Most of them stayed on from the speakeasy days to repair the ravages wrought by what they had consumed in the back room. Many of them were married to men in high places. There were other bankers to see Zoe through the Depression, convinced by their wives' argument that the worse things got the better face they all had to present to the world if they wished to survive.

Sometimes this argument was part of very private conversations between Zoe and the men she found to keep her financially afloat. But not one of the transactions on which her survival depended was negotiated within the chaste white walls of Gramercy Park.

None, that is, until Erich Mannheim came into her life.

It was no coincidence that Erich was a man whose appearance, origins and sense of values were all in direct contrast to those of the young French army officer who was the only man Zoe ever really loved. Perhaps because the child she had had by Paul de Byron had reached the age of rebellion, perhaps because Erich Mannheim lived for making money – and Zoe could identify with the cause with all her soul – she allowed the Swiss banker to lay siege to her as she had allowed no man since her return from Paris.

At a distance of two thousand miles Zoe had successfully cultivated the sense of *chic* which had first excited her in Paris. And Erich Mannheim, who loved Paris as only the sybaritic Goth can, knew the moment he set eyes on her that that was where she belonged. He did not know for some time that it was the one place on earth forbidden to her.

On her way to Sue's house on her seventeenth birthday, Leonie Byron, walking fast, thought of her father. Halfway through the Jean Harlow movie she thought of him again.

The break with birthday tradition achieved, she had discovered in herself the need for other changes. She needed to ask more questions.

Not for the first time, she remembered how her mother always assiduously avoided any talk of Europe, and especially of France. Her father's name had not been mentioned for three years – not since the day she had learned the truth about her birth.

When they left the cinema she made her excuses and took the subway home, staring straight ahead as the car swayed and rattled on its way. Out on the street again she walked quickly through the park and into the apartment building. She already had her key in her hand as she stepped out of the elevator.

The apartment was in shadows, and a slight touch of cool air on her face as she closed the door surprised her, making her wonder if her mother had accidentally left a window open somewhere. In the drawing-room the curtains were drawn against the sunlight. She sat on a sofa, and noticed that the champagne glasses were still on the table, unwashed. It was unlike her mother. In Maddie's absence Zoe kept everything in order against the eagle-eyed inspection of her return.

Automatically, Leonie picked up the tray of glasses and rose to take them into the kitchen. Her footsteps made no noise on the deep white carpet of the drawing-room. But she stopped dead in her tracks as from the direction of the master bedroom came the sound of her mother's low, delighted laugh.

Her face scarlet, she put the tray down carefully and listened, looking round as if for somewhere to hide from what she knew she should not witness. There was a brief silence. For a moment she found herself hoping that she had imagined things, that her mother was alone, perhaps had laughed out loud at some private thought. She re-crossed the drawing-room to the hall, and paused close to her mother's bedroom door.

She was in time to hear a man's voice. Guttural, intimate, and known to her. Erich Mannheim's tone was unmistakable, although it was a tone she had not heard in a man's voice except in the movies. She trembled slightly, not knowing what to do next. Then, as she turned to escape, the bedroom door opened.

She rounded on Zoe in time to glimpse through the half-open door the blond, close-cropped head on the high soft pillows of her mother's bed.

Her eyes not leaving Leonie's face, Zoe put a hand in hers and almost led her back into the drawing-room. She wore a white silk pyjama set that Leonie had always liked, but now she was aware only of the outline of her mother's nakedness beneath the silk. She bit her lip, her eyes heavy with a rush of tears.

Zoe made her sit down. 'I'm sorry it had to happen this way, baby,' she said at last.

Leonie shook her head, swallowing a sob. 'I'm *not* a baby, Mother. I've not been that for a long time. Not for three years.' She could not resist the stab at the fact of her illegitimacy.

'You're still my child.'

'Not only yours. That's why I came home early. I suddenly knew in the movies what I really wanted to do today.'

'Of course, honey. Anything.' Zoe seemed to welcome what appeared to be a reprieve.

'There's a letter I want to write. And something I have to ask.'

'Go ahead.' Zoe walked to the bar and took a cigarette.

'Please don't do that, Mother. This is too important. After what's happened I won't take no for an answer.'

Zoe put down the cigarette and moved to the window. A bar of pale gold striped one of the sofas. Outside, the afternoon was carefree, summer at its height, but the room in which mother and daughter faced each other seemed sculpted in ice.

29

'What has "happened" does not give you the right to become an adult in the space of a single afternoon,' Zoe said warily, her eyes still on some imaginary scene of interest in the street below.

'Look at me, Mother. Please.' There was a movement from the direction of the master bedroom, and Leonie glanced over her shoulder, willing Erich Mannheim to leave them alone for a few seconds more.

Zoe turned back into the room. 'As I said, I'm sorry.' She touched Leonie's flushed cheek lightly, brushing back a stray wisp of dark hair. 'You know this is not the way things usually are.'

'No, Mother.' Leonie resisted the impulse to slap the soft hand with its scarlet nails away. 'That's just what I don't know. There's so much I haven't been told. That's why I've made up my mind. I want – I *am* leaving New York. The school. Everything. I want to go to Europe. To my father.'

CHAPTER THREE

The pearls sprayed in a long, milk-white line across her dressing table. She watched them as she lay in the darkened bedroom where she had run after her outburst, not waiting for a response from her mother. It was almost an hour then before the sound of the vestibule door falling softly into place told her that she and Zoe were once more alone in the apartment.

A moment later there was a tap at the door and Zoe came in, fully dressed now in a cocktail gown of dark blue lamé. Her hair was brushed back from a face that had been made up with particular care, and Leonie knew that the skin was deathly white beneath the delicate mask.

'Are you going out?' She eyed the blue lamé as Zoe crossed the room towards her, touching the back of an antique chair upholstered in velvet as she passed.

'Remember when we chose the things for this room?' Zoe perched in her usual place on the coverlet. 'We had such fun in those days. Perhaps we should do it all over again. I could buy a house. Pity you're too old for jump rope. A yard would be nice, wouldn't it?'

Taken unawares by the total absence of pleading in her mother's voice, Leonie listened dumbfounded to this sudden dream of domestic bliss. Perhaps there was something really serious between her mother and Erich Mannheim and it had triggered off a nostalgic mood. Somewhere at the edge of Leonie's mind was the glimpse of a blond head on a white pillow. It was as if that presence still clung about them both, and she lay motionless, aware of the weight of her mother's body close beside her on the bed.

31

It was Zoe who deflected the images, reaching out gently to smooth her hair. Leonie shook her head impatiently, the exquisite cut of her bob making the gesture superfluous as her hair fell back into place of its own accord.

'You know,' Zoe persevered, 'I've decided I like your hair short after all. Best in summer, too. And Maddie was always the only one who could tie those braids.'

Her daughter nodded miserably. If it had not been Maddie's day off . . . if she herself had not rejected the birthday routine. . . if. 'Is Maddie staying over at her sister's place?' Sometimes Maddie took a whole twenty-four hours' break and they made Monday morning breakfast for themselves.

'Oh, honey, I have a working breakfast . . . someone from Europe. No, not the someone you're thinking. From Paris. But after what you said just now I didn't want to bring France into the conversation.'

'I meant what I said. It's not just because of today. But that did make it kind of final. And if I am going to Paris, Mother, it's the best time. Semester ends next week, you know. Lots of girls leave at seventeen.'

'You're not giving up school now. And you're not going to France. There's a lot you have to learn, and not only at school.'

'I know enough now to want to see my father.'

'You know nothing!' Zoe got up and began to pace about the room. 'Hell, you might as well get it straight once and for all. Those very welcome cheques – if you set one foot in France they stop. Just like that.' She snapped her fingers.

'Does it matter? I'd not be costing you the school fees.'

'That's not the point. I want so much for you. You are a de Byron. It's something I never thought to tell you, but the family pays us to keep our distance. Leonie, your very existence makes them uncomfortable.'

'You mean you bargained with them? Over me?'

'Not with your father,' Zoe said quickly, coming back to the bed. 'Don't ever think that.' She hesitated. 'I had no choice. It was how I got home. How I was able to keep you. The only way.'

'I don't believe it!' Leonie swung her long legs to the ground and stood staring down into her mother's upturned face.

'It's true. If you go to Paris, the contract ends. And if you came back to New York there'd be no money here for you either. I'd see to that.'

'You'd go so far to stop me?'

'I won't have you hurt as I was hurt.' Zoe's voice was harsh with suppressed emotion.

'There are things you haven't told me, aren't there? You're trying to shock me out of going. But you won't succeed. I know we're loaded, Mother. If you really wanted me to go on with school you'd not have to depend on the money from my father.'

'The money comes from the family lawyers. I thought you knew that.' Zoe's face was a mask. She wanted the conversation over, fast, before she blurted out the cruel truth: that Paul de Byron did not even know of his daughter's existence.

Leonie pulled on her shoes, her face briefly hidden as she said, 'So you let other people keep up the paternal act for him after the first, really important part?'

She waited, certain of the blow that did not come.

'If you want me to slap you for that you're going to be very disappointed, baby.' Zoe made for the door. 'You've been watching too many movies. But just every now and then the script gets it right. Like when the mother say's she'll cut the daughter off without a cent if she tries anything foolish.'

'You mean it, don't you?'

'I told you, I don't want to see you hurt. Paris would be a mistake.'

'Mistake? That's a bad joke, after what happened here today.'

'I've said I'm sorry. Leonie, try to think of something else. I have this early start tomorrow. Maddie's left supper in the ice-box. Let's eat. Let's plan a vacation. I'll go round to the travel bureau when my Paris connection leaves tomorrow.'

'Which of your Paris connections would that be, Mother?' Leonie had followed Zoe into the drawing-room.

'So it's true that the young can be merciless,' Zoe said lightly. 'I think I need a drink before I answer that particular merciless question.'

Leonie flung herself down in her usual corner of the sofa while Zoe went to the bar. 'Well, isn't this just the perfect end to a perfect day.'

Zoe raised her glass, managing a small smile.

'You wanted your birthday to be different, darling.' In her heart she knew that she had never mourned the past so much as at this moment, and would never again come so close to telling Leonie that she had been wanted, and that her parents had loved each other, a long time ago.

Next day at school Leonie thought of nothing but the string of pearls bathed in their own translucent light. She was pretty sure they were very valuable. Erich Mannheim paid top price for everything from an orchid to a bunch of daisies; she knew that from the gifts he had brought to Gramercy Park before. And the way he had used the apartment on her birthday freed her from any obligation to honour the gift, she was sure of that.

She remembered that two of the girls in her class had hocked their christening silver to raise the price of the gas to drive into Vermont with two boys while their parents were away. Or perhaps she could sell the pearls outright. Sue would be sure to know the best places to go, as one of her relatives was in the jewellery business. She made a mental note to slip the white leather box into her school bag that night before she went to bed.

'My God, Zoe, that's a Charles James you're wearing.' A woman lounging in an armchair in the foyer of the Waldorf waved a long cigarette holder in Zoe's direction and admired her white sharkskin evening cloak through a veil of smoke.

'Four thousand dollars said so when I paid for it, Marcia,' Zoe smiled, her eyes searching the early evening crowd for Erich's tall figure. 'Cash, of course.'

'Of course, darling.' The woman watched Erich critically as he made his way to where Zoe stood. 'A good investment, by the look of things.'

'Marcia, you really must get around to my new facial soon. Give me a ring, won't you?' Zoe took Erich's arm and they moved away towards the dining-room.

Over dinner, Erich Mannheim began his campaign to persuade Zoe to join him in Paris that fall. He told her of the rich pickings to be found there for a woman of ability. He tried to tempt her with descriptions of how she would be fêted, admired.

She reminded him that she had been to Paris once before, and knew only too well that she had something that appealed to the French. It had been her downfall. They drank champagne quickly, too quickly, and as Erich ordered a second bottle Zoe began to tell him about Leonie's reaction to finding them together at Gramercy Park.

'She wants to go to France. To meet her father.'

'Then what are we waiting for? We could travel together. Your daughter is a charming creature. It would give me the greatest pleasure to escort you both. Let me see if there is a suite left when I go back on the *Normandie*.'

Zoe told him he was mad, and he suggested that it was time she too went a little crazy. She began to get slightly drunk. Then in the cab home she told him all that had happened in Paris the last time, and what would happen if Leonie broke their contract with Charles Vincent and Paul's Tante Berthe.

Erich listened carefully. 'I do not see your problem, chérie. You are a wealthy woman in your own right. There must be something else that makes you reluctant to let the child meet her father.'

35

'I don't want to see her hurt, as I was hurt.'

'And?'

'And I have not told Leonie that her father does not know of her existence.'

The cab had drawn into the kerb outside the apartment, but the Swiss banker made no move. 'Zoe, look at me.' He took her face in his hands and turned her head towards him. A streetlamp lit the cab's interior with a harsh yellow light and the delicate network of lines beneath Zoe's eyes showed that she was tired and had drunk too much.

'It's late. I should go in.'

'I am coming with you. We cannot avoid the child just because of what happened.'

'It's no good. I can't go to Paris with you. Now you know why.'

'On the contrary, now that I know the truth I insist that we go. I have plans for you. For us. And in Paris you shall be able to do what you should have done years ago.'

'Which is?'

'Which is to find this Paul de Byron and tell him that he has a very beautiful, very charming daughter . . .'

They found Leonie sitting up late, at the kitchen table with Maddie, wearing the tangerine sweater and the pearls. Zoe became angry, and wanted Leonie to go straight to her room. But Erich soothed her with a look, and watching them together Leonie was suddenly aware of the influence this powerful, alien man had with her mother.

As if he sensed her thoughts, Erich clicked his heels and bowed to her. 'Thank you for wearing my pearls.'

'Thank you for the gift, Mr Mannheim.' Leonie wondered if he would display the same chivalry if he knew she was already planning to sell them.

Zoe broke in again, insisting that Leonie go to bed. Leonie kissed her, and kissed Maddie goodnight. As she turned and walked towards her bedroom she was suddenly sure that

Erich Mannheim watched her progress with the same annoying mixture of amusement and admiration he had so far reserved for her mother. Resisting the urge to run the rest of the way and slam the door on his presence, she turned on her heel instead, her hand on the door handle.

'Goodnight, Mr Mannheim.'

'Goodnight, Mademoiselle Byron.'

Alone in her room, Leonie unfastened the pearls and placed them carefully in their case, then tucked the case into her school bag between an atlas and a copy book. When Zoe came in ten minutes later to tell her that Erich Mannheim had gone back to his hotel and it was time her lights were out, she was reading innocently in bed, her eyes avoiding the school bag where it lay on a chair ready for the morning.

For a moment she was taken by surprise by the obvious fatigue on her mother's face. She let her book slip to the floor as Zoe sat at the foot of the bed. Her mother retrieved it.

'Scott Fitzgerald. How very apt.' She put the book on the bedside table. 'But don't kid yourself that his smart little love stories show the way things are.'

'At least they're full of surprises, just like life.'

Zoe got up, and leaned to kiss her. 'If it's surprises you want, then go to France by all means. But not yet, please. OK, you'd love Paris. But when you're older, not now. It's a city for throwing your hat over the moon – but not till school's out. I should know.' She shook her head.

Leonie realized that Zoe was perhaps not quite sober. With the ruthlessness of the adolescent she found something briefly reassuring in the sight of an adult with her defences down.

'And there's something else.' Zoe seemed to mistake the silence for compliance. 'You find life full of surprises? If you go to Paris before I give the word I can promise you the surprise of a lifetime.' She averted her face, words trailing away as if she were exhausted by the secret of two decades.

'Don't let's talk about it any more, Mother,' Leonie said, relenting. She reached out to turn off her reading lamp. Zoe

37

shrugged and moved away, silhouetted in the light from the drawing-room through the open bedroom door.

'Goodnight, Mother.'

'Sweet dreams.'

The jeweller was a small, stockily built immigrant with five o'clock shadow, a permanent frown, and expressive hands embellished by several heavy rings. Leonie, waiting while a down-at-heel middle-aged woman returned the contents of a small jewel case to her purse, wondered if the rings had been bought from people desperate for cash. But it was wealthy Sue who had told her where to go. A series of elderly aunts had died and left a quantity of old-fashioned personal mementoes to her mother, who had got a good price from this shop near school.

She brought the pearls from their white box, trying to look unconcerned. The jeweller handled them, shaking his head. She felt suddenly sick. Surely Erich Mannheim had not tried to fool her – or Zoe, of all people? – with some worthless imitation?

'Good pearls. Very fine.'

She breathed again.

'But perhaps too good? For me to buy them from a young lady who should, I think, wear them, not sell.'

'I need the money. For a family reason.' She knew it sounded lame.

'*I* need time. Perhaps one day, and some proof of identity. The police department – it is the usual procedure. . .' The beringed hands finished the sentence while Leonie stood there calculating that if she showed the worn label inside her school bag it would give away her age and lead the trail straight to the school and so to her mother.

Then as if it were a mere afterthought the jeweller mentioned a figure for the pearls that was beyond anything she had dreamed. Enough for a long stay in Europe, if she travelled as cheaply as possible. Paris suddenly seemed a

38

reality within her reach. The purple ink initials on the endless cheques would become a name, and the city forbidden to her as real as New York.

'You wouldn't talk money now if you thought I had stolen the pearls.'

'Perhaps not, young lady.'

'Then I plan to come back. This time tomorrow?' She looked around, as if to memorize the place. On a high shelf strung with cobwebs a small bronze buddha smiled down at her. The faded price tag tempted her for a minute, and she wondered who could have been so hard-pressed as to let him go.

The old-fashioned bell above the shop's door rang sharply as she stepped out on to the sidewalk again. Walking quickly home she remembered that she had tucked her skating club card into her ice boots at the end of the previous winter, and that the photograph made her look all of nineteen. She ran through the vestibule, making straight for the closet in her room. On the floor, with other things she had outgrown, she found the boots, and in them the club membership. Under the boots was a pile of old copy books, a red scarf Maddie had given her, and wrapped in the scarf the passport her mother had insisted she get a year ago, when they had planned a trip to Mexico that had come to nothing in the end.

Within three days she had booked a cancelled berth, tourist class, on the *Normandie*'s return trip to Europe.

That same night her mother announced to Maddie over a late cup of coffee after Leonie was asleep that she was booked on the same crossing.

'For as long as I'm away the apartment is yours. Have a vacation. You've earned it. Leonie can go to summer camp for a while.'

'You've never left her before.' Maddie's face was all accusation. She did not have to be told that Erich Mannheim was to travel with Zoe.

'It's for her sake that I'm going. There's something I have

to do. Before we find ourselves in deep water.'

'Deep water, that's your place in life. Always has been. How do I know you'll ever be back?'

'I'll be back.'

'You got caught up before in Paris, France.'

'I was different then.'

'Then why does the very mention of the place make you blush under your new-fangled white face-paint, Zoe Byron?'

The next night Zoe got home sooner than usual from the salon and ate an early supper with Leonie in the kitchen.

'I asked Maddie to leave us alone.'

Leonie held her breath. The left-over cash from the pearls was hidden in her closet. She believed she had convinced the jeweller that everything was above board. Had Zoe, with her acute sixth sense, found her out so soon?

'I'm going on a business trip, honey. With Erich Mannheim; no use hiding that. You know we're close.'

Leonie waited, eyes lowered. She almost knew what was coming. Erich Mannheim was due to sail for France some time soon. In her anxiety to get her own headlong flight to Europe under way she had completely forgotten that she was not the only one about to cross the Atlantic.

'Erich has plans for us, in Paris. Big plans. I have to listen.'

'You said we'd never go there.' Leonie's heart thumped against her ribs, as she still wondered how much her mother knew of her own plans.

'*We* are not going, Leonie. But Erich has persuaded me that it is time I broke the taboo. For business reasons. I can't go on denying that Paris is the mecca for the beauty business still.'

'And the allowance? You said it would stop.' Her voice was almost petulant. She felt vaguely disappointed that Zoe was about to steal her thunder. She had no inkling that Zoe wanted to get to France to warn Charles Vincent et fils that Paul de Byron's daughter might one day take her destiny

40

into her own hands and that the outcome would break her heart. The plans Erich had made for her had given Zoe the perfect cover. She had almost convinced herself that it was now her dearest wish to get into the big time, and the international cosmetic empire Erich had dangled before her eyes would be ample compensation for losing the allowance from the de Byrons.

What she would not admit even to herself was that for years now the monthly letter from the lawyers on the boulevard de la Madeleine had been a luxury she did not need – except as a symbol of her link with a family that had rejected her. Very soon now Tante Berthe, if she were still alive, would once more hold the fate of a young American girl in her hands. But this time it would be Zoe's daughter.

Now she planned the coming visit to Paris, in defiance of all she had undertaken there so long ago, as eagerly as she had approached her first euphoric journey to Europe. At the end of the tunnel she saw herself free at last in the city that was meant for her . . . as Erich well knew. But he was not aware that the lioness still had the sharp maternal instinct that had made her protect Leonie every inch of the way to Gramercy Park. And even as Leonie herself was preparing to quit the nest Zoe was bent on a last, primitive bid to save her from hurt.

'I have decided there are more important things than the allowance.' Zoe poured more coffee, and held the pot out for Leonie's cup.

Leonie shook her head. She had to be alone, and she had to think. If her mother got to know now of her secret it would ruin everything. Selling the pearls was bad enough, she knew. But to defy her mother to the extent she planned would bring Zoe's anger down on her head in a way that neither of them might ever recover from. What she had done in the past few days was much more serious than cutting her hair or smuggling herself into an unsuitable movie.

'I wish it was someone else, that's all.' She took refuge in starting to clear the table, and turned her back on Zoe to take the dishes to the side.

'I know that's how you must feel now. After what happened. But you'll change, I know you will. One day you'll reap the reward, too, of what a man like Erich Mannheim can do for us.'

'I doubt that, Mother. I just don't know where we stand any more.'

'When I get back we'll have that vacation.' Zoe changed the subject. 'I promise. And you might like to get to summer camp. It's not too late, is it?'

'What about Maddie?'

'This is her home as well as ours. And I need her here.'

'Can I think about camp? Another day or two, Mother?'

Zoe looked up quickly from her coffee, and for a second Leonie thought she had sounded too compliant too soon.

'If that's what you want, baby.' Zoe lit a cigarette and for once Leonie let the hated pet name go by.

In her bedroom she began to go through her clothes, and thought wistfully as she slid the hangers along the rail of the closet, unable to make up her mind, how her mother would have leapt into action if a client had asked her advice on what outfits to take to Paris at this time of year. But to the child of Zoe's own summer love affair eighteen years ago, the famous Byron salon advice service was inaccessible.

She chose two cotton dresses, and the silk she had had from Zoe for her birthday. She would travel in sports clothes, which had the double advantage of comfort and saving their weight in her luggage. She had to be able to carry her own things down to the sidewalk and into a cab. The case had to be small enough, too, to escape Maddie's eagle eye.

Maddie. She rejected the thought of leaving her without a word. But Maddie was capable of bringing in the whole New York Police Department to prevent her getting even as far as the Hudson, she knew that. She would write her a note. A letter. Poor Maddie was going to have a real vacation, alone at Gramercy Park.

*

42

It was quite dark, after ten, when Leonie took up a vantage point at the portside rail on C Deck, watching the late arrivals down on the floodlit waterfront. She had noted when she boarded the *Normandie* an hour earlier that A Deck passengers had their own gangway. Now a huddle of press men waited eagerly at its foot for anyone who might make news for the early morning editions. A camera flash lit the dark canyon of water between the ship and the quayside as a minor movie celebrity spilled in a white fur wrap from a chauffeur-driven car. The reporters drifted away once they saw who it was. White furs in August, indeed, their hunched shoulders seemed to say. Under cover of the actress's fleeting moment of fame, a tall man in a dark coat and wide-brimmed black velvet hat slipped by the press and climbed the gangway with a long, easy stride belied by his white hair.

'Know who that is?'

Leonie turned to the boy who had joined her at the rail. She had been aware of his presence when she first came up on deck. He had been walking alone through the knots of people saying goodbyes. He was about five foot ten, with strong shoulders and a quick, light step. He wore gold-rimmed spectacles, and behind them Leonie saw that his dark brown eyes increased his vaguely foreign appearance.

'That's the conductor of an orchestra with which I hope to play one day. Berlin. He's a Czech.'

'You're a musician?'

He clicked his heels in mock formality. 'I play piano, a little. After my year in Paris I shall, I hope, play a little better.'

Leonie looked at him with new interest. Here was someone about her own age who was going to Paris, and for a year. To him it seemed the most natural thing in the world. She suddenly felt less alone, and less terrified by what she had done, or planned to do. 'My name is Leonie. Leonie Byron.' In a rush of bravado she gave her surname its French pronunciation.

'You're French. I thought you were when I saw you . . . when you came up on deck.'

She had her reward. To be taken for French the first hour on the *Normandie* must mean something. Then she shook her head, not wanting to lead him on. 'I'm not sure. It's a long story.'

'We have almost a week. Long enough? By the way, my name is Heller. Max Heller. I go to the Paris Conservatoire this fall.'

His voice trailed away as somewhere along the quay a hundred yards from where they stood a band broke into a Strauss waltz. As if at a signal, a party way above them unleashed a shower of confetti and coloured streamers. They laughed, and turning to brush the confetti from her shoulder Leonie saw a slim figure in silver place a white-gloved hand on the rail of the first class gangway.

They had said goodbye three hours ago, Zoe dressed as she was now for an early dinner at the Waldorf. They both knew better than to mention that it was Erich Mannheim's hotel. From there Zoe and her banker would go straight to the boat. Leonie calculated that she herself had plenty of time before then to board and find her way about. Then she had planned to lose herself in the crowds who did not travel in the limelight, and somehow avoid her mother for the duration of the crossing.

Max Heller felt her tense. 'You know those people?' His eyes followed hers to Erich Mannheim, a tall figure barring the way to a pushy reporter who was trying to get something out of Zoe while the flash of the cameras now came thick and fast.

'Of course you do. There's an uncanny likeness.' Max Heller took her elbow. 'Want to get closer?'

'No. Thanks. That's just what I don't want.' She began to turn away.

'Then this must all be part of the long story?'

She nodded. 'The tall man with blond hair is my mother's . . . banker. He's Swiss German, I think. The woman –'

'It's your mother, isn't it?' He grinned down at her and she smiled back, grateful that to someone of her own generation at least Zoe had begun to look her real age.

Drawn back to the rails in spite of herself, Leonie put her chin on her hands, staring down at the elegant woman who could wave a photographer away and yet make quite sure that he caught her best profile. Then head in air Zoe Byron climbed aboard and by one of those freaks of timing and placing, in spite of all the push of the crowds and the music and crying and cheering that was part of the beginning of an Atlantic liner crossing, her eyes met those of the girl who watched her progress from the distant other world of tourist class.

For a split second the years fell away. Leonie, in her dark pyjama suit, chin in her hands, bobbed hair caught in the night breeze, was the girl Zoe had been on that crazy voyage with the Princeton men. Leonie, stubborn as the girl who had persuaded Aunt Abbey to let her go to Europe, stared back at her mother with the same unyielding eyes. The ship's officers began to move the visitors on to the exit gangways. The band began to play 'Auld Lang Syne'.

In the intangible, yet complete, exchange between them as Leonie looked into her mother's face, both women frozen in a silence and stillness that cut out the turmoil around them, something totally unexpected happened to Leonie. The dull ache of anger and isolation she had felt each time she let herself into the apartment after the incident on her birthday gave way to a sense of relief. She was suddenly glad of her mother's presence, of the one witness who really knew what her journey was about. She was less afraid. Her purpose made more sense than ever, if she could win her fight with her mother in the few days on neutral, sea-locked territory before they reached France.

She nodded. A small nod of recognition, including the boy at her side.

'Oh yes,' she said. 'That's Mother.'

'The press seem to know her. Is she some kind of celebrity?'

'One day. I think she will be, one day . . .'

45

CHAPTER FOUR

Erich Mannheim threw back his blond head and roared with laughter. A gold filling in a line of strong white teeth caught the light. Leonie and her mother waited, both taken unawares by his reaction.

'Will you please say that for me again? I have to hear it again.' He took a champagne bottle from its cradle and filled Zoe's glass, still chuckling.

Leonie took a deep breath. 'I said that I sold the pearls to pay for my passage.'

The banker walked towards her across the soft stateroom carpet, glass in hand. She held her ground. There was something ominous behind the laughter that she could not place. A supreme audacity, perhaps. To match her own.

'Then, Mademoiselle Leonie, I drink to you. To your aristocratic disregard for my gift. To your imagination. It is all quite superb. I assure you, I find it superb.'

'I'm glad someone can find something to like about all this.' Zoe put down her glass untouched. 'I'll talk to you later, Leonie. Alone. Meanwhile I want to know what poor Maddie has been told. She'll be crazy with worry. You might at least have thought of her.'

'I wrote to her. She'll understand. I left the letter on her pillow. She thought I went to the movies with Sue.'

'Very cute. I didn't know you had this power of deception in you, baby. It really makes me look at you with new eyes.'

Erich cut her short with a gesture towards the clock on the stateroom wall. The whole suite was art deco, the theme of orchid pink and silver. Zoe, still in the silver lamé Chanel copy in which she had come on board, looked like some

46

elegant bird that had flown to roost in its natural habitat.

'I thought we were having a quiet evening first night out.' Zoe scowled at him. 'And as I said, I want to talk with my daughter.'

'You have all the time in the world to set things right with Leonie. Tonight I have people I want you to meet. By the time we give the party for you everyone who is anyone on this voyage must be fighting for an invitation. We have to start working on it.'

'Well, if it's work, then I don't mind . . .' Zoe pulled off her shoes and sat on one of the wide twin beds.

Leonie, watching them, was struck by the way they had discarded all pretence. Now they were in their own world. Erich Mannheim was no longer the intruder; Zoe herself seemed to have given up trying to maintain any formal behaviour with him in front of her daughter.

'You'll have to leave us, honey.' Zoe looked over at her as if sensing her thoughts. 'This is a business trip, after all. And there's nothing we can do about you tonight, I guess. Will you have dinner?'

'I think there's a restaurant, Mother. It looked quite cosy when I passed.'

'And you're sharing a cabin, I suppose? Erich, we have to get this child into something else. I'll see the purser first thing tomorrow –'

'No. I'm not moving, Mother. I'm sharing with a teacher, from Chicago I think. There's no problem. I want to be on my own.'

'And clothes. What about your clothes, for God's sake? We bought you nothing. If I'd known. How could you do this to me?'

Leonie knew that Erich was laughing to himself as Zoe rattled on. It was so like her, faced with a monumental rebellion, to be annoyed that her daughter had the wrong clothes for the occasion.

'I have plenty to wear if I stay tourist, Mother.'

'That's true, I suppose.' Zoe massaged her toes. 'But

47

you'll have to be at the party. If it gets out that you're on board and don't come to the party people will think the worst.'

'Let them think it!' It was the first sign of anger Leonie let through. 'But if it's any consolation to you I packed the blue silk. The dress you gave me for my birthday.'

'Thank goodness for small mercies. But don't think you're getting off lightly. We'll talk. You come to lunch with me, tomorrow. Don't try to get out of it.'

'You put a good face on things, Liebling,' Erich said when Leonie had gone. He crossed to where Zoe still sat, and held her glass to her lips.

'You were far too tolerant of what she has done with the pearls.' She sipped champagne.

'I thought it genuinely amusing. She is her mother's daughter.'

Zoe ignored the remark. She stared at their reflection in the long ornate mirrors that panelled the room. 'All I have to do is to get to those Paris lawyers first.'

'Are you going to change?' He touched the top button of the silver jacket.

'Is there time?' She sighed, and stretched her legs, curving towards him like a cat that seeks a familiar touch.

The crossing was smooth, and next day Zoe was one of the first to take up a vantage point at the pool in the July sunshine. Erich had started early on creating interest about her among the first class passengers. By the time Leonie found her mother, led by a steward who had first tried to bar her from A Deck, there was a group of strangers already at her table.

'We'll have our talk tonight. After dinner. Come to the stateroom about eleven.'

'There are other things happening, Mother. Do we really have to say any more?'

'So amusing,' Zoe told the others. 'My daughter insists on

travelling tourist. She is paying her own way.'

'Why, that's admirable. Desmond, don't you find that typically American? So democratic.' A dark-haired woman with an upper-class Dublin brogue touched her husband's arm. They both scrutinized Leonie as if she were a thoroughbred pony they were about to buy for their stables.

'Wholly admirable.' The husband raised a monocle. 'These American girls are splendid.'

'Glad you like us.' Zoe smiled one of her most stunning smiles.

'I hope you'll not stay below deck all the crossing,' another man said to Leonie.

'No. We do sometimes come up for air. And there's my mother's party. Perhaps I'll see you then, Mother? . . .'

The mention of a party sent a buzz round the table. Leonie took the opportunity to slip away before Zoe made any more attempts to tie her to a meeting. By the time they reached France she hoped that the novelty of what she had done would have paled beside everything else that was happening to Zoe. With any luck they would reach Paris in a state of truce.

Later she walked the deck with Max Heller, and lunched with him in the restaurant on C Deck. He told her that his people had left Austria in '33. He had a sister in New York. His parents had gone to the west coast, where they both lectured at local colleges.

'They couldn't say no when I got the scholarship to the Conservatoire. I think they were just relieved that it was Paris and not Berlin.'

He told her that his family had been among the numerous professional people who had elected for a self-imposed exile from Austria in the early thirties. It was a sacrifice, an uprooting made for their children. Some of them had even sent their children alone to families in the States or in Britain. The Nazi creed and its significance for Jews was far

49

too much of a reality for relatives in Germany, and was creeping too close.

Leonie remembered the wealthy Jewish girls at school in New York. The way they went home quickly after class, and did not mention the recent past. One girl's mother did not speak English. Another had died suddenly 'on the journey'.

By the time they had finished lunch the restaurant was deserted. Max strolled over to an upright piano that stood on a dais at the far end of the room.

'Mozart might be a little out of place, don't you think?' Leonie teased him.

He opened the piano, and smiled. 'Mozart is never out of place.'

But moments later the empty restaurant echoed with a brilliant, virtuoso version of a Scott Joplin cakewalk, and Leonie, intrigued and surprised by his choice, watched him in silence until the last chord died away.

'You should give a concert!'

'How did you know? Matter of fact, I'm already signed for the captain's last night entertainment – the Czech conductor I pointed out to you before we sailed knew I was on board. It seems my professor told him I was on my way to Paris. Anyway, I could hardly refuse. It means he'll hear me play.'

'Mozart?'

'Perhaps. Bartok, for sure. The old man will like that.'

'There are ways, then, of gatecrashing to first class,' Leonie said later as they went in search of a deck tennis match.

'You won't be gatecrashing the captain's party,' Max answered. 'You'll be my guest. Otherwise I won't go.'

Midway through their game Leonie became aware that they were being watched. She looked up, to find that from the raised observation gallery on one side of the playdeck a group of first class passengers was following the match.

'Look,' she whispered to Max. 'Now we know what it's like to be in a zoo.'

Max stood hand on hips and stared up at the onlookers, his spectacles glinting in the afternoon sun.

'Stare away, shipmates,' he said for Leonie's ears only. 'A few nights from now it's my turn for the platform. I'll make them sit up on their gold chairs and ask for more.'

Leonie had never met this kind of arrogance, and she warmed to him for the way he continued to outstare the audience until it broke up and drifted away.

That night she stayed in her cabin and wrote to Sue. 'I have met a real-live musician. He plays beautifully, and when I'm with him I laugh a lot. He's all of nineteen, but not so "gauche" as the kids at home of that age. I guess European boys have more poise, and that's a poem in itself, don't you think?'

She finished the letter in stages over the next two days, then sealed it ready for posting in Le Havre.

When she found somewhere to stay in Paris she planned to write a really long letter to Maddie too.

Zoe was the first to arrive at her own reception, and made her way through the marble columns of the stateroom Erich had booked for the occasion to where he waited for her at a side table near the dais. A steward came up to her and Erich scowled as the man grinned a welcome, so that the grin switched in a split second to the professional frown of concentration.

'They know what I drink here this time of day,' Zoe explained as the Greek steward went in search of a club soda. 'And I don't want anything stronger before the party gets under way.' She did not add that her acquaintance with the man went back a long way: right back to when she had traded a case of champagne for a case of 'communion' wine at his taverna on Eighth Street. She smiled inwardly at the thought of the profit she had made on the deal.

They checked through the guest list for the last time. Erich pointed out the names of one or two people he wanted Zoe to cultivate.

'Although in that gown I think perhaps you need do very little this evening but simply exist.' He eyed the line of white silk cleavage that reached almost to her waist. 'That is, if anything you do is ever simple, Liebling.'

'It's not going to be simple for me in Paris, Erich. You know that. Please don't make too many arrangements for the first two or three days. I can't settle to anything until I've made contact with the family.'

'You shall have your three days. But that is all. Then we have much to do. And the first thing is to find premises.'

They had already come to the decision to open a salon in Paris, bringing the image of Zoe's established success in New York straight to the fore. Erich was using the crossing to implant the image amongst the wealthy European women who were likely to bring her custom. Some of them, he found, had already heard of her in New York. But it was going to be a challenge, to woo them from their lifetime devotion to the great French houses.

'The name. The name is going to be of supreme importance.'

'Once I have seen the family there will be nothing to stop me calling myself de Byron.'

'Do you really want to call attention to your unfortunate story in such a way? You would do better to make a fresh start with these people, believe me. In New York the name would have a certain allure. But for the set I want you to attract it would not have the same . . . impact.'

'Let me think about it.' Zoe frowned. 'Give me a cigarette.'

'Not now. Your first guests have arrived.'

Leonie paused at the head of the marble staircase and fought the instinct that had rushed out at her without warning, making her want to turn on her heel and run back through the maze of the ship to her cabin.

The scene before her was an extension of those Sunday afternoons on Long Island among the idle rich. There was even an Italian fountain playing gently in the centre of the stateroom where her mother was holding the reception.

She heard her name called. A path opened for her in the crowd of guests as her mother came towards the stairs.

She began to walk down, knowing that she was the focal point of attention. Her chin went up in the familiar defensive gesture. Zoe reached out both arms in an exaggerated welcome. 'My daughter,' she said to the people close enough to hear. Then, taking her hand, in a low voice: 'Darling, the blue silk is perfection. You look divine.'

Leonie allowed herself to be propelled towards a table where there was still a vacant chair. An elderly woman, attractive in a muted, elegant fashion, smiled a welcome. A younger man and a boy of about Leonie's age half-stood.

'My daughter, Leonie Byron. I told you about her. Leonie, this is Lady Hume. Her son, Viscount Hume. And –?'

A steward hovered with champagne.

'My grandson, Gavin.' The woman inclined her head. 'Do stay with us, my dear. We are feeling so gloomy after the wonderful time we had in your city.'

Leonie liked her, although it was a jolt to be thrown in at the deep end by Zoe's blatant choice of a titled family as her companions for the evening. But there was something about these people that put her at her ease. When Zoe left them she found herself talking of New York and hearing about the Humes' estate in Scotland. They were going home via Paris, to collect a niece who was at finishing school there.

To her relief, no questions were asked about her own plans in Paris. Her mother had chosen well; these were not the same chattering, inquisitive breed as many of her circle in New York.

She wondered why they had been invited. Erich Mannheim would be sure to have a sound reason. He was not the sort to be impressed merely by a title. The viscount would have to be chairman of a handful of companies at least, if not a member of Erich's own banking circle.

She did not have to wait long for the explanation. Lady Hume told her that her family had ancient connections with France, as far back as the fifteenth century. 'I'm afraid we fought for the land we have there, then lost it, then gave in gracefully. But more recent ancestors of mine were in the Peninsular Wars. They drifted back into France over the Pyrenees, and settled in one of those exquisite little towns. Some claim that it was our family who introduced the first game of golf into France.'

Her grandson made a face. 'Did we lose that too?'

'Gavin is too young to be a cynic. It's all pretend,' Lady Hume said. 'Don't let him frighten you off. If we were staying longer in Paris he would be a useful guide. He was at school there.'

'Grandmother has not told you that she prefers Paris to Edinburgh and that all the family has to go to school there so that she can keep on visiting,' Gavin told Leonie. 'She's so caught up with the place that she's bought a club there. So that she has somewhere to stay.'

It was then that Leonie knew what lay behind the Humes' presence at the reception. An aristocrat with a base in Paris that must be a hive of exactly the clientele Zoe would want to attract.

'You are very like your mother.' Lady Hume changed the subject. 'How beautiful she is.'

Across the room Zoe stood between two distinguished-looking middle-aged men who were paying her their undivided attention. She managed at once to listen to one, to make the other feel it was he she wanted to hear, and to watch the whole room with cool appraisal, as if to say, 'This is my scene. All these people are here because this is how I want it to be.'

Yet at the same time Leonie knew her mother was probably bubbling over inside with excited anticipation of

54

the things that were to come from the occasion. Things that Erich Mannheim had shown her were within her grasp.

The conversations died at a drum roll from the small band on the dais behind where Zoe stood. Erich appeared from the crowd and mounted the platform. Leonie noticed how lightly he moved for so big a man. He held up his hands for silence.

The speech was a masterpiece of public relations. The beauty business was hardly mentioned. The guests were persuaded that the reception had been devised solely to give them a good time. Then, at a signal to a steward, the lights dimmed. A single spotlight came up slowly, on Zoe herself. A ripple of applause went round the stateroom and subdued murmurs of 'bravo' greeted the slim white figure.

Zoe smiled into the dark void beyond the spotlight. 'Ladies and gentlemen,' she began, in a low voice that carried to every corner. 'I hope we'll meet again, in Paris, where I plan to launch a very special new concept in beauty. The perfect blend – New York and Paris.'

She paused. Down the years she heard the voice of a young French army captain telling her how his grandparents had been ruined, and their vineyards saved by the grafting of good stock from America. *They made excellent companions.*

'I hope you will remember this night, on this magnificent ship, when you see the name of my project launched in Paris. Look for the name, just to please me, won't you?'

There was a ripple of applause, and someone called out: 'All very well, Zoe Byron. But what name?'

'Just one word. Anyone can understand it. It's the same in many languages. A beautiful word . . .' She faltered, and to a sceptical onlooker it could have been yet another accomplished ploy in a gifted performance. 'The word to look for is . . . *"Caresse".*'

It was Erich Mannheim who led the clapping that greeted the announcement, and as the lights brightened he came down from the platform and walked quickly to where Zoe now was standing with her back to her audience. Only Erich saw that her eyes were bright with unshed tears.

He gripped her elbow tightly. 'You never cease to astonish me,' he murmured. 'It is perfect. How did you think of it?'

'Oh' – she gave him a mocking look – 'I thought of it like most of my best ideas. All on my own.'

Watching them, Leonie realized that she had once more underestimated her mother. Zoe was still her own creature when it came to the world she had built for herself. This time Erich Mannheim was the victim, lost in admiration of the impression she had made. His contribution had been the organization, the ferreting out of the right people for the occasion, the attention to detail that made a brilliant evening go with effortless ease.

But Zoe Byron, who had pulled herself out of humiliation and poverty and insignificance long before she met him, had needed only herself that night – to make sure that no one who had been at the reception would ever forget her.

Max Heller had gone to his cabin early, the barman in the C Deck restaurant told Leonie when she returned from the party. She was tired herself, and went to her own cabin, where she was glad to find that the teacher from Chicago was already asleep.

She undressed in the dark. As she tucked her purse under her pillow she checked for the card Lady Hume had given her, with the address of the Paris club. Not that she would want to join. Max had promised to find her a room on the Left Bank in the student quarter. One of the advantages of being in Paris in August was that it was deserted, and the best of the cheap lodgings were there for the picking.

But she had liked the Humes. They made her feel at ease with them. And Lady Hume's admiration of her mother had been genuine. She was the kind of woman who valued achievement.

As she fell asleep, Leonie wondered how different the last night at sea would be, and whether the same crowd would attend the captain's entertainment. She wanted everyone to hear Max play.

Something made her decide not to wear the blue silk dress for the concert. She wanted to look different. But the cotton frocks and the sports clothes that had begun to look very childish since she left New York were hardly suitable for what was to be the most formal evening of the trip.

She found Zoe alone in her stateroom in the afternoon. Erich had left her to get on with the complex business of packing. They were to disembark too early next day to leave anything to be done after breakfast except say their good-byes.

Leonie asked her mother if she would be at the concert.

'Of course,' Zoe said. She took a chiffon dress from a closet. 'I was keeping this out to wear. Like it?'

'I don't want to wear the blue silk again. Don't get me wrong, Mother. I like it. Very much. But –'

'What's so special about tonight? I never knew you to be bored so soon with a dress.'

'Someone I know is playing. He's going to the Conservatoire in Paris, on a scholarship. He's asked me to the concert as his guest.'

'So, it's like that? A shipboard romance?' Zoe closed a suitcase and sat on the lid, studying her daughter.

'No, Mother. Not like that. I like him. He's good fun.'

'And may I ask his name?'

'Max. Max Heller.'

'Oh. Well . . .' Zoe looked round the stateroom at the disarray of clothes, and as if she had suddenly lost interest said: 'If there's anything here you think is right for a friend of the pianist . . . you only have to say.'

Leonie found a pale cream silk shirtwaister that fitted her and set off the tan she had acquired in the few days at sea. 'Can I have this?'

'Be my guest. All I'd say if my advice were to be asked –

57

which I'm pretty sure it won't be – is that it needs something. Something very simple. Such as a really good string of pearls.'

They looked at each other for a split second, each of them assessing whether it was worth a fight. It was Zoe who smiled first. 'You're my daughter. It's too damn obvious sometimes. Here –'

She pulled a leather jewel case from under the bed and unlocked it. On the top tray was a row of necklaces on red velvet. Zoe always took care of her jewellery. Her thin hands sorted through the gold and silver until she found what she wanted.

'This –'

It was a very fine gold chain, soft with age, and a small heart-shaped amethyst pendant.

'It belonged to Aunt Abbey. You never knew her – she died before you were born. She'd have liked you to have it. She knew what adventure was all about.'

When Max came to fetch Leonie from her cabin he told her that she looked exactly right. 'Virginal. Cultured. St Cecilia would be proud to call you her own.'

'St Cecilia?'

'The patron saint of music. I need her tonight. I'm nervous.'

'You? Nervous? You have the nerve of the devil.'

'Not on the platform. There my soul is laid bare. After the concert we'll get drunk.'

'What would my mother say?'

'From what I've seen of your mother, Leonie Byron, she'll be leading the fray.'

Leonie sighed, and followed him to the main stateroom. True to the picture he had drawn, it was filled with line upon line of precarious gold chairs. The firstcomers filled the front rows already. Leonie found a seat on its own at the end of a row. Max disappeared backstage, and as she waited she watched the arrivals. Her mother and Erich Mannheim, severely correct in formal dress, were among the last. Erich waved his programme as a greeting. She was glad that they had to find places further back. She was as nervous as Max himself, and wanted to give all her concentration to making the evening a success for him.

Everyone stood up as the captain's party came in. On his right was the elderly Czech conductor from Berlin.

As Max came on to the platform she felt a small flame of pride in her new friend warm her whole being. He bowed, and for a fleeting moment he was a total stranger. The artist, remote from his audience, preparing to perform in isolation. Someone coughed, and there was a grating sound as a gold chair shifted its ground. Leonie thought later that she had imagined it, but at that moment she could have sworn that Max flickered the merest hint of a grin in her direction.

She was to remember Max that night for the rest of her life. He began with Mozart and, his audience ensnared by the brilliant, lucid playing, went on to a Bartok piece that jarred them from their complacency and had them shifting uneasily in their chairs. The Czech conductor led the applause, after a split second of stunned silence. Max stood and bowed, only once. Leonie noticed then for the first time the way his thin wrists and strong hands emerged from a tuxedo that was obviously not his. Her heart went out to him. And as he walked from the platform she stood, leading a second burst of clapping.

Max went backstage during the next item, but joined Leonie in the interval just as Zoe and Erich approached her.

'Mother, this is Max Heller. My mother, and Mr Mannheim.'

Erich broke the ice, surprising Leonie with his knowledgeable praise of Max's performance. Zoe watched Max's face, as if summing him up.

'I thought you were European,' she said. 'But from your accent you could be pure Brooklyn.'

'I take that as a compliment. I caught the accent from an

uncle in New York. My people live on the west coast.'

'That must be lovely.' Zoe sounded slightly bored, and Leonie interpreted it as her mother's way of making quite sure that this young man of European extraction did not feel too welcome.

'We are sure to meet in Paris, if you and Leonie continue to be friends.' Erich Mannheim covered up for Zoe's tone. 'You must come to my apartment. I have a rather good Bechstein.'

Max thanked him, and told him that in the kind of room he expected to be able to afford in the *quartier latin* there would only be room for a small upright, if he were lucky.

Leonie was taken by surprise at the mention of Erich's apartment. She had not known he actually lived in Paris. So her mother at least would have somewhere to stay.

'We'll make sure Leonie gives you the address,' Erich went on.

'But I'll not be staying with Mother,' Leonie cut in. 'I plan to find a room in the student quarter too.'

'As you like.' Erich shrugged. 'I had forgotten that you had a little money of your own. It will last longer on the Left Bank, perhaps. But you must spend at least the first night with us. I think your mother will insist.'

Zoe looked at him gratefully. 'That's right, honey. Until we have the family problem sorted out, at least. Give me forty-eight hours?'

It was past midnight when Leonie and Max joined the last-night revels on C Deck. They took drinks to a quiet corner and Leonie told him more of her story. Her life in New York, her mother's background, the reason why she had to get to France and find her father.

'Be very careful, St Cecilia. Don't get hurt.'

'Why do you say that? That's what my mother said.'

'Perhaps she knows more than you do.'

'I think I know it all. Such as it is. I even know the address of my father's lawyers.' She recited it, parrot-fashion. She was suddenly blindingly aware that two days from now she could be face to face with Charles Vincent in his offices in the boulevard de la Madeleine.

'Do something for me?' Max touched her hand lightly.

'If I can.'

'Let your mother see it through. You've come so far, but I have a feeling that the next steps are up to her.'

'Why should you think that?'

'It's no more than a hunch. But she could have put you off the boat in New York if she really wanted. She saw you in time, I know that. She could still insist that you stay in Le Havre and take the next crossing back home. But she hasn't done either, has she? It's as if she's given in. I think you should let her have those forty-eight hours.'

'Perhaps you're right.'

'Better than walking in on an unsuspecting father after all these years?' He did not add that in his short life he had already found out that people are not always there when you seek them out. Not even always alive.

'I must see him, Max.'

'Look, I'll call for you first thing. We'll find somewhere for you to stay. I'll get a list of rooms from the Conservatoire – they're sure to keep one. You'll be my first guest.'

She nodded, grateful to have the first hours in Paris under some kind of control. Once she knew where to find her father, no one would be able to advise her what else she must do. Until then, there was no one she would rather have at her side than Max Heller.

It was almost daylight by the time the *Normandie*'s lights were dimmed and the last C Deck passenger crawled into his narrow berth.

Max said goodbye to Leonie. He had a train ticket through to Paris. Erich Mannheim's party was to drive from Le Havre. With Zoe's luggage to consider it was the only possible way for them to travel.

Leonie sat in the back of the high bull-nosed Mercedes surrounded by her mother's hand baggage and extra coats. Sleepy after the late night before, she dozed off soon after the

61

start of the journey, then woke to a rush of dark green branches overhead and a landscape of wide fields bathed in golden light, as they drove through an avenue of poplars on the long, straight road to Paris.

CHAPTER FIVE

The line from Paris to Briteau was always bad. Mireille de Byron sat on the desk by the library window, bare brown legs swinging in mock impatience. A storm had been in the air for two days now, and the telephone crackled and died and broke back into precarious life.

'Yes, my father is at home on leave. No, he is not in the house. He has just left for the fields. Yes, I could fetch him. If the matter is urgent? One moment, please.'

From where she sat she could just see her father's oldest tenant, Louis Fabri, his dark blue Basque beret bobbing in and out of sight as he took the winding path to the terraced fields below the château grounds. Beside him her father's grey head, hair cropped close to the finely shaped skull in military fashion, came into view.

She ran down the drive, dry dust spurting beneath her sandals. A small brown and white King Charles spaniel raced through the archway from the stable block at the side of the house and followed her, barking at her heels.

'Papa! Papa!' She lifted the crossbar of the heavy wrought-iron gates as the two men turned to face her, then went towards them at a slower pace.

Paul de Byron watched his daughter's approach with the familiar tug at his heart that grew sharper each summer. This year it was even worse. The long white-blonde hair was caught high on the crown of her head with a knot of black velvet ribbon exactly as Yvette Massine had worn her hair when they first met.

'Papa. Telephone for you. It is Etablissements Vincent, from Paris. They say it is urgent.'

63

'It had better be.' Paul de Byron put his hand on Louis's shoulder. 'Will you go on? I'll join you as soon as I can. We are short-handed enough.'

'Wait till I get my hands on Jacques,' the old man grumbled. 'Trust him to disappear before *le grand travail*.'

Paul smiled. 'Your son will come back, you'll see. He always does.'

Neither of the two men noticed how Mireille reacted to the mention of Jacques Fabri, hiding her face from them as she bent to fondle the dog's soft ears.

Father and daughter walked back towards the house in silence at first, a yard or so apart. It was always like this at the start of the long vacation, as they sought for ways to communicate after the year-long separation.

'The storm is still there, waiting somewhere in the mountains.' Paul gestured towards the endless blue hills beyond the house.

Mireille kicked at a stone. 'I wanted to fly my kite.'

'Not until Jacques can go with you. And then no further than the meadow above the stream.' Paul quickened his pace. 'Did you leave your books in the library? I'll not be long.'

'I'd rather join you in the fields, Papa.'

'Your English tutor will want to see you well prepared.'

Their footsteps echoed on the black and white tiles in the main hall. Mireille watched the library door close, then ran lightly up the wide stairs to the first floor landing. At the far end the door to her father's suite of rooms stood half open. Moments later, holding her breath, she picked up the telephone extension on his bedside table.

Mireille lived in Bordeaux with her mother's parents, Henri and Marguerite Massine. They had taken her home with them when Yvette died at the château, a week after Mireille's birth. It was not only the obvious, practical solution, but also a subtle revenge on the young soldier-aristocrat whom they held responsible for their daughter's death.

Paul de Byron agreed to the arrangement when he was still numbed with grief. He had little choice. His army career kept him away from Briteau most of the year. The dowry settlement from the Massines was stretched over ten years, and the estate – to which Mireille was now sole heir – was already eating up the money. There was no one but Violette, the old cook-general, or the Fabri family, to look after his newborn daughter.

He consulted briefly with Tante Berthe in Paris. Since Paul's father's death she was the last of the older generation of de Byrons, but her influence still reached to the estate in the distant Pyrenees.

'It is true they are mere *haute bourgeoisie*,' she told Paul. 'But the Massines are shipping merchants. It is an honourable enough trade. And they have that great town house. All the servants one could ask. What is more important, there is the lycée. For the modern young woman a good classical education is important. Your daughter will need such background, as the heir to Briteau.'

It was his love for his dead wife that made him impose one condition on Henri Massine. He wanted to watch Yvette's daughter grow, and to teach her to love the land that her mother, in the brief year of their marriage, had learned to love. Every summer she was to spend at Briteau. As an infant, with a nurse from the Massine household. Later, alone.

It had not been easy. The Massines seemed to do their best to undermine Paul's relationship with his daughter. They alternated between spoiling her and subjecting her to rigorous discipline. At the château she reacted, running half wild with the young son of the Fabri family all summer. The Massines visited her there each year after the harvest, registered disapproval, reminded her that her real home was with them, and returned to Bordeaux before nightfall.

This year, with her Baccalaureat only twelve months

away, they had insisted on hiring an English tutor who would arrive in a few days' time.

Deprived of the freedom that Briteau symbolized for her, deprived of the company of young Jacques Fabri who had – he said – gone climbing in the higher mountains close to the Spanish border, Mireille pretended to study for the first few days. Then she began to wander the deserted rooms on the upper floors of the château. It was sheer boredom that made her pick up the phone and listen to the call from young Charles Vincent, her father's family lawyer.

Paul's face was a mask as his lawyer gradually broke to him the news of Zoe's arrival in Paris. Yes, he had known an American girl of that name. A long time ago. He thought she had returned to New York soon after their . . . meeting. It was a long time ago.

'I should perhaps have informed your aunt, Mademoiselle de Byron. But at our last meeting she did not seem in the best of health. This time I thought it best that the matter should come to your notice.'

'This time?'

'Paul.' The young lawyer's voice was hesitant. 'We are friends? What happened was arranged by my father, and your aunt. I have always been sworn to secrecy. But I am not sure I would have kept this secret had I been in my father's place then, as head of the firm.'

'What secret is this, Charles? I am very busy. If there is some family skeleton that has at last to be wrenched from one of my aunt's many cupboards, then please tell me now, without any frills.'

'It need not be a skeleton, my friend. From what I know of your life there may be nothing but good to come of all this.'

'Then why are you so afraid to tell me?'

'Paul. When the young American woman returned to New York, you should know that her papers bore the name Byron, that she travelled first class, that it was all arranged so by the two old people. Now, on her return to Paris, she breaks her vow to them. And with her she brings a daughter, who is just seventeen years old.'

'I see.' There was a long silence on the line. 'Please go on.'

'I have seen the girl, Paul. She is an exquisite child – yes, still a child. Her mother has never dared tell her the most painful part of her story. That you, her father, have never been told of her existence.'

'Where is she?'

'Here. In Paris. She is very independent, and has a room on the Left Bank. She asks to meet you. What am I to say?'

'To the mother – that I can never see her again. Is that understood? I gather that you and my aunt have made it worth her while. I do not know what kind of woman it is who kept her secret from me. But I have my wife's memory, my own child, to think of. Briteau is no place for . . . Zoe.'

'As your family lawyer I have had the chance through all this to save the estate considerable expense in the coming years, Paul. By returning to France the woman has forfeited her expectations from us. Your Tante Berthe has always honoured her part of the bargain. Now, she would consider it to be null and void – I know her well enough for that. I also have the impression that the mother wishes to make the break final herself. She is quite a strong character –'

'Please. No more of the American. Tell me, how have you left things with the child? What is her name?'

'Leonie. Her name is Leonie. I think you will find it in your heart to meet her, Paul. And somehow I do not think you will regret it.'

'I cannot come to Paris. It is out of the question. My leave only allows for the harvest, you know that.'

'Then why not invite her to Briteau? I could put her on the night train to Bordeaux.'

'I need time. One week.'

'For God's sake, Paul. She's only seventeen. She's come all this way to seek you out.'

'One week.'

67

*

'*Bonjour, madame. Comment ça va?*' Leonie tapped on the window of the small apartment belonging to the concierge, then began the long climb to the room Max Heller rented on the top floor.

They had found it quite by chance, the day Leonie moved out of Erich Mannheim's apartment. The day her mother had told her the de Byrons' lawyer was ready to receive her. The room Leonie now rented in the tall, crumbling house next door had been advertised on the notice-board in a student café. Max himself was not pleased with the place he had found through the office at the Conservatoire. It was with a family in the suburbs, too far out. He had only accepted because they had a very good piano.

They paid a week in advance for Leonie's room. Now, Max told Leonie in English, all they needed was to find somewhere for him in the same district, with a piano.

'If monsieur wants a piano,' the landlord said in fluent English with an American accent, 'then I can recommend the adjacent house, and the empty room on the top floor. Madame la concierge will no doubt hand over the key. She is not likely to wish to climb five flights of stairs again in her lifetime.'

'How do you know there is a piano there, monsieur?'

He put expressive hands to his ears. 'How could I not know? The last *locataire* was also American. He played *le jazz*.'

The piano would have looked exactly right in a movie set for a far-west saloon. It also took up one third of the small attic room, and as Max opened the lid and sat down Leonie moved away and perched on the narrow bed.

'I shall play Bizet, of course. In honour of Paris. And of Picasso, close by in the rue des Grands Augustins – did you know you were neighbours? And perhaps "Trail of the Lonesome Pine" – they say it's Gertrude Stein's favourite song and I swear I saw her in that patisserie on the corner.'

'Do you think you should play at all?'

68

'Why not?'

'You haven't paid a sou to the concierge.' Leonie looked round the small room, loving its isolation and its simplicity. Through the window the rooftops of Paris looked like some legendary forest between them and the river.

'When she hears this she will give me a week rent-free,' Max grinned.

He began to play. It was a wild Bizet improvisation, rocking the piano, and making Leonie put her hands to her ears. 'I think they'll wish the jazz player had not left.'

'Oh, I'll play jazz if that's what you want.'

'No!' She jumped up and went over to him. 'Let's pay your rent, and go get my cases. Then let's go out and explore.'

For the next five days they walked everywhere. Paris unfolded for Leonie like some giant high-summer flower. The streets were deserted in the evenings, except for the tourists. It was true that the city emptied in August.

Zoe insisted after Leonie left Erich's apartment that they have supper together every other evening. She had to be sure of maintaining control of the events she had set in motion by her visit, the first morning in Paris, to the offices of Vincent et fils. Her daughter knew nothing of the emotional drain the interview with Charles Vincent made on Zoe. She merely gave Leonie the news that the lawyer would see her the next day, alone. There was something in Zoe's eyes that forbade questions after that.

Leonie's encounter with Charles Vincent had been very short, a matter of minutes. He had asked her where she studied, whether she spoke French, whether she had plans for her future.

'I only wish to see my father. That is my plan. Then I can decide whether or not to go back to New York.'

Charles Vincent replied that he thought her mother had a project to found a company in Paris. It sounded very ambitious.

'My mother will succeed. She always has,' Leonie told him.

He did not tell her that if her daughter was anything to go by then Zoe Byron was certainly a woman who produced results. The exquisite girl-woman who sat on the other side of his desk, nervous as a thoroughbred, eyes fiercely defending the mother who had reared her in the jungle that was New York, surprised in him a need to protect, even to defend. He was not sure that he could refuse Leonie Byron anything she asked.

They arranged that he should talk with her father and find a time and place where they could meet. He explained that the château owned by the de Byron family was a long way from Paris, and that her father would in all probability be there for the grape harvest. That is, if he were not away on manoeuvres.

'Your father is a military man.' He answered the question in the dark blue eyes. 'And a landowner. He has one child. One other child, that is. I shall tell you more if – and when – the meeting can be arranged.'

She knew that the interview was at an end. 'This other child?'

'A girl. Paul de Byron has, as I now know, two very beautiful daughters, mademoiselle.'

In the end it was Max who took her to the Gare de Lyon for the train to Bordeaux. Word had come from Briteau that her father would meet her at the local station next day with a car. She would change trains in Bordeaux at dawn.

'Don't let them frighten you,' Max said as he closed the compartment door. She leaned from the window, and asked him how he knew she was so scared.

'When you're scared – which is hardly ever – you put your chin in the air. Hasn't anyone ever told you that before?'

She shook her head. The times before when she had been afraid – of school, of her illegitimacy – she had run to Maddie, or braved it out alone. 'I'd feel better if I could really speak French well,' she said.

'Oh, I bet the château is full of people wanting to try out their English on you. And if you can't stand it, you only have to whistle.'

70

The train began to move, and she drew back into the carriage, pressing her hand in farewell to him against the window. The lights high in the station's dome caught her face, making her look very pale. She suddenly could not bear to watch Max any longer, and turned away. As the train drew out of the city it gathered speed and she saw that the sky was quite dark. Ahead of her were all the hours of a summer night in which to think about the man she was soon to meet. But now that the encounter was so close she found herself gripped by panic, almost as if she had imagined it all. As if she had never surprised her mother and Erich Mannheim in Gramercy Park that birthday Sunday afternoon, never even wanted to meet her father. In a few weeks she had by her own will destroyed an ordered, sheltered life, discarded her childhood. She found herself inexplicably resentful of the way Zoe had just let it all happen. Max was right. There had been time for her mother to get her off the boat in New York. Was it because she had once made the same voyage that she had allowed Leonie to go on to Paris? Or was it that she had seen her chance, in that split second in which mother and daughter had met each other's gaze across the crowds, to rid herself of all responsibility at last?

All Leonie knew for certain was that she wanted Zoe with her on the long night journey to Bordeaux, and that Charles Vincent had made it clear to her at their second meeting that it was the one thing he could never allow.

It was about eight next morning when the small local train slowed and came to a halt on the track. Leonie took the opportunity to stand and stretch her legs. The hard wooden seats of the French trains had made an ordeal of the journey. On the bench opposite, a small boy slipped from his mother's lap and pressed his nose to the window.

'*Les gitanes! Les gitanes!*'

She followed the boy's eyes to a gap in the railway bank a little further along the line. There was no level crossing or gate, but just a dirt track where the road crossed the rails.

On the road was a Romany caravan, a string of oak-banded, polished houses on wheels, drawn by sturdy horses with gleaming, well-groomed coats. A trio of dark-haired dark-eyed men led the procession; naked children ran at their heels, waving at the train. A small, crooked smokestack on the roof of one of the caravans belched a grey cloud that wisped away on the breeze. Long rods slung beneath the bellies of the vans clanked with cooking pots and the gypsy families' few possessions. Behind the last van a line of more horses followed, roped together, shepherded by a young boy.

Watching them pass, Leonie had an impression of watching another world. The men walked with great purpose, not looking to either side. The horses were unlike anything she had seen in Central Park or in a western. The naked children were as free as the mountain air that now invaded the compartment through an open window.

As the train gathered speed again the child returned to his mother. A peasant in the far corner sniffed disapproval and grumbled that the train had been delayed for the gypsies. Then he produced a stick of white bread from a deep pocket inside his coat and offered it to Leonie.

She shook her head, thanking him, and asked the mother of the boy if it was long now to the station where she was to be met by her father.

'Five minutes, perhaps ten, mademoiselle,' the woman told her.

Her heart began to thump unbearably, and to cover her nervousness she pulled on her jacket over her cotton dress and began to edge her case out from the space under her feet. Then things happened very fast. The woman had miscalculated, or had wanted to put her mind at rest; the station was only yards along the track from the level crossing, and a handbell rung somewhere on the platform announced their arrival. The train drew to a halt and Leonie put her head out of the window.

On the platform a guard in blue overalls was throwing a

crate of screeching hens into the train. A peasant, dark blue beret at an angle, thin cheroot at the side of his mouth, watched impassively. Two women in long black skirts and dark shawls left the train and walked towards the station house where a ticket collector waited.

She opened the door, and dragged her case after her as she dropped to the platform. It was already very hot, yet the thin mountain air caught at her throat. She put a hand to her eyes, and saw the figure of a man walking towards her along the station platform.

He was about forty, perhaps older. He was very thin, and his grey hair was cut *en brosse*. He walked steadily, and held himself very straight. She remembered that her father was a soldier.

She stood, her case at her feet, and watched him draw closer as the train moved noisily out of the station.

The man gave a curt, welcoming nod. He took her hand briefly, and she found herself smiling into hazel eyes devoid of expression. Nervously, she looked down at her baggage, and as if welcoming the interruption her father took the case and gestured towards the ticket collector.

'I was not sure you would know how to recognize me.' Leonie was the first to speak.

'There was no need. Charles Vincent gave me a very good description.' Paul de Byron spoke in English, and she gave him a grateful look, then turned to hand her ticket to the collector. Her father did not tell her that had he met her without warning, in any place at any time, he would have known at once that her mother was the American girl who had enchanted him in Paris the year before Leonie was born.

His silence was his way of concealing the shock of the likeness, and the way in which the years had fallen away as he walked towards his daughter. In the past few days he had relived the time with Zoe again and again, unable to understand how he could have let her go. But Tante Berthe must have been convincing. The American child had left Paris without a word, she had told him, like all her kind. She

73

had probably spent all her money. Certainly, she had met some compatriot who had talked her into going on through Europe with him, or even back to New York. What did he expect?

And he believed her. Even the old man, Charles Vincent, had played her game for all these years.

He had tried to understand. After all, once he thought that Zoe had really left Paris he had made no effort to trace her. Could he have loved her, letting her go like that? It had not been so simple. His father was ill; the demands of the land all fell on his shoulders. He had only weeks before returning to his regiment once his wound had begun to heal properly. In those weeks he had flung himself into working on the estate at Briteau. Yet always at the back of his mind was the thought that he would get back to Paris soon, and find the beautiful Zoe.

Tante Berthe's account of Zoe's disappearance had left him angry, and then philosophical. It was more than three years before he looked at another woman. Then Yvette Massine had come to Briteau for the harvest, and he had fallen in love again.

Their marriage had surprised in him a taste for domestic life. His absences from the château were agony, and each time his regiment released him he made for home and the girl with white-blonde hair like a man possessed. The love of his life had soon supplanted any memories of Zoe. Now, years after Yvette's death, Zoe had returned as if from the dead herself, in the body of their daughter.

As he took Leonie's hand he did not see her as a child, his child. She was for a fraction of a second the girl at the tea party eighteen years ago. He did not feel her flesh, but a white glove. He did not see the childish cotton frock and the thin jacket, but a grey suit and a fresh white blouse. His eyes stared unseeing at the reality, and his daughter knew that he did not want the ghost of a presence she had carried with her all the way from New York.

In the rough road outside the station Paul de Byron

nodded in the direction of an ancient, bull-nosed Citroën. She followed him, waiting as he put her case on the back seat. Then she sat rigidly at his side as he backed and turned, aware that the two women who had left the train with her were watching her, black eyes alive with conjecture.

'We must drive for perhaps thirty minutes,' her father told her. 'You are tired? Hungry, perhaps?'

'Thirsty. Not tired. It is all too . . .'

She fell silent as they drove through the village street. On each side whitewashed cottages, their doors wide open, flanked a narrow track, and down the centre of the road ran a wide, bubbling stream that Leonie sensed must come from the high hills she could see ahead. She gave a low laugh as a family of ducks ran ahead of the car, then took to the stream in a flurry of protest.

For the first time Paul smiled. 'They will soon be someone's good dinner. I really do not understand why they object to us.'

She turned shyly to look at him. But the smile had already gone, and he manoeuvred the car on to a side road with grim determination which she thought was feigned.

The road narrowed a mile or so further on, and then became a single track from which terraces fell away steeply to one side. Their only protection from the slopes was a line of great rough-hewn stones painted white, and she braced herself, keeping her gaze away from the drop as the car gathered speed.

'Not long now.' Her father turned the car off the mountain track on to a gravel road. 'This is already part of the estate.'

They drove on a slight incline, through long terraces of vines. There were people working in the fields, and Leonie noticed that although they turned their heads at the car's approach their hands did not pause as they tended the vines.

Where the terraces ended a road crossed their route, and Paul de Byron braked as a horse-drawn wagon appeared suddenly from nowhere and passed them at a crazy, thunderous speed, the contents of the trailer rolling from side to side, apparently to the complete unconcern of the young man who held the reins.

Leonie was aware of haunted, near-black eyes in a thin face. She knew that the hands would be as supple as the leather they held. His deeply tanned skin was like that of the gypsies she had seen an hour before. He had their same air of resolute freedom. And as he drove past the master of Briteau he acknowledged him with the merest flick of the reins and a brief glance at Leonie.

'That is the son of my oldest tenant. Jacques Fabri. You will meet his family, if you work with us.'

'I'd like that,' Leonie said. Her father's dry tone had not escaped her. He did not add that this was the first time Jacques Fabri had appeared at Briteau for some weeks.

'But first, you will meet the rest of my family.' Paul drove the car past a high hedgerow and on to the curve of a long drive. Ahead of them the château stood as it had stood for five hundred years, square built in red brick, turret windows glinting in the sun, wide steps leading to a heavy oaken door that opened slowly as the car came to a halt.

At the top of the steps stood a girl who Leonie thought was three or four years her junior. She had long white-blonde hair caught high on her head with a knot of black velvet ribbon. She was fair-skinned, but her body was golden with the summer in the mountains, and as she stood very still waiting for them Leonie thought of a gazelle that might run from them if they moved too soon or too fast.

The image faded when Leonie looked into her sister's eyes. Ice-blue resentment greeted her, belying the young girl's hand held out in well trained adult welcome.

'You are Leonie, of course,' Mireille de Byron said. 'You will forgive me? If I am – a little *nerveuse*? I did not know until recently that I had – a sister. But then' – turning to Paul with a swing of the long fair hair – 'I am not sure that my father . . .'

Paul de Byron silenced her with a look, and the frisson of

jealousy that had touched her spine when she saw Leonie walk towards the house at his side took root.

When her father had told her a little of the past, enough to explain the identity of the young American who was to spend a few days with them at Briteau, she had behaved well. There had been time to control the anger and bewilderment she had felt when she heard the conversation with Charles Vincent. It had been necessary, if she was to keep from her father the fact that she had broken his strict code of conduct by eavesdropping.

Now her remarks, delivered in excellent schoolgirl English with an arrogance that spoke of years of privilege, cut through Leonie as she had intended. She turned to Paul de Byron instinctively, as if seeking protection, but he walked ahead of her, reaching the top step before he turned.

'Leonie,' he said. 'This is the daughter of my marriage. My daughter Mireille.'

CHAPTER SIX

Paul de Byron deposited the Paris-new suitcase, chosen by Zoe three days before, at the foot of the main stairs. His two daughters watched him as he crossed the hall, Mireille coolly critical, as if defying him to make his escape before any real conversation became a social necessity; Leonie uneasily aware of the small cloud that had materialized out of the distant past as she touched her sister's hand.

'We shall meet at dinner this evening.' Paul turned, addressing Leonie. 'Violette will look after you – there is always coffee ready in her kitchen. Mireille will show you to your rooms.'

Leonie thought that this stranger who was her father had not once let down his guard since the moment she had walked towards him on the station platform at Briteau.

'I was hoping to do more than that, Papa,' Mireille broke in. 'Someone must make the grand tour of inspection with our guest, surely?'

'Today is a working day for us all.'

'I can study twice as long tomorrow.'

'Briteau will be there tomorrow, also. Today your – sister – needs to rest.'

It was an order, given in the certain knowledge that it would be obeyed. He was gone before Mireille could argue further, and she made a face, beckoning to Leonie to follow her through a heavy swing door which closed silently behind them, leaving them in a dimly lit, stone-flagged corridor, a flow of cold air touching their faces.

The woman who looked up from the scrubbed work table that dominated the kitchen was in her late fifties, perhaps older. Dark, almond-shaped eyes scrutinized the newcomer, then softened slightly, as if Leonie had passed some first intuitive test. Violette nodded a greeting, broad hands still kneading a twist of dough in the swift, vigorous movements of long custom.

'There is fresh bread in the pantry, Mireille. Welcome to Briteau, Mademoiselle Leonie. Your father has spoken to me of you – a little, but enough. You understand me? You speak French?'

'I am taking lessons in Paris.' It was Zoe who had insisted, booking her into a sedately exclusive school for foreigners that had been recommended by Lady Hume.

'If you understand Violette's dialect then you already know more French than I do. We can think ourselves fortunate that she does not speak Basque,' Mireille called from the walk-in pantry across the kitchen, and emerged with a basket of bread in her hands.

'It is the oldest and proudest of languages, ma fille. But the Basques are jealous. Briteau is not in their territory – so we do not speak their tongue. Now, fetch coffee for our guest. You understand that much, I hope, of your old Violette?'

She gave Mireille a sudden smile of such rare sweetness that Leonie, watching them, had to fight down a rogue wave of homesickness for the kitchen at Gramercy Park and Maddie's teasing. She took a gulp of the hot, black coffee and found it the best she had ever tasted. The tears held back. Violette watched approvingly as she spread dark plum conserve on the rough white bread and began to eat.

'Ah, bon. So at last we have someone at Briteau who knows how to eat. Since Pierre left for Paris there is no one here who eats.'

'The bread is very good,' Leonie told her between mouthfuls, unexpectedly hungry.

Mireille drew a chair in close to the table, and put her chin in her hands. 'Pierre is the favourite around here. Violette's grandson. He studies in Paris, to be a famous doctor, and he has an Italian motor cycle – he is very spoilt – and rooms in the *quartier latin*.' She paused, her attention distracted by a scratching at the outer door on the far side of the kitchen. A dog barked sharply, demanding entry. 'Charlie!' She pushed back her chair and ran to the door.

'No dogs in my kitchen!' Violette was ready for her. 'The name is absurd, for one thing. And the dog itself too small. Give me a hunting dog, or nothing.' She wiped floury hands on a cloth with an air of finality.

'Now you know why your daughter lives so far away, in Madagascar!' Mireille blew her a kiss from long, slim fingers as she shut the door against the dog. Leonie glimpsed a high hedge, neat rows of vegetables in dry, sunbaked soil, a brown hen pecking at nothing on a cobbled path.

'Pierre's mother is married to an engineer. They work in the far-flung colonies, and they are very rich,' Mireille told Leonie as she came back to her place at the table. 'Of course, they have no foolish little dogs. But Charlie is different. He is accustomed to the city. He likes to be indoors. *En famille*.'

'Then let him return "*en famille*".' Violette held her ground. Leonie had the impression she was witnessing a single skirmish in a long-tried battle. 'He can go back with your grandparents, when they condescend to visit us for their one day. Life in the country is too much for them all, *évidemment*.'

At the mention of Mireille's grandparents Leonie sat very still. Every moment since her arrival had held something for which she had been unprepared. The plan to leave New York and find her father had seemed so clean-cut. The reality was something else. A whole gallery of unknown faces had followed Zoe in Paul de Byron's life, and perhaps faded in their turn. Leaving the child, Mireille. And the child's grandparents.

'Come and inspect your rooms, américaine.' Mireille jumped up again. 'Charlie will return to Bordeaux with me, only with me, at the end of the summer – and you know it well, ma chère Violette.' She placed a brown arm round Violette's plump shoulders, making her peace.

*

80

They carried the luggage to the first landing and paused, looking down into the silent hall. From the landing a series of corridors led to the bedrooms. Mireille explained that the doors at the top of the main stairs were those to Paul de Byron's own suite.

'My father could not run this place without Violette, you know,' she said as she led the way on through a carpeted gallery. 'And besides . . . we love her . . . and she loves us . . . Charlie as well.'

The walls of the gallery were lined with oil paintings. Portraits from another era stared out from darkened canvas. Mireille made a face at an eighteenth-century beauty, and gave a mock curtsey before the portrait of a man twice the beauty's age.

'He had three wives. One must respect that, n'est-ce pas? It has style. The de Byron style, perhaps.'

At the far end of the gallery they took a narrow staircase and pushed through a door which Mireille explained gave access to the oldest wing. Here the ceilings were lower, striped with blackened beams. At the end of a short passage they came to an oak door set in a pointed stone arch.

'*Voilà*, your very own rooms, away from us all. And with the best view, of course. We give them to all of our visitors.' Mireille tugged at the iron latch and the door creaked heavily inwards, sending a swirl of dust flecked with sunlight up from a bare floor.

Leonie gave a smile as if of recognition. The room was all welcoming silence. A faded blue silk coverlet on a high, carved bed. A single very modern painting on the facing wall. A long window in a deep sill. She crossed to it, drawn to the view.

Directly below, a short drop to the cobbled path, was the kitchen garden. Beyond its high hedge a rough meadow, nine or ten acres of short yellowing grass, cut through by a stream that had twisted its way down from the foothills of the Pyrenees to disappear to the west of the château into a copse of gnarled trees. The water ran very fast over giant flat stones. A miniature humpbacked bridge linked the ground close to the house with a worn track that also soon became lost in the low hills, beyond which grey rock climbed steeply to where the distant mountains formed a circling barrier.

'The sea is not far away . . . perhaps forty kilometres. And to the south, beyond the mountains, there is Spain.' Mireille stood at her shoulder. Her voice was no longer petulant. She seemed preoccupied with whatever lay beyond the forbidding ridge of the Pyrenees.

It was some moments before she broke her mood with a more characteristic shrug, and began to wander about the room, showing Leonie where she might keep her clothes. To one side of an ornate wardrobe, a flight of four worn stone steps led to an alcove, and a closed door.

'Your sitting-room. *En suite*. But it is very cold, even in summer. The bathroom is further along the corridor. We passed it on our way.'

She left her, promising to call her in time for an English tea in the library if she did not appear for lunch. On weekdays time was precious, and all the other members of the household except for herself and Violette stayed in the fields, and ate alfresco for the midday meal.

Leonie unpacked, then on an impulse tried the handle of the door at the top of the stone steps. It swung open easily, on to a square of whitewashed walls and bare floor, with a high ceiling and a grey stone fireplace that dominated one wall. There were deep chairs either side of the hearth, covered in worn tapestry, and a small secretaire under the single window, which shared the same view as her bedroom. She shivered at the damp disuse of the place and turned back, but a fall of plaster in the chimney made her pause.

She went to the fireplace and knelt. Above the iron firebasket, four or five feet away, was a crumbling stone ledge. Higher up, footholds almost as wide as the hearth itself, hung with cobwebs and black with the smoke of fires long dead, led to where the wide chimney opened sharply on to an oblong of clear sky.

82

She lay on the blue silk coverlet for some hours, drifting in and out of sleep. Across the room the soft leather of her new suitcase gleamed a reminder of Zoe, and of her own promise to Charles Vincent that she would not mention her mother's name at Briteau unless Paul de Byron himself opened the subject. Mireille had clearly put her in her place, as a visitor, in a room which was hers by courtesy, and not by right. As a visitor she would keep her promise. But it would not be easy.

It was Mireille's laughter that woke her, from somewhere in the garden. The sun had left the room and she lay for a moment regaining her bearings. A man's voice answered Mireille's laugh, in a volley of French too fast for her to understand. She slipped from the bed and ran to the window, in time to see a vaguely familiar figure walk to the iron gate in the high hedge. It was the driver of the cart that had crossed their path as she and her father arrived at Briteau.

As Jacques Fabri reached the gate he seemed to sense that he was watched, and turned, scanning the upper windows. She drew back, too late. He raised a hand in salute. Then Mireille called to him, and he grinned, and walked out of view. There was something in the smile, a tug of attraction perhaps, that she found more disconcerting than the arrogance of his manner earlier in the day.

In the library she found Mireille poised, a youthful imitation of some old-world chatelaine, over a silver tray laid with porcelain. The room gave on to a terrace at the front of the main house, and was softly lit by the northern light of the French side of the mountains. Between two heavily draped windows there was a small grand piano, highly polished, music sheets stacked neatly in the base of a duet stool worked in petit point whose colours were a fresh ribbon of brightness in the otherwise sombre room. They were the first articles of furniture she had seen in the house that seemed to have received any real care. Yet the piano lid was closed, a gold key glinting in its lock.

To one side of the room a third window looked out over a courtyard edged with a low stone wall and a brilliant yellow flowering border. Beyond the wall was an archway, and a small tower marked what Leonie guessed was the stable block, topped by a blue enamelled clock, tarnished hands tight together as if in some perpetual noonday prayer.

'This is where they shut me up for the summer.' Mireille surveyed the book-lined walls with distaste. 'And it will get worse. My life is one long examination. Was it like that for you, in New York? And was it so unbearably hot?'

'I didn't wait to find out. August can be the worst. And my graduation . . .' She left the sentence as unresolved as the subject itself, and traced a finger the length of the piano lid, thinking of Max Heller, as Mireille poured weak tea into the delicate cups.

'It was my mother who played. Rather well, they say.' The voice was quite matter-of-fact. 'I never knew her, of course, so to be sad is to be – how do you say? – unreal. There is an empty place, if you like. But it has always been there. Perhaps it is the same for you, with Papa?'

Leonie, caught unawares, bit her lip, having no answer she wanted to give. She took a leather chair across the hearth from Mireille. There had been a fire the night before, and the scent of apple wood reached out to her from the soft white ash.

Mireille changed the subject, telling her that they would explore Briteau the next day, a Saturday, as her father had instructed. On the Sunday they would all go to church. It was *de rigueur* – as it would be to dress for dinner that night.

She wore the silk shirtwaister, keeping the blue dress in hand for some more formal occasion, should it arise. At the first, non-committal glance from her father as she took her place at the long dining-table she guessed that her choice had been the right one. She could not know that Paul de Byron was quite unaware of her clothes. Each time he set eyes on her he grappled with an image of her mother, the bright innocent of almost twenty years before, an image more seductive than anything experience, or time, or her own beauty salon, had achieved for Zoe in the years between.

They ate roast duckling, followed by a cheese with the bite of Roquefort which Violette herself had made. It was Violette, too, who served at table, joining in the conversation as she did so, and nodding approval between each course at Leonie's empty plate.

Mireille chattered endlessly, as if to postpone the moment when they would fall silent, and Leonie's arrival in their lives at Briteau would be the only subject left to them.

After an anecdote about a classmate at the lycée in Bordeaux, she casually mentioned her grandfather, Henri Massine. Leonie noticed an almost imperceptible hardening of Paul's jaw as he reached for the decanter, although his glass was still more than half full.

'You drink wine at home, in New York?' He offered the decanter to Leonie, a blatant attempt to sidetrack his other daughter.

Leonie went scarlet. It was the first reference Paul de Byron had made to her life with her mother. Charles Vincent had not groomed her for the moment when her father himself would introduce the forbidden subject.

'Of course they drink wine, Papa. They are not peasants, after all.' Mireille watched Leonie's face, a smile at the back of the blue eyes betraying that she sought entertainment as much as hurt.

'We had champagne on my last birthday,' Leonie said quietly. This man who was a stranger should have known that she had her first glass of wine at fourteen, that she adored the movies, that she wore a brace on her teeth until almost a year ago.

'Your birthday?' Mireille pounced. 'I hope Papa sent you something special?'

Leonie did not miss the barb behind the shield of innocence. *I did not know until recently that I had a sister.*

'That is enough, Mireille.' Paul spoke softly, in French, and Mireille lowered her eyes, sipping her coffee, the damage neatly done.

'I have not been neglected.' Leonie's voice shook a little as she came to her father's rescue, hoping he would know somehow that she referred to the never-failing monthly cheque as well as to Zoe's own brand of caring, which had not faltered for seventeen sheltered years. The pain that the anonymous payments from France had given her since she had learnt of her illegitimacy suddenly seemed insignificant beside her need to get through the rest of the dinner without confrontation.

She thought there was gratitude somewhere in Paul de Byron's voice when he answered at last. 'Your sister will not neglect you, either, Leonie.' He looked her full in the face for the first time that evening. 'I am sad that this is my busiest time, and then – as always – as soon as the harvest is done I return to my regiment.'

'Monsieur Vincent explained to me, in Paris.' She wanted at that moment to call him *Papa*, the diminutive, affectionate title which Mireille had always been able to take for granted. But she sensed it was still too soon. If, that is, it was ever going to be right.

'We are glad, all the same, to receive you. It was important that you should meet us.' Paul de Byron raised his glass. The moment of approaching intimacy had passed. He was the formal host, making the guest in his house feel wanted. For a while.

Mireille took an apple from a dish and bit into it fiercely.

It was the nearest either of them was to come to a speech of welcome.

*

86

The clack of wooden shoes on the cobblestones in the kitchen garden was the first sound she heard next day. From her bedroom window she could see the heads of the estate workers, the women with coloured scarves tightly swathing dark hair, the men in blue berets and paler blue overalls, mingling in groups at the kitchen door.

Shrill orders in patois came from inside the house. A small boy ran to the gate carrying a roomy wicker basket. A burly man followed, clapping him on the shoulder in rough encouragement as he pulled open the heavy iron gate. The estate workers followed in ones and twos until the garden was deserted, and Violette herself appeared, scattering grain at the strutting yellow feet of the hens.

A movement in the fields beyond the stream caught Leonie's eye. She opened her window and heard Mireille's voice, a child's treble at this distance. A man was running, sure-footed, in the rough grass, his back to the house as he let slip the wire of a kite from the spool he held expertly close to his body. A morning breeze from the hills whipped at the kite, a sharp triangle of red with a curling green tail against the pale sky. Mireille followed, shouting instructions, long blonde hair flying loose, wnile Charlie, a ball of brown and white, rolled and jumped at her heels.

Watching them, Leonie felt the pang of isolation. They belonged to their landscape, a trio of shifting, wayward clouds in the arms of the wind. Then a giant bird, wide piebald wings echoing the shape of the darting kite, swooped from the ridge of pines above the meadow, came in low and rose again. The dog barked in useless defiance, and ran towards the vulture as it wheeled towards the treeline. Mireille called him to heel, and walked to where Jacques Fabri stood watching the bird until it had disappeared. Then, as if its coming had changed his mood, he handed the kite to Mireille, ruffling her hair. As he walked back towards the house Leonie drew away from the window, quickly enough this time to be sure that she was not seen.

*

The Briteau estate sprawled in each direction from the château itself for a mile or more, bordered by the foothills to the south and west and the vineyards on the steep terraces to the north.

In the course of the promised conducted tour Mireille made no mention of her early-morning kite flying, but her manner seemed to Leonie the closest to happiness since they had first met. When they had visited the main gardens and the stables, she suggested a walk out on the road towards the village. Ten minutes along the track that led from the main gates brought them to a main road, and the end of the Briteau land. At the junction, a low whitewashed house surrounded by outhouses built round a courtyard stood in its own half-acre.

'It is the home of the Fabri family, my father's head man and his wife,' Mireille explained. She did not mention their son. 'The whole family will be at work on the terraces today.' She turned away. 'They have served the de Byrons for centuries,' she said in a stiff little voice, as if reciting some lesson learned from a guidebook. 'And I suppose they always will.'

At dinner that night Paul de Byron asked Leonie her impressions of the estate.

'It is much bigger than I thought it would be. Like a whole village.'

'Quite. We are almost – how do you say? – self-supporting. If it came to it, we would survive, I always think. We could feed ourselves, for some time at least. And of course there is the wine. A form of currency that never loses its value.'

'I did not take Leonie to the *caves*, Papa,' Mireille cut in. 'I thought she would see them soon enough, if she is to help with the harvest.'

'You will work with us, then?' Paul spoke lightly, reaching for bread from the long basket Violette had provided. But the gesture seemed to serve as a cover for the fact that he needed to know Leonie's answer.

'I'd love to,' she said quickly, meaning it. It was a way of instant belonging, after all. Even Mireille was not allowed to join *le grand travail*.

'Good. Then tomorrow you shall meet many of your fellow workers. At church.'

They left the house soon after a late breakfast, the girls walking on either side of their father, Violette trailing several yards behind and grumbling quietly to herself each time Paul checked his watch and quickened his pace. It was on her advice that Leonie wore the low-heeled pumps in which she had last walked to and from school on the harsh summer pavements of New York. When Paul de Byron went anywhere on foot, his faithful cook-general had explained, he automatically adopted a marching step.

The church was on the main road to the village, and at the junction from Briteau two figures appeared in the doorway of the house as if by clockwork. The man, an older, bearded version of his son, nodded a greeting to Paul and touched his beret to the women; his wife fell in beside Violette, a quick, black-eyed assessment of Leonie achieved in seconds.

'Your son does not honour us with his presence, Camille,' Violette observed, all innocence.

Camille shook her head. 'One does not ask such things of Jacques. If he wishes, he will be there. He left the house before daylight. Who knows where he is by now?'

As they walked on the houses became more frequent. They passed a shabby single-storeyed building with its front door open on to the edge of the road. A child too young to walk half lay propped against the doorway, two olive-skinned girls playing at its side. When they saw Paul they ran out to him, and walked backwards in his path, grinning up into his face. He smiled – the first real smile Leonie had seen from him – spreading his hands in a small benediction that was half tolerance, half dismissal.

89

The church, a squat building in grey stone with a square Norman tower, stood on a rise of ground in a field starred by worn paths and scattered graves. As the de Byron household approached they were joined by groups of farmers and villagers in black suits, the women in dark dresses patterned, if at all, with small flower designs or polka dots. Their legs were encased in dark, thick stockings, strong legs in low-heeled black shoes.

At the west door the men removed the ubiquitous blue berets and stood back in twos and threes as the women went on ahead into the church.

'Follow me. Do as I do . . .' Mireille whispered as Leonie hesitated. They walked into the packed church, the dim light soft after the day outside. Leonie was aware of white walls, high archways, and a sharpness of incense in odd contrast to the monastic simplicity of the surroundings. They walked the length of the centre aisle as if, Leonie thought, it were a walk to the scaffold, heads and eyes swivelling in their direction until they reached the front pews and Mireille halted their progress at last by genuflecting, a token bob, her hand on the high armrest of a bench carved with a swirling letter B.

As they slipped into the vacant places beside Violette and Camille Fabri, Violette handed Leonie a worn leather missal, the place marked with a thin, ageing blue ribbon. She studied the order of service blindly, a blur of French and Latin, then stood with the others as a bell rang and the curé and his entourage of well scrubbed, white-robed village boys made their way to the altar.

It was then that Leonie realized that the main body of the church was lined with a gallery. She looked up, to find a dozen or so men from the village staring down at her in frank curiosity. At the end of the gallery closest to the altar stood her father and his manager, Fabri père. Paul de Byron faced straight ahead, eyes unseeing, his rigid military bearing still held in this simplest, most familiar and unmilitary of ceremonies. Louis Fabri shuffled a little, coughed, and

90

leaned round to watch a late arrival further along the gallery.

Leonie, following his eyes, found herself looking into the thin, dark face of Louis Fabri's son. She bent her head, copying Mireille, thankful for the distraction as she knelt on the hard wooden rail of the pew and the curé's voice began to intone the service. As she closed her eyes she was aware that Mireille's thin, golden body in its formal Sunday dress had tensed – and that the very last thing on her sister's mind was prayer.

After the service the women found Paul de Byron and the two Fabri men waiting at the west door of the church. They began to cross the field to the road in a silent group, until a step on the narrow path behind them made them pause. The curé called to Paul as he drew closer, a tall, ageing man with a thick crop of white hair above a pale, ascetic face. He was slightly out of breath, and smiled ruefully, patting a comfortable paunch, then bowed to Camille Fabri and Violette.

'I could not let you leave without a word.' He addressed Paul in French. 'Your telephone call . . .'

'Of course.' Paul turned to Leonie, and drew her forward. 'Monsieur le Curé . . . my daughter, from New York.'

'Welcome, mademoiselle. You are welcome.' He spoke excellent English, and held Leonie's hand in a firm grasp. She was taken aback, and at the same time reassured, thanking him nervously, her chin going up a fraction as Mireille turned away towards the road with ostentatious indifference.

'Yves Pascal,' the curé introduced himself. 'Your father is a good friend to us all at Briteau. His daughter is therefore welcome.'

She liked him on sight, if only for the way in which he had contrived to make the meeting seem natural, a matter of course after a Sunday morning service. And as he moved away to talk to a villager who had waited for him, she had a

91

sense of loss, as if an ally had presented himself only to go elsewhere.

'Now the village will have to accept you.' Jacques Fabri fell into step beside her, then called to his mother: 'You see, I have come to take you home.'

He pointed to where a horse-drawn cart edged with narrow wooden seats waited on a grass verge beside the road.

'I thought it was strange to see you in church,' Violette scolded him. It was apparent that they were old adversaries from the way Jacques shrugged and smiled his response and Violette marched ahead of them, tut-tutting to herself. 'There is room for us all, I hope?'

The cart rocked and swerved its way back to the estate, the horse at a fast trot, the passengers swaying as one man. Mireille sat stiffly, glaring at the driver's back; the older women grumbled aloud and held on fast with work-worn brown hands.

Physically closer to her father than she had been since their drive from the station on the day of her arrival, Leonie was acutely aware of the disciplined, unyielding figure beside her that moved at one with the curve of the road. The image of Erich Mannheim, mouth wide in laughter, eyes not laughing at all, came to her and was blotted out as the cart manoeuvred clumsily on to the path that led to the château. Far below to their left the terraces blurred green and grey in the midday light. She held back from the impulse to lean against her father's shoulder.

'Tomorrow,' Paul said, 'you start work with us in the fields.'

Mireille's eyes narrowed as Leonie smiled, sitting very straight beside her father as they lurched through the gates of Briteau.

In the next few days, the early morning found Leonie in the kitchen dispensing packed food to the workers under

Violette's direction. Later she followed them to the terraces, and worked side by side with a local girl who knew some English and taught her what to do. The other workers – students and itinerants who came to Briteau each summer – hardly noticed her arrival. Some of the students spoke English, and her own French progressed almost without effort in their company. By the end of the week she could understand most of what was said around her.

At dinner on the Saturday night Paul de Byron informed Mireille that her grandparents, Henri and Marguerite Massine, were unexpectedly motoring down from Bordeaux and were already en route. Henri Massine had a client to see some miles north of Briteau, but they would be at the château for lunch next day.

'It is to be a brief visit only. We will not go to church. They wish to see that you are being serious about your work.'

'Papa! Surely the English tutor can report to them? What else is he for? And how do they think I spend my time, while my sister works with you all? Do they know that?'

There was a long silence. Paul de Byron said at last: 'You will leave that subject to me, of course, ma fille. You are pale. Your pallor proves how much you are working. Perhaps this evening you should both take a walk. It is a warm night.'

Leonie stared at her plate. The thought of coming face to face with the Massines next day found her unprepared. Their granddaughter's hostility, balanced as it was by her occasional moments of friendliness, was still a problem. She realized that she did not even know whether the grandparents were aware of her existence. But she could well imagine the problems it would create when they were. Her father's silence was an eloquent witness to his own dilemma.

After dinner Mireille called to Charlie from the terrace, and he ran out from the stable block, then raced ahead of them, barking in a manic display of delight at his liberation.

'It is a pity that tomorrow is Sunday, and you will be here at the house, not in the fields for your lunch. I think it will be difficult for you. My grandparents have no thought for me, either. It is *méchant*, don't you think?'

Leonie took refuge in throwing a stick for Charlie, patting his head when he dropped it back at her feet. Before she had to answer, Mireille pursued her annoyance with her grandparents. 'They will have their problems, also, now that you have come into our lives. The Massine family has a great interest in my father's estate, you know. My mother was very, very rich. Without her money . . .'

'I have not come here for any part in the estate, Mireille. You are too young to know, anyway. Perhaps I do not have to meet your grandparents.' Leonie's voice trailed off helplessly. She knew that Mireille was in a quarrelsome mood. There was nothing she could say to disperse it.

'I think one day you will have no choice. And why not tomorrow? The lunch will be *merveilleux*. Violette always excels herself at these visits. For my mother's memory, I think.'

'It is too soon.'

Mireille gave a small, tight-lipped smile. 'It will always be too soon for my grandfather to know of your existence —'

She broke off then as the figure of a man appeared in the distance, on the road that led to the village. As he turned into the drive Charlie raced to meet him. Jacques Fabri paused to fondle the dog's ears, while Mireille stood very still.

'You are ready for an early start tomorrow, I hope?' Jacques asked her as he walked towards the two girls. He walked very slowly, Leonie thought, but with a step that resembled a coiled spring.

'Tomorrow? My grandparents are to lunch with us. I can go nowhere tomorrow. Not even to church.'

'You asked to look for the eagle's nest again. In the col between the first hills and the mountains. It was all fixed.'

'There is an eagle, and its young. They have been here for many years,' Mireille explained to Leonie. Then, to Jacques: 'How could it be fixed, when we have seen nothing of you all this week? Where have you been?'

It was true. Some of the estate workers had grumbled at

his absence; when he did work with them, he was the best they had. Leonie had watched for him too, as the others arrived each morning in the kitchen garden. Then, as the sun moved high in the sky and he had not arrived, she knew he would not be there to walk back with them all when the work was over, between the vines, singing, arms round each other . . .

'No one asks me that, Mireille de Byron. No one asks me where I go, or when I shall return. I am here – it is simple.' He crushed a Gauloise under his heel. 'Are you coming tomorrow or not?'

'I'll come, if you like,' Leonie said quietly.

Jacques looked at her, then back to Mireille, and grinned.

'That means yes, he would like you to go with him, ma soeur,' Mireille muttered. 'What luck you have. You escape my grandparents, and you go to find eagles in the hills – all in one day.'

'At dawn, then?' Jacques asked.

'At dawn,' Mireille translated as if she were delivering a sentence of execution.

Leonie nodded. Her excitement at what she had done made it easy to ignore Mireille's acid tone.

'At the bridge.' Jacques spoke to her, slowly, in French. 'You can see it from your window, I think?'

Knowing he referred to the morning when she had watched him she coloured slightly beneath her sunburn.

'Papa will be very pleased to have his problem for tomorrow solved. Or else he will be very, very annoyed. In fact I do not think it wise to let him know of this at all. Why don't you just do one of your clever little disappearing acts, after all, Jacques? And take the américaine with you?' Mireille's eyes blazed with unshed tears. She called to Charlie in a voice knifed with anger, and began to run back along the drive towards the house in the last of the evening light.

Jacques watched her go, apparently unmoved. 'She is a beautiful child. My friend for many years. But a child. You understand?'

95

'I think so.'

'Then – *à demain.*'

'Till tomorrow.'

She walked quickly away, hoping to catch up with Mireille, not altogether sure that she trusted her remarks about Paul de Byron's being better left in ignorance of the plans for the next day. She was still close enough to Mireille's age to remember what it meant to lose a friend to someone else. She had known since the Sunday in church that Mireille was in love with Jacques, even if it was, as he had implied, a childhood friendship that had grown on her side into a first, calf love.

Besides, she thought, as she called to Mireille to wait for her, and her sister paused and turned towards her, she did not want to make an enemy of Mireille. She needed all the allies she could find, as what had started as a quest for her father grew daily more of an ordeal in which she herself seemed to be on trial.

In Paris it had been dark for an hour. On the steps of Erich Mannheim's small, modern apartment block in the avenue Kléber Zoe refused a passing taxi from the commissionaire, and began to walk.

Ten minutes later she turned into a narrow street off the Champs Elysées and stood looking up at the crumbling façade of a tall, double-fronted building. The windows of the three upper storeys were close-shuttered. The dark slate roof dripped from the recent rain into crazily complicated gutters that had somehow survived two centuries of neglect.

On the ground floor, either side of a faded, once elegant door, there were two shop windows. Their plate-glass frontage looked blankly on to the deserted street, a 'For Sale' placard in the place where Zoe had once seen a dress she could not afford, and a silver hairband . . . which she had bought to wear on her first date with a young army officer she had met at a tea party the day before.

She stood back from the building, staring up at its graceful, derelict façade. Her eyes went back to the spot where the silver hairband had glinted at her, price-tag concealed in a swathe of chiffon, almost twenty years ago.

She spoke aloud, as a stray Paris cat, her only audience, slipped by in the darkness, as elegant and hungry and alert as Zoe herself had become in the years between.

'This time,' she said, 'I buy the whole damn place.'

CHAPTER SEVEN

Leaving the chauffeur to park his new navy-blue Peugeot in the courtyard of the converted eighteenth-century warehouse which was the Massine company's headquarters, Henri Massine took the steps from the quayside to the office doors at the purposeful trot of a small, stout man. Unlike the majority of business houses in Bordeaux – and in all of the larger French cities – Etablissements Massine did not close for high summer. The white-painted shutters of the windows overlooking the estuary of the Dordogne remained open all the year round; shipping, the proprietor never tired of reminding his staff, was an unseasonal business.

On the afternoon of the Friday before the proposed visit to a client near Briteau, Henri Massine took the briefest of siestas after lunching at home before driving the return mile to the heart of Bordeaux's commercial quarter to supervise the closing of the company's books for the weekend. His petty megalomania made of him as much of a prisoner as he made of those who served him.

On the drive back to the office he informed Raymond, the chauffeur, that they should be prepared for an extended journey on the Sunday. They were to visit his granddaughter, Mademoiselle Mireille.

Raymond watched his employer push through the office doors, then limped round to the driver's seat and eased the Peugeot into gear with a lover's touch. A difficult birth had left him with a slight malformation of one hip – enough to disqualify him from the usual compulsory two years' national military conscription, and to leave him with a passion for the speed and manoeuvrability of anything on four wheels.

Checking his watch, he saw that before he would have to collect Henri Massine again he had time to make a call on the widow whose comfortable apartment in the old quarter of the city he made a home from home on Sunday evenings. The weekend's change of plans meant that he had to let her know he would not see her.

The understanding he had with Marie-Louise Fontaine was based on mutual respect. Each treasured their day-to-day independence. On Sunday afternoons Marie-Louise cooked to her heart's delight; on Sunday evenings Raymond, a good-looking, usually taciturn man, assumed the role of armchair philosopher, regaling her with accounts of life with Henri Massine. He endured his employer's bustling autocracy with the amused detachment of a man who knew exactly why he stayed in his job. He would suffer much more than he had to, allowed as he was a free hand with the family's cars.

Madame Massine, on the other hand, had his sympathy. She had no real compensation for her role as her husband's whipping-boy. The fortune she had brought to him as the only daughter of a shipping magnate – with whom his own company was to amalgamate some years later – kept him civil enough in the early days of their marriage. But with the death of their only child their relationship had become one of frigid politeness in public, and when they were alone all pretence vanished, in the shadow of the husband's frenzied ambition and the wife's incurable grief.

In the years that followed Yvette's death at Briteau, Marguerite Massine raised her granddaughter in the small eighteenth-century mansion on the outskirts of Bordeaux with the assiduous attention to discipline that was her inheritance as a member of the *haute bourgeoisie*. Her husband supervised the details of the girl's education as if it were a carefully planned commercial operation from which he expected a good return. But for Marguerite each day of Mireille's childhood had been passed as if through a haunting mirror, reflecting the pale blonde beauty of the lost daughter, cold to the touch.

The grandmother, anaesthetized by the role of parent to her own daughter's child, and by the sedatives which the family doctor still issued to her on a strictly supervised basis, did not nurse the same hatred for Paul de Byron as her husband. Yvette had loved Paul, and borne his child. Her mother knew that Paul had loved her. The château and its traditions, its beauty, had the qualities that had eluded Marguerite both in her own family and in her marriage. If Henri had given her the slightest chance she would have chosen to stay there with Mireille each summer. The place had a healing effect on her, knowing as she did that her daughter had experienced real happiness there.

But Henri Massine allowed Mireille the summers at Briteau out of no love for the past. They were merely part of his long-term plans for her future. He had continued to invest his daughter's dowry in the estate even after her death, although he had seen to it that the original marriage settlement contained more than one loophole should he wish to withdraw. But, just as he had seen Yvette's marriage as a step up the social ladder for himself, he saw the estate as a passport to an even more brilliant marriage for his grand-daughter.

By the time Mireille was of age she would be to all intents and purposes chatelaine of a small empire which Henri Massine himself had kept financially stable. He did so grudgingly, so long as his son-in-law was alive: if Mireille were to reach the heights Henri Massine planned for her he had to tolerate her father. It was after all a small price to pay for so handsome a return on his money.

At the back of his mind there was also, always, the spectre of his own origins. A great-grandfather with more Spanish-Moroccan blood than French had lingered in Portuguese West Africa long after the slave trade became illegal, and amassed a fortune from the illicit export of black flesh. It was a profitable business, especially once it had gone under-ground. But it was risky.

At last, when things got too dangerous, and Afroretribution began to rear its head in particularly horrifying forms, Señor Massot beat a hasty exit – leaving his common-law Portuguese wife to her fate – and surfaced alone in southern France.

In the seething human marketplace that was the late nineteenth-century port of Marseilles, 'Señor Massot' underwent a sea-change. His new papers as M. Massine, Frenchman and shipping agent, cost him half the small fortune he had realized on the gold which he had brought out of Africa.

With the other half he courted, and won, a fortyish maiden daughter of the city's second largest shipping company. After the birth of their only son – which her family saw as some kind of miracle – Massot persuaded his father-in-law to finance the new offices in Bordeaux. Within eighteen months of leaving Africa he had installed his new family in the mansion that was to be the home of the Massines from now on. But it had been a long haul.

In the Bordeaux headquarters of the agency of which Señor Massot/Massine had been the founding father, his descendant Henri spent the last Friday afternoon on which he was to be blissfully unaware of the existence of Paul de Byron's first child. There was, as always, much to be done. A telephone call to a subsidiary in Hamburg, a letter to read and sign for his Bristol agent, a query to be made on a suspiciously high demurrage charge for a cargo he had contracted out to a firm in Marseilles.

Henri Massine bent diligently over his desk, a pleat of flesh folding over a high white collar at the nape of the short neck, pince-nez on a black ribbon firmly on a nose that had in recent years begun to betray his life-long affair with the region's claret. The list of tasks checked off, he rang for his clerk, handed over the letter for dispatch to Bristol, and, alone again, rustled through his address book and picked up the telephone. The call he placed was to the university city of Oxford, in England.

Denholm Collins was in the middle of packing a clutch of worn textbooks into an ageing pigskin hold-all when the phone rang in the study that adjoined his bedroom. The college switchboard informed him that they had a call for him from France. The clipped tones of Henri Massine's voice on the line made him hold the handpiece further from his ear. He answered in formal, fluent French.

Yes, Monsieur Massine could be assured that the arrangements for his journey to Briteau were in order. He should arrive at the château in about four days. His work at the university was over for the summer; the agency had made it perfectly clear what was required of him as tutor to Mademoiselle de Byron. He looked forward to the engagement, and he was certain good progress would be made before the summer was over.

'*Bon.* Then I can inform my son-in-law that he is to expect you next week without fail?'

'I will telephone the château from the local station when I arrive.'

'You have the number?'

'*Bien sur.*'

'And you know that it is most important that my granddaughter should work very hard this summer, in both English and classical studies?'

Denholm Collins began to feel grateful that the granddaughter was not to have her special coaching in the bosom of her family in Bordeaux. His voice, when he answered after a pause, was dryly precise.

'I was educated in France myself, Monsieur Massine. I know what it is to face the Baccalaureat.'

In the spotted antique mirror above the telephone table the sardonic, clever mouth smiled back. Nothing mattered, so long as he could get to his beloved France. He smoothed his thinning sandy hair across a high forehead. His grey eyes were tired after the summer term's efforts to get his less able students through their finals. He would bathe, dine in college, and then take the train to London. There was time to make the journey slowly, with a two-day respite before he took up his new duties.

'Then it is settled.' The line went dead.

Denholm returned to his packing, thinking that at Briteau, in a corner of France he knew and loved, the workers would just be leaving the terraced vines, their shadows lengthening as they walked home on the dusty roads.

On the Saturday night Leonie sat up late in bed, trying to read a French children's book she had found in the library. She still had not told Paul de Byron of her plans for the next day; he had been working at his desk when she and Mireille had returned to the house, and Mireille had assured her it was best to say nothing until the morning. But with a dawn start, Leonie wondered if there would now be an opportunity.

She was about to put out her bedside light and try to sleep when her door creaked open and Mireille crept in, finger on lips, a pair of heavy walking shoes in her hand.

She dumped the shoes unceremoniously at the foot of the bed, and stood, hands on hips, surveying the jacket and skirt which Leonie had left on a chair ready for the morning.

'Those are of no use. You must have a warm hat, I think, and a scarf.'

'That's ridiculous.' Leonie found herself still smarting from Mireille's behaviour earlier. 'It's high summer. But – thank you for the shoes. Do you think they will fit?'

'Haven't you noticed? You and I have several things in which we are very alike. It is true I am fair, and you are dark. That is no doubt because of our mothers. But we have certain things in common – we share a father, after all.'

103

She left the room, leaving Leonie to wonder if she would ever get used to her abrupt changes of mood. This sudden overture was typical, after the anger of earlier in the evening. And the bright red scarf and matching ski hat which Mireille brought back with her five minutes later were as cheerful as her conspiratorial grin.

'I almost came face to face with Papa. He was on his way down to the library, for another cognac I expect. No one is able to sleep in this house tonight.'

'I still wish we had told him.'

'I will tell him the truth about your absence at breakfast, I promise. You will have gone too far by then for him to come after you. As for being annoyed – I am sure he will be pleased that he does not have to entertain both you and my grandparents at the same table.'

'What will they say, when they know about me? Are you sure they do not already know of my existence? All these years. Surely something is known?'

Mireille sat on the bed. Her resentment seemed to have gone altogether. Perhaps this was what it was really like to have a sister, Leonie thought. It was a cat and dog existence for some of the sisters she knew in New York.

'Do not even think about it, ma chère,' Mireille said in an odd, cold voice. 'I can promise you that my father has never told my mother's family that you exist.'

There was a silence, and Leonie had the distinct impression that Mireille waited for more questions. As if there was much more yet unsaid.

'Ah well . . . try to sleep. You will walk very far, tomorrow. It is very high. It is wonderful, there in the mountains. You will see . . .' She jumped up abruptly. '*Bonne nuit*. I will think of you tomorrow.'

Leonie turned out her light and curled into a ball, shutting her eyes tightly against her anxiety about the next day, the past, the whole uncertain future. Zoe, who had directed her every move for seventeen years, seemed a distant, intangible figure. Now that her rebellion against her mother had come, in a wild rush, it had a frightening tinge of permanence.

She slept, and dreamed that she was running through the streets of New York, a white leather box clutched in both hands. The crowds on the sidewalk parted, and someone snatched at the box. She ran on, stopping dead at the gaping entrance to the subway, as the jeweller who had bought Erich Mannheim's pearls appeared at the front of the subway steps and climbed slowly towards her.

At first light Jacques Fabri was at the bridge in the field behind the château. He leaned on the parapet watching the water nudge at the flat grey stones, the eternal Gauloise at the corner of his lips pinpointing the black eyes in the tense sallow face. Where the stream grew deeper a carp moved out of the shadows, slipping into the mass of ferns that made dense, green-black borders along the high banks, which when the sun rose would run a double ribbon of emerald across the rough grass.

He had slept briefly, but well. The previous week he had gone almost three days without sleep, while he watched for the two Americans.

It was almost a year since the Internationals had moved up against the Republicans on the Madrid front, and the world outside had given them a few weeks before they would be routed. But the price had been high. The casualties filled the overcrowded, undermanned camps on the Spanish side of the Pyrenees. Now, with the long summer nights, the walking wounded had become a human traffic which Jacques and his kind guided across the mountain tracks and into France. The Americans were journalists who had come to report on the civil war in Spain, and stayed to fight.

Jacques Fabri had been a political animal since his schooldays. He had toyed with membership of the local communist party at eighteen, and not even his family or close friends in the village knew whether or not he had become a card-carrying member. But he had first helped the

105

Internationals quite by chance.

He had been clearing an outhouse at the Fabri home very late one night, heard a sound outside, and turned to see a man fall to the ground in the yellow light of the lantern slung on the lintel. Without thinking to call for help, he dragged him through the door, and waited for him to come round.

The stranger was an Irishman, who spoke French fluently, persuasively, with the charm of his kind. Sensing an ally in Jacques, by dawn he had convinced him of the worth of the International Brigade's cause, and of the need to get the wounded out of the camps that were only a few miles inside Spain, to the south of the Pyrenees. They had need of a contact who could work on the French side. Halfway between the Spanish border and Briteau there was a cave, on a high pass. It was the headquarters of a bear of a Spaniard, Luis, who lived there as a recluse, a price on his head for the murder of a dozen of Franco's men. He could not bring himself to go completely into exile. Instead he planned to open up an escape route for his allies, with the cave as the halfway house.

For some time now Jacques Fabri had been the guide for the exhausted, still fanatical men who assembled in the cave before the long walk down into France. The two Americans who were his latest success were going back into Europe to raise funds for the camp they had left only days before. Jacques had seen them on their way, and knew that there would be a time lapse, for reasons of security, before word would come of others who waited for him in the heart of the mountains.

No one at Briteau knew of his activities. His father chose to think that his frequent absences were due to some involvement with a woman who did not live in the village; it was something he could understand, and even justify, swaggering to his drinking companions that his son was a man. His mother instinctively guessed there was more to it, but knew better than to ask questions.

*

106

He sensed rather than saw the American girl come through the gate in the kitchen garden. Something in his make-up – the macho quality instilled from infancy in the males of the region, perhaps – did not allow him to watch her approach. But her long-legged, colt's walk had been engraved on his mind's eye for some days now.

Leonie crossed the field, drawn as if by a magnet to the pinpoint of Jacques's cigarette. The ground was soaked with the night dew, and she was glad already of Mireille's shoes.

When she reached the bridge Jacques threw down his cigarette and touched her arm casually in greeting. '*Bien. Tu n'es pas en retard.*'

'I am never late,' she said in English.

'We will talk French today,' he told her. 'It will be good for you. But you will find there will be little need for words.'

'You do speak some English, then? I thought you understood some things.'

'Yes. Some things.' He began to walk ahead, taking the first slope above the bridge at a quick stride. She followed easily, and at the treeline he turned and watched her cover the few yards between them.

'Not bad.'

An hour later they emerged from the pines and faced a steeper slope, where the grass barely covered the patches of rock that marked the edge of the grey foothills. Jacques said that in an hour, if Leonie continued to do so well, they would reach the col. Then they would eat the food he had brought, and find the eagles.

'I thought the sun would be out by now,' she said. 'It is still cold.'

'At this time of year there can be a mist. We shall see.'

They reached the col as he had planned, and sat on a small table of grey stone, looking down into a shallow ravine that lay between them and the mountains. Jacques told her that there was a path. But the foot of the ravine was still shrouded in a heavy, unshifting mist.

They ate a dark, strong sausage sharp with garlic, and

long cuts of bread from a baguette Jacques had carried sliced in two in his rucksack. Afterwards he produced bitter chocolate, and told Leonie she should not eat too much as it would make her thirsty. But they could drink later; there was a pure stream close to the eagle's nest.

The silence was at first oppressive, until Leonie's ears became accustomed to the small sounds about them – stones shifting like children in their beds, and the trickle of a secret stream somewhere on the far side of the ravine.

The bleat of an isard, the mountain goat that lived wild in the region, brought Jacques to his feet, scanning the far side of the ravine.

'We must go on.'

Leonie did not know the word for fog or mist. She looked doubtfully into the crevasse, and he laughed.

'I know every inch of the way. You follow in my steps, you understand? And once we are on the mountainside, like the goat over there, we can run!'

They climbed steadily then, not speaking. For half an hour a pale sun waited behind the clouds, only to disappear. Leonie grew warm as they climbed, her breath coming in small, panting gasps on the cold air. The smell of pine needles made her take deeper breaths as they entered a thick patch of trees. Jacques told her that they were almost there. Minutes later they stepped into a clearing and found themselves looking up at a rock face almost a hundred feet high. A wind that had come from nowhere drummed at their ears, buffeting the scrub plants that clung as if defying the laws of nature to the sheer stone wall before them.

Suddenly, as if borne on the wind itself, a male eagle swooped across the tops of the pines, and made a darting reconnaissance above the two figures. 'He will not come too close,' Jacques said softly as Leonie involuntarily ducked her head. 'He has other things to do.'

They watched as, on a ledge halfway up the rock face, the female parent dipped and jabbed at the flies encircling the remainder of the eaglets' last feed. Then, at the approach of the male, she beat her wings and flew from the ledge, leaving him space to land and drop his new kill.

Two eaglets staggered from the nest that was half concealed by an overhang of rock, and began to peck at the furred carcass. A strip of skin torn away, the flesh gleamed a vivid red, and the young birds grew excited, their necks lengthening as they pulled at the meat.

Leonie shuddered, and turned away. Jacques laughed. 'Only two eaglets this year. But they still fight. You must watch – the stronger one will try his wings once he has fed.'

He was right. The male parent wheeled away in his perpetual search for food, and the mother re-alighted on the ledge. The larger eaglet drew back, flapping grey-white wings, then lurched forward, hanging clown-like over the edge of the rock as his mother used her beak to scare it back to safety.

'It is family life,' Jacques said. 'The parents stay together for always, you know. Only each other.'

She thought that family life as she knew it had not been quite like that, and wondered how many summers Jacques had brought her half-sister to this secret, magical place, to watch the sleek heads of the young eagles tear at their prey. It was a primitive world, alien to all she had known, and yet the high grey rock face had the same threatening presence as the New York skyscrapers on a winter's day, and the mist that now came in suddenly and threw a shroud over the whole scene had the same dank permanence as a fog from the Hudson.

'I hope you are not thirsty, after all,' Jacques said. 'I do not think it wise to try to reach the water. We must wait, and shelter for a while.'

She followed him, glad now of the warm hat and scarf from Mireille. The close ranks of the pine trees seemed to bar their way as they retraced their path, the brushwood snapping sharply beneath their feet in the stillness that had fallen over the mountain.

Jacques stopped when they reached a clearing and threw

his rucksack against the base of a tree, checking over its contents as he squatted on his haunches, ignoring Leonie.

'We have no need to worry,' he said. 'There is more meat, and more chocolate. Are you thirsty?'

'No, but why do you ask?'

'I told you. We must wait.' He stood up, and looked at her, as if assessing how much he should tell her. 'We must rest. Here. The wind will clear this soon.'

'When? How long?'

'Who can tell? Your pretty red hat must act as a light. Keep warm. Be patient.'

She sat, leaning against the rucksack as he lit a Gauloise and began to pace to and fro across the clearing. Something told her that he was prepared for a long wait.

'We were not to know,' he said at last, his voice tinged with an apology which she knew by now he was unlikely to put into words. 'At this time of year the whole day should have been clear. But – sometimes the mountains like to surprise us.'

'I could not stop them, Papa. Truly. Their minds were quite made up.'

Mireille stood on the far side of Paul's desk in the library, straight and slim in a new formal cotton dress worn for the pending visit from her grandparents. She brushed her hair back from one shoulder with a quick, impatient gesture, waiting for her father's anger.

'Truly? This is a new word for you, Mireille. Why should I doubt you? After all, Jacques Fabri is acting entirely in character. And Leonie – your sister – is a guest, and will want to see all she can of the region.'

Mireille said nothing, hiding her disappointment. She had not forgiven Jacques for his swift invitation to Leonie once he knew she herself was unable to go into the mountains. She had tried to smother her resentment of Leonie herself, offering her the shoes and warm clothes the night before, but there still lingered the slight hope that the incident would turn Paul de Byron against the newcomer, and her half-sister would be packed off back to Paris next day.

What she had not expected was her father's almost offhand reception of the news she had brought to him after breakfast, as the household came quickly to life in preparation for the Massines' visit, and Violette had shut herself in the dining-room laying the table with the family silver and putting the final touches to the flowers.

'I suppose it will be easier, without her,' Mireille tried. 'My grandparents . . . it could have been hard for Grandmère.'

'Your grandparents are not children. I will have to let them know of Leonie, of course. I will do it today, face to face.'

'And I, Papa? What am I to say? That I have a sister, after all these years? Someone else here at Briteau for the summer? What will they think of that?'

'We do not know for certain how long your sister will be here with us.'

'Then what am I to say?'

'You will say nothing.'

'But what will you say to her yourself, when she comes home?'

'There will be all day for me to think about that, ma fille. Now – I suggest that you too go about your day. I have some papers to study before your grandparents arrive.'

Violette was decorating the cold entrée dishes as the Peugeot turned into the drive. Raymond tooted the horn as they drew up at the front of the house, and she frowned, checking the time on the clock above the stove. Whatever her private opinion of the Massines, the meals she prepared on their rare visits to Briteau were a matter of pride. The timing of the whole affair was also a matter of importance; she knew from the days when her young mistress Yvette Massine had been

111

alive what a petty tyrant the father could be. The day would no doubt be the usual clockwork exercise, from the instant he stepped from the car and ran a proprietorial eye over the house, to the moment when he clapped his hands for Raymond and the long return journey to Bordeaux began.

It was Raymond who came into the kitchen to tell Violette that the Massines were ensconced in the library and aperitifs had been served. He took the glass of wine she put in front of him, and sniffed the air appreciatively. He and Violette, old friends, would eat together in the kitchen, and their menu would be precisely the same as the family's.

'I hope the great man is in a good mood.' Violette opened the conversation.

'Oh, the usual. Why? Has his granddaughter been up to some of her tricks?'

'Worse. Far worse. Monsieur Henri Massine is in for a very big surprise. There will be a new face at the family table today, mon vieux. And heaven help you on the journey home.'

'Oh? A long-lost relative? Someone from Paris?'

'Yes, and no. Not quite family. But close. Born on the wrong side of the blanket, la pauvre. Paul de Byron's elder daughter.'

'Ah, so the de Byrons are not perfect after all.' Raymond grinned as she shook her head disapprovingly. 'How old is the girl? The dates are always of the greatest interest in these matters.'

'Old enough to steal a heart or two. Her father's included.'

In the library Marguerite Massine sat facing the long windows on to the terrace, a glass of mineral water in one thin hand of which the wrist was weighted with a set of gold bracelets. The understated elegance of her grey linen suit matched the severity of the blonde chignon, the slim legs tucked neatly to one side, the lack of expression in the eyes that watched the mist drift in over the grounds of the château. If she heard the small talk with which her husband and son-in-law had opened the encounter, she gave no sign. Her thoughts were, as always when she was at Briteau, with the daughter who had died there. Her grey eyes lit softly, for a moment only, as they moved to the piano, then the mist that held the garden in its grip seemed to close down on the woman's face.

'Why not take a turn in the garden with your grand-daughter?' Her husband called across to her, rather as if he were addressing a child that had run out of things to do on a rainy afternoon.

'It is too miserable out there. Can't you see?' Mireille broke in, but moved to where her grandmother sat and perched on the arm of her chair, one leg swinging, an arm resting close to Marguerite Massine's blonde head, but not quite touching.

'Perhaps I can see your room, chérie,' Marguerite said. 'I have bought you some new stockings, and the white shoes we could not find before you left. Let's go. We can try the shoes for size.'

'As you wish, Grandmère. But I am sure they will fit. I have stopped growing, you know.'

'We thought that when you were twelve. Look at you now!'

They left the room without a backward glance, but Mireille, catching a fleeting glimpse of her father's face in a mirror by the door, saw his accustomed mask of discipline reassert itself as he stood and crossed to the chiffonier to replenish his father-in-law's glass. *This is it*, she thought. *He'll have to tell Grandpère about her now.*

As his younger daughter had anticipated, Paul saw his chance, and took it, with a kind of military precision, making straight for the truth. Briefly, he told Henri Massine of Leonie's presence at the château, of the American mother he had met after the war, of the recent telephone call from Paris that brought the fruit of their liaison to Briteau.

'When I return to Bordeaux, you realize, mon cher Paul,

113

that I go straight to my lawyers?' Henri was as brief in his reaction as Paul had been in telling the story.

Paul shrugged. 'That is your privilege. I cannot say I am surprised. But you have no reason to fear for Mireille's future from all this.'

'You may think that now. But what of the mother? How long will it be before she follows on the daughter's heels? I am a man of the world, Paul. These things have a way of taking over if one does not put them properly in their place.'

'And where is that?' Paul as always had to struggle to conceal his dislike of Henri's domineering manner.

'Why, in the bedroom, of course. Tell me, does the daughter resemble the mother? Eh? Has she sent her on to arouse your memories?' The older man finished his second drink at a gulp, winking at Paul as he held out his glass again. Paul ignored the silent request, and walked to the window, his back to the small fat man whose face hardened the moment his son-in-law turned away.

'My family knew rather more than you do, Henri, how to manage these things, I can assure you. I was very young. We both were. It was taken out of my control.'

'Ah. No more than a peccadillo. *Bon*. Tell me, then, how it is that the child has reappeared in your life? All these years. No wonder I have had to support you and this great barn of a place. How many more of your brats are peopling the New World, tell me that? How many more surprises may I – and my poor Marguerite – expect to sustain?'

'There was only the one. And the mother has never been near this place, or even back to France for that matter. She was – I am ashamed to say – bought off by my family. Even before the child was born.'

'Well, mon vieux, let us hope it will not prove too costly a business this time. You will have to make sure that we are not embarrassed by this little ghost from the past, that is all. Tell me, where is the child?'

'My daughter is a young woman.' Paul concealed his growing anger with his father-in-law successfully, but

114

inwardly the shower of vulgar insinuation that the news of Leonie's existence had evoked made him vow to handle his daughter's future from now on in his own way – as he should have done for seventeen years. 'And you will not see her today, Henri. She has gone on an excursion into the mountains. With my permission.'

In Mireille's bedroom on the floor above, Marguerite Massine knelt at her granddaughter's feet and fastened the straps of the white shoes she had brought from Bordeaux. 'There. They are just right, n'est-ce pas?'

'Perfect.' Mireille got to her feet and danced a few steps lightly about the room. 'I hope I have the chance to wear them, that is all. My English tutor arrives in four, five days, and for me that is the end of any parties, or tennis.'

'You may wear the shoes in the evening, darling. You still dress for dinner, I hope?'

'Oh, yes. Even when Papa is very tired. Nothing changes.'

'I am glad to hear it.' Marguerite walked to the window and gazed down at the terrace. 'After all, this is your life. The way it will be for you one day. It is best that you become accustomed to it.'

Mireille watched her grandmother thoughtfully. 'Well, some things change, of course. Sometimes there are quite big, quite amazing changes, Grandmère.'

'Oh?' The woman spoke absently, her thoughts far away, with the daughter who had walked in the gardens of the château, and never come home to her. 'Such as?'

'Such as my new sister. My elder sister. From America?'

'You are joking, ma petite.' Marguerite turned round, momentarily shaken from her nostalgia. 'You mean you have a cousin, perhaps? From another branch of the de Byrons?'

'No, Grandmère. A sister.' White-faced, Mireille went to her, and held both hands out like a suppliant seeking the alms of the other woman's attention. 'She is here, at the

115

château, for the summer. Maybe longer. Papa tells me nothing.'

'Now, now, Mireille.' Marguerite took the slim hands and drew the girl to her. 'Grandpapa will know what is to be done. You have made some kind of mistake, I am sure. Everything can be arranged. Now' – she led Mireille to a chair, and gently pushed her into it – 'you must tell me all you know about this – sister, and then we will do your hair, and go down to lunch. Is that understood?'

As the family took their places at the long dining-table, Violette stood on guard by the chiffonier, where a great soupier from a Sèvres collection that had been in the family for generations heralded the first course. She watched covertly as Marguerite Massine took her place on Paul de Byron's right and Henri strutted to the carver chair at the far end of the table. As Mireille pulled out the chair opposite her grandmother, Violette chose her moment to ask what had become of Mademoiselle Leonie.

There was a heavy pause. Mireille gave her grandmother a warning look. Henri Massine shrugged, took a large crust of white bread from the basket at his elbow, and gestured to Paul that it was he who must answer Violette.

'It is all right, Paul.' Marguerite Massine's low voice broke the silence. Mireille put out a hand as if to stop the conversation before it was too late. 'It is all right, my dear,' Marguerite persisted. 'What you have told me had to be told.'

'So you know?' her husband cut in. 'So – eat your lunch, and let us leave it at that.'

Uncharacteristically, she looked him straight in the eyes, and smiled. 'I suppose *you* know more than I do, Henri?'

'We will not discuss the matter at this table – where I may remind you your daughter presided as chatelaine of this house. It is her name, her memory, that we should respect . . . by leaving the subject where it belongs – in my notary's office. Nowhere else.'

'My wife was respected, you know that, Henri. And loved. More than most women,' Paul said coldly.

'My poor Yvette.' Marguerite looked vaguely round the table, as if answering her husband at all had taken what strength she had to spare for the time being. 'I should like some of that good soup, Violette. It smells quite delicious.'

'Madame, perhaps first I should clear the placement for the – the young lady? I am sorry, I believed there were to be five today.'

'No, Violette.' It was Paul who answered, an edge in his voice. 'My daughter is out today, it is true. No doubt she will not be back until our other guests have gone. But her place remains.'

As the Peugeot drew away from the house Paul looked up at the sky, then turned on his heel and walked quickly through the stable yard, making for the ground at the back of the house from where he could see the foothills. Mireille stayed until the car was out of sight down the drive, waving to the white-gloved signal of Marguerite's thin hand until her pale face in the rear window mingled with the half-light of the late afternoon, still in the grip of the mist, and was gone.

'Not many cars on the road in these parts at any time,' Henri said to his chauffeur as they reached the village. 'Once we are out of the district the air will clear anyway, don't you think?'

Raymond nodded, eyes fixed on the road. He knew there would be little or no conversation between his passengers for the whole of the long drive ahead. But his mind was well occupied already, with the account he would give to Marie-Louise in a week's time of the bombshell that had exploded in the heart of the well ordered world of Henri Massine.

Three thousand feet above the winding road that led the Peugeot north and away from Briteau, Leonie broke a small

117

piece of the chocolate which Jacques Fabri offered her before he told her that there was every sign they would have to stay on the mountain until morning.

She listened calmly, munching the chocolate, her shoulders hunched against the chill of the mist that had now settled in the col and moved on between the trees, silent and intent as a hunter.

'You are not afraid?' Jacques looked down at her with a smile that concealed his growing admiration of the girl's unexpected nerve. After all, she was no more than a child, in spite of that way she walked and those dark blue eyes with their message of things to come.

She shook her head. She knew from the climb earlier in the day that if anyone was safe in the mountains it was this man. 'Only – my father. He will be very angry.'

'Probably. But that is tomorrow. Today we must keep warm. And be patient.' He took the rucksack from behind her and unzipped a side compartment, tugging out a folded waterproof sheet. 'We sit on this. We stay very close to each other. Like this.' He sat beside her, and pulled her to him before she had time to protest. His arm went tightly about her shoulder. 'Do not fight me, little américaine. It is a question of survival. No more chocolate until morning. Tonight – a walk about us, not more than a few yards – and perhaps a piece of sausage. If you are good. Then you can sing me some American songs.'

Surprisingly, she slept while it was still light, and awoke to find Jacques on his feet, looking down at her, his broad shoulders silhouetted against a starred night sky and the swaying branches of the pines.

'There is a wind,' she said. 'Does that mean we can go back?'

'Not yet. But at first light.'

She yawned, stretching her limbs, and got to her feet. The air was like ice, but she gulped it in in long, deep breaths, and in an unexpected rush of well-being found that she did not care whether they stayed on the mountain for ever.

118

'You do not know the mountains yet.' Jacques studied her face in the light of the match he held cupped in his hands as he lit a cigarette. 'But one day I think perhaps you will.'

They parted at the bridge where they had met more than twenty hours before, and without looking back Leonie began to run across the field to the garden gate, where two or three of the labourers already stood waiting for their packed lunches from Violette. Aware of their knowing glances as she passed them, she was able only to mutter a reply to their morning greetings, and almost fell through the kitchen door in her anxiety to get the encounter with her father over.

'Ah. So the vagabond returns. And wants her coffee and brioche, no doubt, as if nothing has happened?'

'Violette, please don't be angry. Yes, I'd adore some coffee. Very hot. And I'm starving!'

'You will need your strength. Your father went straight to his desk this morning, and ordered coffee to be taken to him. Why not be the one to take in his tray? It will help, I am sure. If anything can help you now.'

'But my hair – my shoes –' Leonie looked down at her rumpled clothing. 'I can't see him like this.'

'Two minutes in your room, and I'll prepare your father's tray. As for the conduct of Monsieur Fabri, his mother will hear from me.'

Ten minutes later she faced Paul de Byron across the wide leather desk. He nodded as she poured his coffee, and took the cup without thanking her.

'I am sorry. If the mist had not come down I would have been back before dinner last night.'

'That is not the question, Leonie. The point is how could you do this thing? Do you not know the danger you were in? And without my knowledge. Without my permission.'

'It was not what I wanted. It all happened without any real plan.'

119

'Surely you do not expect me to believe you went against your will? Your conduct so far has not been that of a child of so little character.'

'I meant to tell you. To ask you. But the time went. Mireille said . . .'

'Mireille has had quite enough to do with this already. You will keep your sister's name out of this. The Fabri family will also have to answer for their son's conduct.'

'I don't think Jacques Fabri would let anyone answer for him.' The remark was out before she could think, and as Paul de Byron's eyes blazed at her impertinence her chin went up a fraction.

'Oh, so now you know all about the people who have lived here all their lives? Perhaps you can tell me, then, what this escapade will do to the good name of this family?'

She blushed at once, her eyes filling with tears at the injustice of the implications in what he had said. 'There was nothing to hurt your good name. Nothing.'

'These things appear differently to us. It is not New York.'

'You do not have to tell me that! I am working in the fields with the others, am I not? If I wanted New York and my old life I would not have come this far, or stayed so long. It is not easy . . .'

Paul got up from his desk and walked to the window, his back to her.

'Perhaps I should go to work now. The others are waiting,' she said in a small voice.

Before he turned to her her father suppressed a quick, gentle smile. 'You are surely too tired. And the matter is not closed.'

'What else is there to say? You have told me I have hurt your good name. The de Byron name.'

'Well, Leonie, I wish for a promise from you that you will not repeat such behaviour. And that you come to me with any plans you may have to go so far from the château.'

She thought his terms were fair enough, and nodded, recognizing from her quarrels with Zoe that they had reached a watershed and actual punishment was not in the air.

'I do not want to go far. I want to belong.'

'That is something we have to earn, even those of us who were born here. Don't you see that?'

'Yes, of course. But – how can I even begin to try, if I don't know who I am? I don't know if I am ever to be accepted. I am a visitor only, sleeping in the guest-room, helping out with the others, the students who are only here for a while every year. I don't even know what to call you . . .' She trailed off miserably. It was the longest speech she had made to him since they had met.

'Why, there is no problem. You work for the rest of the summer. You go back to Paris, like any other student. We will discuss what happens then, when the time comes. And – you call me Papa. It is quite simple.'

She wanted to run to him and fling her arms about him, but something held her back. The centuries of restraint that had made her father the soldier and the aristocrat that he was spoke to her in the slight shrug of resignation and amusement he gave as he went to his desk and picked up his cup.

'The coffee is good today. Please tell Violette I said so.'

Leonie was not to know that the way in which Henri Massine had received the fact of her existence had touched a stubborn nerve in Paul's make-up. Her own manner as she stood before him, taking what he had to say in part sorrow, part defiance, had also touched him. She was vulnerable in defeat, and it was the first time she had assumed the role of his child – a beautiful, wayward child.

'Off you go, if you are to catch up with the others,' he said gently. 'You are sure you want to work today?'

'Of course. Shall I see you at dinner?'

'Nothing has changed. I have only this paperwork to finish today. And after all, your sister will want to hear if you saw the eagle's nest.'

'Oh yes, we found it.'

'How was it, in the mountains, eh?'

'It was beautiful . . . Papa.'

121

CHAPTER EIGHT

In spite of a rail strike that threatened to make prisoners of those Parisians who had not yet migrated for the summer of '37, Denholm Collins found his way to Briteau at leisure and on time. Within a week he had won Mireille's interest, helped at first by chance when Charlie took to him on sight, and later by his years of experience as tutor to undergraduates in whom childish arrogance was invariably a signpost to the need of approval.

There was also in the French girl a hidden, embryo sense of humour that had not been smothered by the rigours of life as Henri Massine's granddaughter. Mireille learned colloquial English best of all from the word games Denholm introduced by way of a concession. In turn, she taught him the Truth Game currently in vogue at her lycée in Bordeaux. On their first Saturday evening as teacher and pupil they were still engrossed in a contest when Leonie came down to the library dressed for dinner.

It was the first time she had worn the blue silk Zoe had chosen for that last, fateful birthday in New York. Skin a deeper olive, and her hair – longer now – streaked bronze by the sun, she exuded a radiant vitality, and a confidence that stemmed from the moment Paul de Byron had let her know, after the escapade with Jacques Fabri, that she could openly address him as her father.

Denholm's arrival had also put her more at her ease; she was no longer the only visitor; there was a newcomer to supersede her novelty value in the village. The fact that he spoke her language, as well as fluent French, gave her someone to whom she could turn when she was stuck for some expression. The talk at dinner had grown more animated each night, and now, on the Saturday, she had a sense of occasion.

'You look far too elegant to play games, ma soeur. But you may sit and listen, if you are good,' Mireille said in greeting.

Denholm gave Leonie a welcoming, half-admiring smile. Mireille's English, he told her, was fast expanding in all directions – not always orthodox. She had just got through a round of the Truth Game with ten out of ten for humour.

'And perhaps eight and a half for lies?' Mireille cut in.

'You're a clever little liar, I grant you that,' Denholm answered. 'But I see through you. Just as I see through the short cuts you try when you translate aloud. You forget that I know the texts by heart.'

'Then you should be grateful that I make them less boring, mon professeur! And this year is of no importance. In three years' time I have the second "bacc." – and one has to translate a complete oeuvre from English. Think of me then, when you will be safely back at your old university.'

'My *ancient* university, thank you. They had a choice of translations in my day. Something from Shakespeare always included.'

'Something more modern, I hope.'

'Why not American?' Leonie asked Denholm.

'American *is* modern.' Mireille jumped to her feet, dismissing the whole of the literature of the New World in a sentence. 'Now, I must change for dinner.'

'Is Papa home?'

Mireille had seemed to accept that Leonie now had the right to call Paul father. She reacted, if at all, with no more than her customary, all-occasion shrug. There was a slight bristle in her walk as she went to the library door and turned, giving Leonie the blank look which the latter knew by now could hide either hostility or friendship.

'In the kitchen, I think. He is choosing wines. Pierre is home for a week or two and tomorrow night there is to be a dinner party. The food will be very good – not only for

123

Violette's beloved grandson. There are people invited, from nearby and from Paris. You really should have kept that dress for tomorrow, ma soeur.'

When she had gone Denholm made a show of putting the books on their work table in order.

'I hope my college dinner-jacket will not put us Anglo-Saxons to shame. Time was when my ancestors owned every inch of this land. But I forget sometimes – you have the best of both worlds. And in that dress you look worth a dozen members of the Aquitaine aristocracy.'

'Thank you. My mother chose it.'

'Clever woman.'

'Not always.'

'Sorry.' He knew enough of her story to guess he had edged the talk on to shaky ground just as he had intended to boost her morale. 'Will you rejoin her in Paris?'

'So much depends. I had started at a college, to learn French. I don't want to leave here yet. Perhaps after the harvest my . . . father . . . will know what I am to do . . .'

'Maybe your roots go deeper than you know. Some of the French believe that it was the local fishermen, some early version of an Atlantic fleet, who were the first to discover America.'

'You're kidding?' The thought made her eyes brim with laughter. She smiled for the first time since she had walked into the room. 'Try that out at the dinner party tomorrow night, why don't you?'

The numbers for the dinner were evenly matched: a childless couple who owned a neighbouring château, both about the age of their host; a Parisian doctor and his wife holidaying in the Pyrenees. Denholm Collins and Violette's grandson were told by Mireille that they had the privilege of taking herself and Leonie into dinner.

Pierre Giraud was nothing like his grandmother. Leonie, studying him across the table while the soup was served, wondered if the severe brown hair cut *en brosse*, the strangely light, yellow eyes, and the thin face, resembled his father's. Pierre was in his mid-twenties, in the final years as a medical student. His manner with the older doctor was suitably courteous and attentive, but underneath the pleasant manner lurked an impatience, perhaps with the man, perhaps with the occasion itself.

The doctor's wife, very reserved in the shadow of her husband's pomposity, was *chic* in black linen, a string of good pearls filling the curved neckline of a dress that was obviously couture. She spoke for the first time at table when Paul asked her if she had seen his Tante Berthe recently. He had plans to visit her when his leave ended. He would travel back to his unit via Paris.

Tante Berthe, she told him, was 'as always'. The apartment near the rue de Rivoli was stifling, but she refused to leave it for the summer. Her work for the Red Cross was quite indefatigable. For her age she was still so energetic.

'She has a finger in every pie,' she concluded, in her rapid, idiomatic French, too quick for Leonie. 'She would run everything, if we let her – even our lives, I think.'

Paul blotted out a picture of his aunt eighteen years ago standing in the doorway of his room at her apartment, and merely nodded, signing to Violette to serve the second course.

Pierre broke in, asking the doctor's wife which plays she had seen in Paris that year, while the doctor dryly remarked that in his day they had money only for food, not for such frivolities as the Comédie.

'Oh, when I want to eat I come home to my grandmother.' Pierre smiled up at Violette as she lifted the covers from the Sèvres dishes, and with the aroma of small white onions cooked in brandy, lamb in rosemary and garlic, and beans nestling like emeralds in a glaze of butter, a respectful silence settled at the table.

The soufflé of wild strawberries and raspberries from the château garden that followed was a less serious affair, and the conversation flowed freely. The light red estate wine was replaced by a Sauternes introduced by Paul as a foreign visitor, but one he allowed at his table in summer.

His neighbour, a broad-shouldered, clear-eyed man with a complexion tanned by an outdoor life, raised his glass in agreement. Marcel Darnand had farmed his family land – some miles to the west of the village – all his life, and jealously guarded the vines from his own minuscule vine-yard for his own consumption. They were his inheritance from a region he loved with a fanaticism that would have surprised him had he ever thought about it. He was a working farmer, with a local reputation as an employer second to none. He and Paul de Byron had many things in common, unspoken between them . . . the St Cyr codes of honour, country, duty. In his spare time Darnand read philosophy and politics, while his wife Edith – a small, vivid woman with a quick laugh and sharp blue eyes – bred horses. They were a wealthy, cultivated pair, more typical of the French élite, perhaps, than anyone Leonie might meet in Paris.

Darnand monopolized Denholm Collins from the moment they all drifted into the library.

'We must be grateful for a quiet evening,' he said as Mireille opened the windows on to the terrace and wandered into the garden, Pierre following. 'There are nights – and days for that matter – when we have to endure the German planes. They fly far too low, perhaps too stupid to have realized what a danger these mountains can be. There is no attempt to disguise their identity. The Fascists have simply closed ranks, and in Spain the Bolsheviks won't stand a chance.'

'You'd think the Germans would have other pre-occupations,' Denholm said. He had spent some time in Berlin two summers before and was in no hurry to return to a city he found torn between survival and self-indulgence. The family he stayed with, teachers, had failed to hide the shortage of food from him after the first few days. 'Versailles left an open wound . . .'

'If the Americans had not backed down from their German investments in '29 there would have been less of an opening in the early '30s for these doom merchants. We cannot always blame Europe for what is happening – what is going to happen. We have simply provided Hitler with a natural enemy, my friend, and he is quite sincere when he addresses the business fraternity with promises to tear up the Versailles paperwork. As he also swears, no doubt, to tear up the Picassos.'

'Talking of Americans' – the doctor's wife took a brandy from Paul and walked over to where the men stood – 'last year we were in London for a conference, and people talked of nothing but this Mrs Simpson and your king.'

'Not our king any more,' Denholm said politely. 'And may I ask what the French talk about?'

'Money!' It was Madame Darnand, wrinkling her straight nose in pretended distaste. 'Always money.'

'And in your case horses, ma chère,' Darnand teased. 'Tell me, Mademoiselle Leonie.' He turned to where Leonie had been sitting in silence, just as Mireille came back into the room. 'Do you ride? I believe there are no horses here at Briteau. You would be welcome, some Sunday perhaps, if your – my friend Paul agrees.'

'Oh, yes, Papa, do let's say yes!' It was Mireille who answered, running to Paul. 'They have two ponies. Please say we can go.'

Marc Darnand had intended the invitation as a chivalrous postscript to his remarks about Wall Street. The girl was, he had suddenly remembered, at least half American. She was also a beauty, and intelligent with it. La petite Mireille would soon have her nose put out of joint – and seemed to know it.

'You can see how my daughter feels the lack of all she is accustomed to in Bordeaux.' Paul bowed to Edith Darnand. 'But even there the horses do not equal yours. I hope that one fine day you will provide our stables with excellent – if rather expensive – stock.'

127

'You see?' She raised her glass to him. They smiled at each other with the tolerance of long acquaintance. 'In France it is always a question of money.'

'There are other things. Our splendid inheritance – yours and Marc's, ours here at Briteau.'

'Not so fast. It could all go, at any time,' the doctor said darkly. 'Do you know, Paul, that your aunt was telling me, last time I called on her to check her perfectly sound if rather stubborn heart, that by ancient Basque tradition – stronger than law, eh? – a seigneur can appoint any heir of his choice? I think she must have been thinking of changing her will. You know what these old people can be like.'

'I hope my aunt *is* well,' Paul said sharply. 'When was this?' He tried to calculate the exact date of Zoe's arrival in France and her subsequent visit to Charles Vincent. It was a relief to hear the doctor mention a time some weeks before.

Berthe would of course have been told of the new situation by now, entailing as it did the end of the monthly cheque which she had secretly masterminded over the years. If it were not for the harvest he would have gone straight to Paris himself and had the whole business out with her. As for making new wills – he planned soon to call on his notary himself. The after-dinner talk of Germany had reawakened a recent premonition that his active service as a soldier was not over yet.

Henri Massine had threatened legal action, but it was not in his nature to do anything hasty, in spite of his bravado. Nor would he put his granddaughter's rights at risk. The land was mortgaged, it was true, but not to Henri Massine. Paul could still take a leaf out of the book of the Basque seigneurs, and make some provision for the elder daughter whose existence had been concealed from him for so long.

During the last, hot days of the work on the grape harvest he watched Leonie, and knew that he was right. The girl had spirit, and the ability to work. She fitted in well – with the students, the itinerant workers, and his own estate staff. Perhaps a little too well with Jacques Fabri, who now worked side by side with his father as the need to bring the harvest in on time became the one thing that mattered.

On the Saturday night at the end of *le grand travail* the traditional party for all the workers was held in the field behind the main house. Violette began to cook at dawn, Pierre Giraud set long trestle tables under the trees, Mireille laid them with white cloths while Charlie dashed in and out yapping at them all. Later Pierre hung coloured lanterns along the garden path and the high brick wall, and an accordionist from the village arrived early and downed three glasses of wine in quick succession.

As always at the harvest supper, Paul and his household served at table. Mireille insisted that her English tutor was also now one of the family, and Denholm and Leonie stood side by side in the kitchen preparing the serving dishes under Violette's eagle-eyed instruction as the first guests began to arrive.

'Long way from New York,' Denholm said as the accordionist struck up a fast waltz in the distance.

'I like helping in the kitchen. It's not so different.'

Denholm watched her as she arranged cold meats on a large white dish. He thought how the coltish figure had filled out, and how the sharpening lines of the child-woman's face had taken on an uncanny likeness to some of the faces in the de Byron family portraits that lined the walls of the gallery. She had the classic potential of the hybrid. Spirit, adaptability. The future might hold anything for this American girl who chopped parsley expertly, like any young peasant housewife, on a wooden block in the great kitchen of her father's house, with long brown fingers scarred by the work of the past weeks. If, that is, there was to be a future for any of them.

The dancing began just as darkness fell. Paul made a short

129

speech of thanks, explained that he did not dance, and ordered Pierre to lead the first waltz with his grandmother. As the clapping and laughter died down, Leonie caught Jacques Fabri's dark eyes on her. She touched Denholm's sleeve. 'Please dance with me.'

As Denholm took her hand she was relieved to see Jacques walk over to where Mireille stood with a group of young girls from the village and ask her to partner him. His eyes met Leonie's again as the waltz ended, but it was some time before he asked her to dance, and when he did so he held her stiffly, at a distance, and did not smile or make small talk.

From their places at the top table, his parents watched, the mother impassive, the father disapproving. They had heard all about the night Paul de Byron's elder daughter had spent in the mountains with Jacques from Paul himself. Their faces said that if anyone slipped away from the coloured lights and into the meadow by the stream where all was darkness it was not going to be their son.

'My father does not like to see people amuse themselves,' Jacques said at last.

'Is it my fault?' They reversed quickly, and Leonie gave a low laugh, catching her breath.

'No.' Jacques did not smile. 'I have stayed too long at home. Only my parents know it, but now the harvest is in I am leaving.'

Leonie stopped dancing, and looked into his face in dismay which she made no attempt to disguise. Without realizing it, she had grown too close to this strange, elusive French boy, in the long days they had worked together, and in an intimacy that had been born quite innocently in the night they had spent in the mountains.

'When? When are you going?'

'On Monday. I report to the military headquarters in Bordeaux. For my two years' national service. It is time I went. My father and I will part in anger if I leave it longer.' He could not tell her that the military training was also something he wanted, and that he was joining the army with

130

the approval of the organization in Spain.

He gripped Leonie's waist before she could answer, pulling her back into the dance, but the music ended soon after, leaving them facing each other in a heavy silence before Jacques dropped his hands and stepped back.

'Tomorrow I go to church for the last time. My mother expects it. All her friends will want to weep.'

'I'll not cry for you, Jacques,' she said steadily. 'I think you will come back.' She turned, and walked quickly to where her father stood watching the crowd. She was unaccountably glad to find him alone.

'Are we going to church tomorrow, Papa?'

'If we are not too tired. And then in the afternoon you go riding. The Darnands have just telephoned. They invite you and your sister, to lunch.'

The Darnands' brown, cream-trimmed Daimler was parked outside the church when the de Byron household arrived for matins. They had arranged to drive the sisters back with them for a light lunch before an afternoon's riding, and would return to the château with them for cocktails. Taking her place in the pew beside Mireille, with Edith Darnand on her other side, Leonie realized that she was not likely to see Jacques again before he left for Bordeaux.

His mother had not walked with them to church, and when she did arrive took a place in the pew just behind them, whispering a greeting to Violette as she rustled her prayer book and undid the buttons at the wrist of her black gloves. 'We came with the horse,' she said. 'Jacques drove.'

Leonie wondered if the information was directed at her rather than at Violette, if it said, 'I, Camille Fabri, have my son under control at last in spite of what any foreign miss might have tried.' She dared not look up to the gallery where she knew Jacques and Fabri père must by now be taking their seats. But throughout the service she was aware of Jacques's presence, and knew that his eyes were on the nape of her neck as she knelt for the prayers.

There were the usual knots of black-dressed parishioners waiting outside the church to talk with the curé or gossip amongst themselves, but the moment the two Fabri men emerged Camille broke away from her own small group of women friends and called to them. She wanted to return quickly to the house. She had been late with the preparation of their meal, after all the excitement of the night before. Monsieur de Byron and Violette also wished to return with them. And Monsieur le Curé wished to give Jacques his blessing.

Mireille stood at Leonie's side and watched Yves Pascal shake hands with Jacques. Then, with no more than a casual wave in their direction, Jacques walked ahead of his parents and jumped into the driver's seat of the waiting cart. The two girls waved to their father as Jacques flourished the whip and the horse broke into a canter, sending Violette and Camille into each other's plump arms.

'He does not want to say goodbye,' Mireille said. 'He has finished with Briteau.' Her voice was flat, and gave nothing away. But as they settled into the rear seat of the Daimler she turned to look back. Leonie noticed that under her golden look she was pale, and for the length of the drive to the Darnand château she was silent.

Paul de Byron spent the afternoon in his suite of rooms on the first floor, planning his new will, and writing to Tante Berthe to warn her that their approaching meeting would be a challenge to them both.

> I respect you too much, ma chère tante, to take a whole page in which to accuse you of keeping my first child from me all these years, however noble your motives. But now she has come into my life I find her quite worthy of my name, as I believe you will also find her. I also believe it can only be to the good that I make some provision for the

future by which Briteau does not come entirely under the control of my beloved Yvette's family. You know enough of the personalities involved not to ask me my reasons! . . .

The letter signed and sealed, he telephoned Charles Vincent at his home, apologized for interrupting his Sunday, and briefly outlined the draft of the will he would like him to prepare before he came into the office on his way through Paris. 'You will be discreet, Charles, I know. And you will make quite certain that I do not visit you at a time when –'

'When a very determined, very elegant American lady calls on me? No need even to ask, my dear fellow. But you are missing something quite extraordinary. Perhaps you know that already?'

'I have our daughter to tell me that. She is quite exceptionally lovely.'

'Be careful, Paul. All that my father and your aunt did was for the best.'

'It is too late, that's all I know. Too late to make amends with the mother.'

'But the child . . . that's a different story, eh?'

'Shall we just say I have plans.'

The fact that Leonie had not taken riding lessons in New York put her at a disadvantage at the Darnands', for the length of an afternoon in which Mireille seemed, perversely, to set out to win their hosts' approval and put Leonie in a lesser light. During lunch she talked in rapid, idiomatic French, in contrast to her silence in the car. She paused occasionally to explain some phrase to Leonie, in laborious English, when simpler French would have served. She referred constantly to Bordeaux and her grandfather's business, and complained that she had not been able to help with the harvest this year and her tutor had been a tyrant.

Edith Darnand knew it for the child-like performance it was, but it was not easy to stem the flow. In her limited

English she tried to put Leonie at her ease when they went to the guest-room and tried out a riding habit for size. When Leonie told her she had never ridden horseback, she promised she was an excellent teacher. But as soon as Mireille was on her pony she rode off at a canter, and with a word of apology Edith told Leonie that she must ride after her before she did anything foolish.

Five minutes later Mireille trotted meekly back into the stable yard, Edith leading. She waited while Edith gave Leonie her first lesson in mounting and handling. Then she trotted off at a gentler pace, sighing that it would take more than an afternoon to teach a New Yorker to ride.

Leonie took the treatment as long as they were with the Darnands. But the moment they were back at Briteau, and the Darnands had joined Paul and Denholm in the library, she followed Mireille to her room. She intended to make her promise never to behave like that again, whether they were alone together or not. Now that Jacques Fabri was to leave there would be less reason for jealousy. And in the few days left before Mireille herself returned to Bordeaux she wanted somehow to make peace between them.

She knocked on the door of Mireille's room, but there was no reply. After a while she turned the handle, and went in, to find Mireille sprawled on her bed in a paroxysm of silent weeping.

Leonie stood stock still, not knowing at first what she should do. It was the only time Mireille had shown her vulnerability so openly, and it had taken Jacques Fabri's departure from Briteau to bring her to it.

'Mireille.' Leonie closed the door and walked over to the bed. 'I think I know what the matter is. Don't cry so. He'll be back, I know he will. This is his home.'

'It will be too late,' Mireille said between sobs, her head still buried in her pillow. 'I will be too old.'

'Too old for what?'

'For flying our kite. For the eagle's nest.'

'That's not true. Things like that don't change.' She

wished she believed her own words.

'How do you know? Her sister sat up, eyes still streaming. 'You've never lived here. You can't love these things as I do. You don't feel things . . .'

'I came here to tell you that I *do* feel.' Leonie sat on the edge of the bed. 'That I can't take much more of the way you are with me. This afternoon at the Darnands' – why did you have to put me down like that?'

'Like what?'

'You know very well. What have I done to you? Now that Jacques is going, I thought we might be friends.'

After a silence, broken by a series of small sniffs: 'Sisters always quarrel.'

'So you do accept me as your sister?'

'I have had no choice. But my grandfather will fight it, you'll see. There will be nothing but trouble now. If you knew how I have hated this summer.'

'Mireille. Listen to me. We may not see each other again for a very long time. Maybe not ever, if your grandfather is really so against me. But the summer is not over, is it? One more week, for Papa too. Couldn't we make a go of things, just for the time left?'

'I have to work.'

'Denholm is not so bad. I like him a lot.'

Mireille nodded, and blew her nose into a small white linen handkerchief. 'Me too.'

'Well then? Seven days?'

'Then my grandfather's car will come for me, and it will all be over.'

'Why not take Denholm back with you, as far as Bordeaux? The strike is still on. It will help him to get home.'

'Perhaps. I will ask.'

'Good. Now – I want to speak to Papa, alone, before supper. Can you wash your face and come down and say thank you to the Darnands before they go?'

'You are giving all the orders.' Mireille got to her feet and

135

went to her dressing-table. She began to brush her hair, and their eyes met in the mirror.

'What else are big sisters for?' Leonie said.

She stood with her father on the terrace after the Daimler had disappeared down the drive, Charlie in pursuit and Mireille calling him ineffectually to heel. She told him that she had many things to ask him, and he suggested that they take a walk in the meadow behind the house until Violette called them in for their meal.

Avoiding the details of what had happened that afternoon, Leonie told him that she felt she must use her time in France, whatever else happened, to learn to speak French perfectly – 'like a Frenchwoman, Papa.' If he would not let her stay at Briteau, then she intended to persuade her mother to allow her to continue her studies in Paris, not in New York. Maybe she would go to the Sorbonne one day. It was what she wanted – to belong. The summer in Briteau had been the best summer of her life.

'A daughter belongs with her mother,' Paul said carefully. 'Ma pauvre petite Mireille . . .'

'Papa, I have had many years with my mother. In New York, that was fine. But in Paris . . .' It was not the moment to explain about Erich Mannheim. 'Besides, I already have a room, in the *quartier* . . . and friends. It is just –'

'Just the money, perhaps? Paul allowed himself to smile.

'I did have some money,' she said quickly. 'But –'

'It is soon gone, eh?'

He told her then that all her questions were already answered. In the past weeks she had earned her place at Briteau – a place which was hers by natural right, if not by law. She had worked hard, behaved well (most of the time), and had proved herself to be a daughter of whom he could always be proud. But she should go to Paris. And there he would make no arrangements not approved by her mother. What he had in mind was a select finishing school, with international pupils, all of good family.

136

'If you are to claim your place with the de Byrons, then such a training is necessary,' he explained. 'The money will be found somehow, because it is important.'

There was, however, one condition. A year from now, the summer after her first year at the finishing school, she must come back to Briteau.

'Do you think you can promise me that?'

'Oh, Papa! Just try me!' She flung her arms round his neck, and he held her close for a brief moment, before he gently disengaged himself.

On the Monday, Leonie tried all day without success to ring Zoe at Erich Mannheim's apartment on the avenue Kléber. She wrote a short letter to Max, telling him that she would be returning to her room, that the rent was due again, and he must promise it to the concierge for the following week.

It was mid-week before she reached Zoe on the telephone. She had been in Zurich, arranging finance for the European venture, and had been persuaded to go on to Milan, where she had gone as 'wild as wild silk' choosing fabrics and designs for the new salon. All next week she expected deliveries. Leonie had the impression that she was just one more package to be delivered at Erich's apartment. 'We'll be staying with him, of course, until the opening. "Caresse" will be big news.'

'Mother, don't you want to hear *my* news?'

'You'll be getting ready for school. Maddie expects you.'

'No, Mother. I'm writing to Maddie myself. It's not going to be like that. A lot has happened.'

'One summer holiday with – your father – does not change the world. I allowed it because you were so damn stubborn. We can't discuss it on this line, anyway.' It was the usual bad line to Paris, but it did not mask the hardness that had crept into Zoe's voice.

'I'll call you when I get to Paris, Mother.'

'You'll come straight here.'

'I'll call you.'

CHAPTER NINE

When Mireille and Denholm had left, the château seemed to Leonie to become a place alive with ghosts, the hallways and stairs and high rooms stifled and silent in the shadowy heat of the summer that had almost gone. Charlie had left with his mistress, a blur of soulful eyes in white fur in the Peugeot's rear window. Paul spent hours at his desk on paperwork that had to be dealt with before his return to his regiment. Violette's grandson went back to Paris. The estate workers no longer gathered under Leonie's window in the early morning, their sabots noisy on the stony path.

There was less than a fortnight to go before the end of his leave when Paul emerged from the library as Leonie crossed the hall on her way to breakfast in the kitchen and asked her not to go far from the house that afternoon. She had taken to long walks alone in the past few days.

Madame Veron, her father explained, would be calling on her from the village. 'The dressmaker. She is very skilled, they used to tell me. I have asked her to make you one or two things. You cannot arrive in Paris just as you are. The season is changing.'

'But, Papa – there is no time.'

'They used to tell me that Madame Veron could make a dress in a single day.'

The dressmaker arrived at two, parking a gleaming bicycle in the drive with the precision of a limousine. Her trim figure and the well cut alpaca two-piece she wore reassured Leonie as she took the stairs to the guest suite at an efficient little run, her chignon of fair hair bobbing in its silk net above square navy-blue shoulders that would have inspired confidence in Worth himself.

It was obvious that Jeanne Veron knew her way about the château, and – guessing that she had worked for Yvette de Byron – Leonie went meekly through the business of measurements and choosing fabrics from the swatch-book that the dressmaker had brought with her.

She wondered, all the same, why her father – who until then had seemed to take so little note of such things – should suddenly have decided it was important she should have new clothes.

She was to get her answers at dinner the night before they left for Paris. They ate, as usual, in the dining-room, two places laid by Violette at one end of the shining mahogany table. At first Leonie had found their solitary evening meal awkward, and then – even when they were silent – it had become a pleasant, peaceful routine.

This time, when Violette left them alone, Paul told Leonie that it had been arranged for her to go with him on his visit to his elderly aunt in Paris. He hoped that the family apartment – in a house that had once belonged to the de Byrons – would become her home, while she attended a finishing school in the nearby Place Vendôme.

'It is what you asked of me. And you were right to ask, ma fille. You will learn perfect French. You will meet many young women of good family.'

The mention of the school pleased her, but only momentarily served to palliate the shock of the idea of living with an ageing Frenchwoman whom she had never met. Tante Berthe's reputation for severity had preceded her in several remarks from Mireille.

'Of course it is what I want, Papa,' she said carefully. 'It's fine. I had no idea it was all fixed. But – I already have a place to stay. My own place. My friend – friends – expect me.'

'Oh yes, on the Left Bank? It would not be at all suitable.

139

You will see. From my aunt's apartment you can even walk to the Collège Madeleine. It is for the best.'

'Your aunt has never met me, Papa. She knows nothing of me.'

'On the contrary.' The irony in his voice did not escape her. 'Tante Berthe has always known about you. From the day you were born, even before.'

'Then she knew my mother?' The word was out. All summer she had managed to keep her promise that Zoe was not to be mentioned at Briteau, and now it was as if she had brought her to her side as an ally. She did not want to live with her mother and Erich Mannheim, and she had set her heart on the small room in the house next to Max Heller and his crazy piano.

'Yes.' Paul seemed to have forgotten the taboo he had imposed through his notary. 'She did know your mother. She has been my agent for almost two decades, in seeing that you were provided for. She, and of course my man of business.'

'Oh.' *The violet signature.* 'So the family knew about me all along?'

'My aunt knew.' Paul realized at that moment that he was too proud, maybe too ashamed, to bring himself to tell her that for the first seventeen years of her life he had not even known that she existed. She was still a child, not to be so hurt. Perhaps in protecting her from the hurt he was role-playing, and making up for all the lost years.

He had written to Berthe again, in answer to her own brief note confirming the time and day, a Friday, she would receive him in Paris en route for his unit. In his letter he had this time expressed in plain terms his anger at the deception of eighteen years ago.

Now it seems to me all that matters is the child. I have told you of her qualities. I intend to make certain that those qualities are used well. She enrols at the Collège Madeleine for the new *trimestre*; my own colonel's daughter is a pupil there. It will be for two years, and it is

140

important that for those two years Leonie de Byron enjoys the right background. If I am to forgive you for the past it will be because you agree to provide that background. For my daughter.

Berthe de Byron had telephoned her reply early one morning. 'You have – I see from your letter – decided to give this girl our full family title? It seems then that I have no choice, and – if I like what I see – well, we cannot have a de Byron running round Paris for two years without a chaperone, eh?'

'Thank you. I knew I could depend on you.' Paul smiled, knowing that the sharpness of her voice concealed her interest in the turn events had taken.

'And money? I suppose you have not thought what all this will cost?'

'This time it is I who will pay, my dear aunt.'

'By raising yet another mortgage?'

'I will see Charles Vincent. When you and I have talked.'

Replacing the receiver, Paul had unlocked a drawer in his desk and removed a soft leather address book. He gently touched the gold initials Y. de B. tooled on its cover before leafing through its pages. At the entry for Jeanne Veron, *couturière*, he paused.

His plan to launch his daughter, the product of a brief love between a small-town American beauty and a Frenchman of good family, had begun.

For the train journey to Paris, Leonie wore a straight tweed dress in *prince de galles* checks, with a crisp linen collar, pearl buttons at the shoulder, neat cuffs above short white gloves. In her suitcase was a second pair of gloves, which Madame Veron had insisted was *de rigueur* if she was to arrive in the capital city of la belle France *comme il faut*.

She sat straight-backed beside her father, neither of them speaking as the train chugged through the familiar local

141

landscape bordered by the distant hills, then began its long haul through the anonymous plains of Les Landes.

As the local travellers alighted at one or other of the stops along the line – villages that presented a face as deserted as the landscape itself – they nodded to Paul and his companion, making no more of her than any young French girl on her way to college for the first time. Madame Veron had merely put the finishing touches to a transformation that the summer at Briteau had begun.

They left their luggage at the Gare de Lyon and break-fasted in a small all-night café near the station before they took a taxi to the rue de Rivoli. The district was one of uniform decaying elegance in grey stone, the houses in the streets behind the expensive shops shuttered tight against a changing world. In the rue Louis, where the de Byrons had lived for two centuries, the apartment building that had once been their town house was built round three sides of a small courtyard, the shade of a young plane tree in its centre dappling the yellowing bricks of a disused well.

Paul tried the latch of the high wrought-iron street gate and finding it locked rang the bell at its side. As if the bellpull worked some invisible chain a small bent figure appeared within seconds at an inner door, and the concierge shuffled to meet them, keys jangling against a long black skirt, woollen slippers silent on the tiled yard.

'Ah. Monsieur Paul. And you are early.' The woman's complaining voice was more habit than mood. She selected a key adroitly, and the gate swung inward as she performed a kind of backward staggering dance under its weight.

'You forgive me, of course, Jeannine? After all, we are old friends.' Paul slipped a coin into the pocket in a fold of her skirt, and she walked back into the house with a more sprightly step. The smell of strong coffee pervaded the darkened hall as she opened the glass door to the cramped kitchen, her *loge*, which led to her own apartment. 'You will soon become accustomed to my aunt's visitor,' Paul told her as he beckoned to Leonie to follow him, and she moved forward, sensing the sharp eyes of the professional observer still on her as she climbed the stairs beside her father.

Berthe de Byron greeted them in the narrow, flock-papered hallway of her apartment, her strong, gnarled hand barely touching the American girl's fresh white glove. Berthe was tall for a Frenchwoman, as elegant and unbending as eighteen years ago, the steely eyes betraying nothing of the shock of recognition as they bore into Leonie's, noting the olive skin that could have belonged to a girl from Provence, the dark hair tied back smoothly in a black ribbon like any young French *collégienne*'s – and the chin held a fraction too high, blue eyes blazing, the girl's shoulders as square as Berthe's – yet the whole image still a reflection of the American girl who had faced her with such poise so long ago.

'*Tiens. La petite américaine.*' The greeting was kindly enough. They moved into the salon, where coffee waited. Paul stood gripping the back of one of the small army of polished chairs that stood like sentinels across the room. He always found the apartment claustrophobic after Briteau, but the apprehension about the first encounter between his aunt and his daughter made things worse. He believed that the discipline which was second nature to his aunt would ensure her good behaviour. What he had not been able to anticipate was his own emotional reaction, as he stood in this room where he had once faced Berthe with Zoe's innocence and beauty, and now faced her with their daughter.

'You manipulated us all then,' he thought. 'Now you need us. You are getting old. Things will be different.'

Nursing his memories of Zoe as she was then, he sipped his coffee, silently watching as Berthe put Leonie through her paces. She wanted news of the harvest. She did not get to Briteau as much as she liked. She had been a mother to Paul since his own maman was killed in a car crash – a woman too daring, too frivolous – and la petite Mireille was more to her grandparents than to her great-aunt Berthe. The less said of the family in Bordeaux the better. To change the subject, what of New York? She wanted to know details of Leonie's

143

schooling. She congratulated her on her knowledge of French.

'You speak with great clarity, great simplicity. That is good. You will do well at the Madeleine. You will find other American girls there, you know, of the highest family. And of course les anglaises. They tried Switzerland. But the best families always come back to Paris to "finish". I think they hope that their girls will learn to cook – or at least be able to direct a French chef.'

'Papa chose the college for me.'

'He has your interest at heart.'

There was a pause. Leonie dreaded the moment when the matter of her staying at the apartment would be broached. She was not certain she would be a match for Tante Berthe.

'You knew my mother?' It was nerves, or the need to remind the old Frenchwoman that she had other contacts in Paris, somewhere else to stay. She felt her father tense.

Berthe was quite unshaken. She nodded slowly. 'She came to tea. More than once. She was very beautiful. Very intelligent.'

'She still is. She is in Paris. Did you know?'

'*Tiens.*' Berthe poured herself a second cup of coffee, and gave Paul a sideways, accusing look. This was not the direction she wanted the conversation to take.

'Surely Charles told you?' Paul said.

'He told me many things.' She took refuge in a feigned old woman's vagueness. It was a ploy she used frequently, and usually to effect.

'You arranged things . . .' Leonie spoke very softly, eyes bright with challenge.

'I looked after things. I always did for your father. I have told you.' She gestured helplessly, as if she had done what she had done and that was it. Then she sighed, allowing herself a gentle smile. 'As I will look after you. If you will let me.'

'I want to go to the Collège Madeleine. I want it very much. But my mother also intends to stay on in Paris. And I have friends here.'

144

'Your friends will be welcome. And your mother has much to do, ma petite. I hardly think she can object if you make this apartment your home.'

'So you know about her? She's very successful.'

'Everyone is talking about her, child. *Tout Paris*.'

'I see.' She wondered if '*tout Paris*' also knew about her mother's Swiss banker. The old woman was right, all the same. Erich Mannheim's apartment was the last place from which she could be a student at the Madeleine. And she owed it to her father. He should not be disappointed in her. Besides, there was something about Tante Berthe that she rather liked. 'I came to France on my own, you know,' she went on. 'I wanted so much to find my father.'

'Then that is settled.' Berthe stood up, and Paul got to his feet quickly. 'After all, you cannot find your father and then so quickly lose him. When he is on leave, it is here that he comes to stay. Briteau is too far. He will want to see you. What could be simpler?'

She led them into the hallway, telling Paul to send for the *bagages* from the station, and as the telephone rang in the salon she left them, with orders that Paul should show his daughter her room. She was to have his old room, of course.

They stood together in the doorway, then Leonie crossed to the window, and looked down into the courtyard. 'I can see into the well.'

'I remember. This was my room. When I was . . . younger.'

'Oh, I see.' She was suddenly painfully aware of the high bed, the white lace coverlet neatly folded down from the great soft feather pillows.

Paul walked over to where she stood, her face averted. He touched her gently on the arm. 'All you need to know is that we were very young. And that I loved your mother. And that she loved me. It was a cruel world. A world just after a war can be like that. I hope you will never have to learn that for yourself, ma petite.'

She turned to him. 'Thank you, Papa. I'm glad you told me you loved her.'

145

'It is the last time we have to talk of these things. You know that my wife's honour, the way things are at the château, cannot be put at risk?'

'I know that. You didn't have to tell me.'

'Now all will be well, you will see.'

Just then Berthe called to them that she had to go out that morning, and Leonie should hurry if she was to make her calls in Paris and be back before dark.

'Do I have to stay here tonight?' Leonie whispered to her father. 'I have to see my mother. And it will take hours to clear my room . . .' She did not tell him that she wanted time with Max, before the world of the rue Louis closed in on her for good.

'It is best. You will ask your mother, of course. You can telephone from here. But the college registers its new pupils on Monday. Tante Berthe expects you to settle in before then.'

'Oh, very well.' She picked up her bag, wanting to find Erich Mannheim's telephone number.

'I will put you in a taxi. Then I have to talk with my aunt. You understand?' Paul grasped her shoulders lightly and kissed her quickly, a formal kiss on each cheek.

'Shall I write to you?' she asked.

'Of course. I must hear of your progress. My aunt has the address. But I do not promise always to have the time to write back.'

The commissionaire at the apartment block in the avenue Kléber crossed the narrow pavement and opened the taxi door. Leonie, remembering something of the panache with which Max Heller distributed *pourboires* whenever he had the cash to spare, added to her cab fare and earned an approving nod over her head between cabby and doorman. Once in the foyer, she gave the Swiss banker's name and said that she was expected.

The lift, as fragile and gilded as a birdcage, jerked to the top floor, and opened on to a reception hall in Erich Mannheim's apartment, which ran the whole of the floor. As the lift gate opened a bell rang somewhere, and the door opposite the lift shaft swung inwards. Zoe, in a dark blue and white silk dress with loose jacket edged with pale fur stood arms outstretched as Leonie walked to meet her.

'Baby! You look *so* French! And the dress. Let me see.' She twirled her daughter with a scarlet-nailed hand. 'Hm. Cut, good. Colour . . .' She kissed her on the forehead, and then held her very close for the briefest of moments. 'I've missed you. I've everything to tell you.'

Leonie returned the kiss warmly. 'Me too, Mother. I'm glad you were in.' She looked about her. At the opulent, slightly self-consciously so, town hideaway of a wealthy patron of the arts – the Bechstein on a dais; the furniture hand-made in heavy, carved woods; the walls almost covered by paintings from the French schools of the past three hundred years, including some bold modern work. The windows were mansard, cut into the gabled roof of the block, and thickly veiled with heavy white silk. There was a scent of cigars, and of Zoe's own products.

'Don't fret. He's not here. We were on our way to lunch but he insisted I wait for you. He can handle the guy we were meeting.'

'I said I'd call. You don't have much time, I know. But I do have to make sure you know what I'm doing next. I want that. And my – my father insists.'

Zoe led her to a deep sofa and sank into its cushions, patting a place at her side. Leonie sat down.

'So. You found him. Did that make you happy?' Zoe lit a cigarette. 'Did he talk about me?'

'I am happy, yes. And he did talk about you. But not until today. I don't think he wants the past to stand in the way.'

'In the way? It's sure as hell shaped what's happening so fast now.'

Her speech seemed freer, tougher. She looked quite magnificent, yet there were lines of fatigue beneath the eye

147

make-up, and the hair grew now in a longer bob, slightly curled, in what surely had to be intentional disarray.

'He wants to do so much for me. And it's what I want, Mother. You're staying in Paris? The new company is what *you* want?'

'It's what comes next for me. It makes a whole lot of good sense.'

'Aren't you excited, Mother? You used to love this sort of thing.'

'Of course I love it. It's just very, very hard work at the moment. You've caught me at the end of a long week.'

'I'm sorry. But I have to make arrangements. My room . . .'

'You're not going back to that dump? Does Paul de Byron know where you were staying?'

'Yes. And he thinks as you do.'

'So, you're coming back here? Erich will want that. He likes to have you around, did you know that?'

Leonie bit her lip. 'No, Mother, I'm not staying here. Papa has arranged for me to go to finishing school, a college in the Place Vendôme. And he insists that I stay in a family apartment, quite near. I can walk to classes, he says. I – we – were there this morning.'

'Well, I'm glad you felt you should come and tell me all this. After all, we go back a long way, child.' Zoe stubbed out her cigarette viciously.

'You know I don't want to live with you and –'

'Erich and I are business partners, and it's more strictly business every day, believe me. And soon I'll have the place off the Champs Elysées finished. There's room. It doesn't have to be exactly as Paul *de* Byron says.'

'I think it does, Mother. If you still want a future for me, as a de Byron, it looks as if this is the way it has to go.'

Zoe pouted, then whispered almost to herself. 'My God, why didn't it hit me first time? I think I know where you're staying.'

'She says she knew you. She remembered you.'

'Unforgettable me. Does she still look through you with those eyes?'

'I think Papa's frightened of her too, if that's what you mean.'

'I *was not frightened* of that woman. That old woman, she must be now. Don't you ever say that.'

'Mother –' Leonie was shaken by the white anger in Zoe's face.

'I did it all for you. I fought her every inch of the way. And what about New York? Maddie too. Do you really want to give it all up?'

'You've walked out on it yourself, Mother! This way we're at least both in the same town. And I've been writing to Maddie. She knows everything, and she's looking on the whole thing as a vacation – for her too. I'll go over at Christmas, if you like. I'm sure Papa –'

'If *I* want it, you'll go. You'll do that for me.'

'Of course. You know I will. I miss the apartment, and Maddie. Do you think I don't miss you too? It's just that everything's changed.' She found herself fighting back sudden tears, of sheer exhaustion after the journey from Briteau, of homesickness for the château, for Maddie and New York, and of fear of the new life waiting for her at the rue Louis.

'Some things haven't changed, after all.' Zoe sniffed, and sought for and found a minuscule handkerchief in the silk jacket. 'We still cry, for one thing. And for another – I still like a little champagne at this time of day. How about it?'

It was the old truce. Zoe fetched the champagne. They lunched alfresco in the kitchen, like old times. They talked of Maddie's situation, and with her third glass of champagne Zoe confided that she had even thought of making a gift of the Gramercy Park apartment to Maddie. 'She's earned it, for God's sake. A Christmas gift. You can tell her when you go over.'

'You might need to go back yourself one day, Mother.'

'A long time off, maybe. And Maddie wouldn't throw me

149

out if I went barefoot, do you know that?'

'I know.'

Zoe went on to pump Leonie about her own financial situation, and sensed she was short of funds. She gave her enough to pay off the week she would have to meet if she got out of her room on the Left Bank, with some over 'for goodies' for the first weeks at the Collège Madeleine.

'Since you've made up your mind, we'll let you do it in style. I'll have to explain to Lady Hume why you've dropped the place she recommended.'

'The Madeleine is something different, Mother. Not just French for foreigners. She'll understand.'

Zoe told her that the Humes had returned to London but that Gavin had promised to bring his grandmother over for the gala opening of the premises of 'Caresse'. It was scheduled for a month's time, in time in fact to catch a peak Christmas trade.

They parted in the street, Zoe putting Leonie into a cab for the Left Bank, and taking her own on to the Champs Elysées. They were both light-headed after the champagne, and laughed as they kissed, making no definite date to meet again.

In the confines of her cab, Zoe took out a hand-mirror and examined her face. The driver saw in his own mirror a wealthy foreigner, with as much style as any Parisienne. The hair a little tousled, perhaps. The mouth just a little too red. But she left an exquisite scent behind her . . . and a tip to match. And like many a cab driver in the weeks to come he remembered the premises at which he dropped her. Especially the name painted by hand, in palest orchid pink, across the two windows. *Caresse*.

On the pavement outside the house where she had lived for just a few days on her arrival in France, Leonie found the landlord sitting on a three-legged stool, unshaven face lifted to the afternoon sun, immobile as a mongrel dog that had run out of games. He recognized her as soon as she left the cab, grinned, and put two hands to his ears. She knew at once that Max must be home. The Conservatoire term would not have started yet.

Arranging to leave her things in the landlord's own ground-floor apartment she told him she would not be long but had to see her musician friend next door before she moved out altogether. She gave him the address of Tante Berthe's apartment in case she had missed Max while she packed up her room, or in case Gavin Hume wanted to find her on his return to Paris.

'I hope you can find someone to take my room, monsieur. I am sorry to be leaving.'

'But you nearly lost it, mademoiselle. To another of your countrymen. Then he preferred the studio which became vacant at the back of the house. He moves in today.'

'An American? A student?'

'*Peintre*. What else? And from New York. Your own city. A Mistère Tonee Shaw.'

'Tony Shaw. Nice name. But Paris is my city. I'll pick up my bags in an hour.'

Max Heller was at home, but the house was silent. She knocked on his door, breathing a little quickly from the long climb, and when he called for her to come in found him sitting on the bed, his glasses on the side table, sheets of music scattered at his feet. She was taken aback at first by some change in him, an aura of inertia, but he shook it off a split second after she came into the room.

'Max! Who were you expecting? I thought you'd at least play me in.'

'No one. Only you. Come here, Mademoiselle Leonie. It *is* you, I presume? You're changed so . . . and it's terrific.'

'You've changed too, Max. Something wrong?'

'No, no. I need to work, that's all. It's family. My mother's sister tried to get out – Mother's not too well, it seems – and

151

she's — disappeared. We've heard nothing. My mother's taken it badly.'

Leonie did not know what to say. Some of the talk at Briteau that summer had taught her that such things could happen, but she had not been prepared for it to happen to anyone she knew, close to home. Max assured her his family had contacts who would monitor what went on once they picked up the trail. His aunt was a well known academic, a psychiatrist. She could not just disappear.

Reluctantly, Leonie told him her own news. She watched for disappointment. But to her surprise Max's mood at once changed. He congratulated her, kissed her, and insisted on playing 'La Marseillaise'. 'We'll show these Frenchies they've got someone special. And when I call on your aunt I'll wear the tuxedo, day or night, I swear.'

He always made her laugh.

'Don't stay away, Max. Promise?'

He went down with her to collect her things, and offered to go back with her to Tante Berthe's apartment, just as far as the door. She agreed, sensing that he did not want to be alone.

As they carried the luggage to the pavement a tall, fair-haired figure turned the corner, laden with canvases and a worn duffle-bag. Leonie was at once aware of grey eyes that gave nothing away yet saw everything, of immense confidence, even arrogance. The boy was perhaps twenty, perhaps more, but would always look young for his years. His clothes were clean, but very shabby, belying the innate style with which he wore them.

'Hi.' He nodded to Max, obviously knowing him at least by sight. He put his bag on the pavement and held out his hand.

Max called to Leonie to leave her luggage and come and meet Tony Shaw.

'Well.' The sharp voice, New York to the last fibre, went with the eyes. 'I see the wealthy are deserting the ghetto.'

'Don't give us that, Shaw,' Max said. 'Your people could

match Leonie's mother, dollar for dollar.'

'Ah, but do they always deliver on time? No pretty suntan for me.'

'If you'd spent two months working on the vine terraces with the other students you'd have a tan yourself.' Leonie spoke to the world in general, hoping she could hold back the blush that was hovering at the base of her throat.

She was saved by the appearance of a taxi at the junction of the street, and dropping white gloves at her feet waved a slim brown wrist and ran. 'Like the proverbial gazelle,' Tony said. 'But the voice is New York city.'

'She's been in the mountains all summer,' Max told him.

Tony nodded. 'Yes. I can see her there. That would be somewhere she could belong.'

'The name's Leonie de Byron,' Max said. 'And she's still very young.'

CHAPTER TEN

Turning left out of the courtyard in the rue Louis, Leonie began the short walk to the Collège Madeleine on the autumn morning on which classes were to start. From a house at the corner of the rue Castiglione two small boys emerged and walked ahead of her on their way to school. Twin figures in first-day-at-school new jackets topped by stiff navy-blue sailor hats, the ribbons starched with bows that stood out like small car signals. From trousers cut shorter than any she had ever seen back home the boys' long legs protruded, the legs of starveling birds were it not for a recent Midi tan. Beside them marched their English nanny, in the nut-brown coat and felt hat of the Norland-trained girls who could command such high salaries amongst Parisian families whose back gardens were the Tuileries, who shopped locally at Rouff and Charvet, and called in at the Ritz for English tea.

The Collège Madeleine was in a courtyard on the far side of the Place Vendôme from the Ritz. Its limestone walls had been cleaned white for the new scholastic year. Double glass doors stood open to allow for the inrush of pupils who would be punctual at least on the first day.

The girls arrived alone in chauffeur-driven cars or taxis, in twos and threes on foot. They grouped and gossiped in the reception hall, and Leonie, knowing no one, was glad when the middle-aged woman who manned the desk called to her: 'Mademoiselle de Byron. *Une amie vous attend.*'

She pointed with gold lorgnettes on a black ribbon at a girl who sat quietly reading a magazine, obviously not a newcomer. Leonie went over. A remote-looking blonde in a cashmere two-piece, the girl stood and held out her hand.

'My father knows Capitaine de Byron. He is the colonel of the regiment. He asked me to welcome you. If you like I will show you round before the bell goes for class.'

Tante Berthe had mentioned that Paul's colonel had a daughter at the college. There was a military coldness and precision about the girl herself as she took Leonie on a conducted tour – the large library where private study was encouraged, the small refectory for midday meals, a miniature garden dotted with elegant benches, and by contrast a series of cloakrooms and toilets so primitive that Leonie had to blot out a treacherous vision of the pretty bathrooms at Gramercy Park.

They parted as the bell rang, Leonie guessing they would be unlikely to meet up again; the colonel's daughter had gone through the formalities, but with ill grace. For a wretched moment as she made for the first-year classroom Leonie wondered if the story of her birth had gone the rounds of her father's regiment. She walked into the classroom head high, gripping the leather satchel, with its gold initials L. de B., which had been a gift from Tante Berthe the day before. She just hoped for her father's sake that he was on friendlier terms with his colonel than she would ever be with the daughter.

The first-year students who made up Leonie's study group were of more promising stuff. To balance the nationalities – and make sure that the English-speaking girls had some French-speakers to set the standard for their accents – there were two French girls in the group, three English and three American.

One of the English girls, tall, with a long, almost bony frame and a lean, boyish face to match, had a vacant seat beside her, and seeing Leonie's satchel called out to her to join her. She introduced herself as Sarah Bentley, a friend of the Humes. Gavin Hume had seen her in London before she came over to Paris, and his grandmother had heard that Leonie was to be at the same finishing school. She had something of Lady Hume's quiet, commanding presence, and would probably grow old in the same elegant fashion. Now she wore no make-up, but her complexion gleamed like a country girl's, and her shoulder-length dark brown hair was brushed carelessly back over her shoulders.

'Can't wait to get out of here and see something of Paris. Are you lunching with anyone?'

Leonie agreed to leave the premises for the lunch hour and find a snack in a brasserie nearby. It would be more fun, Sarah said. As if fun was life's main purpose. Leonie liked her at once. She was direct, and full of life.

In the mid-morning coffee break they were joined by one of the French girls. 'Lise Verdier.' She held out a plump hand. 'I heard Miss Bentley say your name. It is a name I know. I come from Bordeaux, and my father is friends with the head of Massine shipping. I think you must have some connection with his granddaughter Mireille?'

There was something greedy in the French girl's face – perhaps a hunger for gossip, perhaps a lust for attention. Leonie noticed that she wore very expensive, slightly showy clothes, which did little to conceal the remnants of puppy fat. If she were connected with the Massines, there was no point in hiding the truth from her. Sooner or later everyone would know. Leonie plunged in. 'Yes, I'm Mireille's half-sister. We spent the summer together at Briteau.'

'Poor thing.' Lise shrugged. 'She has to have some change. If you knew the life she leads with that grandmother. It is church, mass, doctors, and more mass. They hardly let her out of their sight. And she has to study . . . *mon dieu*, how she has to study.'

'Yes. She had to work in the vacation.'

'Well, we're not going to let a little thing like work spoil the term-time, I hope,' Sarah cut in.

At lunch-time Lise Verdier attached herself to them. They found a small brasserie in a cul-de-sac off the square, and while Sarah and Leonie drank a single glass of wine and ate long, crusty ham sandwiches, Lise ordered the plat du jour, and attacked the hors d'oeuvres while she waited. They arranged to meet later in the week, Sarah promising to have plans to see Paris organized for them all. 'You come along too, Lise,' she said – as if she took it for granted that she and Leonie had teamed up – 'you never know when we'll need a real Frenchwoman to get us out of scrapes.'

In spite of her schoolgirl slang and her truancy, Sarah had the underlying good sense of her breed. Leonie knew within the first day that she could safely take her back to the apartment. Lise Verdier, on the other hand, might not pass the steely scrutiny of the aristocratic Berthe. Yet the details Lise had supplied of Mireille's life in Bordeaux had helped her understand her sister more. The childhood friendship with a man like Jacques Fabri, nursed each summer until it became an adolescent love, she now saw was also a symbol of freedom. Losing Jacques must have meant to Mireille the loss of so much more.

On the first Saturday, Sarah had organized a trip on a *bateau mouche*, from which they would see all Paris, and learn the bridges of the Seine, before the rain came and the leaves fell from the trees along the quays. They took the boat at the Pont de l'Alma, close to the Tuileries, and as they passed the Louvre and the rows of *bouquinistes* along the banks came into view Leonie realized that they were close to the *quartier latin*, and she would be able to walk to see Max quite easily from the rue Louis.

Next morning, promising Tante Berthe that she would do her homework for college that afternoon, she set out early, and crossed the river by the iron footbridge of the Pont Neuf. She walked quickly, seeking the turning off the boul' Mich' which would take her to Max's place. As she climbed the stairs to his room she could hear him playing. She knocked, and waited, and knocked again. Max opened at last, and she was again struck by the tension in his face.

'How are things, Max? Still no news?'

'No. But come in, come in. I got your address from next door, and I meant to write.'

157

'Nothing serious?'

'No, of course not. Far from it. There's a party. The American painter, next door. We're using his studio, and he said to invite you. And any friends you like to bring along.'

'Oh, him. Will he be as rude to my friends as he was to me?'

'He liked you, idiot.'

'Funny way to show it.'

'It's his way.'

'What was the name, again?'

'Shaw. Tony Shaw. He's a New Yorker. You ought to be there.'

'I came to see you. I'm fine, but I miss this place.'

'Then come to the party.'

It was a birthday party for an American Tony Shaw had met at the Louvre. He had found him copying a painting, badly, he announced by way of introducing him, and had persuaded him to give up his art at once in exchange for the good life.

'And he can be very persuasive, believe you me,' the guest of honour said.

Sarah, the only one from the college Leonie had wanted to bring, laughed out loud, and Tony looked across the studio at her, a long, interested look. Leonie remembered the grey eyes, and the arrogance of their first meeting. Perhaps Sarah, with centuries of membership of the ruling classes behind her, would prove a match for him. But she edged away later in the evening when Tony sat with Sarah and began to sketch.

'Those bones,' he said, before Sarah could object. 'I can't let them out of here before I've got them on canvas.'

'What fun,' Sarah said. 'No one's ever admired my bones before. It's like being a really good horse.'

'You said it,' Tony grinned. 'The English . . . God, I love them. Everything so well defined. You know where you are.'

The words were not directly for Leonie, but she caught them from where she stood trying to listen to a Polish sculptor who wanted Max to give up playing Mozart and work towards a Chopin recital to raise funds for refugee families at Christmas. Max agreed to the recital, but not to giving up Mozart. They were trying to choose a venue where they could arrange a concert at such short notice and be sure of an audience.

'I could ask at the Collège Madeleine,' Leonie said. 'There's a refectory . . . I think I saw a piano there.'

'The piano is no problem,' Max said curtly. 'But the college won't do.'

'Why not?' She was disappointed, wanting to help.

'Just look around you next time you're in class.'

'I don't understand.'

'It's very mixed?'

She nodded.

'But there's one ingredient missing. Think about it.'

She frowned. Max had come to meet her on the previous afternoon, and walked back to the rue Louis. She had been last out of class, going through a short translation with a French tutor who was inclined to fuss. She found Max waiting in the courtyard, watching the students leave for the day.

'Are they too rich for you?' she tried, hoping to tease an answer out of him.

'I don't object to money. I don't even object to what I saw. It's a fact of life, that's all. A fact of life for the select village of that arrondissement, and for all I know many others.'

'You mean –'

'No *Jews*, Leonie. No Jews.'

'I see.'

'You'll understand one day. There's something like it everywhere. It doesn't just go with money . . .'

'What's this about money?' It was Tony Shaw. 'You know I don't like that word used in my home.'

Max smiled, and put an arm round Leonie. The bad

159

moment had passed. 'It's all right on Wall Street, I hope. In your father's office. And this is a very good party, Shaw. Did I remember to tell you that this is a very good party?'

They were both a little drunk, Leonie thought, but Tony flushed at the mention of Wall Street, and turned away. Max had told her that he was so dedicated to his work that he accepted help from his father because he had no choice. Living and studying in Paris was his whole life. But the dependency made him bitter. Sometimes he was difficult.

'I don't see why he has to feel like that about it,' Leonie said. She wondered what Tony Shaw would say if he knew that she had recently accepted help from her own mother, whose line of business was so much more frivolous than Wall Street's.

'Perhaps we'd have to meet his father to know that. I'm lucky, with my scholarship, and all the backing I get from the family. That's the way it is with us. Traditionally. And music means as much to them as to me.'

They parted at the door of the studio. Leonie and Sarah planned to share a taxi. But Tony, swaying a little, tried to bar Sarah's way. 'I'd like to take a longer look at that bone structure.'

Leonie stood impatiently, lips tightening by the second. It was already later than Tante Berthe would like her to be back.

'That's easy.' Sarah slipped under the arm Tony had placed across the door. 'I'll be at Max's recital. And I'll bring my friends.'

The recital was held on a Sunday night early in November, in the ballet rehearsal room belonging to a drama school off the boulevard St Germain. It began to snow lightly as Leonie left the rue Louis, wanting to be early to help Max and his friends set out the chairs and distribute the hand-written programmes.

The room was almost full when Sarah Bentley arrived

with five or six friends, all obviously English, older than Sarah, and very well dressed. Waving to Leonie, Sarah made her way unselfconsciously to a space near the piano and sat down on the floor, her friends following suit. Leonie thought she had never looked so self-possessed – nor so close to being beautiful.

As Max took his place the sculptor who had organized the event came to the front to speak for the refugee cause. Leonie noticed Tony then, at the back of the room. During the applause that followed the speech he made his way down the side of the audience and stood, his back to a tall curtained window, where – Leonie thought – he could watch Sarah's profile.

Max played for an hour almost without a break, with more flair and more authority than he had shown all summer. The audience was intent, and kept very still, settling quickly between each of the Chopin pieces as if it could not be too soon before they heard him play again. The second half of the recital went superbly, and the sculptor told Max as the last of the audience left that the collection had amounted to more than double what he had hoped.

Sarah lingered, eyes glowing, and kissed Leonie and Max, thanking him for the evening. She waved casually to Tony as she left, and through the doors of the hall Leonie saw the group of her friends waiting, the snow settling on the dark hats of the men and on the women's furs.

'I'll walk you home,' Max said to Leonie. 'Wouldn't you like to walk back in the snow?'

'We'll all walk.' It was Tony, smiling, arms round them both. 'It will be good for Max to unwind. And we'll sleep better for it. We all have to work tomorrow.'

They walked past the still lighted cafés down the boul' Mich' and kept to the Left Bank at first, shivering at the sight of the dark water slapping the stone quays. In spite of the late hour and the cold there were couples down on the quayside, embracing under the bare branches, even a solitary fisherman, his line a sharply drawn shadow on the towpath, so that Tony made them stop and watch in silence, until the man moved and turned, throwing them a suspicious look.

Crossing the river to the Tuileries gardens they found the paths there already under several inches of unbroken snow. They walked arm in arm, not speaking, enjoying the ritual of planting their feet in the soft white carpet, and lifting them heavily, to leave their footprints, the first of winter, for the morning.

'We've given something back to Paris. A nocturne,' Tony said. He stopped to study a scattered group of thin metal chairs piped with snow. The noise of the city seemed a long way off, as the night began to die. 'The debt I owe this place . . .'

Leonie liked this mood, in which Tony did not drive himself or his companions. She broke into a run, laughing, and the others followed. She was still ahead when they reached the end of the gardens, where Leonie usually crossed to the great terraces of houses and turned into the rue Louis.

She had a key to the courtyard these days, and let herself in quickly, putting a finger to her lips. The light was still on in Jeannine's *loge*. But then it always was. She stood on the inside of the gates, hands gripping the rails, and thanked Max. It was not until Tony put his hands above hers and grinned down at her that she realized she had tried to avoid the moment when they would all quite naturally kiss each other goodnight.

'Mind you work hard, poor little rich girl,' Tony said. 'You owe it to Paris.'

'And to my father,' she thought, as she said aloud that if he mentioned her imaginary riches again she would bring her work round to his studio and make him learn French with her.

He laughed and said she would be welcome any time, so that she almost stamped her foot in the snow. But from that weekend onwards, with Tony and Max as her examples, she began to study in earnest, and Sarah and Lise had to play truant more often than not without her.

The thought of returning to New York for Christmas seemed less and less attractive, and she found herself avoiding Zoe. At weekends she got into the habit of turning up at Tony's studio with her work, as she had threatened. He had looked surprised at first, but the second time she called he had cleared a place for her books amongst the chaos. As soon as she settled to work, he began to draw. When she asked to see what he had done, he refused, and while he made coffee for them one Sunday morning later she wandered over to a set of canvases stacked against a cupboard and idly turned one round. She had half expected to find a portrait of Sarah; the studio was full of sketches of women's faces, and there had been several of her lying about the first time Leonie brought her work to the studio.

But the painting was a composite – of a thin, dark-haired girl in a check tweed dress walking as if in a dream down a New York street, and on the city skyline behind her a girl-woman with the same face, against a mountainside.

She stood frozen before the canvas, seeing herself as Tony must have seen her that first time, and disturbed by the things he had seen in her since. She could not tell whether the painting was a token of admiration, but she knew it was honest.

'You're half-grown, you see.' Tony came up behind her. 'If you must pry you must expect to learn some truths.'

'It's the mountains that are real. New York is the dream, isn't it?' She turned to him. 'You aren't angry that I've looked?'

He handed her the coffee, and stared critically at the canvas as if it were the work of a stranger. 'I think I must do some more studies of you,' he said. Then – 'By the way, I have to go to some reception at my father's Paris bank. As his representative. A very smart affair, and I can't get out of it. I think I should take a really genuine, respectable young Frenchwoman with me. For effect.'

'I'm sure you know plenty.'

163

'On the contrary. I know only one girl in town who might answer the description. And I think you should wear that dress – and of course bring the gloves.'

The reception was on an early evening the following week, and Leonie wore a two-piece in fine coral wool made from a remnant Jeanne Veron had in her store at Briteau. Tony called with a cab for her at the rue Louis and laughed appreciatively when he saw her, saying he liked a little independence of spirit in a woman.

'What's more, you look stunning.' He held her elbow as they stepped out of the lift on the top floor of the bank's headquarters.

'I'm glad you think so, because there's someone over there who cares very much how I look. Did you know my mother would be here?'

Tony followed her eyes. 'Wow. I'd have known who she was the moment I saw her. Are you going to introduce us?'

Leonie had no choice. Zoe was halfway across the room to them, glass in hand. At least there was no sign of Erich. Zoe, in a muted outfit in shades of pale beige, contrived to look as if she had belonged to the select banking circles of New York and Paris since she was born. Within minutes of meeting Tony she had established that she was with the same bank as his father in both cities. So Erich was not her only financial stand-by in Paris, Leonie thought, and wondered what her mother was up to now.

'You've been avoiding me, I know.' Zoe put a free hand on her daughter's shoulder. 'But you look divine. I'll forgive you.'

'I've been working. They push us hard at the college.'

'I'm glad to hear it. And you'll be relieved, I expect, to hear that you don't have to go to New York this Christmas. If you don't want to.'

'It was going to be difficult. But what about Maddie?'

'Maddie and I have come to the perfect agreement. She is

164

to enjoy a little semi-retirement, and Gramercy Park is at her disposal, rent-free – in exchange for a few little favours now and then.'

'Is she pleased? What does she have to do?' Leonie thought sadly of the note she had left for Maddie on the night she quit New York.

'Just be there if ever I run for home.' Zoe turned away, eyeing the other guests as if she wanted to decide who was important enough for her to talk to next. But Leonie noticed a little quiver in her voice, and as her mother walked away Tony said that her face had an infinite capacity for suffering.

'I'm glad you see it. We have such fights. But somehow I'm on her side.'

'Better you don't live together. You must tell me the story some time.'

Over dinner in a small restaurant later, she told him. The years in New York. The need to find her father. The meeting with his notary. The summer at Briteau. She managed to keep Erich out of the talk, merely hinting that of course her mother had admirers, always had.

'She works. I'll say that for her,' Tony said when he heard something of the reason for Zoe's presence in Paris.

'She's worked all her life.'

'It's the only way. Cosmetics, what the hell. And think how her patrons can just slip out of that salon off the Champs Elysées and round to lunch at Maxim's before the effect of the treatment wears off.'

'No need to put her down.'

'Not guilty. It's a social service, kid. She earns her money all right, and I like that.'

'I know you do. Wouldn't you prefer to be able to say the same of yourself?'

'Touché. But it will come. I'd like to be independent of my old man. Sooner than later.'

'I feel the same.' She had told him how the de Byron family and notaries had rallied round to make her two years at college possible.

'Then why not get a job? Even just for the vacation?'

She thought about it. If her father came to Paris on leave at Christmas she would be able to see him. But not so much if she had a job. She was tempted, all the same. 'What could I do?'

'There must be dozens of things. Ask your mother. She must know a lot of people by now.'

'I don't think I could. But –'

'But what?'

'I'll take a vacation job if you promise to look for one too.'

'Oh, thanks, Leonie. You've made my evening.'

At Saturday morning *petit déjeuner* she told Tante Berthe her plan, mentioning it casually as she poured coffee for them both in the apartment's small dining-room. As she sat down and raised her cup to her lips she surprised a look of fury on the old woman's face.

'Why . . . Tante Berthe . . . what is it? What have I said?'

'You are not serious. This idea of work, when you have your studies. The vacation is to be for your books if you are to make use of the time at the college. Do you not realize what it is costing your father? It is the most expensive establishment in Paris, and he has mortgaged a great part of Briteau to pay for you there. Did you not know this?'

'I had no idea. I thought you and he always arranged things. I was told nothing except the date on which I was to come to Paris and start school.'

'That was the day your father sacrificed the only land that is still really his. So that you could become a true de Byron. This you should know.'

'I don't know what to say. I'm glad you've told me. But it doesn't alter things. I think I ought to try to make money for myself.'

'That will come. In two years. There will be many doors open to you then. One does not expect a de Byron to sit at home these days. Your – sister – is also receiving the highest education, to equip her for life.'

166

'Mireille works so hard.' She pictured her sister with her grandparents, and Charlie, and wondered how they would spend the coming holidays.

'That is how it should be. And it is my place to see that you do the same.'

'But I do, Tante, I do. How can you doubt that?'

'*Bon.* I believe you. Then we say no more.'

If Tante Berthe had known that her disclosures would lead straight to Leonie's truancy on Monday morning she would not have finished her *petit déjeuner* with such satisfaction. By ten o'clock Leonie was in the offices of Charles Vincent et fils, demanding to see her father's lawyer.

His male secretary informed her that if Monsieur Vincent could see her at all it would be only for five minutes. He had to visit an important client at his home in the suburbs before lunch. The implication was that no one could be less important than Leonie de Byron, and she sat meekly in the *salle d'attente* on a worn leather chair, one of a dozen carved with a flourish that hardly suited a lawyer's premises, she thought. But she had to remind herself more and more recently that Paris was not the new, new city of her birth.

When he came in from the street, Charles Vincent recognized her at once, and greeted her warmly. Yes, of course he could see Mademoiselle Leonie for five minutes, he rebuked his secretary. What was the problem?

Facing him across the wide desk, in the chair where her mother had sat at almost the same age and faced his father, she asked him if what Tante Berthe had told her was true.

'I am not allowed to tell you all the facts of your father's relationship with you, you know that, mademoiselle. He is a man of great discretion. Great quality, I may say.'

'But is it true – that he has mortgaged the last of his land for me? I just cannot believe it. I don't want it to be true, can't you see? It's the last thing I would want.'

167

'Then if you can promise me that you will not go to your father with this?'

'I don't like to hurt his feelings.'

'That is what you would do, mademoiselle, if you reject what he has done for you.'

'But he has already done so much . . . All those years . . .' Her eyes filled with tears, of anger, of memory of the payments that came without fail to New York for her month after month.

There was a silence. Charles Vincent looked down at his desk. Berthe de Byron's secret was safe with him. He could never, in any case, bring himself to deal this exquisite young girl the blow that was in his power, by telling her Paul de Byron had not known she was born. One day perhaps. Preferably never.

'Then you must tell me what you want. But I promise nothing,' he said at last.

'I can't leave the college. I would have, but Tante Berthe is so angry with me . . .'

'Angry? How could that be?'

'Because I want to get a job. This Christmas. And for longer, if I can. She thinks it will mean I can't study.'

'I'm sure it will.'

'No more than going on the town every night like the other girls. I have no real social life. I know I could do both.'

'One day, you will have money of your own. You will earn it, and then we can talk, perhaps.'

'If I did get hold of some money! Could you come to some agreement with me? I'm sure you're good at secrets?'

The innocence of her remark shamed him, and he said bleakly, 'It is my profession.'

'Then you and I will have a secret, Monsieur Vincent. One day, I swear to you, I am going to pay back every cent of what it has cost my father to bring me to Paris. Does that surprise you?'

'I think you will always surprise us, Mademoiselle Leonie. But I think you are being very ambitious about this.'

'I've made up my mind. Do we understand each other?'
She stood and held out a gloved hand.

He saw her to the outer door of the offices, earning a *moue*
of disapproval from his secretary on his return.

'You'll learn some day, Emile. Each of our clients is of
equal importance.'

Back at his desk he thought that he too had learned
something that morning. If he were not mistaken, the girl
who had called on him, without an appointment, eyes
shining, would be a client of Vincent et fils for a long time to
come.

CHAPTER ELEVEN

Leonie received a gilt-edged invitation to the buffet party marking the opening of the premises of Caresse, and while Tante Berthe was out telephoned Zoe at the number printed on the other side under a map showing the salon's location. She told her of her decision to earn some money, and said she wanted to talk. Zoe responded with a slightly mocking air, saying she was glad her daughter was showing some independence; it meant she had inherited at least one of her mother's qualities.

Leonie had to admit that she did not feel as independent as all that: it was her mother she was hoping could give her a job. She needed money for extras, to have fun.

'Anything, Mother. I'll sweep up if that's all that's going. Or reception? I'm really fluent in French now. I'll do anything.'

Zoe trod carefully. Her pleasure at the thought that her child might be asking to come back into the fold was not good business. Nor did she like the idea of employing anyone who went back every night to the rue Louis and the bosom of the de Byron family.

'It's not so easy, baby. But I'll see.'

'Thank you, Mother.'

'Come half an hour before things start. Will you have that beautiful young New Yorker with you?' She had done her research after their meeting at the bank, and intended to encourage the friendship between Tony Shaw and her daughter.

'May I?'

'I'll be disappointed if you don't.'

170

*

The Caresse salon ran the length of the ground floor of the old house off the Champs Elysées, and above it were more treatment rooms and Zoe's office-cum-sitting-room. On the top floor Erich Mannheim had a large office of his own, from which he ran the business side of the venture, and his own affairs.

There were flowers everywhere: expensive hot-house blooms mingled with wild flowers flown at vast expense from the south; orchids the exact colours of the themes that ran through the decor of the whole building; white roses from England sent by Lady Hume.

Zoe led them upstairs to her sitting-room. She looked better groomed than the first time Leonie had seen her on her return to Paris, and had lost weight. A slim, bird-like figure in a sleek black haute couture ankle-length gown, her only jewellery a pair of diamond ear studs and a large matching ring on her right hand, she sat at her desk and smoked 'a soothing cigarette before the fray'. She was in fact icily calm, and Leonie thought there was something missing – perhaps the enthusiasm that had always made her mother such a dynamic achiever. Everything at the salon seemed almost too much under control.

'My business partner will join us. We'll have some champagne when he arrives,' Zoe said to Tony. 'What do you think of the place?'

'Of its kind, perfection,' Tony admitted, and grinned at Leonie. 'It'll have them by the ears.'

'And by the wallets, I hope.' Zoe smiled lazily. 'Does your father have any involvement with the cosmetic business in New York?'

'Not that I know of.' Tony's grin vanished.

'Have I said something?'

'No.'

'Tony's like me, Mother. He wants his independence.'

'That's why you're here, of course,' Zoe said, putting out her cigarette. 'I haven't given it that much thought. But it'll

171

have to be just spare time, you know that. I won't have you working as well as studying. For one thing, there's no need. I understand you're well cared for, and I'll not have you waste all that schooling I put you through back home.'

'Mother!' Leonie would have argued back, but just then the sitting-room door opened and Erich Mannheim appeared, a tall, bulky figure, blue eyes smiling a prepared welcome, white hands held out to Leonie as if she were some long-lost child.

Tony sensed Leonie stiffen. He himself took an instant dislike to this man who apparently had the run of the place. But it was an authoritative figure; the man had real presence.

Leonie shook hands as quickly as Erich would allow. Relinquishing her grasp slowly, he continued to smile. She introduced him to Tony, and told him he was a very talented artist. Erich said that he felt outnumbered – three Americans to one Swiss.

'Don't let that worry you now, Erich darling,' Zoe said airily. 'You're the one serving the champagne, and we need you.'

As Erich handed Leonie a glass he contrived to stand with his back to the others, and looked down at her with blatant admiration. 'You are perfectly lovely this evening, child,' he whispered; then, aloud: 'Zoe, ma chère, your daughter does you credit. I think the life here in Paris suits her, don't you?'

'She has a taste for it. And it's proving expensive. We were just talking about getting her some work.'

'It has to be part time, you said so yourself.' Leonie frowned at her. She did not want Erich Mannheim involved in her plans.

'But I don't see your problem.' Erich took her glass, and led her to face a large mirror on the far wall.

'Come.' He beckoned to Zoe, who joined them. Mother and daughter stood side by side, as they had stood after the quarrel when Leonie cut off her hair at Gramercy Park.

'What do you see?' Erich stood at their shoulders.

172

'Style. I see style. Thank God.' Zoe sipped her drink and put a stray curl in place. Her diamonds sprayed reflected light as she moved. Leonie said nothing.

'More than that. Look again. Look at your daughter.'

'Erich, you know I hate games. People will be here any minute.'

'I'm not joking. I'm amazed you don't see it for yourself. The face. The body. The colouring, even. All exactly what we have talked of for the spring campaign.'

'New York comes to Paris?' Zoe frowned, knowing at once that he was right – Leonie was the living embodiment of the image she wanted to project for her new products.

Erich went on eagerly, talking this time direct to Leonie. All she had to do was to lend them her presence, from time to time. They could leave the rest to him. Art work. Photography. Work would start straight after the opening, and the new face of Caresse would be launched on an unsuspecting Paris after Christmas.

Leonie looked over her shoulder to where Tony sprawled in an armchair. His face was expressionless, and she knew he had already sensed her hostility to Erich Mannheim.

'What do you think?'

Zoe walked away from the mirror, not wanting to betray just how much she would like Leonie back under her wing. But her business instincts told her that her real consideration should be Leonie's suitability as the model for packaging Caresse.

'We could try it,' she said flatly. 'Perhaps just a try-out. The spring campaign.'

'Then we can say the matter is settled.' Erich put an arm round Leonie's shoulders, but she moved quickly out of range, with a mute glance of appeal in Tony's direction.

'You need the work.' Tony grinned. 'Sounds like the answer to a maiden's prayer.'

'There'd have to be a contract,' Zoe cut in. 'Family's family, but business . . . that's something else? Don't you agree, Tony?'

173

Tony raised his glass. 'To something else . . .'

'Thanks, Mother. I just hope I can do it.' Leonie turned back to the mirror, a critical frown on her face as she scrutinized her own image.

'Don't let me hear my daughter ever admit to failure in advance.' Zoe laughed uneasily. 'And now – I must join my guests.'

As they took the stairs to the ground floor she let Leonie and Tony go on ahead. Touching Erich's arm, she told him she ought to be angry with him. He had forced her hand, given her no time to think things through. And she was not at all sure that she really liked his idea.

'You are fooling yourself, my dear,' he answered. 'There is a kind of victory in this – your daughter coming to you for money after all that has happened. You love it.'

Annoyed, she dug her fingers into his arm. 'And my daughter gets treated exactly like any other employee of this company. You do get my drift?'

'The girl wants work. There will be no problems.'

'Don't sidestep with me, Erich.'

'Did I ever?' He spread his hands in mock innocence, and they moved on into the reception to a scatter of applause.

The contract for the work Leonie was to do for the spring publicity was signed before Christmas. Leonie's copy was posted to the rue Louis, and tucked inside was a Christmas card from her mother and a cheque. 'Retainer, darling,' Zoe told her when she telephoned to thank her. 'Have fun.'

The college had broken up for the holidays, and as soon as the cheque had gone through Leonie went shopping. She bought and boxed a Paris hat for Maddie, from Lafayette – a confection of sequins and veiling on a white velvet base. She bought gifts for Tante Berthe and her father, and wine for Tony and Max.

She lunched with them both at the studio on Christmas Eve. Tony teased her about her new job, and admitted he

174

liked to think of her creaming the profits from the Swiss banker to whom he had taken such a dislike. But if he detected that her studies were coming second he threatened to tell Berthe de Byron the whole story. He intended to work over Christmas himself. She found him a hard taskmaster, but at least he led the way.

The Christmas vacation went quickly. Paul de Byron came home on leave to the rue Louis for only forty-eight hours, and seemed tired. He spoke little about his work, except to say that they were under heavy pressure with training schemes for new conscripts. There was a spring manoeuvre that entailed a great deal of extra planning. He had got away with only minutes to spare to catch the Paris train, and still wore his uniform. It was the first time Leonie had seen him in it, and it made her feel there was a distance between them again, until the traditional Christmas Eve dinner, with Berthe presiding over a formidable, endless meal, made Paul relax a little.

In the morning Leonie found a wooden sabot outside her bedroom door filled with nuts and crystallized fruits and a small orange. It was the custom, Tante Berthe explained when she thanked her. At breakfast they exchanged gifts. Leonie had bought a silk scarf for Paul from a boutique in the Place Vendôme, and doeskin gloves for Tante Berthe. They both murmured approval. By her place at table there were three packages. They watched her as she opened them. There were embroidered handkerchiefs from Tante Berthe, a leather diary from her father. In the third package, badly wrapped and postmarked Bordeaux, was a red-knitted hat. Tucked in the hat was a note from Mireille: 'Charlie sends his love.'

'Well.' Tante Berthe pushed back her chair. 'That is Christmas, for another year. Very pleasant. It is good to have you here, Paul.'

'I sent nothing to Mireille,' Leonie said anxiously. 'Papa – will you see her?'

'Never until summer.' Paul spoke with resignation, as if it were a habit long unbroken.

175

'I'll send her something. There's a girl at college who knows the family, you know. Lise Verdier.'

'Verdier . . .' Paul looked at his aunt, eyebrows raised. 'So they managed to get their girl into the Madeleine?'

'They manage most things, that family,' Berthe grunted, clearing the plates on to a tray. 'But I do not think you see this Lise so much, eh?' to Leonie.

'Only in class these days. I work in the library afterwards.' She hoped to get Tante Berthe accustomed to her absences in the weeks to come, not intending to tell her about the work for her mother. The matter of money had been taboo since Berthe had objected so fiercely to anything that would disturb her studies and her father's plan to make her a true de Byron.

'*Bon.*' Paul folded his silk scarf neatly back into its wrapping. 'Now tell me, have you any plans to see your mother today?' He spoke casually, but secretly hung on her answer.

She told him that her mother was away for the vacation, in Switzerland. They were to meet at New Year.

'Then we can take a walk.' Her father smiled. 'In the Tuileries. If you would like.'

'I'd like that very much, Papa.'

An hour later she walked at his side, aware of the interested glances from passers-by at the handsome man in the military cloak and blue kepi.

On the balcony of their suite in the lakeside hotel in Zurich which Erich always used for his Swiss vacations, Zoe stood looking out across the water, dark glasses hiding her eyes, the collar of an ermine coat – Erich's Christmas gift – turned up against the cold.

They had come to Switzerland against her wishes. There were things she wanted to do at the salon while it was closed; and she would have welcomed a little solitude. They had driven by night in the Mercedes. Erich said the car knew its

176

own way, and in spite of ice on the roads they arrived as planned. He told her while they drove that he wanted her at her best when the salon opened for New Year. She would soon see the wisdom of leaving everything behind for a few days.

What he really wanted, she found as soon as they arrived in the hotel, was a renewal of their love-making, which had become intermittent, almost non-existent, during the weeks of gruelling work it had taken to launch Caresse.

Dismissing the hotel maid who had come in to unpack for Zoe, Erich put out the 'Do not disturb' card under cover of handing the woman a tip, and locked the door.

'You can unpack for yourself. Later.' He began to undress Zoe, and, too tired to object, she let him make love to her with the brutality he sometimes liked to use in bed.

At these times he never kissed her, or called her by her name. There were other words, mostly in German, and when he made love in his own language he became demanding.

It was almost dark when she woke after a third bout of love-making and said she wanted a bath. Erich told her to dress for dinner, and returned in an hour carrying the ermine coat. 'Put this on. Happy Christmas. We're dining out.'

They drank cocktails in the bar of the restaurant, and he informed her that they were to have company. Two Swiss property developers.

'You said we were to rest. Do nothing,' Zoe grumbled. 'Now all this.'

'I hope you don't refer to this afternoon, or this morning. I think you liked it.'

'I'm wearing the coat. I'm here.' She drained her glass as two men approached their table.

'I should have told you, Liebling,' Erich said softly. 'I have plans. I intend to buy a much larger apartment here. Perhaps a whole block. I am selling my other place in Switzerland.'

'That's your privilege.' She gave a hard smile as Erich greeted his guests.

'I was telling Madame Byron,' Erich said as they took their places for dinner, 'that things look very uncertain. I want a place that gives total security. Perhaps in a year we will both be glad. I have two days, perhaps three, to go into any developments you think would suit my purpose.'

They talked in millions of francs. Erich was not easy to please, and the dinner was hardly a social occasion. It was almost one when they reached their hotel.

While Erich took a bath, Zoe telephoned the hotel desk. 'Get me New York.' She gave the number of Gramercy Park.

'Maddie! What time is it with you?'

'Christmas time, child. Happy Christmas. Did you see the hat? From Leonie? My sister wants one just like it.'

'I'll get it. I promise. And I'll bring it over in person.'

'Oh, yeh? Such as when?'

'Next year, Maddie. It's a promise. I'm homesick. I'll take a vacation. Will you have me?'

'If you're alone. You know why.'

'I'll be alone, Maddie. Merry Christmas.'

'You never cry,' Maddie chided her. 'I can hear you. Dry those eyes and ring off, honey. I don't like the sound of those tears.'

Tante Berthe did not object to Leonie spending the day out once Paul had returned to his unit. She packed a lunch for herself and Tony, and walked slowly through the Tuileries, remembering how it had felt to stroll there with her father on Christmas Day.

Tony had planned to work over Christmas. He hated conventions, and what he called 'being made to make merry'. She found him sitting staring at a canvas, covers over much of his recent work.

'I'm concentrating,' he said. 'How *was* the de Byron Christmas, by the way? The hat must have been knitted by an aunt.'

She pulled off the red-knitted hat and shook her hair,

laughing. 'I like it. It has memories. And I'm *not* changing it for you, Tony Shaw.'

She told him more about her father's leave while they ate cold cuts from Tante Berthe's post-Christmas larder.

'It was strange,' she said. 'Seeing him in uniform. He seemed like someone I didn't know at all. But I liked it. I was pretty proud of him while we were out, too. Don't you think those blue officers' hats are quite stunning?'

Tony stopped eating. 'What is all this about hats? And no, I don't think anything military can be stunning. It can only make it easy for them, make a game of war.'

'What do you mean?' She had never seen him so serious.

'Think. Think hard. What is the most unlikely, the most terrible thing I could ask you to do now, this very minute?'

'You're going to tell me, so tell me.'

'To walk out of here, go down the street, and kill another human being. Wouldn't you say that was unthinkable?'

'The army is my father's profession,' she said in a low voice.

'And it keeps you.'

'No longer. He mortgaged land to bring me to Paris, don't forget. And I'm paying it back. Don't put your own guilt on to me, Tony.'

'Sorry. But it's not guilt. I've never talked about all this, but to me war is the final obscenity. We should cultivate our garden, as the philosopher says. I could never fight, Leonie, not in a million years.'

'I understand that. It's good. But I don't know why you turn it against my father. Someone has to fight.'

'I'll never accept that. But I do have my reasons. It's my own father that gets to me. I saw a list of his biggest clients when I was last in his office. At least two arms manufacturers. It broke me up for days. I came back to Paris hoping to start selling my work. That was when I met you, remember?'

'You were tough to get on with. It's better now. Isn't it?'

He poured more wine for her, shaking his head. 'I've got to get free of it all.'

179

'You'll not give up your work?'

'No. I'll make something happen.'

That night they called on Max and dragged him out to a small theatre showing a farce that had attracted a student audience. They sat on wooden benches surrounded by the noisy, articulate French of the *quartier*. As the three 'coups' backstage dramatically silenced the audience, Tony took Leonie's hand.

The play was too fast, in sophisticated language, and she found it hard to follow. Tony's hand in hers made her think of their conversation earlier that day, and she made up her mind to back him in finding some way of earning money. She had the impression that it was the most important conversation they had had since they became friends.

In the interval they stayed in their seats, laughing at the series of advertisements that were screened from an old-fashioned lantern slide on to the curtain drop. The copy seemed to have been left over from another era – a bicycle advertisement featured a girl in a bloomer suit, a local delicatessen had its praises sung by a portly, frock-coated Italian with moustaches a foot wide. When a Renoir beauty dressed in nothing but a Grecian drape appeared on behalf of a *crème-poudre*, there were catcalls and whistles from the audience.

'Wait till it's your face up there.' Max leaned past Tony and spoke to Leonie.

Oh, God, she thought, I didn't reckon on that. Maybe I'll be so unrecognizable that Tante Berthe will not get to hear of it.

The work on the publicity for the spring campaign went badly from the start. Zoe dismissed a photographer who turned up late for a photo session Leonie came for after a day at college. The next photographer was too slow, the third too creative, Zoe thought. It was a fortnight before a set of pictures arrived on her desk. She telephoned Leonie to ask her round next morning, a Saturday, to see them.

Leonie was finding the whole operation a strain, but the first weekly cheque made it worth it. She put it in the bank, planning to go to Charles Vincent when she had saved a sum big enough to convince him she could succeed in her plan. At the weekends she stayed in her room and worked, so that Tante Berthe suspected nothing. She did not want to go to the salon that Saturday, as she had an essay to write on French social customs.

'Will Erich be there?' she asked on the phone.

'Yes, he's working upstairs. We're under great pressure, baby. Don't be late.'

The ground floor at Caresse was a hive of activity; treatments went on until late on Saturday night, and the salon was enjoying a first-flush success. But Zoe knew it had to be followed through, and fast. She was chain-smoking when Leonie arrived, and wearing a red two-piece that made her look pale under her make-up.

She flicked the proofs over the desk to Leonie one by one, making cutting remarks about each of them. There was nothing there that captured the American/Parisian theme. It was all too harsh. The samples of graphics she had had in that morning from an agency were just as bad.

'Erich's joining us for coffee,' she said. 'We've got to rethink.'

Leonie wanted to get back to the rue Louis, and was saying she had to get her essay written when Erich walked in. He offered to drive her home as soon as they had talked, and she looked helplessly at her mother, hoping Zoe would object. But Zoe was preoccupied, and let it go. A few weeks ago she would have suggested a taxi.

'I think I'm what's wrong.' Leonie sat heavily in the chair by her mother's desk. Erich laid a hand on the back of the chair, leaning over her to scrutinize a proof.

'No. We are right about you. What we need is someone

181

with whom we can really communicate. I'll brief the agencies again.'

'There's no time for all this to start up again.' Zoe sat back, giving him an angry stare.

'There's always time for perfection,' he said firmly as he put a sheaf of photographs back into their folder. 'This photographer falls short. The next will be better, you'll see.'

'Maybe you're right.' Zoe lit another cigarette. 'I'm too tired to make decisions this morning.'

'I'll take your daughter home, then we'll plan a quiet day for tomorrow.'

Leonie did not see that she could object to the offer, but as always when the Swiss banker touched her she tensed inwardly as he took her elbow and walked down to the street at her side. To her delight, she saw Tony waiting outside the salon, and waved through the window.

'I'll go back with Tony,' she told Erich.

'But I insist. I'll see you home. I'll drive you both.'

'Tony lives off the boul' Mich'.'

'My dear girl, I know every inch of Paris, and I will not take no for an answer.' He looked down at her with an almost insolent stare that made her shiver, and she made up her mind that she was not going to be alone with him if she could help it.

Tony explained that he had called at Tante Berthe's apartment to carry Leonie off to an exhibition that afternoon, and had guessed it was work that took her to the Champs Elysées.

'Don't worry, I was very tactful. Your aunt thinks you're on a purely social call to your mother. I thought you'd need lunch.'

It gave her the excuse she needed to avoid Erich Mannheim. The exhibition was on the Left Bank, and they could lunch at the studio. Then, she said, she really had to get home and study. But it was worth losing an hour or two at her essay to get rid of Erich.

He drove them to the studio, and Tony asked him in for a

drink, enjoying his obvious annoyance that he was not to drive Leonie to the rue Louis.

But once inside the studio, Erich's manner underwent a dramatic change. Tony had for once neglected to cover his work. The room was strewn with drawings in charcoal, studies for paintings, sketches of a girl's face in all moods, all lights. Leonie stood in the middle of the room staring about her. She knew now why Tony always kept his work from her. Every one of the pictures was a portrait of Leonie herself; exquisite, graceful work of extreme originality that lifted them out of the run-of-the-mill portraiture that so many artists came to Paris to work at.

'But this is extraordinary.' It was Erich who broke the silence.

'I didn't know I'd have company.' Tony started piling the drawings on to a table. 'I'll soon have this lot cleared up.' He did not look at Leonie.

'No, don't do that,' Erich Mannheim said sharply. 'I want to see this. Leonie will tell you I am an "amateur" – in the best, true sense. I collect modern work. I am very impressed.' There was no hint of condescension about him as he walked about the studio, admiring the drawings.

'I can sell, when I am ready for an exhibition,' Tony said. 'But I hadn't thought of showing these.' His hostility was just under the surface.

'No. That is not my idea either. Did you know of our problems at Caresse? We are still without the artwork we need.'

Leonie marvelled how Erich Mannheim could forget his annoyance, his personal feelings of a moment ago, and switch to a business matter as if it were the only thing that concerned them. She knew at once that he was right. Tony was exactly what they needed for the spring campaign. But knowing as she did what he thought of Erich she did not think he would play ball.

She was wrong. Tony saw in the offer the chance to become independent of his father at last. Working with

183

Leonie was a bonus. Taking money from Erich Mannheim was the cream in the coffee. It was just the kind of situation he liked.

He told her all this later, when Erich Mannheim had gone back to the salon to instigate a contract. They walked to the exhibition, and later back to the rue Louis, hand in hand.

It took Berthe de Byron less than a month to find out what was going on. A well-wisher called on her with a magazine for which Leonie had by-lined an article written by one of its staff on what it was like to be a part-time model. The fee had been irresistible; her bank balance was growing fast and she had plans to see Charles Vincent soon about repaying some money into the mortgage accounts. Zoe was equally delighted with the free publicity for Caresse. She saw the feature as the start of a new source of clientele. If they could only get Leonie into the *chic* glossies she could double her income that year.

Tante Berthe had the magazine open on the table beside her chair when she called Leonie into the drawing-room and told her that, of course, this sort of thing had to stop.

Leonie apologized at first. She had intended, one day, to explain. But it was too soon. If only Tante Berthe knew why she had disobeyed her. She would be sure to understand, if not forgive.

'It is the family name I care about. You are correct when you say that I might not forgive. And what of your studies? Are you wasting your father's money as well as your life?'

'That's what I mean. Charles Vincent will tell you, if you check with him. But Papa is not to know. I'll tell you everything, if you promise to keep this a secret . . . my father's notary, you, and I are the only ones to know.'

'I will have to hear your story first.' Berthe was implacable.

'Very well.' She told her everything – her distress when she had discovered her father had mortgaged Briteau, her determination to pay him back, the meeting with Charles Vincent. The chance to earn money, when it arose, came sooner than she planned, but she knew she could cope. The money was more than she could ever hope to earn elsewhere, and could Tante Berthe deny that she still studied hard?

'You are as proud as your father . . . and as stubborn as your mother. And I do not like this affair.'

'I'm sorry . . . there's no going back. Tante Berthe, I am under contract, and my mother's business manager can be very difficult.'

'A de Byron does not break a contract, it is true.' The old woman nodded. Leonie remembered what Edith Darnand had said that summer about the French and money.

'Exactly! Won't you let me see this through? Please. And say nothing to Papa?'

'He is sure to find out. Your face on a product – one cannot imagine what he will think.'

'He's not in that world, and all I want is to do what I've set out to do, for Briteau, before he can stop me. As you say, he is proud. Can't we leave it at that?'

'*Eh bien.*' The old woman sighed and refolded the magazine, thinking that the child had eyes that would try a saint. 'But at the first sign of neglect of your studies . . .'

'Oh, you angel!' It was the first time that Leonie had embraced her, and Tante Berthe tapped her wrist in a show of affection before she pushed her gently away.

By the end of May the Caresse campaign had begun to show results. Only by the autumn would they be able to tell if they were lasting, and Zoe decided to leave the salon to her French assistants for the easier months of June and July. She had to get back to New York. Checking with Leonie, she bought the hat for Maddie's sister at Lafayette, threw two dresses and a spare coat into a suitcase, and took a last-minute cancellation on the next boat.

She told Erich that she would come back a new woman,

ready to resume their life together in the way they both wanted. He let her go. The new apartment in Zurich was ready, and he planned to spend the summer turning it into a fortress.

The Nazis had condemned Picasso, and Erich had five originals, a fortune that would bide its time. But in the flat on the avenue Kléber he left one of the five, knowing he could not live in Paris without it. It was a full length portrait of a girl in a white dress holding a blue flower. In his office he left two Braques and a Rodin maquette. It took two journeys in the Mercedes to move the pictures he would not trust to freight. The Meissen china would have to wait until winter.

Leonie turned down Zoe's offer to pay her passage back to New York; she was committed to the harvest at Briteau and there would not be time to get back. She banked three quarters of her year's earnings in an account Charles Vincent had opened for the estate in their joint names, and wrote to her father. She wanted to go to the château straight away, and – if he agreed – to take some guests.

Paul replied by return, from manoeuvres in Normandy. He had heard good things of her from the Madeleine, and of course she deserved a vacation with her friends. If anyone wished to stay on for the harvest, *tant mieux*. He would meet her and her sister at Briteau as soon as his colonel granted him leave. It had always been automatic, but this year they watched for a lull in Europe's problems before he could get home. Meanwhile Fabri père was in charge, and Violette would care for them all.

She telephoned Violette, and between a few tears and the scratching on the perennially bad line heard that Briteau was deserted; not even her beloved Pierre had been to see her. She would open up the bedrooms and start to cook. But for how many?

'We'll be four,' Leonie told her. 'We can share rooms – a painter and a musician, both American, and a girl friend – English. She speaks perfect French.'

The friendship with Sarah Bentley had survived Leonie's

new existence, and as she could drive a car and had a short time to spare before her family vacation in England she jumped at Leonie's invitation. On their arrival at the local station she buttonholed a porter who directed her to the only car for hire in the village.

Tony and Max Heller sat wedged in the buggy of the ancient French tourer, and Leonie gave directions from the passenger seat as Sarah, hair flying, took the road out to the château. They arrived to find the fat white eiderdowns hanging from the upstairs windows like banners of welcome, and a smell of cassoulet in the kitchen that Sarah at once recognized, thus winning Violette's heart for the duration.

In the evening they sat in the library. Leonie lit an applewood fire and sprawled on the carpet, chin in her hands, while Max played for them so beautifully that she was sure Yvette de Byron would have approved. The presence of her father, and of the past, was everywhere. It was the first time she had been in the château without him, and she was surprised to find that her heart ached. For him, and for Zoe, whose face as they parted had softened, and looked vulnerable – a look she rarely let her daughter see.

Tony watched her, and knew that Paris, even New York, were illusions. However successful Leonie was to be, however *chic* her image, it was here that she belonged, with the terraced vines, the crazy roads, the distant hills.

At that moment he fell in love with her. She glanced up, caught the look in the eyes that never gave anything away.

'Will you stay for the harvest?' she asked him.

He told her then that he had in fact very little time. Before they left Paris he had heard from his father that his mother was seriously ill. He was wanted at home.

'I had to come here, all the same,' he said. 'And I think I can get to Cherbourg for a passage.'

'You can go when I go.' Sarah, who had been watching them, joined in. 'Don't worry, Leonie. I'll treat him with care.'

'You should have told me,' Leonie said to Tony.

'You'd have made me go back with your mother if I had. And I think that lady needs to be alone.'

Mireille arrived at the end of their first week, and Sarah exchanged looks with Leonie when they saw that Lise Verdier was in the back of the Peugeot, with Charlie on her knees.

'The house party is complete,' Sarah grimaced. 'Let's hope Violette has enough food in her larder.'

Mireille looked less of a child, her hair braided and caught back in a silk scarf. She ran to Leonie and kissed her warmly. 'It's so good to get away from Bordeaux. You don't know how good it is!'

She explained that Paul had told her Leonie had house-guests, so she had brought one of her own – for a week only. While Sarah settled Lise in the room next to hers, Mireille almost dragged Leonie into the library.

'There's so much I have to tell you. I am giving up classics after next year. I'm going to study medicine! What do you think?' Her eyes glowed. 'My grandfather is quite pleased, you know.'

'Does Papa know this? I think he'd approve.'

'I'll tell him everything when I see him. It means years and years of study. And –'

Leonie waited, sensing there was something else behind this new Mireille.

'And I hope to go to the Sorbonne . . . with a boy from my école . . . he too wants to be a doctor.' She did not ask after Jacques Fabri at all, and that evening responded to the teasing which Max and Tony adopted towards her with great aplomb.

It was as if seeing Leonie with men friends made her less of a threat, and her own friendship with the future medical student lent a bond.

The week of Lise Verdier's stay went quickly and smoothly. They walked in the mornings, lazed in the

188

grounds, ate everything Violette put before them. The Darnands came over for tea, wanting to meet the American visitors, and talked for a long time with Max about his family and their predicament. Max also surprised them with an expert knowledge of horses, and had learnt to ride on the long beaches of the west coast with a campus instructor. Edith Darnand invited them all for the next day. She had a pony she wanted them to see, and a mare so beautiful that Mireille would want to take her home.

It was Tony's last day, and he made his excuses; Sarah drove the others to the Darnands' place. It was silently understood that Leonie would stay behind with Tony. The tourer shook its way down the drive before breakfast, Charlie performing his usual frenzied pursuit as if he would never see Mireille again. They called him to heel, and spent the morning walking in the meadows behind the house.

In the afternoon Violette announced that as the whole world was on holiday she was going to visit her friend Camille Fabri. She closed and locked the garden door with a flourish and marched off down the road to the Fabri house, calling that a cold supper waited in the kitchen for them all.

They watched her go, from the terrace.

'Do you think it's some kind of conspiracy?' Tony said.

They walked back into the house, and once inside she turned to him. 'Tony, I don't want you to go tomorrow. I know you have to. I wish now I was going to New York. We could have gone together.'

'You're going nowhere. Not with these beautiful mountains to guard you. I know where you are this way, safer than New York.'

'Suppose you don't come back?'

'I'm out of bondage to my father. I come and go as I want. And we have a contract, with the formidable partnership that is your mother and her banker.'

She was glad he did not say her lover. Both aware of their dislike for Erich, they had so far left the subject of his true role in her mother's life as a no-go area.

189

'I just wish you could stay for the harvest,' she said. 'You'd love it so.'

He kissed her forehead. 'Another year. That's a promise. And now the house is ours for a few hours, we're going to make love, aren't we?'

She nodded, and held out her hand as they walked to the stairs.

Tony put an arm round her shoulders.

'For you, love should begin in this place.'

CHAPTER TWELVE

With a lull in the threat of war in Europe, Jacques Fabri was granted leave from his military service for the harvest at Briteau. It was a last-minute decision, organized by Paul de Byron, and Mireille and Leonie were drinking coffee at the kitchen table watching Violette at work when she announced that her friend's son was coming home.

'Camille Fabri has enough to do at that house. It is time her men saw that.' She kneaded a twist of dough heavily.

'Jacques can't help conscription,' Mireille said defensively.

'He can help many things, that one.'

Jacques came into the kitchen garden early the next morning, while Leonie was handing out lunch baskets to the estate workers.

'Ah, at last!' Violette greeted him sharply from the doorway. 'So you have remembered your old friends. And you could have gone straight to the fields and done a good day's work by now.'

He held up brown hands, begging truce, grinning at Leonie. She thought he had changed, but it was an outward change: the brutally short haircut and a new precision in his dress. She smiled back. 'The work is running late. Some of the students did not come this year. Things are so uncertain.'

'Then we'll walk to the terraces together, now. We are used to walking, n'est-ce pas?'

'The eagle's nest has been neglected this summer,' Leonie said as they set off down the road, following the groups of estate workers at a distance.

'Mireille should have gone to see them. But I hear she has

191

new friends. And that she is a young woman now. As for you . . .' He looked sideways at her, a careful look. For a moment she thought he was laughing at her, and wondered if there was something about her that told him she had a lover.

'As for me?'

He did not reply. The new, more stylish beauty the American girl had acquired in the past year did not deceive him. The same creature, the creature that belonged in the mountains, was still there under the skin, even if she had lost her virginity – a fact which he had known instinctively the moment he saw her.

There was a split second later that first morning as they worked side by side when he let his hand brush against Leonie's, unable to resist testing her reaction. She looked away, as if nothing had happened, angry with herself for allowing even accidental contact only days after she and Tony had made love.

'So,' Jacques said lightly, 'there is someone in Paris.'

'That is my business.'

'Understood.'

After the break for lunch she made some pretence of wanting to talk with a girl from the village, and fell into work beside her for the rest of the day. From time to time she sensed Jacques's eyes on her. It was the patient, almost lazy look of a man who knew it was best for now to leave her in peace, and – as always with him – she found it vaguely disturbing.

Alone in her room that night, she thought of him again. It was as if he personified the world that was Briteau, and it was that which drew her to him – just as she knew she would now always be drawn back to her father's land.

It was Paul de Byron's presence that had made it possible for her to bear the parting with Tony. The first days had been agony, coming as they did on the heels of falling in love. Then Paul had come home, and taking up the relationship again from the promise of their Christmas together in the rue Louis had served to distance the pain.

192

She drifted into sleep, pleasantly tired from the day's work in the fields, on the bed where Tony had made fierce love to her and she had as fiercely responded. Her last thought was of him at large in New York, that city of bright-eyed predatory girls.

She had never been so grateful to her mother for anything as for the contract with Caresse that would surely one day bring Tony, with his appetite for work and hunger for independence, back to his beloved Paris.

She returned to Paris alone, a few days after Max had left for the start of term at the Conservatoire, and the moment her train got in to the Gare de Lyon she was relieved that her father had travelled direct to his unit in Lorraine, where he was based for intensive winter training in the Vosges. Tante Berthe had told him that Leonie was occasionally 'employed by magazines and such to make a little extra money', and Leonie had silently applauded her tactful preparation of the way should her father ever confront her on the subject. But had he accompanied her back to Paris nothing could have disguised from him the scale of the truth.

Erich Mannheim had used Tony's portraits with his usual unerring business instinct, and what must have been an almost fanatical persistence. The precarious spring campaign had, under his propulsion, escalated into an autumn attack on the market that seemed to have seized the city's imagination.

The face that was Caresse – Leonie's face – stared out at her from every station bookstall, and in the street looked down at her from row upon row of hoardings, glistening in the light wintry rain so that the face came alive, and she found herself running through the crowds of travellers, pushing her way to the sanctuary of a taxi in escape from her own image, or recognition.

By the time she set down her luggage outside the house in the rue Louis she had composed herself, but was still not

193

prepared for the first sign of the changes that were about to come into her life, with Jeannine scuttling from her *loge* even before she had her key from her purse, throwing back the iron street gates, and escorting her all the way to the apartment with a volley of congratulations.

Refusing her *pourboire*, the concierge waited only long enough to inform Berthe de Byron that *la plus belle américaine de Paris* was back, their young celebrity was home, and the street gates firmly locked against those insufferable journalists.

'So. You see how it is.' Tante Berthe's steel-grey eyes held no hint of a smile as she sipped coffee at the drawing-room table, put her cup down with care, and did not ask Leonie if she had had a good journey.

'I had no idea it would be like this, Tante. Have you really had the press at the door?'

'Jeannine exaggerates, of course. It improves the size of her Christmas *pourboire* if she makes a fuss. But yes, at least one reporter traced you from the offices of your mother's salon.'

Leonie refused to believe that her mother would have set the press on the apartment in the rue Louis, if only because she would want any publicity to concentrate on the premises at the Champs Elysées. Perhaps in her absence in New York one of her assistants had revealed Leonie's address. And if Zoe had anything to do with it the woman would not work at Caresse for long.

'I'll see my mother at once. She must be back from New York. Tante, would you wish me to leave? Should I move out?' As she waited for the answer she prayed it would be a refusal.

'That would be nonsense. But there are some things on which I can insist, I think. For your father's sake, and for mine. No press here at the apartment. No late parties during term-time at the Madeleine. Believe me, your social life will become far too demanding if you do not take care. Above all – no scandal. You understand these things?'

194

Leonie was too relieved not to agree. To avoid having to move into the rooms above Caresse, or worse still the avenue Kléber, she would have agreed to anything. 'Of course, Tante.'

Berthe rose and drew the heavy curtains against the early dark. 'Good. One must always hold one's destiny in one's hands, child. And I thought after our talk about your plans for Briteau – what you want to do for your father – that you had chosen your path.'

'But that's not changed. It's more true than ever since this summer. Tante, it was so beautiful there. And just think – all this means there's going to be a lot of money . . .'

Berthe returned to her seat and raised the lid of the silver coffee pot. 'Ah . . .' She poured herself more coffee, and for the first time since Leonie's return allowed herself the hint of a smile.

Leonie leaned forward. 'Think of it, Tante Berthe. Think what it could mean to my father.'

'He must not know?'

'Of course not.'

'He would put a stop to everything.'

'Well, we'll just have to hope there are no posters on the sides of the mountains in the Vosges.'

'My poor Paul. I hate to think of him fighting again.'

'Please don't talk like that.' Leonie felt a cold finger touch her heart. 'Everyone says the crisis is over. It's going to be a marvellous winter – you'll see.'

'How good to be young. So full of optimism.'

'Peace in our time, Tante. That's all everyone wants; you're not alone.' She thought of Tony, and his abhorrence of war. She had defended her father's profession to him, but until now had not thought that a soldier who ran the risk of killing another man ran an equal risk . . . of being killed.

'A false peace.' Berthe compressed her lips. 'Paris will go quite mad this winter. I have seen it before.'

*

195

On the secretaire in her bedroom, Leonie found a neat pile of letters. There were notes from Sarah with a new phone number in Paris and from Lise Verdier saying she had messages from Bordeaux. A letter from Maddie had reached the apartment a week ago, and gave a long account of the good times she and Zoe had at Gramercy Park, together with a shopping list for yet more frivolities for her sister. Leonie was not deceived. It was Maddie who wanted more hats, and silk lingerie, and Maddie who wanted her to deliver the shopping in person that Christmas.

Don't stay away much longer, child. Your mother's trip made a new woman of her, and I'll do the same for you! Your letter from the château was out of this world, and I can't wait to see what Paris has done for my best girl. Your mother says you're a raving beauty now. And there was a boy here last week asking about you. Says he knew you over there. Name of Tony Shaw. We ate cookies and drank martinis all afternoon. See how dangerous it is to leave me alone like this?

There was a letter from Tony, which she saved for last, reading it again when she was in bed, and keeping it under the bedside lamp to read again when she woke up.

His mother's illness had been diagnosed, and she had cancer. There was a long haul ahead of the family, and his father had insisted that she be nursed at home. With his father at the office most days Tony had decided to set up a studio in the house, and work there. It helped if there was a member of the family on call for the professionals, who came and went like small doves of mercy in his mother's room.

He described the visit to Gramercy Park with the same relish that Maddie had shown, and told her that Maddie was her greatest fan. The way she had fled New York had also been revealed. 'Maybe you're a girl after my own heart. To sell those pearls was really something. Herr Mannheim unmanned. And by now you'll be wearing diamonds, no doubt, so sell them at Christmas, and make the return trip. It looks as if I'll be here still.'

Leonie wept over Maddie's letter, but could not weep for Tony. It was as if she shared a numb despair, and the dread of long weeks to come, and had to keep faith at a distance, steeling herself to the long absence and the sadness as she knew he would himself. She woke in the middle of the night and tried to start a letter in reply, but gave up as words failed her when it came to writing about Christmas. She knew it was impossible. The one thing she could not do was to neglect her college work if she was to be able to continue to make money to repay all her father had done for her in mortgaging Briteau. The two went together now. And the Christmas vacation was a brief affair, a few days only. She decided not to mention it – not even to Maddie. If Tony got in the habit of visiting Gramercy Park there would soon be no secrets left for any of them. But she found herself comforted by the thought that the two people she loved so much were in touch.

On arrival at the Caresse salon next day she saw that what Maddie had said about her mother was true; Zoe was in reception downstairs as Leonie's taxi drew up, and through the windows Leonie was able to watch her unobserved as she floated between clients and staff, an elegant wraith in pink-beige tweed, her dark hair concealed under a silk toque, legs thinner and longer than ever in sheer stockings and obviously hand-made Italian shoes.

Zoe turned to see Leonie come through the salon door, and waved a gloved hand, as if to say she would be with her in a moment. The smile was warm, relaxed even. The deep blue eyes were clear and unlined. Maddie's cure, whatever it had been, had worked, and success had done the rest.

They went up to Zoe's private office, and Zoe put a reservation through for a table at the small restaurant opposite. 'We can talk more there, baby. But you don't have

197

to tell me a thing. You look wonderful. Did Maddie write you about Tony Shaw? He visited after I'd left, I guess. And he obviously has a way with him. Isn't it good to think there's someone in New York to talk about us both and make our ears burn?'

Leonie warmed to this Zoe, who in spite of the heady success that had hit her yet again was more like the young mother she had been ten years back. Once alone in the office, they put their arms round each other.

'You're too thin,' Zoe said as she let go.

'You too,' her daughter echoed. They laughed.

Zoe said they had to get down to business. Had she seen the posters, and all those publicity features? They had to follow through, and with Erich in Switzerland for a few days they would spend the time making just a few tiny adjustments to that perfect face on the posters, to catch the next wave of publicity to the most effect.

Leonie let her mother run on until they were settled at their table in the restaurant.

'I have only two days before college starts, Mother. And then I have to work. My French social history paper is due this term, and the French language viva is a horror. I have to study. It's what you want, isn't it?'

'Of course. We'll work fast, then. And baby, you *are* French social history, don't you know that? In the making, at least.'

'I don't know that I want this thing to get out of hand.'

'Nonsense. Have fun. And get rich! Erich will see to that, if you follow his lead.'

Leonie took refuge in choosing her meal, and only after dessert asked what Erich was doing these days when he was not at Caresse. Her heart sank when Zoe answered that, on the contrary, Erich was at the Champs Elysées premises a great deal, running the business side of Caresse from his own office at the top of the building, now that he had installed most of his art collection safely in the Zurich apartment.

'Of course, he's kept that divine Picasso here. I can't think why. I guess it reminds him of some pure, lost love – before yours truly.' Zoe sighed. 'You mustn't mind us, you know. We've kind of settled down since my trip. It did me good to get away . . .'

'From him?' Leonie instantly regretted the words. She did not want to disturb her mother's good mood.

'Everyone needs a break, you'll learn that,' Zoe said lightly. 'And if I read the signs Tony Shaw will be tired of New York and will come back to Paris soon.'

'Don't, Mother. Didn't you know Mrs Shaw is desperately ill? If he comes back, it will mean he's free to leave New York because she'll have died.'

'I'm sorry. No one told me that.'

'I get letters. Not often.'

'Now –' Zoe took her hand. 'This is Paris. We're going to the top of the tree. You have a lot to thank that boy for, you know that?'

She watched her daughter's face for the telltale blush, knowing she was right about the young New York artist's place in her life, and gave an uncharacteristic sigh of content as she signalled to the waiter to serve coffee.

Back at the salon she insisted that Leonie stay on, and ring Tante Berthe to say she would be late. They needed time to get rid of that wild mountain look, divine though it was, and the staff would work after hours if they knew it was in the interest of yet more success for the salon.

Leonie tried to object, and failed. Her mother waved a substantial cheque under her nose – her share of a little bonus system on profits Zoe had set up without consulting Erich – and promised to let her spend a whole week at college undisturbed if she would see through a new treatment, allow the new look, and be at a photographic session next day. *Vogue* wanted just a single full-page photograph. And it would come out in Paris and London. Was Leonie really going to let that go by?

When the salon staff had spent three hours on her face and body under Zoe's direction Leonie begged for a break, and sat drinking lemon tea in her mother's office, her head turbanned in an orchid-pink towel. She still had to have her hair restyled, and try out a new range of colour and texture in make-up that Zoe wanted mentioned in the caption for the *Vogue* photograph.

Zoe had left the room to supervise the mixing of a new face powder for a client who had telephoned in despair only an hour before a diplomatic dinner which would be attended by *tout Paris* when the telephone rang, and Leonie answered.

It was Erich, hard-voiced when he thought he had got through direct to Zoe, effusive when he learned it was Leonie on the line. He had seen all the magazines, all the posters, before he left for Zurich. Had he not been right about that young man's work? How did it feel to be the face that Paris loved?

'When Paris loves, it is an *amour fou*, ma chère. I will get jealous.'

'I can't think why.' She was ready for him, protected now by her love for Tony, and made up her mind to snub him from now on each time he tried to flirt. 'Do you wish to speak to my mother?'

'Just tell her I'll be in Paris by the end of the week. We'll all have dinner, eh? Is she in the salon still?'

'She's been making over my image all evening. I'm not sure Paris will take to it this time.'

'Trust her. Fashions will change if she says so. And change means more sales. Your mother is always right in these things.'

At that moment Zoe came back into the office. Leonie held out the telephone receiver, but by the time her mother had crossed the room Erich had rung off.

It was gone nine when Zoe sat her down in front of a mirror in the deserted salon and showed her the final results of the day's work. It was a subtle masterpiece, keeping the essence of the face that already stared down from every street corner of Paris, and the freshness of Tony's portraits of her, yet introducing a sleekness, even a tinge of hardness, that would make every woman who saw the new look believe she was out of fashion.

'Very *chic*,' Leonie said dismally. 'My eyebrows have almost gone, and my neck looks so thin. Do I have to have all that width in my hair?'

'Glad you appreciate the detail. And yes you do. The new parting makes the hair fall that way. You can be thankful we haven't added bunches.'

'It's not funny, Mother. I hate it.'

'Nonsense. You'll grow to love it. And it's all free, after all. How many women get to grow up in an hour or two at absolutely no cost?'

Leonie thought it better not to continue that line of thought. She was wondering how she could get to a mirror somewhere out of Zoe's reach and remove some of the make-up before she went back to the rue Louis.

Her mother must have read her mind. 'Don't let it get to you, baby. It's all trial and error at this stage, and you're going to have to go through with something new, if not this. Personally, I think it's a tour de force. But you can fiddle a little before you go home. Maybe it's a little too harsh. We'll try a paler version tomorrow, n'est-ce pas? For the photographers?'

She was in the salon next day by eight in the morning, and Zoe had got there first. A battery of the new make-up range on a tray beside her, she went to work fast, and produced a delicate echo of the new look of the day before. Leonie had no choice this time but to accept. There was a pile of clothes to be tried out which the people at *Vogue* had sent over. By nine sharp she was ready for the cameras.

'Perfect,' Zoe breathed, as the daughter who had fled her nest just over a year ago turned a sleek head towards the photographer, raised a thin brow and gave an iced look from dark eyes. '*Très chic*.'

*

201

It rained heavily on the first day of term at the Collège Madeleine, and Sarah Bentley called for Leonie early, brandishing a giant multi-coloured golfing umbrella stolen from a cousin who played at St Andrew's. Leonie borrowed a diminutive, fading black one with an ivory handle from Tante Berthe, and the two girls walked to the Place Vendôme, umbrellas bobbing amongst those of the *vendeuses* on their way to work in the great *maisons* of the quarter.

Leonie found herself returning to college happily, her studies making a refuge from the world of Caresse. The past few days at the salon had brought home to her the ruthlessness that kept her mother's small empire going. Gazing into the mirror in her room at the rue Louis after the photographic session for *Vogue*, she had wondered what Tony would think of the new image, and wished he was there to watch her wipe the make-up quickly from her face at the sound of Tante Berthe's voice from the kitchen calling her to lunch.

At college, like Sarah – striking as ever – she wore no make-up. They lunched at the brasserie, laughing over Sarah's fund of stories of her vacation, and smiling at Lise's news that Mireille's teenage romance with the young medical student in Bordeaux was definitely 'on'.

Leonie noticed that Lise ate very fast, following the hors d'oeuvres with an omelette and two desserts, touching full lips between mouthfuls with her napkin in a token display of good manners. Later Sarah remarked that the silk shirt she wore must have cost a small fortune, and the diamond links in the tailored cuffs were obviously real, not to mention far too large.

'Perhaps a little exaggerated for college wear, don't you think, ma chère?'

'If that's what she likes,' Leonie said.

'I have a feeling that Lise Verdier will always get what she likes.'

*

202

That night Zoe was to cook dinner at the avenue Kléber. Erich was back from Switzerland and wanted to get down to marketing plans for the follow-up to the full-page exposure in *Vogue*. It was to come out in the January issue, so would be on the bookstalls for Christmas – felicitous timing, Zoe told Leonie when she called her. 'Wear the new make-up.'

Erich let her in himself, and caught her in a bear-like embrace before she managed to slip past him and walk on into the drawing-room. The first thing that struck her were the bare walls and denuded shelves – and then the splendid simplicity of the Picasso girl, hanging alone above the fireplace, made her stand quite still in the centre of the drawing-room.

'You like that, I know.' Erich came up behind her and touched her shoulder.

'She's perfect.'

'That makes two of you. Of equal worth.'

'Where is my mother?' She turned and looked up at him suspiciously. 'Isn't she here?'

'But of course she is here, chérie. In the kitchen. Where else? After all, this is a family reunion.'

'I thought it was a marketing committee. Didn't you notice – I've put *the* face on.'

'Ah, yes. Paris will see that face this season – everywhere, and in the flesh. You must be seen.'

Zoe came into the room, slightly flushed from the heat of the kitchen. 'Hi. Dinner's ready, then we can talk. Let me see the make-up.' She held Leonie's shoulders and gave her a long look. 'Right first try. Don't you think so, Erich?'

Leonie moved to the dining-table while Erich opened champagne. They toasted Caresse. Then Erich announced that he had decided they would launch the next publicity promotion with a party on New Year's Eve.

Zoe's face lit up. 'Why didn't I think of that? My little girl launched in Paris at the start of '39. It's a perfect idea. I'll start on the scheme straight away, tomorrow in my office. And the invitations. We'll send them out on December the

203

first, and get in before everyone else.'

Leonie was relieved that they had come up with a project that would not interfere too much with her studies. Her paper on French social history would be in before Christmas, and her viva over well before the end of term.

'I think that would fit in quite well with my work,' she said in a pause.

'This *is* work,' Erich said. 'It may all sound like a game. But the winnings are to be taken quite seriously. You know that?'

'You're right, darling,' Zoe said. 'But the child has to study, and I'll not waste all those years I went through at the grindstone in New York to keep her in school.'

'You must let the past go, Liebling.' Erich refilled her glass. 'New York is turning over quite well on its own. I have just seen the figures.'

'Oh?' Zoe looked annoyed. 'Since when did those figures come in without my knowing it?'

'They are on your desk. You'll see them first thing.'

Zoe got up and started to clear the dishes. 'I only *play* at Hausfrau, you know. Caresse is where I belong.'

'And you adorn it like a queen, Liebling. Calm down; no one is trying to supersede you. Have another glass of wine.'

Zoe left the table and collapsed, gracefully, on to a sofa. 'You're right. But right now I'm worried – about what my daughter and I should wear for New Year's Eve.'

'Something off the peg, but special.' Leonie sat beside her. 'Not the mother and daughter look, I hope.'

'The child is right.' Erich stood looking down at them, a proprietorial gold-toothed smile including them both. 'Those days are also past. And we will drink to that passing. I have some really good brandy. My pictures have left Paris, but my wines seemed quite unable to bring themselves to go.'

The guest list for New Year's Eve read like a Who's Who for

the fashion world, high finance, and the international diplomatic set combined. If one in two accepted, Zoe knew she would still preside over a glittering occasion. She had decided on an early-evening affair, 'so that people could go on to their midnight revels and be disappointed in every other party in town!'

Leonie called in at the salon on the day the cards went out, and saw that Lady Hume's invitation was on the top of the pile going to London. She asked her mother if they could add Sarah Bentley to the list. Sarah knew the Humes, and was the only student from the college Leonie wanted to invite.

'Of course, baby. Anyone who's a friend of the Humes is a friend of mine . . . and maybe we should have given you your own list. How about that boy Max? The pianist. Wouldn't he like to play for us?'

'Mother, I don't think Max will feel much like celebrating New Year. And I'm certainly not going to ask him to play at your party.'

'*Your* party, don't you mean? You'll be the belle of the evening. And I still haven't made up my mind what to wear.'

Leonie gave Sarah the invitation in the foyer at college just as they were on their way out to lunch. Lise Verdier ran to join them, and asked who the love letter was from.

'None of your business, Lise.' Sarah winked at Leonie. She guessed there would be no invitation for the Verdiers of this world at what promised to be the most select venue of all the celebrations for the last night of the year.

All through lunch Lise went like a terrier for the information, and when she saw that Sarah was not going to give it she walked back alone, claiming she had an essay to finish before class. But after school she left alone again, running past Leonie and swinging her bag as if she had nothing on her mind.

When the *Vogue* issue came out, on the last day of term, she was the only student who did not carry a copy into college and congratulate Leonie on the photograph, and during the reception held in the cafeteria the last morning she made a point of standing with a group from another class.

After the principal's speech of farewell for the short Christmas break, Leonie told Sarah she had had enough of Lise's behaviour. She had wanted to send something to Mireille at Christmas, and had bought a studded collar for Charlie. As the girls began to scatter, she went up to Lise and asked her if she were going home to Bordeaux.

Lise did not look her in the face. 'No. My family has a suite booked at Chamonix. There's so little time I am to go direct from Paris.'

'Well, I hope you enjoy it,' Leonie said. 'Happy Christmas.'

'Thank you so much,' Lise sneered. 'And how about happy New Year? Or don't you wish *all* of your friends to last that long?'

That evening there was a call from Paul in Strasbourg. Tante Berthe talked to him first, and then called Leonie to the phone.

'Do not be too sad with him,' she whispered as she held out the receiver. 'There is no Christmas leave. You and I must say we will be happy, and promise to drink his health.'

Leonie listened to her father's voice on the usual bad line, and fought off a rising sadness. Christmas the year before had been a turning point in their relationship. This year even Tony could not be in Paris. Maddie would be in New York, maybe with her sister.

'Are you there? Can you hear me?' Paul had to shout to make himself heard.

'Yes, Papa. I'm here. We'll think of you. We'll drink your health.'

'Promise me something.'

'Of course.'

'Do not leave my aunt alone. Stay at the rue Louis for Christmas. Is that possible?'

'Of course, Papa. I promise.'

As she rang off she sensed Berthe de Byron's keen eyes on her, and knew she was waiting for details of the conversation. Berthe had watched her for weeks, seeing the colour in her cheeks fade as life in the city, the long hours at her desk, and the commitment to a hectic social round that her success as a model had brought took their toll.

'You are too thin, my dear,' Berthe said à propos of nothing. 'Very *soignée*. And I congratulate you on your poise these days. But – too thin.'

'It's the fashion, Tante. And I work so hard.'

'You play hard. Too hard. And that lovely complexion always hidden. Perhaps it is not my place . . . ?'

'You have every right, Tante. You have given me a home here.' She went to her, and put a hand on her shoulder. It was the nearest to an intimate touch that she felt Berthe de Byron would allow. 'And at Christmas I promise to eat so much that I burst!'

'That is more like the child you were a year ago. And we should all be children at Christmas, n'est-ce pas?'

There was a swift, grim quarrel with Zoe when Leonie told her that she had no choice but to spend the holiday at the rue Louis. It had all the stormy suddenness of their old battles in New York, and ended as suddenly, both of them in tears.

Apologies over, they telephoned Maddie together.

'More tears, I expect,' Zoe said as she waited for the operator to put her through.

But Maddie was out.

'Say, why don't you call that boy Tony? Be my guest.'

Leonie almost ran to the phone. It was a problem calling long-distance from Tante Berthe's apartment, as her offers to pay were always turned down.

Tony answered before the phone had buzzed twice, his voice very low. He told her that his mother's condition was unchanged. He was working, sometimes. He thought of her, all the time.

207

'Did you get my letter?' She had written to him saying she could not get to New York for Christmas.

'You write every day. But yes, I did. And it's OK, really. One day I'll be back in Paris. You know that.'

She found she could not reply.

'Give him my best,' Zoe said. 'I have to get my cigarettes. I'll leave you alone for the goodbyes.'

'Will you call in on Maddie?' Leonie asked when Zoe had left her alone. 'I think it'd please my mother. She's missing New York more than she'll admit.'

'I'll write when I've been to Gramercy Park. You can show your mother the letter. I'll make it a real letter for a real family read.'

'Don't joke about that, not for now. Things aren't easy, Tony. I've almost begun to feel I have to protect her. Can you believe it?'

'You'll have to protect her against one thing, if you're as lovely as the *Vogue* pic says you are. Or was it all lighting?'

He told her that a friend had crossed back to the States for Christmas and brought the Paris *Vogue* with him. And that Zoe would be certain to suffer from jealousy if things went on as the *Vogue* photograph hinted they might.

'Tone down the style. If you can. It's not you, not for real life. It's your mother's province.'

'Well, thank you for those kind words, Tony Shaw, and happy Christmas.'

He laughed, the first time his voice sounded as she remembered. 'Who's paying for this call?'

'The company.'

'Then tell me . . . do you remember that afternoon, when the others had gone?'

She told him that she remembered.

While she set the table for Christmas Eve dinner at the rue Louis, Berthe de Byron asked Leonie to light the candles and open a wine from Briteau that she had kept especially for the

208

occasion. Later they sat facing each other across the white linen and heavy silver, and raised their glasses.

'The toast is, of course, to my dear Paul.'

'To Papa.'

Towards the end of the meal Berthe asked if Leonie had decided what to wear for her mother's New Year's Eve reception, and what time it was to take place. Leonie told her it was an early-evening party, and work at college had meant that she had had no chance as yet to look for a dress. She had almost made up her mind to be a true Parisienne, and shop at Galeries Lafayette, in the *solde* which they usually held in the days after Christmas.

'I think a true Parisienne could not do better,' Tante Berthe said. 'And you are almost that now. I see it coming.'

'Thank you. I did have time for other shopping. My father will have to wait for his gifts. But yours is ready, in my room.'

'I'll fetch my gift for you, since you remind me, child. Better still, come with me.'

It was the first time she had been in the older woman's bedroom and she hovered, suddenly shy, in the doorway, until Berthe turned and beckoned her.

On the bed was a large flat couturier box, with a faded monogram in one corner. Tante Berthe told Leonie to open it.

'I have treasured this for some years. It is what you might call an heirloom.'

Leonie raised the lid of the box, and removed a layer of paper tissue. A wisp of black silk lifted like a sigh, and she reached for the dress that lay neatly folded beneath the tissue.

'Oh, I don't believe it, Tante! Is it really what I think?'

Berthe nodded. 'If you know what it is, then you deserve to wear it.'

The dress was a Worth. Cut on the bias by a master, seamed and beaded by a perfectionist of a midinette, the eternal little black dress of the eternal Frenchwoman.

Berthe held the dress against Leonie, critically. 'I was as

209

svelte as you, of course. And the length? We could shorten it.'

'Don't let's touch it. It's perfect. Too good to wear.'

'Never. You will wear it for the reception? And many more times.'

Leonie let the dress fall, and held out her arms. 'I'll guard it with my life.'

'*Bon*. It will go with you always. A true Parisienne would never let it out of her sight.'

They went back to the drawing-room, and Leonie gave Berthe the pure cashmere jacket she had bought with her Christmas bonus from Caresse. The dress lay on the back of a chair for the rest of the evening, the older woman glancing at it from time to time as she might watch a favourite child.

In the write-ups in the Paris gossip columns the week after New Year, not a single journalist neglected to mention that the darling of the reception held for the American venture Caresse was a certain Mademoiselle Leonie de Byron, and that she had complimented her Parisian guests by wearing a Worth original.

The creator of Caresse, herself a beautiful American, had, they said, the true New Yorker style. *Soignée*, ageless, *amusante*.

Erich Mannheim had spent the evening apparently nursing the many business contacts who had accepted invitations and in reality watching Leonie at a distance.

It was Zoe who sent the reporter from *Time* on his way with the remark she said she had overheard from a French diplomat's wife – that after such a party everyone must have gone on to be disappointed in all the midnight revels in town.

The quote made the column.

CHAPTER THIRTEEN

Zoe began the new year by donning black silk tailored pyjamas at eight in the morning, going through her entire wardrobe, and discarding anything with a look that might even remotely be mistaken for girlish. If her daughter was to become the face of the year, she told Erich as she threw a pair of shoes halfway across the bedroom, she hoped it was true that Frenchmen would always be interested in the older woman.

'And I need some jewellery.' She frowned, tugging a diamond Pegasus brooch from a lapel and returning it to a case on her dressing-table.

'Always a good investment.' Erich, still in bed, sipped his coffee. 'Get what you like. I'll see if there's anything special – antique perhaps – coming on to the market. There's a nice little panic in the air, and that usually brings out the really good pieces.'

'Trust you to know what's going on.' Zoe eyed herself critically in the dressing-table mirror.

'One day you'll be glad of it. Not so far off now. Meantime – let's try to enjoy life a little more, eh? We went to sleep far too soon after we got back.'

'Wasn't it wonderful? The whole party, just as I planned. That takes experience, wouldn't you say?'

'And maturity.' He put down his cup as she walked towards the bed.

'Not too much maturity.' Zoe slid between the sheets. 'And I'm not resting on my laurels. I'm going into the salon this afternoon.'

*

211

Life at the Collège Madeleine during the middle term of the second year was a heavy routine of advanced studies laced with cultural visits to the city's museums and lectures by a series of visiting professors culled from the principal's distinguished Parisian acquaintance.

Leonie found it easier than she had expected to balance the work and the demands of success. All she had done in the first year – egged on by Tony – had laid a solid foundation. Zoe too proved an unexpected ally, keeping photo-calls and interviews to times which suited her studies, and taking it on herself to organize her clothes.

Leonie gave in gracefully. The numerous appearances she had to make meant that she was grateful for the deals Zoe arranged with several of the big fashion houses soon after the New Year's Eve reception. Knowing that Leonie de Byron would be seen everywhere that season, they lent out samples of the new lines. Leonie wore them, to charities at the Comédie, to a Sacha Guitry première, to a gala ballet Joos. She wore casuals to a string of Saturday morning *vernissages* for up-and-coming painters in the smart little galleries off the rue Seine. She dressed with the muted elegance of an upper-class French girl for country-house Sunday luncheons in Passy and Versailles. She wore outrageous new numbers from the younger couturiers for the latest *chansonniers* on Saturday nights.

One evening as she sat on her bed applying eye make-up in a hand mirror, she looked up to find Berthe de Byron standing in the doorway of her room.

'May I come in?'

'Of course.' They had become more relaxed with each other in recent weeks. 'You don't mind my going out? Max Heller is playing.'

'I was young once. And you work hard. But perhaps you also play too hard. Perhaps you will tire of all this, and it will leave a space in your life. Space can be so very dangerous.'

'You know why I do it, Tante. Not long now and it will be spring, and this summer I can say goodbye to it all and go back . . .'

212

'To New York,' Berthe said, almost to herself, as if she did not want an answer.

'I do have to see someone there. Two people. But no – I think I was going to say Briteau.'

She had arranged to call for Max in a taxi and go with him to the Czech Club where he was giving a recital. Traffic was dense, irritable and pleasure-bound, and she arrived late, getting the driver to sound his horn. When Max did not appear she got out and looked up at the top-floor windows, but could see no lights. Asking the taxi to wait, she climbed the stairs.

Max was sitting in the half-light from the street lamps far below, in the room's single battered chair, staring at the piano.

'For heaven's sake, Max,' Leonie said. 'We're running late as it is. And you haven't even changed.'

'I don't think I can go,' he said flatly. 'The German army has marched into Prague. Did you know that? I don't have the nerve to play for people who will sit there thinking that any day now Hitler will deny that they even exist.'

She sank on to the narrow bed. 'Sorry. No, I hadn't heard. But I think you're wrong. About the recital. They'll hate it if you don't show.'

'I just can't sit in Paris letting things like this happen – to people I know.'

'Max, don't you see that the music is the very best thing you can do for them now? *Please.* Come with me. What the hell does it matter if you've not changed?'

He ran a hand through his hair and looked round for his spectacles. 'Have you seen what day it is? I never did like to play on the Ides of March. I once made a total fool of myself in a campus production of *Julius Caesar*.'

'Well, you're not making a fool of *me* tonight, Max Heller.' She took his coat from the back of the door. 'And I'll drag you down those stairs – all four flights – and throw you at the

213

piano if you don't come quietly.'

In the taxi he took her hand and thanked her, saying that she had come a long way since the night they sailed from the Hudson. And Tony would be proud of her.

Tony. As they turned the corner of the street she looked back at the house where he had rented his studio. Tony would not have wanted anything to do with what was happening in Europe. He had chosen his own wars: a long battle with his father, with his own genius, and now the quiet struggle for his mother. He was probably sitting by her now, she thought, and in spite of the grip of Max's hand in hers she found herself wishing she was with him, sharing the battlefields of New York.

The end-of-term ceremonies at the college were conducted in a certain behind-the-scenes flurry of anxiety, as if the principal wanted to make short-cuts and bring the year to an end with the least possible fuss. Usually there were two or three lunch-time buffets for staff and girls 'to let their hair down', an evening reception with dancing which this year was cancelled without explanation, and the last-day graduation with speeches, which was attended this time by a thin audience.

Earlier in the week half a dozen American girls had made polite excuses and gone, after the announcement of the German-Italian friendship pact. A Greek girl had been found sobbing in the powder room and had left that day. The only two German students took a formal leave of the principal in private before they slipped away, with no goodbyes to their classmates.

After the graduation ceremony, Lise Verdier sidled up to Leonie in the foyer. The noticeable coolness of her behaviour since New Year's Eve was temporarily replaced by a bright, tense smile.

'Wish I could get to Briteau again this year with la petite Mireille,' Lise said. 'But my people are refusing to make plans. Papa says so much could happen. They even talk of sending me to America – but that I refuse. I am not a child.'

It was the longest speech she had made to Leonie, or Sarah, for days, an obvious attempt at patching things up, perhaps angling for an invitation on her own to Briteau. Leonie did not choose to inform her that Mireille's grandfather had also talked of sending her to the States if the international situation got worse. Her instinct was that the less one said to Lise Verdier about the family plans the better, if she were not to become a leech now that they were leaving the Collège Madeleine and returning to the south.

'I'll be at Briteau. I am sure Mireille will try to join us,' she said non-committally.

'Doesn't your mother mind? With all that's happening surely she'll want you in Paris? And you've made it your *milieu*, ma chère. Everyone adores you.'

Everyone except Lise Verdier, it seems, Leonie thought as they kissed on both cheeks, dissembling to the end. *Bonnes vacances. Bonnes vacances.*

That evening Leonie joined Sarah Bentley for an aperitif at the Humes' club. There were several English families still in residence, but Leonie noticed piles of luggage ready for collection at the desk, and all the telephone kiosks were booked.

Sarah was going to Scotland first, for a long family vacation, then would look for a job. She promised to write as soon as things happened, and gave her London address for replies.

Leonie told her it was a good feeling to earn your own money, and Sarah would be sure to land on her feet. She had so many friends, she thought, looking at this striking English girl who was the only real friend she had made at the college. Sarah would have an entry to any door she chose to unlock in England. Leonie herself was bound to the new life she had created for herself the day she told her mother she would go to France and find her father.

Sarah sensed her eyes on her. 'Maybe I'll get back here,'

she said. 'Shall we drink to that?'

They raised their glasses, both knowing that it was not true.

When Sarah went off to finish her packing, Leonie waited for an empty booth and telephoned her mother at the salon. Erich was away in Switzerland for a few days, and Zoe invited her to the flat for supper. 'We must talk.'

Over onion soup in the large, functionally bare kitchen Zoe announced that she was making a hurried round trip to New York. She had to make sure Maddie had all she needed. She also intended to stash away most of her jewellery at Gramercy Park, in her New York bank, and with various discreet friends . . . 'in case things blow up on us over here and I have to run. You would come with me, of course.'

'There are things here now that might make that difficult, Mother.'

'Baby, we're talking about our *lives* here, don't you know that – our safety?'

'Does Erich know about this? I think that's more to the point.'

Zoe sighed. 'I guess I'd have to try Zurich with him if things moved too fast. But he knows I'd look after my own. And several of my clients have already booked their children out to the States. Did you know there's a real panic setting in? Haven't you seen the signs?'

'A little. At college . . .'

'Now,' Zoe ploughed on, 'I want you to listen.' She told Leonie that she was also taking to New York a set of bonds that would be put away in her name. And that in the meantime, in Paris, she had banked for her a substantial final cheque on the Caresse company account.

'You're going to need it while you decide what to do. And anyway, your birthday's close. Consider it a gift from a grateful employer. Then as soon as I get back from New York we'll talk again. Where can I find you?'

'At the château. I'll call you.'

'Still the same old forbidden territory, am I? I can't think why I'm not more jealous.'

'There's no need.'

'Remember your birthdays?' Her eyes shone too brightly. 'Such plans.'

'The parties were beautiful, Mother.' *And they brought on our worst fight, and got me here to Paris.* She had not the heart to remind Zoe of the truth.

'What will you do on your own?'

'I'll think of something. Don't *worry*.'

Two days later she checked her bank account and knew at once exactly what she wanted to do to celebrate her nineteenth birthday. She called Charles Vincent's office.

When she got through, she asked him if he had any idea what very important date was coming up any day now on the calendar.

'Let me see. It's too early for Chantilly.'

'Are you teasing me, Monsieur Vincent?'

'Mademoiselle de Byron,' he said, 'I have to confess that for reasons of business I have been studying your file this morning, and yes I do know the date of your nineteenth birthday. In three days' time.'

'Of course. I should have known you'd have it on your files.'

'What can I do for you?'

'Take me to lunch. I have news for you. Such news that only Maxim's will do.' There was a silence. 'Are you still there?'

'I was making a note for my assistant to book us a table.'

'He'll hate that.' Leonie grinned at the thought. 'One o'clock?'

'At your command.'

She had lunched at Maxim's before with her mother and Erich, and one or two publicity conferences had taken place over dinner there, but this was the first time she had walked

217

in alone, and she found it gratifying that the maitre d'
recognized her and led her straight to Charles Vincent's
table. One or two heads turned, as they always did since her
face had appeared on so many magazine covers, and a
woman she knew vaguely by sight nodded and murmured to
her companion.

Charles Vincent rose and shook hands. 'I do not often get
to see my clients on their birthdays,' he said. 'This is a
pleasure.'

'I've even brought my own birthday present,' she
answered.

When she mentioned the sum she had deposited that
morning in the account for Briteau the notary for once let go
his professional image and gave a loud laugh of sheer
pleasure. 'Do you realize that this means we can pay off the
whole sum your father borrowed two years ago?'

'That was the idea.'

'Do you always get your own way with such determination? And are you sure? How does this leave your own
account?'

'Oh, I'll not need money this summer. And there's a
deposit in New York, I think. And anyway, after the harvest
this year I must find work.'

'Things may not be so easy.'

'The only problem I can see is how to tell my father what
we have done. I don't want him to feel we have deceived
him.'

'Perhaps too much has been kept from you – from you
both – over the years, mademoiselle. I think he would be
proud of you, though he would find it hard to accept.'

'At first, maybe. I think it's the timing that matters. I want
him to know this summer, so that he needn't worry about the
château. But I don't want any dramatic scenes. He's going to
hate it, isn't he?'

'Perhaps I will tell you something that will show you his
real feelings for you. Would you like me to be the one to break
the news that the mortgage can be repaid?'

'Would you?'

'I'll want your vow of secrecy in exchange.'

'More secrets . . .' She looked doubtful.

He told her that her father had made a new will, and she asked him if he was sure he should go on. Paul de Byron could be very strict in these matters. The notary explained that he wanted her to know what he had to say because everything might change so soon in France.

'Very well.'

'As a French officer your father sees it his duty to ensure the safety of his estates, and of his daughters. Your half-sister is already a wealthy young woman, and will be very rich in her own right one day. In the event of a tragedy – in war, you understand me – as the – the legal . . .'

'The word is legitimate, Monsieur Vincent.'

'The government compensation would go to her.'

'So?'

'To you, mademoiselle – who have just arranged to make yourself a pauper for your father's estate – he leaves one half of that estate. The rest is in trust for Mireille de Byron, until she is twenty-five years old.'

'In trust? With whom?'

'With the trustees, mademoiselle. Myself . . . and you.'

'Oh. And you think that the grandfather in Bordeaux would allow that for one moment?'

'He would have no choice. Your father has the right to name his heirs.'

'Henri Massine hates my father. For what happened to Mireille's mother.'

'It would be a long, costly fight for him. With much scandal.'

'Monsieur Vincent – aren't we forgetting something? There's no war yet. Perhaps there won't be. And my father is very much alive. Why did you have to tell me all this?'

'Because of my admiration. Because of the past. And because you needed assurance of your father's love for you.'

'What would he do if he knew you'd told me?'

219

'He must never know. My father and his father before him have always looked after the de Byron family affairs. I would not like to be the one responsible for losing the business!'

'I'm glad to hear it, Monsieur Charles.' She raised her glass to him. 'But I don't think I'll ever be able to believe what you've told me.'

'Then forget it. Put it away as a good thing to keep by you, until the time comes.'

'That's got to be never,' she said.

They parted on a corner of the Place de la Concorde, Charles Vincent taking a taxi back to his office, and Leonie turning south to walk to the rue Louis. She wanted to let Tante Berthe know that she and Charles Vincent were about to repay the mortgage on Briteau: but letting herself into a silent apartment, the blinds drawn against the afternoon sun, she remembered that Berthe had mentioned a Red Cross meeting that would go on until *le cocktails*.

She made herself tea and washed her hair, trying to take in the news of her father's will. It was out of the question to reveal the notary's breach of confidence to a member of the family, but she had to tell someone, if only to make it real: that her father thought enough of her to make her his heir, and that she need never leave Briteau.

She thought of Max, and took a walk to the Left Bank, buying *pâtisseries* in the boulevard St Michel. The carton began to leak *sirop* as she climbed the steep stairs to Max's room, and as she leaned on his door, licking her fingers, it swung slowly inwards.

It took no more than a second for her to see that all of Max's few possessions had gone.

When she regained the street she found the concierge next door sunning himself in the street on his three-legged stool.

Yes, the young musician had left. In a great hurry. No goodbyes. No messages. No address.

The first thing she wanted to do was to call Tony. The world

220

they had shared for so short a time seemed to be breaking up around her, and hearing his voice would, she felt, salvage something from the wreckage. Then if she talked to him from Zoe's office she would follow with a call to Gramercy Park.

The Caresse salon was almost deserted; with the weeks when Paris would empty approaching Zoe had left her assistant manageress Marianne in charge. The woman was putting last-minute touches to the reception area for the next day and had the outer door keys in her hand ready to close the salon for the night.

'I'll let myself out, Marianne,' Leonie told her as she took the winding staircase to the first floor. 'I have my keys. I want to call my mother.'

'I hope she enjoys herself in New York. Tell her all goes well here,' Marianne answered as she put on her coat.

Opening the door of Zoe's private rooms Leonie was taken aback to find Erich Mannheim sitting at her mother's desk. A brandy glass at his elbow, he was checking through a sheaf of accounts.

'Ah!' He looked up. 'Ma chère Leonie. I was hoping that we would meet today.'

'What are you doing here? They've locked up downstairs.'

The Swiss banker put down the papers and gave her an appraising stare. 'You have just washed your hair, I think? It is quite beautiful.'

'I want to call New York.'

'For your birthday, of course! That is precisely why I myself wanted to see you.'

'I'd like to talk to my mother alone.'

He reached for a velvet jewel case beside his glass and came out from behind the desk. 'First, let me wish you *bonne anniversaire!*' He clicked his heels as he handed her the box. 'I apologize for the fact that it is not in a pretty wrapper. It has travelled a long way, and only just arrived. My gift.'

'Erich, I don't want your gifts – surely you've learned that by now?'

221

'But it gives me pleasure. It is a *faiblesse* of mine. Your mother will tell you.'

'Mother does not discuss such things with me.'

He smiled and gave a wry shrug. 'Let me pour you a brandy while you open the box.' He crossed to the small bar in an alcove by the door.

'I only want to make my calls and then I am going back to the rue Louis.'

'I'll drive you there.'

'No thank you.' She put the box down on the desk, and picked up the phone, thinking he would eventually tire of his cat and mouse game, and asked for long distance international. The operator said there was considerable delay. Lines had been extra busy all day. She said she would try later, and put the receiver down.

'Good,' Erich said. 'Now you have to see what I have found for you.'

She gave a sigh of annoyance as she picked up the gift and walked with it to the window, her back to him. He drained his glass and took it to the bar. She did not see him pause at the door before he crossed the room to where she stood.

He took the box from her hand, and opened it. Inside lay the pearls she had sold in New York two years before.

She gave a small, nervous laugh. 'You don't give up, Erich. Did you think it a good idea to remind me of that day? Did you really think that?'

'It has been a long two years,' he said, 'and I have watched you change with great interest. Into a woman.' He touched her hair, and she stepped quickly back, snapping the box shut.

'I am going to try New York again,' she said, 'and then I am going home.'

He let her go, asking her if she would not change her mind and have a birthday dinner with him. She told him that Tante Berthe had arranged to celebrate alone with her. She could not let down her father's aunt.

As she learned from the operator that the lines were still

engaged, Erich came behind her and put his hands round her waist. With her free hand she wrenched one of his arms from her, then, replacing the receiver, she turned and tried to push him away. He smiled down at her, eyes cold in a pale face, and pinned her against the desk.

'No,' she said. 'Please leave me alone. I'm going now.'

'I have been leaving you alone for months.' She could feel his breath on her neck, and twisted her head away, but could not break his grasp on her waist. 'You know very well what I have felt for you – all these months. For two years.'

'Why do you think I didn't hesitate to sell those wretched pearls? You're like this with all the girls here. They talk, you know. My poor mother . . .'

Erich gave the laugh she hated, throwing his head back, and she took her chance to force his hands away and run to the door. It was locked.

'I don't believe this. Even you would not be so . . . obvious,' she said in a low voice.

Erich, perhaps mistaking her tone for a sign of acquiescence, walked slowly towards her. She moved away from the door and stood hesitating, wondering whether she could reach the desk and phone for help.

'There is no one else in the building,' Erich said. 'I can read your thoughts, ma chère. You think you are going to escape me somehow. But believe me, that will not be possible. Nor do I think you would be so foolish as to make any noise. After all, as you say, your poor mother . . . she has much to lose by any hint of scandal.'

Leonie kept her eyes on him as he came closer, then darted from him again. But as she moved away he caught her dress, and she heard the sound of fabric tearing as he pulled her round towards him.

She fought him for ten minutes, and it seemed an hour. She felt the soft flesh she had always disliked as he forced himself on her, and knew before he entered her that he would be heavy. What she had not been prepared for was the brutality. And the way he talked, in German, during the prolonged, violent attack. Not until she began to weep from exhaustion and despair did he close his mouth, and close her lips with his, coming quickly to a climax. Then, seconds before he ejaculated, he withdrew from her, and told her, panting as he rolled away from her, that he adored her more than ever.

She crawled to the sofa, weeping, and found the torn dress and remnants of her underwear. Dressing awkwardly while he watched her, she fought off the need to be sick. She would not give him that satisfaction. Her tears subsided slowly, to be replaced by a cold, speechless anger.

Erich said at last: 'You need some cognac. We'll have a drink together, eh?'

'Do you really think I'd sit here and drink with you? Give me the key. I'm going.'

'Oh, no. I drive you home. When you are calmer. When I am sure you forgive me.'

'Forgive? You must be mad! This is the end of everything. My mother . . .'

'Think carefully. I do not think, somehow, my dear child, that you will let your mother know what has happened between us.'

'What you did was not between us. You are disgusting.'

'Here.' He seemed unperturbed by what she had said as he handed her a glass of brandy. She took it reluctantly, but once she had sipped it she gulped it down quickly. Erich put his own glass down and sat beside her, an arm along the back of the sofa. She turned as if to strike him, but instead hurled her empty glass in his face. Too quick for her, he fielded it with a large open hand, but it hit him with such force that it broke, cutting deep into his thumb.

He shrugged, pulling a silk handkerchief from a pocket, and wiping the blood carefully so that it did not drop on the sofa. 'I am not averse to a little violence between lovers.'

'Lovers!' Leonie hissed the word, thinking of the time she had spent in Tony's arms before he left for New York. 'You have no idea what the word means.'

224

'And you have?' He grinned lazily. 'I realized just now, of course. You are not the little virgin you would have us all adore from afar. I have already told you – I adore you, but it is the real thing. Not romance. You can run home, it is true. But that will not wipe out what has happened here.'

'You're right,' Leonie snapped back at him. 'Nothing can do that. I'll hate you always. More than I hated you before.'

'Oh, I have always known you disliked me. I have the same trouble from time to time with your beautiful Zoe. But you will get used to this ambivalence. And if you try to run from me this time . . . you will find that I can be very cruel to those I love.'

'I'm going to my apartment,' she whispered. 'If you try to stop me, I'll really fight you this time.'

Until now she had been angry rather than afraid. While Erich raped her she had tried to think of Tony, blotting out the heavy body and the gasping words of the older man. She remembered what girls at school in New York had told her when there had been a rape scare in the city. Sometimes the rapist could not finish. Best to let them try. You hardly ever got pregnant.

She tried to stand, but her legs were too weak and she began to tremble.

'I'll drive you home. Come. You can bathe here.' He began to undress her again, very slowly, with skilled hands. It was with a sense of growing despair that she allowed her mother's lover to lift her in his arms and carry her to the private bathroom attached to the office. Wrapped in Zoe's towelling robe, she sat and watched him numbly as he ran a bath. Then he helped her into the warm, scented water and with surprising gentleness began to wash her, as if he were tending a cherished child.

An hour later he parked the Mercedes outside the iron gates in the rue Louis and told her again that he loved her. 'You don't believe me?'

'It doesn't matter,' she said dully. 'All that matters is that I'll never see you again.'

'Where will you go? Your mother is afraid for you. I hope she will join me in Switzerland if war comes.'

'After what you have done to me?'

'Your mother needs me. And after all, ma chère Leonie, I am not your first lover.'

She was too angry to reply. All she wanted was to get out of the car and run into the house and pack her bags for the summer at Briteau.

'Zoe is vulnerable, more than you think,' Erich went on blandly. 'And a good mother. It is because she has been such a good mother that I believe you will not tell her what happened tonight.'

'It's true,' Leonie said quietly. 'I don't think I could tell her.'

'Then we do understand each other a little. Can't I see you tomorrow? I could be good to you. And you have left your pearls at the salon.'

'They're your pearls, Erich. You'll find someone to take them, while Mother's away. I told you – I never want to see you again.'

She tugged at the car door handle and made her escape. The last she saw of Erich Mannheim was the large fair head glinting in the flame as he bent to light a cigar.

That night she told Berthe de Byron that she wanted to get out of Paris as soon as possible. The international situation had begun to scare her; all her friends had left and there might be no students able to come to Briteau to help in the harvest. 'I have my commitment now, Tante. To Briteau.'

'Yes, my dear child. Charles Vincent telephoned this evening. We are both delighted with you. You have done as you vowed. It is splendid, truly splendid.'

They went to her room to organize the packing, Berthe remarking that she looked very tired. She asked if she had been weeping. No one should shed tears on their birthday.

'Only a little. Because people I love are in New York.'

'There are people who love you in Paris. Not so far away. Did you know that?' The old Frenchwoman sat in a chair by the window, framed against the fading summer light.

Leonie threw down the dress she was folding and ran to her. 'Tante! I'm so sorry. All you have done for me . . . and for Papa. And will you be safe here? Won't you come with me?'

'*If* war comes, then no one will dare to harm Paris. And – well, I have had a long life. A good life.'

'Papa will want you to be at the château, if –'

Berthe shook her head. 'Your father knows that nothing could make me leave my home. And in the end, everyone always comes back to Paris. Someone should wait here for them. So – finish your packing and we'll drink a glass of wine together.'

Leonie went to the wardrobe. 'There's something here I can't bear to leave behind.'

She brought out the box containing the Worth original and lifted it from its wrapper, rediscovering its shadowy, wraith-like beauty and the feel of the black silk.

'You shall wear it at Briteau.' Berthe nodded approvingly. 'Many, many times. It is like Paris, n'est-ce pas? Immortal.'

Paul de Byron did not get leave to join his two daughters until late August. Talks between Daladier, the British and Hitler had failed, and it was a flying visit, allowing him to make plans for a longer absence. Jacques Fabri did not get leave at all. His mother told Violette that she thought this year they would be all women at *le grand travail*.

Leonie spent her first few days at Briteau walking alone in the fields behind the house, trying to cleanse the memory of Erich Mannheim's attack on her, until Violette cornered her one evening as she came back through the kitchen garden and asked her if she intended to spend the summer dreaming, or would she perhaps help a little in the house? From then on she threw herself into the tasks Violette set her, and by the time Mireille joined them the château was in better order than she had ever seen it.

It was a new Mireille, who spent the evenings in the library with her medical books and wrote long letters in her room, cycling to post them daily in the village on the old bicycle she kept in the stables, with Charlie running at her side. Watching her, Leonie noticed that the thin limbs had rounded, and the long fair hair was now always neatly tied.

Knowing from Charles Vincent's deliberate indiscretion what the future might one day hold for them, Leonie welcomed the new Mireille. The resentments of that first summer had dissolved completely with the departure of Jacques Fabri, and with Mireille's own changing interests. The jealousy of the place Leonie might hold in Paul's affections gave way to a shared wish that he was with them at Briteau. The petulance was replaced by a gentle teasing.

'I hate your eyebrows,' Mireille told Leonie within an hour of her arrival. 'But then I suppose you had to change everything to get on those front pages.'

'Pity that blondes don't have eyebrows you can actually see.' Leonie put an arm round her sister's shoulders in mock commiseration.

'Your hair's not bad, *quand même*,' Mireille said.

The night before Paul was due to get home they sat in the kitchen with Violette. Charlie – who had won his way into the sanctum with advancing years – hugged the warmth of the stove. Mireille watched him for a while, and sighed heavily, telling them that several of the families in Bordeaux had booked their children on to ships for Canada. If war came her grandfather wanted both her and his wife to go. And where would that leave Charlie?

'The dog would live well here,' Violette said. 'But what would Henri Massine do with you both away, except make money as usual?'

'You don't want me to go, darling Violette. Good.' Mireille munched a brioche.

'Only your father can decide. And he will want your safety

228

if those Boches bring us to disaster again. Your grandmother, too – he will want to know that she is cared for.'

There was a letter from Sarah Bentley next day. She had
returned to London early from a Scottish holiday, as a phony
emergency seemed to have them all in its grip. They had
been issued with gas masks in square cardboard boxes and
people were already making small fortunes designing *chic*
covers. There was talk in the welfare office where she had
found temporary voluntary work of getting the children and
mothers with young babies out of the city.

Leonie read and reread the letter, and spent the morning
writing to Sarah, and to New York. Borrowing Mireille's
bicycle to post the letters in the village she had to swerve out
of the drive as an army staff car turned in at the gates, and
she glimpsed her father's face, oddly white, in the rear seat.

Paul went straight to the Fabri house, checking with Fabri
père what arrangements could be made for workers if the crisis
took hold and the itinerants failed to turn up. Fabri said he had
recruited several villagers who were too old to fight. 'Too old to
work in most cases,' his wife snorted from her kitchen.

On his return to the house Paul asked his daughters to
walk with him in the grounds before supper. There was a
boundary wall to inspect, a tree damaged by storms that
might have to come down. Mireille ran off to find Charlie,
leaving Paul and Leonie alone on the terrace. It had rained
lightly, and the scent of warm soil mingled with that of the
vines and the flowers Yvette de Byron had planted.

'I am glad to have this time alone with you, my dear
Leonie,' Paul said quickly. 'I have talked with Charles
Vincent. Did you know?'

'Papa – please don't be angry. It was something I had to
do. When Tante Berthe told me what you had done for me –'

'At first I *was* angry,' he said. 'And then I had to admire a
young woman with such spirit – and with the de Byron pride.
I can only thank you, and assure you that I too have made
plans. For many years ahead. And if this war comes, I want
you to be safe.'

She told him the news from London, and the way in which Paris had been deserted early that summer. She thought that nowhere could be safer than Briteau.

But he believed that nowhere in Europe was really safe. 'Henri Massine wants your sister to go to Canada. Did you know that?'

She nodded, biting her lip, suddenly aware that if Mireille went, and Paul was at war, she would be the only member of the family at the château.

'If only for her grandmother's sake, I am afraid I have to tell Mireille that for once I agree with him,' Paul went on.

Mireille rejoined them, unaware that her fate had been decided, and the girls walked each side of their father as he inspected the boundaries of the grounds. Later a slight breeze blew up and the sky darkened. Mireille said that if there was a good wind next day at dawn she would fly her kite in the meadow, like old times.

'And I will find time to fly it with you, ma petite Mireille.' Paul took her hand.

'And I'll watch from my window – like old times.' Leonie put an arm in his.

A week later he drove them both to Bordeaux. Mireille was to prepare for Canada with her grandmother, and two first class berths were reserved for an early September sailing. Violette also wanted supplies. She demanded a large stock of the best olive oil, and asked him to look out for a source of flour in bulk. The village stores were already running short of goods. Fabri père wanted petrol, and new pruning knives. Watching her father prepare the list on the morning of their departure, Leonie thought that she had already begun to learn what the responsibilities were for the guardians of Briteau.

It was Mireille who begged her to drive with them to Bordeaux. Charlie was left, as a temporary arrangement, at the château; if the war scare died she would come back for him at the end of summer.

While Paul searched the stalls in the old market the two girls wandered to the edge of the square, where the caged-bird sellers had their wares stacked on the cobblestones in a ramshackle miniature babylon of small bird cries and dusty, flapping wings.

They stood watching for several minutes. Mireille bought seed and scattered it in one of the cages in which two linnets were perched, silent, eyes darting as the girl approached; then as the seed fell they hopped to the floor of the cage and began to feed.

Mireille stood staring down at the birds. 'I cannot leave them. First Charlie. And now . . .'

'We'll buy them.' Leonie opened her purse and spoke to the stallholder. He named his price, and she gave him a note, saying he could keep the change.

'You will find this prison down by the river,' Mireille said to him as she picked up the shabby wicker cage.

They met Paul as arranged, on the steps of l'église St Michel on the far side of the market. His shopping was as complete as it was likely to be, and he allowed them to persuade him to drive them down to the quay.

In the lee of a terrace of exquisite eighteenth-century houses they parked the car, and Mireille took the bird cage to a high stone parapet above the river. She opened it, and at first frozen into immobility the birds did not take their chance of freedom. Then she scattered seed on the parapet and they emerged, fluttering their wings and chirping to each other before they took flight across the dark water.

As a military man who rarely allowed sentiment to come into his life in any form, Paul de Byron surprised himself with the thought that the two birds were now as lost to the city as his daughters would soon be to him.

CHAPTER FOURTEEN

The war came at first to Briteau in small ways. Violette, who could remember a shortage of food in her own larder in the war of 1914–18, spent a ritualistic five minutes each morning checking the supplies she had amassed all summer in the cellar below her kitchen. The stables were piled high with logs which Paul himself had cut early for winter from the trees he had chosen for felling. His rooms were closed to save heating the first floor, and at night Leonie warmed her bed with a flannel-wrapped brick that had spent the evening in the kitchen stove.

Jeanne Veron came to the house to measure the windows for black-out curtains, and insisted on bringing her bicycle – now a precious commodity – into the hall for safety. The village streets, she said, were like a circus, with small boys lurching about on the large *vélos* left by older brothers who had gone to fight.

When the new curtains were hung, Leonie spent almost an hour each evening touring the house and closing them to a regulation tightness.

The snow, heralding a winter of devastating cold for the whole of France, came on the heels of the harvest. Fabri père had no sooner dismissed his temporary labourers than he himself was called in by neighbouring farmers to help bring down sheep from the snow-capped hills. At first light some days later Violette opened the kitchen door to find her share of a grateful farmer's gift at her feet – the limp carcass of a young mountain goat, which she bore to her cellar with the air of a woman under some Napoleonic siege, telling Leonie, who looked on in disgust, that the day would come when she would eat what was put before her and be thankful.

When France declared war on Germany, less than a month before the snows, Leonie had tried to call Paris. There was no answer from the rue Louis, and she pictured Tante Berthe already in command of a dozen new committees. It was two days before she could get another line through to the capital, to Caresse, and Marianne answered, telling her that it was 'business as usual' until anyone forced them out.

'Your mother has been extremely anxious,' she said. 'She spends hours on the telephone trying to reach you. And now, when you call, she is out.'

'Tell her I'm still at Briteau. And please ask her not to leave Paris without letting me know.'

There was a letter in the next day's post from Zoe, written a week earlier, begging her to make plans to return to New York. Zoe had plenty of friends who could get her a passage. Maddie would give her a home at Gramercy Park until 'this stupid business' blew over.

By the same post a letter from Tony brought the news that his mother had died.

I'll wait for you here. You'll be coming home, of course. You know my feelings about war, and if it comes I want you safe. I shall paint and grow roses until these madmen succeed in each other's destruction. It is something I do not want you to witness.

She put both letters in the top drawer of the secretaire in the room off her bedroom, which she used as a sitting-room when she could not face the empty silence of the library. She had carried logs up to the room, and lit a fire to air it. On evenings when she could not stand the solitude she went down to the kitchen, and within a few weeks she and Violette were in the habit of spending the hours after darkness by the kitchen stove, with Charlie at their feet.

It was on Violette's ancient kitchen wireless set ten days after the fall of Warsaw that they heard the news that the last Polish troops had surrendered. While Violette went into a

233

tirade against *les sales Boches*, Leonie could think of nothing but Max Heller, and the night he had played for the refugees in Paris. It had snowed then, a light first fall, and Max and Tony had walked her home through the Tuileries gardens. Now Max had disappeared on his own quest, not content with charity concerts and a distant good cause, and she knew that if he had gone to find his people in Poland then he was really lost.

She jumped up at the thought and began to pace the kitchen. Violette watched her, in silence at first, then switched off the news bulletin.

'If you and I are to spend a winter here together, mon enfant, we must use the time well. I have no choice – I shall teach you to cook!'

They began that night, with a batch of bread for the coming week, and poached fish while they waited for the dough to rise. Violette made a dill sauce, and they ate the fish, very late, with a bottle of the vintage of two years before. 'Ah,' Violette sighed as she drained her second glass, 'do you remember your first summer here?'

The next night they made omelettes, and Violette declared that she suspected the little American had a gift.

'The simplest things are the true test, you will see. And when you cook for your first guests, ma chère, we will make everything quite simple, and quite perfect.'

They invited Marcel and Edith Darnand for a Sunday lunch, and the Daimler turned into the drive promptly at midday.

'One sometimes needs a little luxury,' Edith said taking Leonie's arm as they moved into the library, where a fire was lit. 'But Marcel says this is the last time we use the car for a frivolity. My horses will come into their own – if I am able to keep them from the army, and the butchers.'

Violette served the meal, accompanying each course with an account of how her pupil had achieved such results under her expert tuition.

'The cook truly has a gift,' Marcel said as the entrée dishes were removed.

'And plenty of butter from somewhere,' Edith laughed.

Marcel asked Leonie if she remembered Denholm Collins, her sister's English tutor from two summers ago. They had kept in touch, and the Darnands found him a very interesting man, who considered France his second home. A recent letter had described the quite extraordinary shortages of food which the English had imposed on themselves within the first weeks of the war.

Leonie remembered the clever face and the way the tutor had of cajoling Mireille into working. She asked what he was doing.

'Oh – some office work in London,' Edith said. 'It is perhaps his health, you know. He will not make a soldier.'

'It seems strange then that he doesn't stay at the university.'

'Not so strange with a man like Collins,' Marcel said. 'I suspect his so-called office work is something more than he is prepared to tell us.'

During the German advances on the northern front early in 1940, Leonie interrupted a violent argument in the kitchen between Violette and Jacques Fabri's father, who claimed that the entire allied military operation was being mismanaged, by men who cared nothing for the future of France.

Violette turned on him for such heresies in the house of a family that had given France its best soldiers for generations. Her own grandson was also fighting now. And where, she wanted to know, was Monsieur Jacques Fabri?

It was the next morning that the village postman, who usually delivered the mail through the kitchen garden, called at the front of the house, and stood, cap in hand, saying that he had an important document for mademoiselle, but that he preferred to give it to her while she was with a companion. Perhaps Madame Violette was at home?

Leonie took him to the kitchen, thinking that perhaps

there was some legal document to be handed over in the presence of a witness, but as they pushed through the swing doors Violette looked up, and went very pale.

The postman was an elderly, red-faced villager whom Leonie had seen sometimes in church. He shifted from one foot to the other, twisting his cap, before he produced a telegram from his satchel.

At first Leonie told herself that it was only a wire from Zoe, with some news of a move now that the active war zone had come uncomfortably close to Paris. Then, as Violette moved to her side and put an arm round her shoulders she began to tremble with the presentiment of bad news.

She sat at the table, and Violette pulled a chair close to hers, while the postman stood watching them open the wire.

'I am so sorry, mademoiselle,' the old man said, as she read the official announcement that Capitaine Paul de Byron had been killed in action.

The two women sat at the long table after the postman had gone, Violette weeping unashamedly and cursing the Germans, Leonie unable to think of anything except that she had found her father only to lose him after so short a time.

'There are things I must do,' she said at last as Violette, the first rush of tears over, poured them each a cognac.

'La pauvre petite Mireille. She must be told. So far away.' Violette began to cry again.

Leonie went to the library and telephoned Charles Vincent's office, which was manned for the duration of the war by an elderly notary who had been his father's friend. She explained what had happened and asked if the lawyer would go in person to the rue Louis and break the news to Berthe de Byron of her nephew's death.

'She is no longer young,' Leonie said. 'She will be very shocked, I think. I do not want her to be alone when she is told.'

She then found the number of the Massine shipping

agency and asked the operator for Bordeaux.

It was a bad line, but did not disguise the thinly veiled excitement in Henry Massine's voice.

'Ah! Now, mademoiselle, this changes everything. I can be thankful that I have sent the heir to Briteau to safety. There my granddaughter will stay until this war ends. But my lawyers will at once begin work on this matter. You will hear from me when you are to leave my granddaughter's estate.'

'I think you should wait until you hear from my father's own lawyers, Vincent et fils,' Leonie said carefully.

'Oh? What do you know of these things? I suppose that old woman in Paris has been meddling again?'

'My father's aunt is not to be troubled, Monsieur Massine. I telephoned you only because I thought that you would feel badly for Mireille, and that perhaps her grandmother could be asked to break the news of her father's death to her. Can you arrange for this, or not? I know it is what my father would have wanted. Poor Mireille . . .' Her voice trailed into silence.

'You know a great deal,' Massine said tetchily. 'Perhaps what you do not know is that I am fully aware of the sordid story of your origins. And that I have the power to take the estate for myself if I wish?'

'Charles Vincent will tell you that the situation has changed. And I believe the French government protects its heroes from men of your kind.' She put the receiver down and Henri Massine spluttered his retort to a dead line.

When Violette came into the library with a bowl of steaming *café au lait*, she found Leonie sitting in Paul's fireside chair, staring into space, her face white with anger and grief.

'What will you do, child?' Violette sank into the chair opposite, watching her drink the coffee. Her eyes were red from weeping, but she had put on a fresh apron and tidied her hair.

'I shall stay, Violette. One day Mireille will come home.

There is so much to do. My father's lawyers will tell us how things stand. And someone has to make sure that Mireille's grandfather is kept away from Briteau.'

'That is all I wanted to hear,' Violette said comfortably. 'Now, you must rest. After a good lunch.'

'I couldn't eat.'

'Nonsense. If we are to look after this place, we need our strength.'

The Germans had marched into Paris before Leonie's twentieth birthday, and Zoe rang from Zurich to wish her happy birthday and beg her to join herself and Erich in Switzerland. She had left it almost too late to get to the States, but if she would live with them in a neutral country till the whole business was over they could take things up where they had left them – Paris would never be harmed. Erich believed they would make it an open city.

'He wants you to come here, baby. And there is the most incredible birthday gift waiting here for you. Just a little special offering from us both.'

Leonie knew then that Zoe had no idea that Erich had raped her. Erich Mannheim was still playing the fatherly benefactor, amused by mother and daughter alike. He must have wanted her to join him in Zurich badly to have risked the problems he would face if both women lived with him in Switzerland. She shivered as she remembered the declaration of love that had followed the rape. For a wild moment she wanted to get her mother out of Switzerland, away from the man who had betrayed her in such a fashion, and – it appeared – was prepared to continue to live a lie.

'Mother, I can't leave here,' she said after a pause. 'There's something I have to tell you, then you'll understand.'

'What is it, honey? Are you in some kind of trouble?'

'No, Mother. It's not exactly trouble. It's something worse. It's my father . . . I wanted to write to tell you. Then I

238

thought my letter might never get to Paris the way things are, and I'd rather tell you face to face.'

'You don't have to tell me, baby. I can tell from your voice. Paul's been killed, hasn't he?'

'Mother . . .'

'It's all right, Leonie. It's OK.'

'I wish you were here with me, just for this . . .'

'I wish it too. It's the end of something for me, you know that?'

'Yes. I'll write. Can you give me the Zurich address?'

'Write soon, won't you? Erich says that everything will close down in France any day now. He can come and go as he pleases, of course. He still has the car. If you change your mind, you only have to say, and we'll get you out somehow.'

She gave the address and number of Erich's new Zurich apartment, and wanted to know if Leonie would talk to him – just to say hello.

Leonie pretended not to have heard the question, and quickly asked what it had been like in Paris before they left.

'Very hot. There's a long hot summer ahead, I guess. And so quiet. The people stood along the sidewalks crying when the Germans came. Now they turn away when they march down the Champs Elysées – every morning at eleven. That awful German music – and the goose-stepping. Very bad for business!'

She said that she had left Marianne in charge of the salon, and things would be sure to pick up again soon. Erich had closed the flat on the avenue Kléber, and moved his things in above the salon. He would get back from time to time, and keep an eye on things for her.

A sudden vision of Erich Mannheim at her mother's desk when she had called at Caresse a year ago made Leonie say a hurried goodbye, and she rang off wondering if Zoe would shed tears for Paul, and who would comfort her if she did. That night she wept bitterly for the death of her father, feeling that both her parents were now lost to her. Paris too, which for two years had bitten at her senses each time she stepped into the street, an intoxicating drug that she had taken eagerly, was now in the hands of an alien army.

Edith Darnand came over on the local bus and walked from the village when she heard that Paul had been killed. Marcel had gone to Tours for the night, to meet a group of businessmen who did not want Petain at the head of the new government about to be formed. Everything was in chaos, the roads crammed with people on the move south, and she did not know when he would get back. She brought flowers for Leonie and told her ruefully that she had to keep her horses under guard since one of her best ponies had just been stolen.

'The gypsies are in flight. Maybe they need more horses to make more speed,' she said.

'You don't think they are stealing horses for food?'

Edith shook her head. 'The Romanies would never eat a creature that is a symbol of their own freedom.'

Leonie offered to lend her Paul's car. They had enough petrol for her to get back, and for the car to be returned when Marcel came home, perhaps. But Edi.h refused, advising her to keep the car under lock and key – petrol included.

The government had shifted to Tours as a temporary measure, then to Bordeaux. On the day of the move Henri Massine was on the terrace of the hôtel de ville to welcome an acquaintance who had arrived in the city with the bands of civil servants who preceded the ministers. Together they watched a flight of French airforce planes dip their wings in farewell as they made for the open sea and the coast of England.

Massine remarked that he thought it was a mistake to leave. The city – like Marseilles – risked some small embarrassment with half the French fleet in the harbour, but that would pass. There was much to be done, and he, Henri

Massine, a patriot, was ready to serve. After all, his poor daughter's husband was a dead hero of the northern campaign, his granddaughter heir to an ancient estate and a proud name.

His companion eyed him quizzically, making a mental note to add him to the list of well placed so-called patriots who might be very useful, and were certainly infinitely disposable, as a link with the German authorities.

Driving his employer home that evening, Raymond eyed him in the mirror and decided that for a loyal Frenchman on the eve of his country's defeat he looked altogether too satisfied with life.

The village of Briteau held its breath when, with the signing of the surrender to Germany, France was split into two zones – the Occupied territory, and the new French government's Vichy region. The line of demarcation ran from a point almost twenty miles in from the coast and south of Biarritz, then north east, to Tours and beyond. Briteau was just inside Vichy France, and therefore would not be under German control. But communications with anyone over the line were forbidden, and with a sinking heart Leonie, studying the poster in the village square, saw that the Darnands' house was in the occupied zone.

The château seemed to her that evening to be landlocked, the only way of escape the criss-cross goat tracks and smugglers' paths across the mountains into Spain. The thought made her restless, and before dark she paid a visit to the Fabri house. She found a gathering at the kitchen table, her father's manager and his workers still in their dark blue berets, a small group of ageing, weathered faces in the lamplight, and the scent of Gauloises heavy on the air.

'It is a cold evening, mademoiselle.' Camille Fabri placed a chair for her close to the stove, which gleamed with the even, white heat of the *boules*: the walnuts of coal used for long burning in the district.

241

'I came to ask for a meeting,' Leonie said to Jacques's father. 'Now that we know Briteau is in Vichy, we can plan. I need your help, now that my father . . .'

A man at the table murmured that in Capitaine Paul they had lost *un grand monsieur*, and Camille crossed herself, bowing her head.

Fabri père told Leonie that she had nothing to fear. Word had come from her father's lawyers; they were glad to have her at the big house. Life at Briteau would go on. Not even the Germans would dare put paid to the wine trade. They might have to declare their assets to those clowns in Vichy from time to time, but figures could always be changed a little here and there. And – if he had understood the new regulations – he himself would have a permit to travel if they sold their wine – a very useful item in time of war.

'A wine cask is also a useful item, my friend,' the man who had praised Paul said, smiling.

'Speak for yourself,' Fabri père retorted. 'You're a small man. We could smuggle you over to the enemy if that's what you want.'

'Your son knows more of that than I do,' the man answered.

'Not a word about my son from now on! You understand me? If he keeps silence, he has a reason. And with Capitaine Paul de Byron gone, for France, we do not worry his daughter with such things.'

They gave Leonie a glass of estate wine, and Camille Fabri walked her to the corner of the road. In the gathering dark they stood and watched an eagle dip over the roofs of the château, then soar out of sight, before Camille sighed and turned back into the courtyard and Leonie took the path home, wondering if her father had been alone when he died, and what had happened to Jacques Fabri.

On a bright morning in mid-November, a French civil servant who had been given Henri Massine's name by a

242

colleague mounted the steps to the shipping offices on the quayside at Bordeaux. Of appearance so discreet that it amounted to anonymity, papers in triplicate in his briefcase, he passed the newly appointed guard without difficulty, and found his way to the room where Massine worked, over-looking the river.

The name of their mutual 'friend' was sufficient. Brandy and cigars were produced, the outer door closed against the curiosity of the spinster of a certain age who was 'all the staff one can find these days'.

The visitor explained that he was looking for men he could trust, men who wanted France to settle into a new era, of order and peace. Several prominent citizens had already agreed to join his organization; Monsieur Massine would know their highly respected names. Their purpose was to make quite sure that what the Germans wanted – in pursuit of order – was carried out. A watch was to be kept on potentially rebellious elements. And to give the team some authority with Frenchmen, it was proposed that the '*Milicien*' be composed of compatriots, and even that a uniform be part of the image.

'You are not talking of espionage, I hope?' Henri Massine asked. 'And as for a uniform – I do not think –'

'Everything is to be quite open, I assure you. We are an enforcement body, if you like. There are people to watch, of course. Reports to be made. And at the end of it – real power, the authority to act.'

Henri Massine frowned. 'And what would one get in return?'

'The respect of those in authority should surely be payment in itself?'

'I have no need of payment, my friend. But with my business, I may in time of war need a small favour from time to time.'

'You are not alone. If you care to come to our next meeting, you will find that that is true.' He gave a date, a luncheon in an upper room in one of the city's prestigious restaurants.

When Raymond drove Henri Massine to the first meeting of the *Milicien* he was unaware of the purpose of the luncheon. With his usual amused detachment he watched for a few minutes once his employer had disappeared into the restaurant. Two or three cars drew up and deposited their passengers, all men of middle age, well dressed. He recognized one face as that of a highly respected local man, and another as that of an ex-gaolbird who had turned straight and made a small fortune.

The following Sunday evening he drew Marie-Louise's head on to his shoulder as they lay side by side in bed. She sighed comfortably, secretly thanking God – in whom she had totally unquestioning faith – for keeping him at home.

'The little Fascist I work for has, I think, found friends of his own kind at last,' Raymond said.

'Oh, one could guess his type would have plenty to do under the *sales Boches*.'

'I wish I could say the same for myself. It is hardly to my taste, working for such a man in these times.'

'You are in a strange mood these days, chéri, I know. It is difficult for you. But you will see – there will be a place for you. So long as it does not take you from me, eh?' She would not be the one to tell him that he was too old for service, even had his disability not prevented him from joining the armed forces in the first place.

'All I can say is that Henri Massine should be very careful. We are not all endowed with such unlimited self-interest.' He shifted irritably against the great soft pillows, and got out of bed, dressing hurriedly, while Marie-Louise watched him thoughtfully in the mirror facing the bed.

By the end of the next lunch party the self-recruited members of the *Milicien* were able to congratulate themselves on the clarity of the outline they had prepared for their duties. They were to be in the main an information service, as they saw it – and would operate in the name of good order during the difficult times to come.

Henri Massine was careful to keep his own possible contribution within as wide a brief as possible. In his line of business – and it would be in the interest of the occupying powers to keep a man like himself in business – he could make many contacts. He even had ready-made information, he implied, concerning a potential trouble area in the free zone. Vichy, he felt, should be regarded with unflagging suspicion. There had always been pockets of freethinkers, at all levels, in that alien line of country bordering the Pyrenees. If pressed, he could name names. But being a careful man, as he informed the assembly, he would prefer first to make sure of his facts. 'Alien' was the word he wished his new friends to keep in mind.

Yves Pascal, the curé at Briteau, called at the château the afternoon Henri Massine was hinting to fellow members of the *Milicien* that he had information to lay. Leonie received him in the library, and Violette brought a supply of hot coffee at intervals during their long meeting.

'You are not at war with Germany, mademoiselle. Your compatriots sometimes take a little time over these things. But believe me, those Americans who are getting out of France quickly have their reasons. Anyone speaking the language of the enemy will almost as a matter of course be considered an alien; at worst a potential traitor.'

'But I speak French, Monsieur Pascal! Admit it, I speak French now like –'

'Yes, and it is because you are half French that I think you should keep a very low profile. You will be seen as an object of suspicion.'

'What nonsense.' Leonie shrugged. 'I can have a travel permit, I can move freely from one zone to the other – that must mean I am to be trusted.'

'But are you? Where do your loyalties lie?'

She looked at him steadily. 'I know enough not to answer that, monsieur. Unless you speak first. Vichy is packed with resistance already – resistance to Petain, as well. We are very close to the border here. Will you be keeping a low profile too?'

'I will play the modest village curé, if you will play the modest chatelaine. The survival of this estate should be your first duty.'

'I think we understand each other rather well.' She smiled.

'I think so, too. We must bide our time.'

'I'm so glad my father told you the truth. He did, didn't he?'

'Later that summer he told me much more. You were well loved. It is my duty to watch over you. Now . . . listen.'

He warned Leonie not to be drawn if local people came to her asking her to join in anything that might lead to a breach of the new regulations. She was in a delicate position. A lead might be expected from the landowners, but a plea for help of any kind might conceal a trap. The penalties for breaking the laws now included death, and she should be careful. If she were approached, she should play for time – and bring the names of those who had approached her to him.

She found herself looking at this man who had been so kind to her in a different light. He was perhaps tougher than she had thought, and more complex.

Yves Pascal had more freedom to travel between the two zones than most of his parishioners, as part of the parish lay over the line of demarcation. It happened to include the Darnands' land, and he told Leonie that poor Edith Darnand had been forced to watch her horses taken off by the Germans. Her husband had been away at the time. But Marc Darnand was a man who would fight the Germans with subtlety, and would find ways of avenging his wife's loss.

Promising to act as a messenger between her and her

friends in occupied France, he left, reminding her to be careful.

She remembered the warning a few weeks later, when she was out very early in the meadow looking for a new source of firewood in the bare winter branches beside the stream. About to cross the bridge on her way back into the house, she was suddenly aware of some slight movement in the treeline above the slope of the field. Then everything went very still, and as she made her way to the gate in the wall of the kitchen garden she was quite certain she was being watched.

Late that night Violette was dozing in her chair by the stove when a scratching at the kitchen door made her head jerk upright.

'That dog. One minute he wants to be outside, the next he tries to get back in,' she grumbled, then looked at Leonie and put a finger to her lips. Charlie was curled as usual in a brown and white bundle at their feet.

Leonie rose and moved silently to the door. She listened for a moment that seemed an hour, but heard nothing. Then, as she was about to extinguish the lamp so that she could look out of the window and see if there was a prowler in the grounds, the scratching came again. When she looked round for Violette, seeking guidance, she found her standing by the table, a knife in her right hand.

'Who are you? What do you want?' Leonie called through the door.

'Put out the lights. Let me in. It's Pierre.'

'Oh, *mon dieu*.' Violette crossed herself with her free hand and ran to put out the lamp while Leonie unlocked the door.

The figure that stumbled in from the darkness was in shabby farmworker's clothes and beret, a long scarf wrapped high round his face. As the women closed the door and relit the lamp, Pierre Giraud took off the beret and scarf with gloved hands.

As she looked at her grandson Violette put a hand to her throat, then led him to her chair. The once bright hair was grey and a scar from some recent wound ran down one side of his face. As he drew off his gloves she gave a cry of protest: his hands were gnarled and blackened with frostbite, the fingers curled awkwardly, protectively, inwards to the palm as if against the next blow.

Pierre told them that he had been on the run for months. He had wanted to leave with the British from Dunkerque, but his unit had been badly organized and he lost his chance when he was called to an emergency field hospital. There had been so much to do; then, when the Germans caught up with them, hell broke out. Even the dying were bundled on to trains for Germany. As a doctor he was ordered to care for the German wounded as well as his own countrymen. For victors the Germans were in bad shape, and they wanted to get cleaned up as quickly as they could.

He had found himself in a convoy of Germans making for Paris. There had been a fight between two drunken officers, and Pierre had interceded – hence the scar on his face. But under cover of the brawl that broke out around the two Germans he had made his escape, and walked the length of France in one of the worst winters they had known. Now he wanted to rest before he got out of France altogether. He had made up his mind to join the FFL – the Free French forces – in London.

'But your hands, my poor boy.' Violette reached an arm round his shoulders, fighting back her tears. 'And my God, you are so thin.'

He told her that he knew how to treat his hands, if they would only give him time and shelter until he could organize his escape.

Violette said nothing, but looked at Leonie, an unspoken plea in her eyes.

'There's a room beyond mine,' Leonie said. 'You'll have no lights, and no fire – nothing that might give you away.'

She did not add that she had no idea how he would ever escape, and that the one man she wanted at Briteau at that moment, the man who would have the answer, was Jacques Fabri.

They prepared bedding and food, and installed Pierre in his hiding-place before midnight. He slept immediately, and the two women returned to the warmth of the kitchen to plan their strategy while they had their first runaway Frenchman under their roof.

'*Alors*,' Violette said, 'you have my friendship for ever, little daughter of the de Byrons. And the war has now really come to Briteau.'

CHAPTER FIFTEEN

It took Pierre Giraud seven days to regain his strength and become difficult. His grandmother brought meals to the room beyond Leonie's bedroom; Leonie kept him supplied with books from the library for the short hours of daylight. At night the rooms were kept in total darkness on the top floor, so that any chance traveller should see nothing from the road that might hint at a change in the routine. Even a curtain drawn at dusk might betray Pierre, if the passer-by were a traitor in the making.

'I cannot stay for ever in this room,' Pierre told Violette on the seventh day of his hiding.

'You are lucky not to exchange it for a real prison, Pierre. That is what will happen if you are seen through a window – or in the grounds.'

'I'm not talking about that,' Pierre almost shouted back. 'I've got to get away – right away. It is my duty to get back to the army.'

'And how pray do you propose to do this heroic thing?'

'Perhaps a little supper in the kitchen after dark.' Pierre's voice softened. 'I could discuss this – with Mademoiselle Leonie.'

'No supper downstairs. You won't fool me that way.'

'Well . . . a talk? I am sure she will know what to do . . .'

The morning after the talk with Pierre Leonie announced she was going to the village to barter eggs for candles at the *épicerie*. It was only weeks from Christmas, and she knew Yves Pascal would be visiting his parishioners in the occupied zone – including the Darnands, who she guessed might help her. The time had come to take the curé up on his promise.

Under the layer of straw that nursed the eggs she concealed a box of nuts and crystallized fruits which Violette had hoarded like a squirrel. They were for the Darnands, who she knew would by now be short of such luxuries, if not the necessities, for Christmas.

Wearing the countrywoman's uniform – long dark skirt and thick stockings, hair bound in a cotton scarf – she cycled into the village and parked Mireille's old *vélo* outside the *épicerie*, a familiar figure to whom the villagers had grown accustomed in the months since the defeat of France – and to any stranger the girl on the shaky cycle, basket dangling precariously from a handlebar, would pass unnoticed, except perhaps for the perfect face.

Leaving the shop, her haul of candles safely concealed beneath the straw in the basket, Leonie was at once on her guard. Across the street two women watched stonily from a doorway as a man she could not remember having seen before in the village approached her, raising an expensive velour trilby with a leather-gloved hand. As she made to ride away, the man barred her path, took a magazine from the pocket of his raincoat, and tapped the face on the cover.

'Mademoiselle de Byron? You will pardon this intrusion.' It was more of an order than a polite query. 'I was to call at your house. And then I saw you here. Saw your face. It is a face that was on every poster in Paris last year.'

He spoke in English, with an almost perfect accent.

'I am sorry, monsieur.' Leonie eyed the two women across the road, hoping to signal in some way that she found the stranger's approach unwelcome, even frightening. One of them gave an uneasy smile before they both turned away. 'I don't think I know you.'

She had spoken in French, and the stranger at once switched languages, as if condescending to conduct the interview in whatever tongue she pleased. '*Journaliste*, Mademoiselle de Byron. I am looking for unusual stories, something to boost the morale of our loyal readers. Perhaps the story of a beautiful young American who has not deserted a defeated France.'

'My father was French.' She looked at him coldly. 'And my days of talking to the press – especially those who do not give a name – are over.'

'Naturally. I understand your caution. After all, you have achieved a certain idyllic anonymity here, in that house . . . so close to the mountains.'

She studied him more carefully. He was still of an age for military service, but too well dressed – and too composed – for a man who might be on the run.

'You could be of great help to a good cause in that house, you must know that.' The man spoke softly. 'Could we not meet again, to discuss such a possibility?'

'I have already told you, I do not speak to journalists.' She turned the bicycle sharply, forcing him to step back in the path of a village woman laden with firewood.

The woman hurried by, eyes lowered, and disappeared into the darkness of a house across the street.

'Not a friendly place,' the stranger said evenly. 'More a place perhaps that a man should pass through, very quickly, on his way to the world outside?'

'Why not?' Leonie mounted the saddle. 'You should go very quickly, monsieur. There is only one story in this village: that we have to survive this winter. There is no time for fiction.'

She rode off in the direction of the curé's house, inwardly so shaken that her feet could hardly grip the pedals.

Watching her go, the man signalled to a car that waited in a narrow side street. As he slid into the passenger seat he remarked that old man Massine was wasting his money. *La petite américaine* had nerve. Games like this would not succeed with her. They would need really strong evidence to catch her out – if, that is, she was up to anything at all.

'I reckon she's gone native,' he chuckled as the car swung on to the Biarritz road in the direction of the occupied zone.

'Some Frenchman's going to be very lucky when she goes the whole way.'

Yves Pascal knew at once that his visitor was afraid. While his housekeeper made hot chocolate he got the story out of Leonie, and told her that she had handled the situation well. If her 'journalist' was genuinely interested either in her story, or in the château's potential as a safe house for allies on the run, he would take her rebuff as routine. It would be a good sign from a clandestine operative's point of view, and he would be back.

'What shall I do if he tries again?'

'You do nothing until we check. There are already small pockets of resistance forming just over the demarcation line, and I could get these people checked out.

She promised to do as he said, but in the meantime she had a more immediate problem. Violette's grandson was in hiding at the château, and wanted to join the Free French forces in London.

The curé shook his head, popping a crystallized fruit into his mouth. 'Forgive me – I think better when I am eating. I promise you, poor Edith Darnand will get the rest of the box! Now, as for our young Pierre, he will have to learn to be patient.'

'But he has run out of patience already.'

'He must know we can do nothing for some weeks. No one can cross into Spain in these snows.'

'He will never wait that long.'

'He grew up in this region; he knows the truth. And he has no choice. But I really do not see his problem, chère mademoiselle. Imprisoned for the winter in a great house with the best cook and the most beautiful young woman in the village. Tell him that much careful planning is needed. You learned for yourself this morning that we may be watched. There are many people interested in this region.'

He could not divulge that from more than one village

253

housewife's confession down the years he had learned just who might be approached if a guide was needed through what for generations had been the secret network of smugglers' paths across the mountains into Spain.

And in Marcel Darnand he had had an ally since the day the Germans moved across the south-west of France to the sea.

From that day, six months before, Marc and Edith Darnand had turned their home into a rendezvous for men who had held key positions in government, either locally or in Paris, and saw it as their duty to stay on in France. With the knowledge and approval of the Free French government now based in London under the leadership of Charles de Gaulle, they made a great show of leaving to join their compatriots in England, but in reality went to earth in France.

They were concerned with amassing information on German movements and supplying London with the facts. They were to organize escape routes for servicemen on the run, both British and French. They were to sabotage the German machine with every method at their disposal.

With his special knowledge of the region, Marcel Darnand was at the head of the group working on lines of escape. On the night he made his first radio contact with his opposite number in London he called Edith excitedly into the secret wireless room above their stables.

'Edith! Listen! Don't we know this voice?'

Edith listened, frowning, shaking her head as the line crackled and almost faded. Then it revived, and the voice of an Englishman asked if it had been a good summer at the château nearby? And had a certain young American girl ever returned? Edith gripped his arm. 'Denholm!'

Her husband put a finger to her lips, and asked again for the code name by which he could be certain the transmission was genuine. It came back, and he visibly relaxed. Yes, he told the caller, the girl had returned. Something told him, from the knowledge he had gained of Denholm Collins's

254

character when their friendship had ripened two years before, that the voice might sound nostalgic but behind the question would be a serious motive. Why else would London have risked even the casual mention of a girl who would be at once under suspicion if the Germans thought the Free French even knew of her existence?

In his London office, in an elegant Georgian house five minutes' walk from Hyde Park, Denholm Collins leaned back in his chair and looked out on to the black skeletons of the plane trees in the square which had become his home since the day war had been declared. He had always known that his health would mean he could not fight, but with his special knowledge of France and his fluent French he had been able to join Intelligence. But now, as he thought of the long summer and the harvest at Briteau – and the girl Leonie – he hated his job. Always choosing other recruits to go into France, always planning their routes of escape through the hills he loved. It took a very special breed to carry out the work planned from the small, anonymous London office – a breed to which Denholm would have belonged himself had it not been for his health. It was the recognition of this side of his nature in another that had drawn him to Leonie de Byron. He had not forgotten her spirit, and the way she belonged so quickly in a place where strangers were rarely, if ever, accepted. Marcel Darnand had been right when he assumed that something rather more than nostalgia lay behind Denholm's query. Leonie had all the qualities Denholm Collins looked for in his recruits.

It was after Christmas, as the thaw in the north of France began, that the Germans began to move their prisoners. For six months the thousands of French soldiers who had not got away had been herded in makeshift camps, or lay forgotten, intentionally starved in hundreds of cases, in barracks almost destroyed by the German advance. The survivors, as spring came, were of some interest. But if they were to be fed, they must work.

Jacques Fabri found himself locked in a train compartment meant for eight passengers with twenty fellow prisoners, on their way to a Polish labour camp notorious for the short life of its inhabitants, on a spring morning which was made for a day in the mountains where he had been born. He had a place against a window, his emaciated face inches from the glass that reflected his expressionless eyes, long unkempt hair, tight lips. The windows were locked. There was no smoking. There were no cigarettes. But he had grown used to that. Used to everything but imprisonment, and anger.

The train crawled, taking a complicated route, stopping sporadically to pick up small groups of German officers in their long grey coats, a handful of prisoners added each time to the already packed human cargo. It was nightfall as they steamed into what was apparently a main junction. All means of identification had been removed from the station platforms, but one of the men in Jacques's carriage said he was sure it was Nancy. He had been there once as boy, en route from his native Alsace for a stay with relatives in Paris.

'God forbid that we end up in Alsace,' a Parisian boy growled from his perch on the luggage rack. 'There are limits.'

'Don't worry,' the Alsatian grinned back. 'We wouldn't have your kind. It's Poland for us all.'

'Then it's *fini*,' the Parisian said, turning to the wall of the carriage.

Jacques was silent, scanning the platform for some sign, for anything that might show a way of escape. In spite of the black-out the station was curiously alive, as alive as on any ordinary day in peace-time. His eyes followed a girl who hurried to the exit with a small boy, probably out after curfew and in fear of her life if she was. A porter, as old as time, staggered past carrying luggage for the young German officer who swaggered after him. Desperately, Jacques tried to catch the old man's eye, but he too seemed to go in fear, eyes blind to anything but the next safe step.

Involuntarily, Jacques's hand had reached up to the top of the window frame as he sought the old man's attention, and it rested there briefly before sliding helplessly down the glass, fingers making a line in the thick condensation of the prisoners' breath. But not before they had touched the catch at the top of the window, and found that it gave to the touch.

An hour after the train had left Nancy, just before the German border, Jacques's thin body was pushed through the carriage window by his fellow prisoners, behind a human screen. The others whispered goodbyes into the void as Jacques fell from the slow-moving train, and rolled down the embankment into freedom. By the time they reached the German border three others had followed. The other prisoners in the compartment were, as they had known they would be, shot where they sat when the first guards came round to inspect at the border.

The long walk south from Alsace began, and continued, at night. The Communists Jacques had talked with in the months as a prisoner had supplied numerous addresses of sympathizers who were now amongst the ranks of the growing resistance movement. The long list of 'safe' houses he needed for his journey to Briteau was engraved on his memory. He stayed only one day at each, then walked on. He accepted food, disguises, shoes as the last pair wore out. He walked as he had so often walked into Spain – surefooted, eyes keen in the dark, no thought but for his destination. He kept, as soon as he could, to the Vichy zone – although even that could be dangerous for a Communist or a resistance fighter, so sure was Petain that only he could save France, and anyone not toeing his line was better destroyed.

But on the last stage of his journey, needing to be sure of how things stood at Briteau, he turned into the occupied zone and made for the last 'safe' house on his list of contacts. The home of Marcel and Edith Darnand.

They sheltered him for two days, breaking his rule, but

now that he was almost safe he was in no hurry to move on the first night. He wanted, too, to arrive at the château in good shape. The peasant boy still liked to make a good impression. No one at Briteau was to guess that the last six months had been a living hell; the walk to freedom had in many ways restored him to his old arrogant self.

The Darnands did not take him straight away to the secret room above the stables. They had learned to be more cautious than that. But they listened avidly when he told them of his own plan: to set up a '*réseau*' in the free zone, and run an escape route into Spain.

'It is rather a coincidence,' Marcel said slowly at last. 'We are in touch with London. With the same idea . . .'

'London!' Jacques ran an impatient hand through his hair. 'London can give me a radio, that is all. We have no time for their complications. All that matters is the choice of local workers, and our knowledge of the mountains.'

'And a trained operator? Have you thought?'

'That too.' Jacques shrugged. 'And a base. I have chosen my base.'

'Not your parents' place?' Edith looked anxious. 'There are penalties for discovery, even for the old.'

'No,' Jacques said. 'I intend to use the château.'

'Then you don't know who lives there now? Did you not hear that Paul de Byron was killed – in the northern campaign?'

'I had heard he was dead,' Jacques said coldly. 'I hope that Henri Massine has not moved in on the estate.'

'Mireille is in Canada, with her grandmother. The grandfather struts about in Bordeaux as a *Milicien*, and we are watching him, believe me,' Marcel answered.

'Then who runs things at Briteau.'

'The American girl,' Edith said. 'She refused to leave France.'

'Really?' Jacques Fabri's expression did not change.

'Yves Pascal keeps contact with her. You can trust him to help,' Marcel told him.

258

'Since when did I have to trust a priest?'

'You will find him invaluable. He has been waiting for the thaw to get one man out already.'

'Oh? From where?'

'From the château, into Spain. You will see tomorrow.'

Jacques began his walk to Briteau at midnight, and at dawn waited in the shelter of the bridge over the stream at the back of the house, watching for some sign of activity. There was a slit of light, quickly gone, as the kitchen door opened and shut and a dog barked. Then a brown and white dog nosed through the garden gate, and began to run towards him. As Charlie reached the bridge he began to bark again, then at a soft call from Jacques slid down the bank of the stream and found him.

His cover broken, Jacques moved fast, skirting the field and the garden wall before making for the kitchen door, Charlie trotting meekly at his side.

It was Violette who opened the door, grumbling at the mud on Charlie's paws, then staring, white-faced, at the man who pushed past her and held her by one wrist, his other hand over her mouth.

'Say nothing. Make some coffee. There is nothing to fear from me. Now – if I release you, you will not cry out?'

She shook her head, and as he freed her whispered angrily that he would wake the house, and why had he not gone to his poor mother?

'My mother is to hear nothing,' he said in a low voice. 'It is too dangerous for her to know that I have escaped. You understand? Whom will we wake? Who else is here, apart from the American girl?'

'If you harm her, Jacques Fabri –' Violette glared at him.

'Violette' – he put an arm round her – 'make the coffee. I know you have someone else here. I have come to help. You will see.'

*

259

It was the smell of the coffee that brought Pierre Giraud into Leonie's room. He apologized for waking her, and told her he would fetch her *café au lait* if she wished. She reminded him that he was not allowed downstairs, and he grinned.

'I thought it was so early I would catch you off your guard. I don't know where my grandmother gets that coffee, but it smells so good.'

'It is very early, you're right.' Leonie came fully awake, and shivered, pulling on a robe. 'Wait here.'

She stood quite still for a second outside the swing door into the kitchen, but hearing nothing unusual went in quickly, blinking in the light of the lamp Violette had set in the centre of the table. Beyond the light, a man sat at the table in the shadows. As she walked towards him, he stood.

She thought he had hardly changed. He was very thin, but it was a strong, spare body beneath the dark overalls he wore. The eyes were as compelling, and as she held out her hand a glimmer of a smile lit the dark face briefly.

'Jacques! I can't believe it's you. How did you get here? What happened?'

'Too much,' Violette broke in. 'He brings us trouble, I swear it. He's on the run, like half of France. We want no trouble here.'

'I can help,' Jacques said as Leonie sat beside him. 'I have come from your friends, the Darnands. They tell me the priest, Pascal, will confirm it if you want.'

'Then you know that the curé is helping us? That we have a problem?'

'Yes, he knows about my grandson,' Violette scowled. 'Now we have two of them to hide before they get out of this poor country of ours.'

'That's not so.' Jacques shook his head. 'I will not be getting out. But I will be helping others. And I plan to use this house.'

Violette threw up her hands. 'So, the Communists have at

last found an excuse to take over the big houses.'

'You will need permission,' Leonie added. 'I'm not the only one who is involved, Jacques. I am here on trust. My sister's future is here. The château must not be put at risk.'

'If France stays under the Nazis you'll lose this place anyway. Don't you know what they're up to? They throw people out of their homes. They're taking over the best places in Paris.'

Leonie nodded. A letter had reached her from Tante Berthe through Marseilles the week before. A German couple had discovered that the apartment above was empty, and had taken out a twenty-five year lease. Jeannine had ways of making their life difficult: there was now never a light on the stairs, and the water seemed to go off at least once a day – usually while the new tenants were preparing their dinner. But the Germans seemed very patient; too patient.

'Look,' Jacques persisted. 'Let me prove how this whole thing would work. Violette here may not trust me, but if I get her beloved Pierre to safety – what do you say?'

They both looked at Violette, who sighed and sat heavily in her chair. 'Pierre's one wish is to fight. To get to London. Half his unit got away with the British at Dunkerque. He'll not wait now that the thaw has come.'

'Then let's get him away. I have it all planned. Leonie –' He touched her hand. It was the first time he had called her by her name in all the three years since she had come to Briteau. 'I'm sorry about your father. My own father must be desolate.'

'Thank you. No one can believe it. But we have to go on. He would have wished it.'

'And don't you think he would have wished his home to be used to help other fighting men? To plan for freedom – to fight back?'

She knew he was right.

It took Jacques three days to make contact with a courier

261

who would guide them to the cave that was to become the halfway mark on the route into Spain. Jacques himself knew the cave from the days when he had escorted the anti-Franco brigade over the Pyrenees and into France. But he wanted Leonie to become acquainted with the route, and to have an escort. There would be many times, he explained, when he would be away.

The courier appeared at the kitchen door in full daylight, suddenly materializing on the path amongst the few hens Violette allowed out at a time. The moment she saw him Violette rushed into the garden, saying no gypsy would get her chickens now that there was a war on.

He stood his ground, looking up into her face with wide green eyes in a wizened face. She noted the thick, dark head of hair and the thin brown limbs. The boy's feet were bare. He was no more than ten years old.

'My name is Manuel,' he said. He had an accent she recognized as that of a family of *gitanes* who had once helped with the harvest. 'I am hungry.'

They left before midnight, taking turns to cross to the treeline above the meadow one by one, leaving fifteen minutes between each journey. Once in the shelter of the trees they walked in single file, the boy leading the way, a slight, shadowy figure wrapped now in an old coat and wearing boots which Violette had found amongst a store of discarded clothes that had belonged to Pierre as a boy.

Pierre knew the paths for the first hour. Then he and Leonie stumbled after Jacques's silhouette, the boy still in front, until the trees thinned and they came to a long exposed slope of grey rock.

They skirted the stone, keeping close to each other, Pierre bringing up the rear and looking back to make sure they had not been followed. Leonie walked easily, her long legs covering the ground as if she had been born to climbing. But they had all begun to tire when Jacques called a halt, and

262

informed them that they were less than an hour from the cave. From there Pierre would go on alone.

'Not alone, monsieur,' Manuel said. 'You forget that I go as far as the plain. And I wait for the car. I wait until Monsieur Pierre is in the car.'

'Do you never go home, Manuel?' Leonie asked.

Jacques gave her a warning look.

'Our caravan was home,' Manuel said in a matter-of-fact tone. 'Then the Nazis took my parents. And our horses. I stayed under the caravan for three days. Then I ran to Luis!'

Luis was the great bear of a Spaniard who waited in the cave for them, a meal of sausage and harsh red wine laid out on a flat stone, the air heavy with the scent of cheap cigars and oil. While they ate, he and Jacques talked quickly: of future plans, methods of making contact, and the numbers of men they could safely shift on each excursion over the mountains. At the back of the cave was stacked a pile of coloured blankets. A shelf of rock housed several rows of bottles. There was only the light from a single candle, deep in the cave, and its mouth was closed by a further blanket, the colour of the rock.

Money changed hands openly. Jacques had already received funds from the Darnands. He and Luis spoke in a Spanish patois and laughed frequently, the quiet laugh of conspirators, or gamblers, who knew each other well.

They slept for an hour before Luis said it was time for them all to go down to the lowland: Pierre with Manuel on into Spain; Jacques Fabri and his beautiful companion back where they came from.

'You will see my companion maybe other times,' Jacques said in Spanish. 'And I am glad you think she is beautiful. Hands off, amigo.'

Luis raised his fifth glass of wine. 'Sorry there's no coffee. I do not risk fire.'

'Oh, we have passed other nights in the mountains,'

Jacques said in French. 'N'est-ce pas, Leonie?'

'It was not so cold. And there were young eagles to watch,' she replied, including Pierre in her smile.

'I remember those eagles,' Pierre said. 'It was so long ago. Go to see them for me, this summer?' He held out his arms, and she stood in his embrace, too sad to answer.

'Look after my grandmother?' Pierre let her go and stepped back.

'It's the other way round,' she said. 'But yes, I'll not let her come to harm.'

They watched Manuel lead the way to a rise of ground where a tongue of thin ice still sprawled on the frozen grass. The boy and the man climbed for ten minutes, then disappeared.

'I'm glad it will be light for getting back,' Leonie said as she turned away, hugging her jacket tightly about her.

Luis gave a short laugh. 'That is one risk you never take. You go back into France by night. Today you rest.'

He produced two pillows from under the pile of blankets and threw them at her feet. Then, taking a hunting rifle propped at the mouth of the cave, he pushed past the curtain. 'Sleep well.'

They lay down side by side, inches apart, eyes on the ceiling of rock above their heads. Suddenly afraid of the long wait in the closed space, she asked Jacques if there were more candles.

'It was different in the pine woods. I don't know why, but I wasn't afraid then.'

'It was summer.' Jacques propped himself on an elbow and looked down at her. 'And this is a first run into danger. A practice run, but real.'

It was the first time since Erich Mannheim had raped her that a man had come so close to her. She remembered the day she and Tony had become lovers, and the memory cut into her like a knife. There had been no word from New York for months.

She looked up into Jacques's face, and thought that he

264

could be as ruthless as the mountains they had just challenged.

'I'm exhausted,' she said.

'Then sleep.'

It was Yves Pascal who delivered the radio transmitter Marcel Darnand had obtained for use at the château. He brought it to the house in broad daylight, concealed in the back of a ramshackle farm cart in which four children from the village sat, hands gripping the sides, eyes fixed solemnly on Leonie as she stood in the drive to receive them.

'Nature study.' The curé gestured to his passengers. 'It is Saturday, and a holiday. We shall tie this brave and somewhat ailing horse in the stables and go to see your gardens.'

As the children dispersed the curé helped Leonie carry the equipment to her rooms. The transmitter was fitted into a suitcase which would go on the shelf inside the chimney of the annexe.

They paused on the first landing, Yves Pascal patting his stomach and catching his breath. 'But I am thinner than when we first met, eh? We are all thinner, for that matter.'

'You were so kind to me, that first Sunday at church.'

'Your father had prepared me well. He was not the most pliant of my flock, but that rigidity concealed much feeling. There were many regrets. You should know that he loved your mother sincerely.'

She thanked him, thinking that this great-hearted man should have been the one to lay her father's body to rest in the quiet churchyard at Briteau, had the Germans not left the French dead to rot in their wake.

That evening Jacques left the hiding-place he had organized for himself on his arrival, in the store-room above the deserted stables, and listened to the first of the twice-nightly transmissions from London. Leonie knew that when he got the 'pianist' he wanted she would probably have to share her rooms so that the operator could stay safely in hiding. But for some reason London was stalling.

One early-evening broadcast came through just as Jacques had returned from a trip into the occupied zone. He hurried upstairs and listened alone, coming down to the kitchen later to insist that Leonie join him for the second, late-night confirmation of the messages for the day.

Violette had grown more tolerant of Jacques's presence since he had got Pierre out of France, but she grumbled softly that it was late and no good would come of these contacts with the outside world.

'If your poor mother knew that you were here, only a mile from the house! How can you leave her thinking you are dead?'

'She knows I am safe; I sent word only days ago. It is best for both my parents that they know nothing more than that.'

Leonie decided not to come down again that night; she could see that Violette was tired, moving heavily as she damped down the stove and extinguished the lamps before opening the door into the garden and calling to Charlie, who had now been promoted to spending his nights on the foot of her bed.

The signal from London came through promptly, and Jacques made Leonie put on the headphones as a series of coded messages followed. Then a voice, speaking in French, made Leonie frown in half-recognition. She waited, sensing Jacques's eyes on her.

'I know this man,' she said quickly. 'He was tutor to Mireille, that first summer.'

'And he remembers you.' Jacques watched her keenly as she listened to the perfect French on the line.

Denholm Collins talked in veiled language to identify himself to her. He told her that a new player was needed for a Truth Game, that all good little French girls had to finish their Baccalaureat, that all eagles had to leave the nest.

266

The transmission over, she took off the headset, shaking her hair free.

'He proved his identity to you?' Jacques began to dismantle the transmitter and return it to its hiding-place.

'Yes. In funny little ways. Very typical of him.'

'He wants you in London, little American. I heard the details today, from your friends the Darnands. They have watched you for a long time now, and they are not going to take no for an answer.'

He told her that Denholm Collins had been in touch with Marcel Darnand ever since the fall of France, and was seeking people who knew the region whom he could train to organize a *réseau* – a resistance unit. 'In our case, escape routes, of course. Collins wants to train you. It would mean that you would need to hide no one else at Briteau – you could run the line, the radio, everything, from here yourself.'

'But I would have to leave here, Jacques! It's out of the question. Who would take care of things? How would my absence look in the village? Everyone's used to me now.'

'It might be a good thing. Violette could announce that your family – your other family – have sent for you. That there is work for you – in Paris, in New York, *n'importe*.'

'My other family?' Leonie sat on the bed, her face bleak at the thought of Zoe and Erich in Switzerland. It was months since the last call from her mother. They had each chosen their way of life for the duration of the war, and their paths were unlikely to cross.

'Everyone knows that Briteau needs money,' Jacques persisted. 'They will understand that you have to work.'

'That's not really true any more, Jacques. And it is *I* who need Briteau.'

'Then is it not true that you loved your father? That you love his memory? He would want this of you. I know it. And you are uniquely able to do this work. There are women all over France who would give anything for such a chance.'

'How would I go?'

'First, with Manuel, to Luis. Then the boy would take you

on into Spain. Car to Lisbon. A plane waiting. London wants you at once.'

'I'd never make it.' She looked round the familiar room, as if seeking some excuse to stay.

'Then I have been wrong about you all this time. Collins too is wrong. Do not waste our time, little American. We thought you had become enough of a Frenchwoman to welcome this offer.'

He stood, hands on hips, looking down at her. She was aware of the old tug of attraction between them.

He was right, of course, about her feelings for her father. Even more so now that she had learned from Yves Pascal that Paul de Byron had nursed such remorse for the past. And loved her mother once.

Then, as if from nowhere, an image of Max Heller came into her mind. Max playing sublimely in the small room in Paris that was now silent – and as desolate as the battle lines where Paul had died.

'I'll go.'

Jacques stepped towards her, and took her fiercely in his arms. She responded without thinking, abandoning herself to her decision and to his kisses as part of the same thing.

'I always knew we would be lovers. One day.' Jacques lay smoking beside her some hours later in the dark. She nodded, remembering the first time she had seen him, and the way he had smiled up at the windows of the room where they had just made love. The long night with Jacques had done much to cleanse her of the brutal rape in Paris. Everything about him was in total contrast to Erich Mannheim.

But as she drifted into sleep it was Tony she thought about, and the way he had made love to her in the same bed, the last time perhaps they would ever meet. She wondered what Tony would think of her decision, and whether he would see it as a compounding of war. She was glad that she did not have to talk it through with him, even though she knew that her training in England was to equip her to protect all she held most dear. Tony could be persuasive. He was capable, too, of rejecting her if she went against his principles. She would have liked to write to New York. But from now on she was bound by laws of secrecy, for there were to be many other people whom she must protect by her discretion.

She moved into Jacques's arms at dawn, and they made love with an obsessive seeking of each other's bodies. It was over very quickly, and Jacques got up at once, dressing without looking at her. She knew then that he would not come to her again before she left for England. He had made his imprint, like some wild creature marking out its territory – and imbued in her the will to fight whether or not they were to meet again.

A week later she boarded a plane in Lisbon, and found it already crowded with an ill-assorted group of diplomats, children, and French refugees. The journey was noisy, the cabin airless. The children were sick in turn. An old Frenchman wrapped in a blanket in the bucket seat beside her snored his way to freedom.

A makeshift, windswept airstrip waited for them in the flat fields of East Anglia like some wide street going nowhere. She climbed stiffly out of the plane and walked quickly, head down, in a heavy autumnal downpour – rain tinged with sleet – so that it was not until she reached the lee of the airport's single hangar that she saw a man in civilian clothes waving, thin sandy hair lifted by the wind – the wry smile on the clever face exactly as she remembered.

'Denholm! How nice to see you.'

'Good trip?' He took her arm, looking round for luggage. He might have been meeting her from a day's shopping in Paris.

She nodded, suddenly formal, then smiled. 'No, it was terrible. Things can't get worse, can they?'

'Sorry about the weather.' He looked up at the sky,

269

unfurling a large black umbrella, and drew her into its shelter. 'At least you can be sure you've landed in the right country.'

The firm hand on her arm reassured her, and she walked with him to a waiting black limousine. The uniformed chauffeur nodded without speaking as she took her place beside Denholm in the back of the car, and she had an impression of total professional discretion.

'Two years since we met,' Denholm said as they skirted the airstrip and turned on to the main London road. 'And now I'm taking you to another country house. Not as ancient as Briteau. Perhaps as comfortable.'

'You should try it now,' she said. 'Violette's cooking is still a miracle. But we're short of fuel.'

'Where you're going to, my girl, you're going to be far too busy to feel the cold.'

CHAPTER SIXTEEN

It was the glimpse of a giant multi-striped golfing umbrella propped in a corner of a bar popular with the Free French forces in London that sent Leonie's thoughts sharply back to the days at the Collège Madeleine. Sarah Bentley had carried her St Andrew's emblem like a trophy through a whole rainy Paris season. Now, after weeks of combat-training in a sea of mud, Leonie had begun to accept the need for the ubiquitous British brolly. It was raining heavily still, on the first leave Denholm had allowed her for weeks.

He had met her at Waterloo after her cramped journey in the crowded, blue-lit train from the country house where a selection of new recruits for the French Resistance lived and worked. Her own training was almost complete, and she had grown used to a grinding fifteen-hour day, little relaxation, endless briefing over endless English tea in the great hall scattered with deep leather sofas, where everyone had to speak French.

She had trained as a radio operator, but the rest of a combatant's schooling went with it, and she was fitter, physically more disciplined, than she had ever been.

Over their first drink Denholm told her that he had good news. She asked if it meant that she would soon be able to get back to Briteau. They spoke in low voices, although the hubbub of service personnel off duty around them ensured that they would not be overheard.

'It's tied in with that.' Denholm smiled. 'You're not going to have to make a jump. We've found a nice little patch north of your place. A Lysander can get down and turn in three minutes if you're a good girl and get out fast.'

She leaned back in her chair, closing her eyes. 'I was dreading it.'

'Now you can decide where you want to eat.' Denholm patted her hand.

As he went to collect more drinks she looked about her. The bar was a venue for every nationality, every uniform in Europe, with a predominance of French and Poles. She wondered how soon the Americans would crowd into London as well now that Pearl Harbor had brought them into the war. Suddenly she wanted more than anything to be back at Briteau in time for Christmas.

As Denholm manoeuvred his way back to their table, a woman in the heavy dark blue tunic and wide trousers of the London Ambulance Service turned away from the bar. Leonie found herself staring across the room into the bright, questioning eyes of Sarah Bentley.

Excusing herself to the man in naval uniform with her, Sarah wove her way quickly towards Leonie, her arms outstretched. They embraced, both on the verge of tears, Sarah saying she had made up her mind they were never going to see each other again.

'And what on earth are you doing in London?' The question included Denholm, and she eyed his civilian clothing. Leonie introduced him as a friend who had known her father, and added that she was just looking around and making up her mind what to do now that America had come into the war.

'If you choose to go back to New York you'll find Tony Shaw having a very quiet time – very low profile. I have friends out there who say he's just disappeared.'

'I guess he would,' Leonie said shortly. 'But it's Max Heller I can't get out of my mind. Did you ever hear anything?'

'Rumours. He got to Poland. End of story.'

Denholm invited Sarah to join them, and Leonie gathered he had decided they could trust her. But she pleaded a late-night rosta. She was living across the park, alone apart from

272

two servants in the old house her parents had inherited in Belgravia. Her current true love was in the Navy, and she had not seen him for six months. Her nanny had refused to leave London, and lived in the attic, declining to come down even in the worst air raids.

'I rattle about in the house when I'm off duty,' she said ruefully. 'I'd wish you'd come to supper one night. Cold meatless sausages and Nanny's substitute banana blanc-mange, I expect, but do come.'

Leonie looked at Denholm, neither answering.

'I see.' Sarah looked serious, obviously knowing better than to press the invitation. 'I must say I did wonder what brought you here.'

'Sarah —' Leonie hesitated. 'If you do come across any of the others . . . from Bordeaux . . .'

'I haven't seen you? Of course. But if you don't contact me when all this is over I'll never forgive you. The Humes will want to know what happens to you. Did you hear that the Germans took their club? You really ought to do something about it.' Her voice sank to a whisper, and her eyes shone. 'Leonie de Byron, you'd make the perfect Resistance heroine.'

'Is that your umbrella over there? I thought I recognized it.' Leonie changed the subject deliberately, wondering what Sarah would think if she knew that her old friend from the Collège Madeleine had recently learned how to murder a man with her bare hands.

Sarah grinned. 'I must take it home before it ruins the carpets. Must go.' They hugged each other, and Denholm stood to shake Sarah's hand.

'See you in Paris?' she said as she passed their table moments later, followed by the naval officer, and retrieved the striped umbrella from its corner.

The Lysander carried three Frenchmen, who were to join a *réseau* in the Biarritz area, and Leonie. She sat facing the grim-faced silent men on the floor of the plane, her body tense with the throbbing of the engine and the knowledge that she was less than an hour from seeing Jacques Fabri again as they crossed the west coast of France.

Everything went as Denholm had planned. They touched down in a triangle of pale flares and turned fast, the passengers jumping clear. As the plane took off again several figures slipped from the shadows at the edge of the field to extinguish the landing lights. Then the three men who had flown in ran blindly, crouching low, for the shelter of the high hedge that separated them from the road.

The whole operation took three minutes, and as the Lysander disappeared into low cloud Leonie found herself alone in a frightening, silent dark. The others had vanished as if they had never existed.

Her instructions were that Jacques would take her to Briteau. She had learned to obey orders recently, and knew that whatever her fears she should wait some time before it became necessary to take things into her own hands.

It was half an hour before she heard the soft whirr of cycle wheels on the road. Her eyes accustomed to the night, she made out the figure of a man trailing a second bicycle alongside his own. She stood back, out of sight; then as the cyclist reached her hiding-place he paused, lighting a cigarette. She saw in the light of the match that it was Jacques, and stepped out into the road.

'Ah,' he said in a matter-of-fact tone, 'it's you. Not bad.' But the kiss with which he greeted her told her that he had missed her.

Twelve hours later she woke from a heavy sleep to find Violette at the door of her bedroom, tray in hand. She stretched her limbs, remembering the reunion with Jacques the night before. He had left her bed before daybreak, but while he was with her neither had slept.

'Welcome home,' Violette said primly, placing the tray on

the bedside table. 'I heard so little last night. You have learned to come and go in silence, eh?' Although she tolerated Jacques Fabri for his part in saving her grandson she had made it clear that she could not be expected to tolerate the affair with Leonie.

Leonie pulled on a robe and got out of bed, shivering, embracing her. 'It's so good to be back. What news is there? And how are things in the village?'

Violette said that her friends the Fabris faced Christmas in better spirits, as their son had called on them a week before, late at night. But there was no sign of Monsieur Jacques this morning. The stables were deserted. She must warn her that her co-worker was often absent these days, and always without explanation.

'He'll contact us if it is necessary.' Leonie was reassuring herself as much as Violette. 'We are in a business that means we are always in hiding.'

'You cannot hide from all of us for ever, mon enfant. But if the village gets to know that you are back they will either keep it to themselves, for your sake, or give you away – for theirs. So let us hope the Germans stay on their side of the demarcation line for the rest of the war.'

Violette's grasp of the local attitude was sound. With America now in the war Leonie's position was more dangerous, and Jacques's unexplained absence so soon after their impassioned reunion meant that she went into her isolation with some apprehension and a sense of loneliness.

By Christmas the radio transmissions, contacts with the *réseau* run by the Darnands in the occupied zone, and receipt of information – mainly from Yves Pascal – to forward to London had become second nature. But the two women at Briteau lived on a razor's edge, Leonie spending her days almost entirely in her rooms.

The routine suddenly lightened two days before Christmas, with the arrival of a crumpled, rainsoaked letter

275

from Mireille. It had come via Marseilles, and was addressed to Violette. There were no references to Paul's death, or to Leonie, and they took it as a sign that she was quite aware of the dangers she could bring down on them if the letter had been intercepted. She wrote about her grandmother, who was so much better away from Bordeaux, and of her first year at medical school with French-speaking Canadians. She asked after Charlie, and said one day they would walk in the fields again and fly her kite.

Violette wept as she read the letter, and tucked it into the pocket of her overall to read, with more tears, when she was alone that night.

On Christmas Eve they decorated the stove with a sabot on each side brimming with fruits which Violette had hoarded from the summer. To avoid suspicion they had agreed that Violette should spend Christmas Day with the Fabris. Leonie would spend a normal day at her post. It was the first Christmas she would ever have spent alone, and she watched from the half-open front doorway as Violette slipped her way down the drive on the ridges of frozen snow that marked the path.

The telephone rang before Violette was out of sight, and she turned quickly away, making for the library, unsure whether or not to answer.

The phone seemed to scream into the silence. She let it ring. When it stopped she drew the heavy library curtains against the endless day, and was lighting the fire when the phone rang again.

She lifted the receiver, but did not speak. At the other end, on a crackling line, Tante Berthe wished her a *bon Noël*. 'Do not speak, ma chère, if you find it difficult. My thoughts are with you. And I have a message. A Swiss friend of your mother has been in Paris. They still wait for you in Zurich. If things get bad, it is there you must go.'

'But all is well here, Tante. You must believe me. *Bon Noël.* Are you well? And Paris?'

The line went dead.

She stood looking down at the phone, wondering whether she dared make a forbidden call to Paris. Deciding it was too dangerous, she went to the kitchen and set a tray with wine and crystal glasses. She took it back to the library and sat by the fire, drinking to her absent family. Her mother and Tante Berthe and Mireille suddenly felt very close to her, and she shrugged off the thought that it was Erich Mannheim who had played a part in bringing them together. She was thinking of Erich again, and of the audacity of a man who seemed to be able to move freely across any frontier at a time when movement was so restricted, when Charlie gave a short, warning bark and ran into the hall.

Moments later there was a knock at the front door, then silence. She stood in the library doorway as Charlie made for the door and began to scratch and whine. To her horror she saw that she had left it slightly open when Tante Berthe had telephoned, and as Charlie persevered it swung slowly inwards, to reveal a middle-aged man in civilian clothes, of military bearing, gaunt face, and thin frame.

'I apologize if I have frightened you, mademoiselle.' He raised his hat, speaking in French. 'I believe I am speaking to the daughter of the house?'

'The daughter of the house is in Canada, monsieur.' Leonie walked quickly towards him, her training telling her that she had time to close the door in his face before he could question her further.

'There is no need to fear me,' the man said gently. 'You are, I am sure, the first child. I know that because your father told me about you. The night before he was killed.'

Leonie looked at him carefully. The eyes were frank, even friendly, the man's bearing so reminiscent of her father that her guard automatically went down as he waited for her to answer.

'Your name? And are you alone?' She tried to keep any warmth from her voice.

'I got here with help from your friends the Darnands.'

She looked down at his shoes, and saw that they were hardly wet from the snow.

277

'So someone is still running a car?'

'My work in the Red Cross gives me some freedom, many helpers.'

She decided to hear what he had to say rather than leave the door open any longer, as they were visible from the drive. Inviting him into the library, she bent to revive the fire, thinking fast as she realized that the visitor had still not given his name.

'Perhaps you will take a glass of wine? It is Christmas,' she said. 'And it's sad not to be with one's family.'

'My family – what is left of it – is in Paris.'

'And you say you were with my father? Before he died?'

'I ran an ambulance unit on that front. Sadly, we were moved on that night. I never saw him again, but I promised myself that if ever I were near his home I would seek out the daughter he cherished so much.'

'I did not think my father talked of such things.'

'My dear mademoiselle, you are suspicious of me still, I can see. Believe me, men on the battlefield do not maintain the barriers they might keep between themselves and others in normal life.'

She was struck by the fact that it was not the first time people had talked of the rigidity she had found so hard to breach in her father being cast aside. And each time he had told another man of her existence. Her eyes filled with tears at the thought that his true feelings for her had to reach her from beyond the grave.

'And I have other reasons for coming here.' He put down his glass, and eyed her carefully. 'Things to say. Perhaps things that our friends the Darnands might not bring themselves to tell you.'

'I would find it easier to listen if you had told me your name.' Her feelings again under control, she made up her mind to make sure that she let him go no further until she was reasonably certain he was not dangerous.

He laughed quietly, and produced a set of papers from an inner pocket. 'You will see that I am a Red Cross worker. It is that which gives me mobility between the zones. But I do not abuse the privilege. The Nazis are perfectly capable of harassment of even a bona fide neutral. You must know that.'

'Monsieur —' She looked at the name on the papers. 'Is it the Nazis you have come here to discuss?'

'I *have* come to warn you. I should let you know frankly that I am not a great admirer of the Americans, and that I do not see their entry into this war as the greatest possible Allied asset. But perhaps they will learn. I tell you this only because there are many Frenchmen who think like me. You should take my warning seriously.'

He told her that in his opinion – and in that of the group of informed, influential men who were working with Marcel Darnand – things would get worse in France before they got better. One day France would be completely overrun, and once the Nazis crossed the border into Vichy her presence at Briteau would put the whole village into jeopardy. It would be then that she would find who were her friends.

'Any one of the villagers might betray you, and for many reasons. You might have to surrender for their sake, or see the village suffer such reprisals as you would never forget if you were captured by the Germans before you surrendered. You do not know how far the Nazis will go to smoke out their enemies. Villagers who now turn a blind eye to your presence – oh yes, they are not deceived so easily in these mountains, mademoiselle – know enough to send you to your death. As it is, it seems to me that you are merely playing at war.'

She said nothing, suppressing her anger at the remark. If he hoped to goad her into betraying what she was doing for the Resistance movement, he would be disappointed. She was more sure of the loyalty of the village than he could know, with Violette at her side.

At last she got up from her chair and refilled his glass. 'I can only thank you for your concern. And for bringing me word of my father's last hours. I do not know what will happen here, but I have more friends than you think. If you see the Darnands, you will tell them of this meeting? Tell them I am well?'

'I shall meet our mutual friends quite soon, in fact.' He looked at his watch. 'There will be a car waiting for me on the road.'

'Poor Edith. She should have her horses. Then there would be no need for her to have friends who can find petrol.' She could not keep the sarcastic edge from her voice. 'Maybe you have American friends who obtain your petrol for you?'

'Please do not take anything I have said as a personal slight.' He got to his feet and held out his hand. 'You need to be warned. I have said you are playing a game. But I know also that it is a dangerous game.'

When he had gone she turned the heavy iron key in the front door and leaned on it, suddenly tired. Charlie looked up at her wistfully, knowing there would be no walks in the snow that day.

At the end of the long year that lay ahead she was to remember her visitor. Once the snows had gone the months sped by, and the line into Spain became a clockwork way to freedom for the men and women who wanted to get to England and continue the war. Jacques worked like some kind of machine. He became less communicative, returning to the remote, slightly amused attitude of the months when they had first known each other. But at night he came to her bed and made love to her in the same wild way of their early nights together, leaving her before dawn to go into his hiding-place for the day.

It was as if their love-making expressed the danger and dedication of their Resistance work. Jacques never used the word love. But he was often tender with her, and though she rarely knew when he was about to make one of his disappearances, she became aware as the summer passed that the tenderness was always there, in the way he made love to her, the night before he was to live Briteau.

He was away on the night in November 1942 when,

threatened by Allied advances in North Africa, the Germans moved south across the length of the line of demarcation and into Vichy France.

Zoe threw down the newspaper she was pretending to read and began to pace the deep white carpet of her bedroom in Zurich.

'You've got to get her out. I don't know how you intend to do it, but I want her out of France.'

Erich looked up from his perusal of a fine arts journal. It was a Sunday morning, the one morning in recent months that he habitually woke in Zoe's bed and they maintained an illusion of companionship as the day wore on.

'I have not given up, you know that. One has to tread carefully.'

'It's a year since you got any word to – Berthe de Byron.' Zoe had found it hard to accept that Erich had called at the rue Louis on a flying visit to Paris. It had been so much her own territory – hers and Paul's – once.

'I am sure the message was delivered. As I am certain your daughter will be the one to decide whether or not to leave France. You both made your choices, long ago. We can only be glad that she is safe.'

'We're not sure.' Zoe lit a cigarette, and stubbed it out almost at once. 'Erich, I can't pretend that I'll ever feel as much for you again if you don't do something about it.'

'Since when did you have to blackmail me into caring about Leonie?' Erich's voice was ominously quiet, and Zoe shrugged and sat down facing his armchair, her long legs visible beneath the fur-edged silk peignoir.

He thought how grateful he should be that she had kept her figure. She still attracted him, in spite of her recent moods, and it was an attraction laced with the memory of her daughter's body.

'I love my daughter, always have.' Zoe lapsed into silence, staring out at the view of the lake and the mountains that formed a barrier between her and the world she had known outside.

'She knows that. I promise you when I next go to Paris I'll look into things again.'

'How can you risk Paris now? The Germans have got France. The roads will be blocked.'

'I have things to interest the Germans, Liebling. There are still my paintings, the few in Paris. And someone should make an appearance at the salon, don't you think? It can hardly be you, now that America is in the war.'

Zoe's restlessness was rooted in the fact that she no longer ran the business, which they had left in good hands, but on Erich's insistence. She had fled with him to Zurich because she believed the war would last months, not years. Now, with the slow running down of their relationship, she wished she had made for New York.

'When? When will you go?'

'If it means so much to you, I'll go in the New Year. Perhaps I could make it a regular trip, to allay suspicion. I have a name . . . a German. Quite a collector. He is in Paris; and they are settling in, you know. A few modern masters on the walls, and it is home.'

She glanced at the small Renoir above her bed. She had always loved the young girl's face. Erich had given it to her the day they moved to Zurich. 'Something beautiful to make the months to come as special as the years gone by.' His way with words had deserted him recently, she thought.

'Somehow I don't think the French are going to notice what is left on their walls from now on.'

Jacques Fabri returned to Briteau once more after the Germans moved into Vichy France. There was no German presence in the village for a while, but in the distance as they lay in bed Leonie could hear the rumble of a convoy of lorries going east. The winter had been less severe, and the roads north of the château were easily manoeuvrable.

Jacques told her that for a while she had to run the radio transmissions alone. There was urgent need for German naval information from Marseilles now that the focus had shifted to the African front. An informer had been arrested and given away the port's *réseau* members. An unknown was wanted to go in, collate the facts, and get them to London. If he found no way to do that in Marseilles, with the Resistance units reforming still, he would come back to Briteau to do so.

He left abruptly, without any real goodbye, and she lay looking into the darkness, realizing that to a Frenchman now she must still seem an outsider. The issues were all heightened by the German occupation of the whole of France; so much more was at stake. The escape lines would become more hazardous – and more necessary – than ever.

Three weeks went by without a sign from Jacques. They were only days from the expected thaw, when the line into Spain from Briteau would reopen. She became afraid that Jacques had been captured, and their network would be at risk. A week later she decided she could not go on alone. She radioed London with a coded message: their line would be closed that spring. Things had become too dangerous. Until she had more help, more backing, she thought it safer to close down.

The late-night messages from London contained no reference to what she had said earlier. But before they put out the code word that signalled 'end of message' a new voice came over the headphones.

It was Denholm. He talked her gently through her problem. If she closed down now she would impose an isolation on herself that she might find hard to bear. She should keep her options open. There was no immediate danger, and they would look into her situation. But whatever happened, communications must stay open.

He cut out before she could answer, and she sank back on her heels in the dark in front of the transmitter feeling vaguely ashamed, like some schoolgirl reprimanded for homework unfinished. She wondered how Denholm could really know there was no immediate danger. Jeanne Veron had cycled to the house only days before – under the pretext of bringing a length of bartered material that might make a dress for Violette – and warned them that German cars had passed through the village during the night, though there had been no German presence next day.

The Fabris, too, were aware of the traffic, which passed closer to their house than to the château. Fabri père had seen a convoy of staff cars, headed by motorbikes, the day before, and had acted the idiot goatherd, standing watching them as if they were creatures from another world. It was an act he was to use more than once in the months to come, when the Germans came closer.

It was in the same guise, a shambling, smiling old man dressed in rags, shepherd's stick in one hand, a small milk can in the other, that he approached the château in broad daylight a week later. Violette sat him in the kitchen while she went to Leonie's room.

'It is no good, this hiding away. The Fabris know everything, or have worked out the truth. They are afraid for their son. But there is something else . . .'

Leonie followed her downstairs. As she entered the kitchen Fabri père got to his feet, and spread his hands in apology for his appearance. 'I have my reasons, mademoiselle. I am not too old for some kinds of war, and I have convinced the few Boches I have seen that I am a fool. So – for the moment they leave me alone. But I have something in my barn that I cannot keep there much longer, without danger to us all.'

He asked her then if the escape line which she and his son had run for some time was, as the rumour in the village had it, closed. Or would she do him a great kindness and remove a young English airman – quite unharmed, and able to walk on his own two feet – from his house that night?

'So you knew?'

'Many of us know. My wife also.'

There was something in the old man's manner that moved

her. A touch of his son's bravado still lingered in the small, wiry body and lined face. The knowledge that he – and it would seem half the village – had kept her secret so well made it hard to refuse him now that he needed her help. The snow had almost gone from the mountain tracks and there had been no orders from London.

The inactivity that had gripped her in a battle of nerves all winter had been her worst enemy yet in this war that had come to France. Now Jacques's father offered her a chance to start up the line again.

With Violette nodding approval, she told him that she would take his Englishman halfway. From then on he would have to rely on the Spaniards. And until she was better organized, would he please not bring her too many more lost young men?

'But where else would I bring these soldiers, if not to the daughter of Paul de Byron?' The dark eyes gleamed at her with the stubborn pride of the Basque men, knowing she had no answer.

Where else indeed, Violette echoed, and thanked her God that the long winter was over at last.

CHAPTER SEVENTEEN

Some weeks after Mireille de Byron's letter to Briteau had reached the château, a crumpled, dog-eared replica from Quebec arrived complete with censor's stamp in the offices of Etablissements Massine in Bordeaux. The elderly woman who was the only staff now left to the shipping merchant placed it on Henri Massine's desk, in prominent view. Usually respecting her employer for his law-abiding ways, she saw the letter as a symbol of incipient treachery. With no one and nothing to amuse her in her own small home on the outskirts of the city, she found the comings and goings of the town's *Milicien* an endless source of interest. It made her feel good to be sent home in a limousine when their meetings were about to start. Her neighbours watched her arrivals through heavy net curtains, and – she thought – would conclude that it was time they found some respect in their hearts for the widow Leblanc.

'I hope that your dear wife is well, Monsieur Massine.' She stood watching him as he examined the envelope.

'From my granddaughter, I think.' He ignored the obvious curiosity behind the remark.

'Quite a young woman by now, no doubt,' Madame Leblanc persisted.

Henri Massine looked at her coldly over the rim of his pince-nez. 'Quite. And may I ask if you have finished the letters for my signature from yesterday?'

He read Mireille's letter avidly, sniffing at the news that she had passed an examination with a Grade B. The sooner he could get her back to the rigours of French education the better. And if she insisted on becoming a doctor, well, after

286

the war there would be need of young doctors. At Briteau as much as anywhere, though he still hoped to see her as the sole chatelaine of her father's estates, as was her right.

The disappearance of the American girl from the château a year before had lulled him into thinking she had perhaps relinquished her claim to the lands now that the war had got so hot for her fellow countrymen. But his own special knowledge of the region meant that he could be very useful to the Germans if it came to a campaign against the activities of the Resistance there. Unfortunately the villagers had been reticent to a man when his agents had first tried to find evidence that the American girl might have joined them. The one meeting with the girl herself had disarmed his representative, but he had never quite believed that the man was as thorough as he should have been – though he had taken his money fast enough.

If the American girl had really left, then it was all to the good. He would bide his time, and if she had in reality gone to ground, then he would scoop her up with any other rubbish he could find for the Germans. His activities in this direction had already ensured that his business survived in what had now become entirely a Nazi-run port. He had promises that his small fleet would remain in his own control, and the contracts were lucrative to say the least.

Madame Leblanc returned with the letters for signature to find her employer standing at his office window surveying the river with a satisfied, rare, smile.

'Your letter from Canada had good news, Monsieur Massine?'

He turned to face her. 'Madame, if you should prefer to go home by *taxi-vélo*, then I have no objection. My chauffeur has other work to do on the car. It waits for you. If you have finished your gossiping.'

She backed out of the room murmuring apologies. The thought of being pulled through the streets by a young boy on a bicycle, and drawing up at the house in a vehicle that one could see on every corner of the city . . .

287

Ten minutes later Raymond deposited her at her door as usual, and returned to the quayside offices to await the end of the weekly meeting of the *Milicien*. Unable to fight because of his disability, he had spent the months since the occupation of the whole of France watching his employer's growing involvement with the hated self-appointed French henchmen to the Germans, and if it were not for his need for the independence which the job brought him he would have walked away from Henri Massine for ever.

At weekends he still saw Marie-Louise, who performed culinary miracles with her hundred and twenty grammes of meat and somehow found the fuel to keep her apartment the warm haven it had always been for Raymond.

It was he who had changed. The philosophy was flawed by bitterness. He brooded on what he was forced to witness of his employer's activities as a *Milicien*. He laughed less, and when he made love to Marie-Louise it was tinged with melancholy, as if what was happening to France had undermined his desire.

That evening Raymond waited for Henri Massine, watching the Bordelais worthies who had gathered at the quayside offices leave one by one.

The last one to go was Verdier, a jumped-up tradesman if ever there was one, and hard enough to trust even in peace-time. Raymond calculated that Verdier had only joined Henri Massine's little band of respectable gangsters as a means to break into a higher social level for himself and his family after the war. They would tolerate him, and then probably destroy him, once France was free again.

Verdier's daughter Lise was conspicuous these days by her absence from the Bordeaux social scene – except when she emerged at nightfall, wearing the latest fashions in evening wear, silk stockings, unobtainable make-up, and took her usual table at the German officers' club behind the hôtel de ville. She was not the only collaboratrice to go unharmed in the city – there were many young women fraternizing with the occupying forces, and it was hard to tell

288

whether they were members of the Resistance using their charms to obtain information or not. In the case of Lise Verdier – an unremarkable *enfant gâtée* if he remembered aright from the summer he had driven her with Mademoiselle Mireille to the château in the Pyrenees – Raymond was certain the collaboration with the Germans was entirely a matter of self-interest and appetite.

Her father and Henri Massine were two of a kind. They would sell anything they could to the Germans. Or anyone. And that included their fellow Frenchmen.

That night the shipping merchant carried his usual briefcase home. As they drove back to the house Raymond saw in the mirror that the little man was leafing through a set of papers with a satisfied smile on his face. He slipped them into a large envelope as they drew up at the front of the house, and seemed in a hurry to get in, telling Raymond to garage the car.

When he checked the car as usual for the night Raymond found the envelope still on the back seat. In his room above the garage he opened it, and read the contents. It contained lists of names, addresses and dates. Amongst them, and dated that day, were the names of two of Henri Massine's rivals in business – both of them also known for their unswerving patriotism, to the extent that their business had been ruined.

He resealed the envelope, and ten minutes later returned it to its owner.

In those ten minutes he had made up his mind that before the war was over he would somehow make an end of Henri Massine.

Leaving the house by a back gate, he walked quickly, an ungainly figure, head down, in the direction of the old quarter. It was almost curfew, and he had better things to do than be picked up by an SS patrol and asked for his papers.

Marie-Louise opened the door at once to his knock, and he pushed past her, asking if he could use her telephone. He would explain everything later. It took almost half an hour to find an operator who would supply two numbers in Marseilles.

The first was the private residence of the owner of a shipping line that had for generations rivalled the Massines'. A woman's voice, slightly anxious, told him that her husband was late home. There had been no answer from his office when she rang him herself, and she had no idea why he had been delayed.

Raymond bit his lip. He could find no words with which to reassure her, but said he would call back if he got news for her. He tried the second number. The phone rang endlessly into the silence of a small office at the top of a warehouse building on the Marseilles harbour. Sprawled across the desk was the body of the elderly, white-haired owner of the building. In the cellars below there were signs of a scuffle.

The Resistance workers who had been in hiding there for weeks had been betrayed by Henri Massine's local contacts. When the SS broke in, having beaten the old man when he refused to answer their questions, the young boy who acted as messenger for the *réseau* made a run for it, and was shot in the back.

They threw the body into their van at the feet of their prisoners. Three of the men were later shot after failing to break under interrogation. The fourth the local SS commandant found of more interest. Clearly their leader, and as clearly not a local man, he refused to admit his real name, his origins, the reasons for his presence in Marseilles. They put him on a train to Paris at the end of the first week, while his face was still just recognizable and he could still stand, if supported on either side by the two junior officers who escorted him.

After three nights in a cell in Fresnes prison, the notorious stone-faced building in a once innocent Paris suburb, Jacques Fabri still had nothing to say. As his further injuries from torture had not diminished his brute strength, the notes on his single page in the commandant's journal stated, he was to be deported to a Polish labour camp. There it was hoped he might break, or be sold out by some other wretch who might see him as a ticket to freedom.

In his bid to destroy an old business rival who sheltered the Resistance group as it re-formed in Marseilles, Henri Massine had quite by chance dealt a blow against the American girl who was his ultimate target.

The news of Jacques's arrest and deportation reached Briteau a month later. Yves Pascal brought orders from London through the Darnand contact. While Leonie sat, white-faced, he gave her the details of all they had been able to discover about Jacques's last days in France. She asked questions to which the curé could give no good answers. Jacques had been seen and recognized on the train from Marseilles to Paris. A prisoner at Fresnes had watched a group detailed for the Polish labour camps move off, Jacques amongst them.

'He will come back. He is a survivor,' Yves said quietly. 'And you too must survive. The Germans are moving in on this area, slow but sure. Your orders are to close down the line until further notice. It is too dangerous, and we must rethink before we put you and any Allied servicemen at risk.'

'Then what am I to do? The village knows I am here. I cannot stay shut up in this place from now on with nothing to do.'

'Precisely. The plan is this: you have new papers.' He tapped his briefcase. 'You come out into the open, as the owner of the château. Perhaps a rather "snob" lady? A touch of Fascism in your attitude might not be lost on our guests. They will want this place, you can be sure of that. But be pleasant. Bide your time. We are all with you. And you could still serve France in this way.'

The irony was that her new papers made her into a Frenchwoman, and gave her the name her mother had sought for her more than twenty years ago. She was to assume an identity which was familiar to her through knowing Mireille – the young aristocrat, highly educated, born to run her father's estates. The curé apologized for the fact that her mother was described as 'unknown'.

'It is the price you have to pay if you wish to stay on here. Any mention of American origins now would mean your deportation or worse. You do want to stay? There is still time to get you out. After all, no one knows better than we do how to rejoin the outside world.'

She shook her head. 'No. This is where I must stay. There's no one for me to go to. My mother is in Zurich. When the war ends I'll find her again.' She dismissed the thought of Tony and New York from her mind. As Yves Pascal said, that was the world outside. 'And I daresay the Germans would find it quite in character that a French officer should have at least one love child?'

The curé smiled. 'The words have real meaning, in this case, my dear Leonie.'

'There is something I must know,' she said as he rose to leave. 'Was Jacques tortured? Was it bad?'

'My child.' He touched her hair. It was the first human contact between them, and by making it he let her know he was aware that Jacques had been her lover. 'He was recognized on the train. He walked from Fresnes prison. He is alive.'

It was the thought of the torture that Jacques's body had suffered that sent her into a black mood in the days that followed. Violette, her own spirits improving now that Leonie's presence was out in the open and the château could be run in some semblance of its old ways, failed to shake her out of a mounting depression. There were no tangible orders from London; no attempt was made to have the transmitter removed. She lived in limbo, torn with fear for Jacques's safety.

'There is so much to do. Why not work in the fields with the poor things we have to use now? If you cannot be happy, please try to be useful, child,' Violette scolded her on a Saturday night as they sat in the kitchen and ate onion soup made with stock from an illegal delivery of bones from the village. 'And the radio in your room. Get it out of the house, I beg of you, before we are murdered in our beds by the Boches.'

'It will go soon,' Leonie said flatly. 'It's not so easy now that they are swarming all over the village.'

'Then go to church tomorrow, and pray that Monsieur Pascal finds a way. We will all go. It is summer – the walk will bring colour to those pale cheeks.'

Camille Fabri and Violette trudged arm in arm to church next morning, Leonie a yard or so behind. She noticed that both women wore the clumsy wooden-soled shoes which were all they could buy, and Violette in a spirit of bravado had tied the wide leather straps across her instep with a plait of laces in the blue, white and red of the tricolour.

Obeying the last instructions she had received, Leonie dressed in an expensive raincoat she had bought in Paris two years ago, and wore dark glasses and heavy gold earrings and necklace. But the plain headscarf bound round her long hair was like a uniform shared with the village women, and the men in the church gallery looking down on the pews where the women sat could not have told the other girls from the mistress of Briteau if she had not taken her seat in the place her father and the de Byrons before him had always used.

There was a German staff car on duty outside the church, the occupants eyeing the ageing men and small boys as they crossed the field through the gravestones to the west door.

Violette genuflected and crossed herself as they came to the de Byron pew, murmuring to Camille Fabri that anyone would think they were French *poilus* in disguise; it was a bad thing when there had to be a guard on the good Lord's house, but a German guard . . . she mouthed a remark that had very little to do with prayer.

They walked back to the château at leisure, remembering the old times when Jacques would rattle them home in the farm cart and a long Sunday luncheon would take up the hours of a summer afternoon. Camille did not talk of her son's disappearance. It was as if she held on to the fact that in the old days, too, he had always wandered home in his own good time.

'So the Boches did not follow us home and spoil our good dinner. Butter on our bread tonight. More than they have, I daresay.' Violette ladled soup from a tureen on the kitchen stove into deep bowls, while Leonie sat at the table, watching the soft light of the summer evening play on the garden. Violette had been right to make her go to church. It had lifted the mood of recent weeks.

'Do you remember the first Sunday? It was this time of year, and we walked to church . . . with Papa.'

'I remember how hard we worked in the days that followed. As you must work now, ma petite. There will be a good harvest this year. The Germans will not interfere with that, you will see. It will cost us a few bottles, perhaps. They can have last year's – it was not so special.'

'You're right.' Leonie straightened in her chair and buttered her tartine. 'I'll see the Fabris tomorrow, and go down to the village to find some workers.'

After supper she went to her room and checked on the radio transmitter, making a mental note to see Yves Pascal next day in the village and hasten the arrangements to remove it before the Germans became too curious about the château.

She sat at the secretaire in the annexe trying to write to Tante Berthe. Letters got through rarely, phone calls never these days, and she put her pen down helplessly, deciding to try to get word from Paris through the Darnands.

Back in her bedroom she started to tidy her wardrobe. It was still not quite dark, and the warm night air pervaded the room, making her restless. From the depths of the armoire she took the box containing the black dress from Worth. Five minutes later she walked into the kitchen where Violette sat in the half-light, and under her astonished eyes performed a stylish mannequin walk the length of the room.

'*Formidable*. It will bring you luck, a dress like that,' Violette said.

'It was a gift from Berthe de Byron.'

'Ah, they say she too was a beauty.'

'Yes. I hope all goes well for her.'

'A woman like that . . . she knows how to treat those animals. And talking of animals, where is the dog? I missed him earlier.'

'I thought I saw a rat in the stable blocks. I've shut him in there for the night. It will be good exercise for him.'

Violette got up to light the candles, and as Leonie crossed to the window to draw the curtains she saw what she thought at first was a reflection in the glass panes of some movement in the room. Then the movement became more distinct, and closer, and she found herself staring into the face of a man pressed against the window.

'Violette,' she said very quietly. 'There is someone outside. Leave the candles. Wait here.'

The man's face was very pale, the hair wild. He mouthed something to her, and pointed to the door. She shook her head at first, then watched the man's lips move silently again. 'Jacques Fabri. I have news of Jacques Fabri.'

Her training forgotten, she ran to the door and opened it. Finding no one there, she stepped out into the gathering dark. In a split second a rough hand clamped her mouth, another gripped her waist, and she was propelled back into the house by a man in ragged, stained civilian clothes, with a day's growth of beard, and the wild eyes she had first seen at the window.

'Close the curtains. Light. Or the young chatelaine is dead.' He gave orders to Violette in odd, clipped French that reminded Leonie of Erich's accent when he talked to the girls employed at Caresse. She attempted to nod at Violette, telling her to obey.

In the light of the candles she tried to turn to look her captor in the face, but he jerked her arm into her back. She stood very still, then, and slowly the man took his hand from her mouth.

'I won't scream,' she said steadily. 'We are alone here. You can let me go.'

'Very well. I want wine.' Violette hurried to do as he asked. 'Then I must know how soon you can get me out of here and into Spain.'

'You behave badly for someone who asks favours.' Violette set a glass in front of him and poured some wine.

'I want nothing from you, old woman. I have been with the *Maquis* for months, and I know how to get what I want when I want.'

Leonie thought that he looked too well fed for someone who had lived rough, as the *Maquis* did, for any length of time.

'I see you don't do badly here.' He drank the wine at a gulp, and got up to take off his jacket. 'And that dress – expecting someone to dinner, eh?' He eyed Leonie's figure boldly.

The two women watched as he removed his jacket, and Violette's eyes caught Leonie's as they saw that he wore a heavy army pistol strapped to his chest. Leonie knew at once from her training in England that the weapon was German, and that in all probability they had a German *agent provocateur* on their hands.

'You gave a name. Before I let you into my house.' Leonie decided to move to the attack, and call the man out into the open.

'Fresnes prison. I escaped, but I saw him go off with the lot for Poland. Someone in a cell with him told us about this place. When I had to leave my *réseau* last week – near Lyon – all dead – I remembered.'

'Then I am afraid whoever it was in Fresnes prison had the facts wrong.' She knew that Jacques would have told no one of their escape line, especially in prison, where men could trade such information for their own freedom. 'We are alone here, as I told you. But – you are among friends. My father . . .'

'Ah, the good captain. I had pals in his regiment.' His eyes ran over the black dress again. 'Very aristo, the good captain. The St Cyr touch. Sorry about his death.'

'He died for France,' Violette said acidly.

'And I plan to live for *la patrie*. That's the difference between us, old woman. Now – a bed and a meal, eh?'

'There is only soup. And the rooms are not aired.'

'Oh, I'll sleep under the dust covers. It'll be a luxury.' He removed the pistol from its holster and laid it casually on the table. 'How about the captain's room, eh? Don't tell me you've let the memory go cold?'

Violette looked at Leonie for guidance, and when she nodded silently, shrugged and got to her feet. 'Very well.'

'Violette,' Leonie said suddenly, 'I think things may look different tomorrow. Tonight we will make our visitor welcome, and then tomorrow maybe we will think of ways to help him on his way. More wine, I think. We'll take it to the library while you heat the soup.'

'You're your father's daughter, I'll say that for you.' The man watched her as she poured the wine from the side table in the library. 'Real class.'

'Thank you.' His was a good act, she thought, but she could match it. She crossed her legs, the black silk of the dress outlining her long thighs.

'Very pleasant. I think we're in for a very pleasant evening. Maybe you'll not want to put me in the captain's room after all?' The man's smile was unpleasant.

'Oh yes,' she said quickly. 'As you thought, the room is aired. And you must sleep before you leave.'

'Leave? That's a pity.' As he held out an empty glass, she noticed that his hand was as steady as a rock.

It was after midnight when they left the library. Violette had gone to bed, after preparing a divan in a small dressing-room on the first floor. She knew that the stranger's accent

297

was either Alsatian – with its shades of old treacheries – or German. In neither case was Paul de Byron's suite to be unlocked for a visitor who got his supper by using threats.

The two women had not been alone together all evening, but Leonie knew that Violette was on her guard. It was tacitly understood that they would play a waiting game. If they made any rash move to get help they would be in worse danger than if they waited till next day to rid themselves of the stranger's presence.

The man held on to the balustrade as they climbed the stairs, and placed a heavy hand on Leonie's shoulder, swaying slightly, as she stood with him in the doorway of the dressing-room and wished him a comfortable night. She knew he was not as drunk as he pretended.

'You have not asked my name.' He shifted the hand to the nape of her neck.

'We do not ask or give names too freely in France these days.' She drew back imperceptibly. 'But we can give you food, and fresh clothes if you wish, before you move on tomorrow.'

'So you've made up your mind to move me on? Tell me, you wouldn't be so foolish as to make me angry? That dress promises something quite different.'

'And you would not be so foolish as to abuse our hospitality?'

He grinned, and stepped back. 'Officer and a gentleman. At your service.'

He still held one hand to his forehead in mock salute as he watched her walk to the stairs at the far end of the gallery.

Leonie did not undress. She lay between the covers, listening to the small, familiar sounds of the house as it settled into silence for the night. She regretted having locked Charlie in the stables. He made a good watchdog, and his presence would have been a comfort. She was thinking of the brown and white ball of fur that he had been, rolling in the fields behind the house that first summer while Mireille flew her kite, when she drifted into an uneasy sleep.

The creak of the door that led to the annexe woke her an hour later. She opened her eyes to find the German looking down at her. His pistol was in its holster, dark against his grey shirt. He held a torch in one hand, and as she moved her head he switched it on, blinding her.

'I move quietly, mademoiselle. I have found what I came for. A very interesting room, this secret sanctuary next to your bedroom. The chimney especially.'

She sat up slowly, blinking. 'What are you going to do?'

He switched out the torch, and sat on the bed. 'I have several choices. I inform my superiors, and you will be removed from this house within the hour – you and the old woman. Or – I move in with a few friends, and together we operate your radio and bring your unsuspecting young men into our nest.

'The line is closed,' she said wearily. 'It was nothing to do with me. This house is not used as you think. It was all over months ago.'

'That brings me to my next idea. The village must know something. Mass arrest of the young boys, perhaps? The women could watch in the square, while we prepare their deaths. Someone would talk.'

'You do not know these people. And I tell you, there is nothing to betray.'

'Time will tell, Mademoiselle de Byron. And that brings me to my last choice. The one I favour. I like this place. I like you. If I bide my time here, say nothing, then eventually proof of your activities will come to hand. Even then, I need not act on such proof. If I had been made so happy here that I did not want to throw it all away.'

He leaned over her, and slowly pulled down the covers. When he saw that she was still in the black silk dress he put a hand to her throat, then ran it over her breasts.

'Would they believe that you were waiting here for more evidence? Are you expected back?' Leonie twisted her body towards him, as if in invitation.

'They knew I might need a few days.' His voice was hoarse. 'I believe you and I may come to an understanding for those few days, or longer?'

'You have put me in an impossible situation. I need time.' She raised her arms and put them round his neck.

Releasing himself, the man stood and removed the holster, then lay beside her on the bed. She slipped from beneath the covers, and lay on top of him, her long legs tight against him. They moved slowly, the man finding her body's shape with his hands, in mounting excitement. Then, pretending to respond, Leonie took his head in her hands and put her mouth on his.

It was a ritual killing, expert, unhesitating. She followed the instructions she had been given in England like a machine, finely tuned to a deadly skill. The man had no time to fight her, and gave a single, coarse oath as his head fell back on the pillows. She lay on top of him for a moment that seemed like an eternity, then shifted from him and leaned over the side of the bed, retching her heart out.

It was growing light as she and Violette closed the annexe door, the dead body stowed in the chimney breast with the equipment the German had come to find.

'Now we are in real trouble,' Violette said as they sat in the kitchen, waiting for the time when Leonie could cycle into the village and get help.

'I had no choice.' Leonie sipped her coffee and put her head in her hands. 'It was something I thought I would never have to do, but when it came . . .'

'No one would blame you.' Leonie had told Violette that the man had put the whole village under threat. If she had given in to him, their lives at Briteau would have been no better than imprisonment.

She cycled into the village with a shopping basket on her handlebars, unable to believe that the sun was shining as if it were any other day. An old man touched his beret to her, and a child ran beside her, laughing.

Looking down at the child, she thought how thin the people of Briteau had become. The well fed body of the man she had killed had disgusted her. She could never have agreed to his offers.

In the village main street she saw a group of German staff cars, and got off her bicycle, pushing it as far as the grocer's store. Groups of women stood in their doorways in silence. She walked into the store, leaving her bicycle propped against the whitewashed wall. She bought rations of bread and fat, her eyes still on the street, and then as an SS officer emerged from a shop opposite the grocer's with a young woman she paid hurriedly and left.

The girl was plump, hair newly permed, legs smooth in real silk stockings. The village women had not seen stockings for months, and that summer the more daring among them painted a thin line of a seam the length of their bare limbs. She stood impatiently as her companion spoke to another German, swinging a large leather handbag. Her arms were tanned, and her face had the glow of a woman who had spent long hours in the sun.

Leonie recognized Lise Verdier at once. She knew that she should turn away, and hope that the clothes she wore would help her to blend, unrecognized, into the landscape. But she could not help herself as she crossed to where Lise stood, anger and incredulity in her eyes.

'Leonie de Byron!' The girl held out a hand, laughing, perhaps to hide embarrassment. 'Well, who would have thought you'd stay in this backwater? And you look as if you belong.'

'You look at home too, Lise. Are you on your way to Bordeaux?'

'One doesn't ask such questions, ma chère, you ought to know that. We've had a gorgeous vacation. Now, who knows?'

'I'm glad you're enjoying yourself.' Leonie failed to keep the bitterness out of her voice.

'Yes. Lots of parties. I get asked by all the top people now.'

The girl's eyes flashed a long-nursed resentment, and at that moment Leonie knew it had been a major error to confront her.

'I'm sorry. Sorry things have changed so,' she said carefully. 'My sister, too; everything changed for her.'

'Can't be bad, away from that old monster of a grandfather. Shall I give him your love?'

'He doesn't know me. When the war is over things will have to be decided.'

'Until then you seem to be having a very quiet time of it,' Lise said sarcastically.

'You could say that.' Leonie turned away, watching the child that had followed her earlier trying to straddle the bicycle with thin, brown legs. 'I must go.'

As she ruffled the child's hair and shooed him away from the bicycle, Lise watched her, eyes narrowed, fighting down a wave of jealousy of the way Leonie seemed to belong here, in a remote Pyrenees village, as surely as she had become part of Paris in their days at the Collège Madeleine.

'Well, au revoir,' she called. 'See you in Paris after the war?'

The sarcasm in her voice was not wasted on Leonie as she cycled off, a casual wave of her free hand as she steadied the *vélo* her only goodbye. She knew it had been a mistake to talk to Lise Verdier. The fact that she had turned up in the village in a German staff car need not in itself be an indication of anything – except that Lise had, as always, her own interests at heart. She could not imagine the ever-hungry Mademoiselle Verdier going without life's comforts even in the face of defeat. But Leonie did not want the meeting to be talked about in Bordeaux. The small but menacing figure of Henri Massine sometimes walked at the edge of her dreams, and she could hardly believe sometimes that she had so far been left in peace to live out the war at the château. She knew he was a man who would bide his time to get what he wanted for his granddaughter – but she had so much more to lose herself, now that she was a member of the Resistance . . . and

302

had killed one of the men with whom Lise Verdier associated.

'Such an innocent, rural scene, don't you think?' Lise said to her companion as they drove off. 'Don't be deceived by those black clothes and the peasant scarf. It's time that snob was taught a lesson. Remind me one day to tell you all about her.'

Until Yves Pascal opened the door of his house to Leonie she had held back the tears of horror and of fear at what she had done. It was not only fear of the consequences of the murder at the château – heightened now by the chance meeting with Lise and the German staff officer – that made her burst into a storm of weeping the moment she saw the curé's kindly, familiar face, but also sheer horror at the fact that she had taken the life of another human being. And almost without thought. It had been a ruthless, professional killing.

'It was a necessity,' she told the curé when he had calmed her, and dried her tears. She sat curled in an ancient chair in his study while he let her talk. 'You know my training. Yet – I had no idea that I would be able to do such a thing when the moment came.'

'If you knew how many people have sat where you are now, in that very chair, with such matters on their conscience . . . You must forgive yourself, as God will forgive you – I'm sure of that. But perhaps the most important thing at the moment is to act.'

She looked up at him gratefully, surprised and relieved by his down-to-earth reaction.

'This war. France's sad situation. They have changed everything. Your father would have understood. Been proud of you.'

'It was in his house,' she said dully. 'I killed a man in his house.'

Yves Pascal laid a hand gently on her head, then went to the window overlooking the village street and drew back a

303

heavy lace curtain. 'Look. There is already a little divine mercy in the air. A beautiful day. What's more, I think the good Lord last night had some plan to help. A very old man – his time had come – died in the night. I was called to him. His widow has little money, and the church is to bury him. We go to their cottage this evening, before dusk. And when we pass the château – it is on our way there – with the cart carrying the coffin I should not be at all surprised if we had a small problem of some kind, perhaps a wheel? And I and my helper, a strong fellow who hates the Boches as well as the next man, will call on you for help.'

'Do you think it will work? Is your helper discreet?' Leonie stood up hopefully. 'I would not want to put you at risk, mon père.'

'You will find that the whole village can be discreet when it comes to a dead German. A short journey with the body in our coffin, a short burial service deep in the woods beyond the château – and *voilà*, you must begin to try to forget.'

It was just after dark that Yves Pascal and his helper struggled through the kitchen door with the body of the murdered man and carried it, under cover of the trees, down the path to where the cart waited at the main gate. It was after curfew, but the priest was used to pleading urgent spiritual duties whenever he was found out after hours. The road past Briteau was deserted, and the cart lurched away in the darkness, Leonie watching until she could no longer hear the rattle of its wheels. A mile further on the cart turned off the road and into a small wood. There the curé and his companion swiftly dug a shallow grave for the German and for the transmitter and radio equipment which at the last moment Yves Pascal had insisted be taken from the château and buried.

'*Voilà*,' the villager who had come to help him muttered as he concealed the newly turned soil with a pile of brushwood. 'You have the radio for which you were searching. You can rest in peace, mon vieux.'

*

Ten days later the Germans returned. It was Manuel who brought the news to the château, and warned the women that a staff car full of SS was parked in the courtyard of the Fabris' house.

'There is no more for me to do in the mountains now,' he said ruefully. 'No one tries to escape any more. Luis is always drunk in his cave.'

'Would you like to stay here at the château?' Leonie could not bear to think of the gypsy boy roaming the hills without shelter or purpose.

'No, no . . .' the boy said quickly. 'I do not sleep in houses. And it is summer.'

'Where can I find you?'

'I will be back. I will watch you. I will know when you want me.'

Jacques Fabri's parents were arrested and detained for some hours in the local prison by the SS. They were questioned about their son's activities in the region. Fabri père shrugged and said his son was never at home, and there was always some woman who would take him to her bed. His interrogator delivered a heavy blow to the side of the old man's head, and Camille gave a slow sigh, as if she herself were in pain.

They were released before curfew, and made to walk home. Later Camille confided in Violette that the incident had given her new hope. If they still needed evidence of Jacques's work for the Resistance movement, then he must still be alive.

Leonie saw the episode as an attempt to frighten the village. There was nothing the SS could find now that might put them all at risk. She was certain that the man she had killed had come from some agent further afield, higher up the SS ladder, and it might be some time before they found that their *agent provocateur* had neither gone on into Spain and discovered the escape line, or made himself a cosy hiding-place with the chatelaine of Briteau.

They had not done the worst they could do to her. The Fabris were home safe. If she had lost her staff the harvest would have been ruined – and there were signs that it was going to be a vintage year.

CHAPTER EIGHTEEN

With the Allied invasion of Sicily early in July and the arrest of Mussolini in Rome before the month was out, the German command focused increasingly on the Italian campaign during the late summer of 1943. There was also always the old threat of the winter to come on the eastern front, where the Sixth Army had been routed earlier that year and the Russians were still regaining ground. In France, the officers of the occupation army either were lulled into a false sense of security by the failure of the Allies to invade that year, or – if their faith in Hitler was flagging – began to plan for self-preservation.

Klaus Werner, temporary commandant of Fresnes prison, had been a frequent pre-war visitor to France, and having observed Franco–German politics with cynical detachment since France's surrender in 1940 knew that Laval's current flirtation with Hitler and compromise would not shift the Germans from Paris. He began to think of his future. His *garçonnier* in a small apartment block close to Erich Mannheim's first Paris home in the avenue Kléber was stacked with a growing collection of important modern paintings on the Third Reich's list of decadent art, and his evenings away from the prison were spent in contemplation of their value.

Erich Mannheim, as a Swiss neutral, was free to visit Paris as often as he wished, but rarely used his apartment. His belongings were stored in the offices above the salon, and business at Caresse was flourishing, so that he preferred to stay on the premises and make sure that the staff remembered who was still the director.

307

With America's entry into the war Zoe no longer risked travelling with him. She lived almost as a recluse in the Zurich flat, sometimes writing to Maddie, but – on Erich's strict orders – making no attempt to contact Leonie. Letters were dangerous, and might give away her American connections. Telephone calls could be overheard – if they got through.

Zoe took the enforced isolation badly. Erich had long since ceased to be a source of physical comfort, and on his return each time they hardly embraced, settling down instead to a discussion of the latest accounts and sales figures, as if it was all they had left in common.

News of another painting offloaded in Paris for a small fortune left Zoe unmoved. The night Erich drove back non-stop to the Swiss border with his entire Meissen collection in the back of the car she refused to help him unpack. In her heart she knew that things were over between them, and she had made up her mind that at the end of the war she would go back to Gramercy Park and Maddie. At the thought that Leonie might not go with her, she felt utterly lost. She lived out the war on a tightrope, safe, yet more unsafe than she had ever been.

On his visits to Paris Erich also held back from the temptation to contact Leonie. Each time he walked into Zoe's office he could see the girl's white face, the long limbs twisting away from his grasp.

He did not regret that he had told her he loved her. It was still true. His adoration of the brilliant, butterfly mother had not been deep enough to survive their unsettled life. Yet it lay between him and the daughter, who he knew would always hate him for it. It was his punishment too that her innocence would always elude him. Once he had imagined that he could persuade her to forgive him. He had been to the rue Louis, hoping to make contact, but the old woman had dismissed him on sight.

These days he avoided the company of the French patriots. He even vetted his German customers in advance.

And the credentials of Klaus Werner – discreet, unmarried, ascetic, lover of French art and endowed with a solid private income – he found to be quite impeccable.

Tony Shaw's father had watched his son apprehensively in the months after his wife's death, certain he would make straight back for Europe when a decent interval had passed. He was not to know that Tony stayed on in New York because Europe meant war. Not until he watched a friend die in a foolish training accident at the controls of a Dakota did Tony volunteer for the AAF. Making sure that he could work as a non-combatant, he trained in the interpretation of aerial photographs, and with his knowledge of France was posted to Europe the week his training was over.

It was on a crazy impulse, he told his father when he walked in at breakfast time eighteen months later as if nothing had happened, that he had gone on a joyride from an air base in the south of England in a reconnaissance flight over France. Everyone did it. Not everyone had to land in a field in central France with engine trouble.

The pilot injured a leg badly in the landing, and insisted that Tony get away on his own. He made for Tours, where he arrived just before dawn and sent help back to the plane. Assistance was available all down the line, and Tony's fluent French made it possible to spot who might be of genuine use. He was taken up in the end by a *réseau* that put him on a route south, by train. With his blond looks and noticeable height they went for the audacious and dressed him as a German soldier. But his escort was caught in a Gestapo check and ran for it. Tony himself got out at the next station and began the long walk south-west . . .

The harvest that year was brought in by old men and children, village housewives and German soldiers. The Germans were volunteers, tired of standing watching the

309

workers walk each day from the village and back. When the soldiers joined *le grand travail* the French ignored them, and worked in silence even amongst themselves. They sat apart during the lunch-time break under the trees. There was no real objection to their presence; it was as if while their guards worked side by side with them the villagers could relax a little, and the work that had always been the most important thing in their lives came into its own again, the war receding, the silence a token of truce.

There could be no magic lanterns, or lights on the tables, for harvest supper. Leonie decided to give an evening meal to the French workers (no Germans were invited) early on the last day of work, before night fell.

It was a Saturday, and everyone went home early from the terraces, returning to the château in what best clothes they had kept by them since the shortages began. The women wore flowered dresses with crisp white collars and cuffs, their long dark hair caught back in gold and silver-mesh snoods knitted from hoarded fragments of cotton or unravelled silk. The men wore wide-trousered suits, shining from recent pressing, late roses in their buttonholes.

The accordionist, wounded very early in the war, took up his place under the trees and drank the obligatory three glasses from the vintage they had bottled the year Leonie first came to France.

Two long tables set out on the grass gleamed with starched white cloths. Violette's larder was stripped for the occasion, and the local rabbit population decimated the week before. At a corner of the table at which Leonie presided – with Fabri père and Camille heading the other – the gypsy boy sat eating steadily from the moment the food was brought in, his dark eyes watching the hills.

There was no dancing. 'No young men to dance with,' Violette said. Fabri père made a short speech, and the guests murmured approval. Leonie stood to thank them all, raising her glass to her father's memory. Low-key and unremarkable though it was, it was the moment for which, without

310

knowing it, she had waited, the proof that she had finally been accepted by her father's people.

As it grew close to curfew the guests drifted home. Manuel disappeared with a shy, silent nod of farewell, the slight figure darting away with the other children, then lost to view down the drive.

Violette busied herself in the kitchen, and wept silently for her absent grandson, and Paul de Byron, and la petite Mireille. Returning to the field to clear the tables, Leonie began to fold a white cloth, which unaccountably fell from her hands and floated to the ground like a wraith in the growing dark.

'Let me help you with that.' The figure of a soldier in German uniform, tall, young, fair-haired, came out of nowhere. Leonie stooped quickly to retrieve the cloth, playing for time. The SS had left the village in peace for some weeks, and it must have been obvious to even the most zealous among them that there had been time for nothing at the château but the harvest. She had let herself be lulled into a false sense of safety, and her fear – which she had been able to keep at bay since the Fabris had been returned from their arrest – came back with a sickening familiarity.

As she straightened, her face a white mask, the soldier walked to where she stood and took the cloth from her hands.

'Since when did a German speak French with a New York accent?' said Tony Shaw.

She walked back into the house in a daze, Tony's arm round her trembling shoulders. Closing the door quickly, she leaned on it, wondering if she was hallucinating, and watched Tony take long strides across the kitchen and draw Violette into his arms.

Violette held him from her, shaking her head in disbelief. 'At last a man in the house. And hungry, eh?'

He sank into the nearest chair. 'I don't know how I walked the last ten miles. And as for watching all that food out there

311

from my cover for half an hour before anyone began to go home . . .'

'You do not eat at that table in that uniform, all the same.' Violette asked Leonie if there were not some things of her father's that might fit him, and while Tony drank scalding coffee laced with cognac she went to her father's rooms on the first floor where she herself had slept since Yves Pascal had removed the body of the man she had murdered from her own.

Tony joined her ten minutes later, and put an arm round her waist, kissing her hair, as they looked down at the thick English tweeds she had laid out on the bed.

'I'm glad I couldn't bring myself to throw anything away,' she said softly.

'They're fine. I wish I'd got to know him.'

'So much has happened, Tony. Your mother – I'm glad you were with her.'

'It was important. It helped with my father. We got to know each other through it, and things are easier between us.'

'And New York? It's like another world to me now.' She sat on the bed, touching the sleeve of Paul's coat.

'Maddie would have you back any time.'

'Maddie.'

'I saw her a lot. That's quite an apartment. She has all her hats in a row on stands in the vestibule – like some counter in a fancy store.'

'There's no point trying to get letters through now. But if you get back to New York soon will you tell her I'm fine? That I love her?'

'I've told her a lot already, Leonie de Byron. It was good to talk with someone who knew you.'

'She knew me so well, once. But I've really changed, Tony.'

'The new image is a knock-out.' He took her hands and drew her to her feet. 'I love the thick stockings.'

'It's the deep-down changes –'

'Look.' He kissed her gently. 'We're going to talk all night – when I've had some sleep. You know I must move on. No hanging around.'

She told him that he could sleep on the divan in her father's study adjacent to the bedroom, explaining that she no longer used her own rooms. The roof needed repair, and they were too damp and too cold, too isolated from the rest of the lonely house.

They both knew she was talking fast to avoid the memory of the day they had made love in her high bed in the room at the top of the château.

While Tony slept, she lit a fire of applewood in the library, and drew the curtains. When he came downstairs they ate a late supper together in the light of the fire, and sat, their arms round each other, on the deep leather sofa facing the chimney, while Tony gave her the story that had brought him back to Briteau.

The death of his friend in the flying accident he saw as a moment of truth, confirming his pacifism, and yet preventing him from being able to isolate himself any longer from what was happening in Europe. The non-combatant job was a compromise, he knew that. It was a word she had never thought she would hear him use. She remembered a conversation they had had in Paris. The most unthinkable thing, Tony had said, was to kill or be killed.

'So here I am,' he said finally. 'You can get me out of here into Spain, I hope? It's all part of the deal with Old Glory. I have to try to get back.'

He sounded cynical, and she guessed it was a cover for his true feelings about the war. Maybe it took a real pacifist to be able to come to Europe and make such a stand, even a compromise, in the face of what was happening. She would never bring herself to believe that the Tony she had known in Paris had changed.

'I don't want you to go. Violette and I have been alone here so long. Long enough.'

'But that's where your safety lies – this innocent set-up.'

313

Tony's voice was sharp, almost impatient. 'It's not safe for you to keep me here.'

It was the old dominance, and she knew she had been right about him; he had not changed. She told him there was no real organized escape route now, but that if they left in the early hours she could walk with him to a point in the hills from which he might find a guide down into Spain.

'And you?' Tony took her in his arms. 'You'd get back?'

'Of course. It would be getting light.'

He kissed her. 'I haven't touched anyone since I was here with you. Do you know that? They laugh at me on the base. Half of them think I'm a fag.'

'Ask them to talk to me.' She smiled up at him, knowing it had been a mistake to show her weakness and ask him to stay.

'After the war. We'll meet at the Ritz.'

'No – the street where we first met, outside your studio. We'll go on to the Ritz for tea.'

'Same time of day, another world. And the last time you were annoyed with me. You dropped your gloves and ran.'

'Maybe I should have gone on running.'

'Don't ever try that, Leonie.' He took her face between his hands.

It was the moment to tell him everything – about her love for Jacques Fabri and its roots in what was happening to France; about Erich Mannheim; about the man she had killed.

'Max was there,' she said instead. 'Do you remember?'

'Max.' He laid his head back, suddenly tired. 'If this war has taken his life too . . .'

She got up, smoothing her dress. She was right. Tony could never accept the things that had to be done in the face of defeat.

When she turned to look at him again, she saw that he had fallen into a heavy sleep, and for an hour she sat by the dying fire, watching his face. Until that night he had never shown her his vulnerable side, and even then it had been for no

314

more than a moment. He would always be the dominant one in their relationship. And if he rejected her she believed that it would be a ruthless, final rejection.

She shivered at the thought, but left the fire to die, and moved to her father's desk. There she lit a single candle and took writing paper from the centre drawer, and while Tony slept, she began to write.

They left the house just after three, under a sky of scudding clouds and a pale moon. When they had crossed the stream they walked briskly, making for the shelter at the edge of the meadow. Then as the ground smoothed out into a climb across steep grey rock they stopped briefly to rest, and Leonie talked about Mireille. She told Tony that one day she would share Briteau with her sister, as Paul had wanted. But Mireille had always been an unknown quantity, and if she was serious about her medical studies it might be some years before the terms of their father's will were fulfilled.

'I'll have to get to Paris as soon as the war's over,' she said. 'Tante Berthe seems to be handling the occupation all on her own, but she'll want me there, I think, once it's over.'

'Everything will be just fine.' Tony took her hand. 'We'll make love in Paris. A month and a day after the nightmare ends. You'll see. I wanted to last night, but not when I had to leave again so soon. It hurt too much last time.'

They climbed the rock slowly, side by side, and made good time. The cave was an hour away from where the track flattened again and led into a small pine wood, and Leonie knew she could get back by daylight. Meanwhile, if what Manuel had told her was still true, Luis would be there at the cave, a fixture, waiting for his wars to begin again. It was a gamble they had to take.

Halfway through the wood a movement to one side made Leonie clutch at Tony's coat. She sensed rather than saw a break in the green-black shadows, then nothing. They waited, holding their breath, then walked on steadily,

315

looking from side to side, until they came to the treeline and the moon broke through low cloud.

They stood, finding their bearings for the track to the cave, until a sound made them tense and turn back, to see the small figure of Manuel running barefoot towards them across the grass.

'You see.' He looked up at Leonie, great eyes pleading. 'I told you I would know.'

'How could I forget? And Luis? Is he still there?'

'Nothing has changed. Our contact in the next valley also.'

'Tony, this is your guide into Spain. He can take you to and on past the cave. You can rest there a little. Don't drink the wine!'

They smiled at each other, making light of the parting that had come too quickly. It was dangerous for Leonie to stay longer, and she could trust Manuel better than herself to find Luis and shelter for Tony.

'If you go now, you'll be back by daylight?' Tony asked, already knowing the answer.

'It's best.'

'It's too soon.' He gripped her hands in his.

She nodded, fighting back her tears. 'You can trust the boy.'

'You have such interesting friends these days.' The teasing was a cover, for a pain neither of them could take. But the words held too much irony for Leonie, and she looked down, not answering, as she felt in the pocket of her coat and found the letter she had written while he slept.

'They're all in here, Tony. All the interesting people, all the things you should know. Read it when you're safe.'

He took her into his arms in a single, agonized embrace, but she was already absent, thinking that when he knew all there was to know about her the meeting in Paris would become no more than a dream, for them both.

'See you in Paris. A month and a day. Be there.' Tony let her go, watching until she disappeared into the depths of the silent woods. Then Manuel tugged at his coat, and they began to climb.

As Leonie came to the bridge a stray vulture, its wings silver in the first light, dipped over the stream and gave a single wicked cry as it wheeled away, and then returned. She crossed and walked along the bank to the spot where it hovered, and in a clump of flattened rushes saw the brown and white fur ball that was Charlie's dead body.

There was an open wound, rough-edged, on the dog's neck. She thought at first that a fox had attacked it, or an eagle swooped down on it, live prey to take back to the eyrie in the mountains. Then as she picked the small body up and held it close she felt that it was still warm, and turning towards the house she saw the waiting Germans, and their dogs.

She walked towards them, her anger somehow giving her courage. They did not move, waiting for her to come close before the lieutenant gestured to the corporal with him to hold back the Dobermanns, and then clicked his heels, bowing to Leonie.

'May I ask what you are doing on my land? And who is responsible for this?'

'I apologize. It is to be regretted, Mademoiselle de Byron,' the lieutenant said. 'An accident. Perhaps the dog ran after you on your early morning walk? Your very early walk, may I say?'

'You may tell me why you are here,' she said, her voice ice, in spite of the pain of her heartbeat. She held Charlie's body very tight, as if it would protect her against what was to come.

'Let us walk back to the house,' the officer said. 'A few questions.'

'I too have questions.' She began to walk, so fast that the corporal panted slightly as he followed them, trying to keep up.

317

'Ours are serious, mademoiselle. A matter of the body of a man found not far from here. And a radio.'

'That is nothing to do with me.' She was glad they still had a hundred yards before they reached the kitchen garden. It would give her time to prepare her answers.

'Yours is the nearest house. Either we can arrest the whole village, or you can come with us and tell us what you know. From what we have observed of your attachment to your father's people, mademoiselle, I believe you will choose to talk to us.'

'You can believe what you like. There is nothing to talk about.'

'Then you will not object to coming to our headquarters, to explain how little there is to know?'

At that moment Violette appeared in the open doorway, and with a cry of rage ran forward to take Charlie from her arms. At a warning look from Leonie, she turned away, and carried the dog to her chair by the stove, where she sat rocking the body against her own strong frame, as if she would bring it back to life.

'And you will want your papers,' the lieutenant added. 'My corporal will go with you to your room to get what you need.'

'What is this?' Violette glared at him. 'I rise early to make coffee and I find the doors open, the house full of the Boches, this little creature dead.'

'Something bad has happened.' Leonie kept her voice as steady as she could. 'The body of a man has been found. And a radio.'

'The radio is a matter of the death sentence,' the German officer said casually.

'We know nothing of such things. All we do here is work.' Violette held Charlie close, staring at Leonie with eyes filled with silent questions.

'Violette, take Charlie to the Fabris' place. Close the house. I want you to stay with your friend Camille while I am away. It will not be for long.'

318

'Long enough for us to find out what you know of the Resistance in these parts,' the German officer cut in. 'And now – those papers. Or shall we take the old woman as well?'

Leonie walked slowly from the room, the corporal and dogs at her heels.

'I have told you – I know nothing,' she said. It was a practice reply, the one she was to make for many days to come, to her many interrogators.

In Bordeaux the night before Leonie's arrest Eduard Raymond drove Henri Massine to the Verdiers' mansion for a dinner with other members of the *Milicien*. The daughter was to be there, and would introduce her latest influential '*ami*'.

Raymond watched the other arrivals, then put the Peugeot into gear and turned to drive into the old quarter of the town. He had a curfew pass, so that he could collect his employer later.

'It has to be tonight,' he told Marie-Louise as they finished their meal. 'The widow Leblanc has passed me a file she found – letters he has typed himself. Someone must stop him. You will help me?'

'Of course.'

'I have the pass. I can get back to you. And you know what he's like these days – he'll have had plenty to drink.'

'He is getting careless.'

'It is an aspect of arrogance.'

'But if the widow knows, surely it is dangerous? And the existence of those letters – why should she have told you?'

'A patriot, and a woman unappreciated – a lethal combination, believe me. But all she will know for certain is that Henri Massine fails to appear on Monday. She will shed no tears.'

Raymond explained that the secret file showed that Henri Massine had been plotting for some time to destroy the American girl at Briteau. It was obvious, too, that Lise

319

Verdier had played some part in the betrayal of Leonie de Byron to the Germans. A member of the Gestapo had been planted at the château, but the deadline for his reports had come and gone without word. The German police were to move in on the whole village if they did not get the girl.

'To send spies to his own daughter's place, that is unforgivable. *La pauvre petite américaine.*'

'I can at least see that he betrays no one else,' Raymond said bitterly. 'If it is the last thing I do.'

Henri Massine left the Verdier house late that night in good spirits, ensconcing himself in the passenger seat with a sigh of satisfaction, cigar between thin lips, while Raymond closed the door with a heavy hand. From time to time on the drive back to the Massine house the chauffeur looked in the mirror at his employer. It was a cold, expressionless look, and it was still on his face when, having garaged the car, he let himself back into the house by the kitchen door and stood waiting in the dark.

The body was found on the Monday, when the chauffeur reported that his employer had failed to appear for the regular eight o'clock drive to the office. There were signs of a struggle, and a knife had been used, not too expertly. There was a great deal of blood. The intruder seemed to have gained entrance to the house by smashing a pane in the glass of the kitchen door. The chauffeur had known nothing, as he had spent the Saturday night with his friend, and Henri Massine had given strict instructions that he was not to be disturbed on the Sunday.

Responsibility for the killing was claimed by two local groups of patriots, and the Gestapo made several raids without success, closing the file with indecent haste on a man whom they had milked perhaps for too long, who had become a natural target. His latest revelation – concerning a village close to the Spanish border in the Pyrenees – had caused far too much trouble, and evidence of the village's guilt was not yet forthcoming. The matter was now out of their hands, in fact, and the main suspect had been transported to Paris for questioning by higher authorities: there was some talk that she might be useful in the inquiries concerning a Resistance fighter who was causing unrest in a Polish labour camp. A man called Fabri.

Verdier and his daughter Lise, breakfasting together on the morning the news of Henri Massine's murder broke, remarked that someone should write to poor Marguerite in Canada. It was a pity her husband had not lived to see their granddaughter inherit those estates at Briteau.

Lise made a mental note to check that the German officer with whom she had been to the Riviera that summer had not forgotten the information she had let slip about Leonie de Byron, after they had seen her at Briteau. When Mireille returned to France to claim her inheritance she would find she had a good friend in Lise Verdier . . . they could look forward to some really good times at the château.

'The thing Henri Massine would really have liked to see,' she said, 'was that American girl put in her proper place.'

New York. October '43.

My darling girl, This is a letter I'll not send. I'll bring it with me, that day in Paris we've promised ourselves. I'll tell you how I got to Lisbon in the back of a crazy truck, stoned out of my mind by the red wine that bear Luis made me drink all day. There was a clipper leaving Lisbon each night, about six – they told me it would be packed with VIPs, fleeing diplomats, and American press. There was just room for a GI – that's me – with a broken ankle – I got it on the climb down into Spain after that day in the cave. Then the real journey home began, with a touch-down in some goddam river bed in Portuguese Guiana, all mud huts and mosquitoes, then Natal, so that we could

321

take the shortest route across the Atlantic. I left them in Bermuda, and got a lift back on a proper plane. I read your letter in Lisbon, where I felt far from safe. Afterwards I wept for you, for us. I don't know how I feel about it yet. But I'll be there at the studio. So I trust you believe in me enough to be there yourself.

Tony.

CHAPTER NINETEEN

Klaus Werner's love of women had always been confined to delight in a haunting virgin face in an early pietà, a gentle Renoir girl in a frivolous hat. He had several close women friends, including a Professor of Fine Art at Munich who had continued to adore him for the three decades since he had successfully avoided her plans for marriage in their student days. Amongst the female staff attached to the army of occupation in Paris there were numerous candidates for his bed; the handsome, fair-haired commandant of Fresnes prison was a man to be cultivated. But, as several French women agents posing as collaboratrices in Paris found, he was sexually unapproachable, in the habit of leaving late-night parties alone, and more interested in the paintings hung in the chic apartments leased by Nazi party members than in the intrigue that surrounded them.

The counter-espionage branch of the Wehrmacht security forces in Paris numbered another serious art-lover, and at one of the parties given for high-up members of the Abwehr Klaus Werner remarked to him *sotto voce* that it would be good to see something later than Watteau while one drank one's martinis. The list of artists proscribed by Hitler had recently lengthened, and both men found themselves paying high prices on the black market for contemporary work.

The Abwehr officer replied that if – he meant when – victory came, things would be no better. Their private collections would remain just that. Yet he still could not resist the game, and had recently made a contact – a Swiss – who had two really important Picassos on offer. But he was proving sticky about price.

'He lives near you when he's in Paris. Erich Mannheim – he has an apartment in the block next to yours. I have the address somewhere. It would be amusing to see if you can beat him down.'

During his next weekend leave, which he spent at his *garçonnier* in the avenue Kléber, Werner left his card at Erich's apartment. The concierge informed him that Herr Mannheim was in Zurich, but that he should be in Paris within the month.

On the desk in his office at Fresnes prison next day Klaus Werner found a new entry in the register of women prisoners. Turning a page that ended with the number of the grave in which a girl from a *réseau* in Normandy had been buried in the prison yard the night before, he read *Leonie de Byron, age 23, parentage French/unknown*. There was a note stamped at the Gestapo offices in the avenue Foch attached to the page, to the effect that the woman may or may not have a connection with the disappearance of an *agent provocateur* in the district where she owned land, but that her importance was that she must have information about Resistance work in the same area. The woman also had probable, though as yet unestablished, American connections.

Leonie took her first turn to sleep on the narrow bed that ran the length of one wall of the cell she shared with the three Frenchwomen. Closing her eyes against the cold glare of the single bulb that lit the place day and night she thought for the thousandth time of the moment the Mercedes staff car had driven away from the château. She had looked back helplessly to where Violette stood on the terrace, weeping openly, Charlie's small tousled corpse still clutched to her body. Then, as they turned into the road, she wrenched her gaze from the house and looked out over the steep terraces to her right, and the line of the low hills that bordered her land.

'It is quite a good view,' the lieutenant remarked. 'And your interest in what goes on in these hills is of great interest to us, Fräulein.'

She noticed that he no longer addressed her by her French title, but was too shocked by what was happening to Briteau, to herself, to make much of it. It was only days later, when the grey-mice female guards scuttled up and down the corridors of the prison speaking amongst themselves in German, and the women prisoners sat in careful silence, suspicious even of each other, that she realized she had been uprooted and thrown down in a world where the army of occupation made the rules.

Her first meeting with the prison commandant did nothing to assuage her growing fear. The exquisite politeness with which the tall blond German offered her a chair, a cigarette, a chance to save herself if she would give information, was more frightening than the threat of torture. Her training in England had prepared her for either, but not for the exhaustion and latent terror that would make her doubt her own ability to withstand interrogation.

'I know nothing. We care only about the land, at Briteau. Your own soldiers would tell you the same.'

'And the dead man? The body found on that land?' Klaus Werner, who had come to the position at Fresnes only because of the repatriation of the previous commandant for reasons unknown, found that he had to make a show of consulting the Gestapo notes in front of him to conceal his reaction to the girl's beauty.

He had interviewed dozens of women before they went to their interrogation and had become accustomed to solid, strong girls from the provinces who would not break physically and were too blindly patriotic to give in to mental pressure. There had been the occasional sophisticate, an agent who had played at collaboration; one had even pleaded a special case as they had met at an SS party. There had been English women obviously in love with the French men they would, or would not, betray. But this young French aristocrat with the well controlled fear in those eyes . . . she sat across from him, straight-backed, proud rather than arrogant, with the exquisite face of a madonna. It was her stillness that made him think of a woman in a painting . . . and with a slight frown he suppressed the thought of what torture might do to that stillness, if she took too long to break.

In a flat, ceremonial voice he recited the possible consequences of lack of co-operation. The château might be forfeit, her village certainly under risk of destruction.

'I know. It has happened elsewhere. But you have forgotten – I know nothing.' Leonie refused a cigarette, and stared at Werner coldly as he lit his own.

'There is one other thing' – she knew that he meant before she would be taken from his office, out of his sphere of influence perhaps – 'but I was a frequent visitor to Paris before the war, and I am certain I have seen your face, many times. Perhaps you were an actress, a Comédienne? I am a great admirer of Racine.'

'My family . . . my father would not have wanted that. I was at school here, that is all. Then I went home, to Briteau.'

'And your mother? I see there is no entry in your papers concerning your mother. Would she have approved of something more theatrical, perhaps?'

Leonie sat quite still, remembering the birthdays so well staged by Zoe, the innate style that turned every head as she entered a room, the seventeen years for which Zoe was the only parent Leonie had known. The only parent she could claim, if she were to save herself and Briteau, was the man her mother had once loved.

'I cannot say,' Leonie said. 'It is something else that I simply do not know.'

The beatings began at three the next morning, when she was pulled from the floor of the cell by a woman dressed from head to foot in grey, the coarse material brushing Leonie's face as her head was pushed under a cold tap somewhere at the far end of the corridor, then marched down three flights of steps to a thick-walled room bare of any furniture but a set of heavy chairs and a lamp that lit the place as if it were the set for a low-budget movie.

It lasted for four nights, and as she returned to her cell each time the other women became more friendly, making a place for her where she would feel least pain, congratulating her on the fact that her interrogators had not touched her face.

'Can't think why, américaine.' They had soon detected the New Yorker beneath her near-perfect accent. 'Maybe the commandant fancies you. Though you'll be the first, from what we hear.'

When they were sure the grey mice were not too close, they brought out the only reading material they had between them – a 'Courier de l'Air' leaflet dropped over Normandy by the RAF weeks before. The girl who had died the night of Leonie's arrival had left it to them, a small legacy. It had news of advances in Italy, a new front soon to get started in Holland. It was a signal of hope, to women who knew that their situation was hopeless.

On the fifth night of her imprisonment, Klaus Werner reviewed Leonie's situation. He wanted to get away quickly for the weekend. Erich Mannheim had left word that they must meet for drinks and talk about pictures. The entry for Leonie in the register stared up at him accusingly as he looked at his watch. 'Her face has not been touched?'

'There was a moment – we were almost sure she knew what we were talking about. The murder. But no, your orders stand. Her face is untouched.'

'If we get her to admit to the killing,' Klaus Werner said, 'it's the death sentence. I think we'll let her settle down this weekend. Then you can move in for some more treatment. I think we should be certain.'

'Very well.' His lieutenant clicked his heels and left the

office, while Klaus Werner closed the register and locked it in his desk.

The telephone number Erich Mannheim had left at the *garçonnier* was of a place off the Champs Elysées, and Werner arranged to meet him there on the Sunday morning. He decided to walk, and crossed the Champs Elysées only minutes before the ceremonial daily march-past of the occupying forces. It was a show of strength he found particularly distasteful and unnecessary; they were well settled in Paris now, and what shadows were waiting for them to the north and west were still a long way off. The hectic, headlong goosestep procession down the most beautiful thoroughfare in the world seemed to him a sacrilege – and ill-advised.

The sound of the distant brass band as the march began reached him as he turned off the main street and came to the salon. The orchid pink name, 'Caresse', was freshly painted on each of the side windows, but behind the signs they were swathed in dark curtains, as was the glass door. He rang a bell. Within moments the door was opened by a heavily built, ageing man with staring blue eyes and a careful smile. They shook hands, and Werner followed Erich Mannheim to Zoe's old office on the first floor.

There was a bottle of Dom Perignon in an ice bucket on a side table, long fluted glasses ready beside it. The air was heavy with some expensive but slightly alien scent which Werner – always the gallant with the women he deigned to escort – could not identify.

Opposite the chair which the Swiss banker had placed ready for him was one of the Picassos. A girl in blue, simplicity itself, the artist at his most engaging and in-genuous. On the far side of the room, at just the right distance for the perspective, a cubist landscape of a small Mediterranean town, seen perhaps from a hill above the houses, Picasso in brighter mood.

328

But Werner, after a quick look at the two paintings he had come to see, was distracted by a larger picture which was stacked against a wall, almost as if it had been dumped there unceremoniously, to be examined at a later time.

'Who is the girl? In the New York scene.' He did not put the question until he had the first glass of champagne in his hand. There was no hurry. If he bought the other paintings he could ask for this one at a good price.

'Not for sale, I'm afraid,' Erich Mannheim said abruptly. Then: 'That is, it belongs to the artist still.'

'He's an American?'

'Commercial. Not important. We used him for our first season.'

'I know the girl's face. Do you remember her, Herr Mannheim? Do you know where she is now?'

Erich began to sweat lightly. He crossed to Tony's painting of Leonie walking in a dream New York landscape, and began to turn it to the wall.

'No. Don't do that.' Werner's voice was sharp. 'I simply asked if you have any idea where this girl is now?'

'Then my answer is no. She left Paris when the war began. Disappeared.'

'She is French?'

Suddenly wary, Erich shrugged indifference. His dossier on Werner, quickly assembled when he found the commandant's card at his apartment, included his position at Fresnes. 'Very French.'

'Herr Mannheim, I really want to buy that picture. You may ask your price. It is not so much the girl's unusual beauty, but the mood of the whole thing. Now I wonder, why did the artist see her in that New York setting?'

'I cannot imagine.' Erich made a pretence of wanting more champagne, and held the bottle out to Werner, who refused. 'I don't understand your interest. As I said, the artist is without importance.'

'Perhaps I would not altogether agree with you on that. But my interest is that I do happen to know where Leonie de

Byron is, Mannheim. And I think you may be in a position to help her. I need more information.'

'You are trying to tell me that you are holding her at Fresnes prison.' Erich sat on a chair facing Werner, and leant forward, sweating freely now.

'Precisely.'

'And you must know that as a Swiss neutral I do not play these games? I value my travel pass too highly, for one thing.'

'I am sure we could do a deal, all the same.' Werner kept his eyes on Erich's face, trying to fathom what this cold, wealthy man knew and felt about the girl.

Erich took a deep breath. 'I would be interested only in securing her freedom.'

'Ah.' Werner produced a silver cigarette case and offered it to him.

Erich stood up, and walked over to Tony's painting, then turned. 'The Picasso of your choice. No information. No charge. I want the girl.'

The grey-mouse attendant called Leonie from the cell the next evening when she made her rounds. The other prisoners watched in silence, suspicious of any change in the routine. As the door clanged into place and the guard's business-like footsteps mingled with Leonie's painful, shuffling walk, then faded, one of the women whispered, '*Courage, américaine.*'

'In here.' The guard pushed Leonie into a washroom on the first floor of the building, and another uniformed German woman stepped forward, a large towel over one arm, and pulled a shower curtain back briskly from a partition beside the primitive toilet.

'You're a lucky bitch, sharing our bathroom,' the attendant said in German. Leonie, too dazed to try to understand, stood impassively as between them they stripped her.

When she walked into the commandant's office she was

330

wearing a plain woollen skirt and jumper two sizes too big for her, her hair, still damp, was scraped back from her face, and she shuffled forward to take the chair Werner offered in the old laced shoes in which she had been arrested and which had been confiscated when she arrived at Fresnes.

At a sign from Werner the women who escorted her left the office. Leonie, prepared for a final, deadly sentence as a judgement on her obstinacy, kept her eyes on Werner's face. The shower and clean clothes had given her new courage, but it was courage only to face an end to things. She realized as she sat down and refused the offered cigarette that she had been nearer to breaking than she thought – she could not go through the whole routine of interrogation again from that polite overture to the first, blinding blow.

It was as Werner lit his cigarette that her eyes strayed to the open door of the adjacent office, and she saw the tall figure of a fair-haired man waiting, his back to her.

In a soft, unhurried voice Werner told her that she was fortunate in her friends, and that he was about to give her her freedom. She must be discreet, never talk of what was to happen. And there was a condition: she must go with the man who waited for her in the next room.

'Herr Mannheim?' Werner called to Erich, and as she heard the name Leonie came back to life.

'No!'

She stood quickly, forgetting her pain, and gripped the back of her chair, keeping it between them as Erich walked in. The first thing he saw was the proud, unmarked face, before his eyes fell on the bruised hands that gripped the chair, and he became aware of the odd, involuntary crouch of a body that waits for violence.

'Leonie. Listen to me. I have reached an agreement with these people. The details need not concern you. All that matters is that you can be in Switzerland, with your mother, hours from now.' He took a step closer to her, and saw in her eyes that her hatred of him was stronger than fear.

'I thought – hoped – I would never see you again,' she

331

said. 'And now you think you can collect me, like some piece of merchandise? How can you be so sure I will go?'

'If you value your life –'

'It is because I value my life that I refuse.' She glanced at Klaus Werner, who stood watching them in fascinated disbelief. He saw that there was more between this man and the girl than he was ever to know. 'Don't *you* see that?'

'Your life may well be forfeit,' he said. 'I have delayed the decision as long as I can.'

'You cannot know what you are doing, if you think I prefer to go with this man. I refuse. You cannot force me.'

'Leonie –' As Erich touched her arm in a last attempt to reach her she turned towards him and spat in his face.

It was a gesture of helpless fury, against all that had happened in the prison, against what Erich had done to her, against the long path along which he had led Zoe to useless, sterile safety.

Erich's hand dropped to his side. He spoke to Werner. 'I can talk again with you?'

'It's no good!' Leonie hissed the words. 'I must see this through. This is where I belong now. And no deal you can make over my body will persuade me to go with you.'

Werner and Erich exchanged looks. For a single, absurd moment, Werner found himself glad that the girl was not leaving with this man. He pressed a bell on his desk, and indicated that Erich should return to the inner office.

'You will leave the way you came in, Mannheim. And please, take your gift with you.'

While Leonie was escorted back to her cell, the commandant opened the drawer in his desk and brought out the register of women prisoners. At the foot of the page for Leonie the line waited for his signature for her execution. He paused, and wrote: *Sent to Ravensbruck concentration camp. Inquiries continue.*

In Zoe's office, Erich began to pack the last of his collection

332

of paintings. He drank a brandy and sat smoking for an hour before he carried them down to the waiting car. It took him five minutes to drive through the curfew under the dim blue street lights to the rue Louis. It had begun to rain, and he tugged impatiently at the bell to the courtyard gates, cursing softly in German as Jeannine trotted, keys jangling, from her *loge.*

He said that he had to see Mademoiselle Berthe de Byron on urgent business, and Jeannine answered tartly that he should have telephoned, when he would have learned that madame was not well. Pressing a generous *pourboire* into her hand, Erich asked her to give his name, and to say that his visit concerned Mademoiselle Leonie.

'Very well, if that is so,' she sighed. 'It is not quite time for bed, and I will see. Let us hope that the Germans who live above are not making too much noise for once.'

Berthe de Byron was waiting for him in the hallway of her apartment, her white hair and pale face giving her a ghostly look under the weak centre light. She walked ahead of him into the drawing-room with the deliberate gait of stubborn old age, and did not offer him a chair, but stood waiting for him to explain his visit.

He told her that he had discovered that Leonie was in Fresnes prison and accused of every kind of offence against the regime. He did not think the commandant would lightly pass the death sentence, but she was in danger. The family should do all it could to check on her welfare, to make certain that if she were moved they knew where she was sent. There were records kept of all such things, and a family of the de Byrons' status would perhaps stand some chance of getting better treatment for her, even of engineering her freedom. He did not refer to his own efforts to make a deal.

'Leonie is strong,' Berthe said at last. 'Strong-willed, also. It is the strength of the mother, the will of my nephew Paul. Of course I will inform our family notary. I am sure your advice is good. But tell me – what of her mother? I should like news of her.'

Erich, taken aback, murmured that Zoe Byron was in Zurich. 'I was not aware that you knew her.'

'In recent years,' Berthe said, 'I have sometimes thought that perhaps the mother is the more vulnerable of the two.'

'In recent years?'

'I have known Zoe Byron for a very long time, Herr Mannheim.'

It was not until she heard the courtyard gates click into place behind her visitor that the old woman limped to the hall cupboard in which she had hurriedly concealed her walking stick on his arrival. Returning to the drawing-room she allowed herself – for the first time for many months – the luxury of tears. As she dried her eyes on a fine lace-edged handkerchief she saw that the Swiss banker had left his card, with the address of the Zurich apartment, on the small table beside her chair.

Deciding to drive overnight to Zurich, Erich took the Nancy road in a dank, persistent rain that anticipated winter. He wanted to get out of Paris, away from the haunting memory of Leonie's face and the knowledge of what she still had to endure. On the passenger seat were the two Picassos which Klaus Werner would now never own. Piled on the back seat, and protected by the last of the clothes Erich had kept in Paris, were Tony Shaw's paintings of Leonie.

He drove very fast, the car holding the road superbly as always in spite of the treacherous surface. Repairs were a thing of the past since the disaster of the northern campaigns, and the roads were an obstacle course of cave-ins and small craters.

He was halfway to Nancy when the sirens went, but he heard nothing above the whine of the car's engines and the heavy thud of the windscreen wipers as they swept to and fro against the glass.

The RAF plane was on its way back from Germany, a rogue bomber that had been deflected from target and lost its companions. Ahead of the Mercedes by less than a mile a convoy of German lorries forged through the dark, going east with supplies. The British pilot's observer guessed it was as good a moment as any to offload the remaining bombs, and as they bounced in a sure, destructive line along the convoy, the last fell directly on the Mercedes.

In Zurich, Erich's apartment was in darkness when the telephone rang. Zoe, who had not slept, switched on her bedside lamp and lifted the receiver.

It was Tante Berthe. 'I know it is foolish of me,' she said in French. 'They say these calls are impossible, but, my dear, I talked and talked to the operator, and got an old woman's way. It is to tell you that I have had a visitor, and that you must have courage. As your daughter, I know, will have courage also. And when this war is over, you will come to me here. Perhaps both of you.'

'Tante Berthe,' Zoe said, 'I know better than most people that when you make up your mind about something everyone else might just as well give in gracefully. But – calling after all these years – something has happened, hasn't it?'

Berthe told her all she knew, and, as Zoe's questions and tears began, assured her that Charles Vincent's office also knew of Leonie's arrest, and the family's many friends would do all they could to save her.

'I have spent half the night on the telephone, my dear. If there is anything more I can do, you must ask.'

Zoe said she would start inquiries in Zurich with the American Red Cross, and would come straight to Paris herself. Berthe cautioned her not to do anything so foolish. As an American with no pass she would find herself in prison as soon as she got through – if she got through at all.

'When we get her back,' Berthe's voice betrayed apprehension, and a plea for forgiveness, 'will you tell her the truth? That it was I who ruled that her father should not know of her existence?'

Zoe hesitated, the years falling away to the afternoon

335

when she sat in the drawing-room at the rue Louis and found that in Paul's aunt she had an implacable adversary.

'No,' she said. 'We must never tell her. Paul knew her when it mattered. And I think my daughter should not have to suffer any more.'

The news of Leonie's arrest spread through the village within an hour, and Yves Pascal – already alerted by a rumour of the discovery of the German's body in the woods beyond the château the night before – cycled to the Darnand's to tell them. He had tried to telephone the château in the early hours, when a villager had told him that the Germans had unearthed a corpse, but there had been no reply – and it was more than he dared risk, with the place now swarming with Germans, to break the curfew and go there in person.

Edith Darnand asked him if there was any proof that Leonie had killed the German. If there was, then her life, and maybe that of the whole village, was at stake. Marcel was less emotional. He said dryly that they could only hope that the girl's character and her training in England would equip her to face interrogation.

Later that day he transmitted the whole story to London, and the decoded message reached Denholm Collins's desk that night. Denholm read and reread the cold, routine words, remembering the last time he had seen Leonie, in London, and the moment during the harvest dance at Briteau in the summer before the war when he had realized her true potential. As he went through the ritual of filing the report with the Free French and the Special Services, he tried, and failed, to blot out her image. It was he who had given her name for training, and he who had indirectly turned her into a woman who could kill.

Two days later he heard that his double agent in Paris, a young girl from Normandy, had been executed in Fresnes prison, and knew that yet another link in the trail that might have led him to Leonie de Byron had been broken.

The vigil by the telephone in the Zurich apartment became a way of life for Zoe. She stared unseeing at the modern masterpieces that lined the walls, smoking endlessly, never prepared for the terror each time the bell rang. Sometimes she told herself as she lifted the receiver that Leonie's voice would be on the line. Sometimes she convinced herself, for a moment that soon passed, that it would be Erich, back from whatever mysterious errand had recently meant his complete disappearance.

It was a call from Caresse that alerted her to the fact that Erich was really missing. The manageress told her that he had never come back to sign some letters he had insisted were urgent, and had not checked on a new consignment of perfume reserved for certain unnamed friends in Paris.

Zoe gave nothing away. She said she expected the director to contact her with a date for his return and that in the meantime she would deal with urgent queries by phone. Asking casually when Erich had last been seen at the salon, she ran her finger down his desk diary, hoping to find an appointment that would give some clue to what had happened. The last entry was *Paris*. It was the week that Leonie had been arrested.

The next day she sent for Erich's Swiss lawyer, explaining that she wished to discuss something extremely confidential. He and Erich usually met over a working lunch, and he was hardly known to Zoe. She knew, however, that he was one of Erich's board of directors at the bank.

Accepting a whisky, he took the news of Erich's disappearance without surprise. None of them queried Erich Mannheim's movements these days, he reminded her. Surely all that mattered was that he still ran her Paris company so well?

'That's just why I'm convinced something is wrong,' Zoe said. 'He would never leave things undone there, and he rings at least once a week while he's out of Switzerland.'

The man studied her under lowered eyelids. He would

have thought such a woman merited a call rather more often.

'If he is in trouble, Madame Byron,' he said, 'Erich will find some way of letting us know. And you must surely be aware by now that he is perfectly capable of looking after himself?'

'But – he could have been arrested –'

'Nonsense.' The lawyer smiled at the thought. 'It is out of the question.'

'Or injured – or worse – I don't know what I should be doing about this.'

'What you should do, madame, is stay calm, and deal with your affairs – with my help if you wish – until your – colleague's return.'

Zoe leaned forward, her eyes dark. 'I sometimes think Erich is dead,' she whispered.

The lawyer frowned, and put down his glass. 'If Erich Mannheim is dead, madame, it will be many months before we can accept such a disaster as either official or legal. Where is the body? Where are the people who must know? You will have to go on with your own life, as I have advised you. You will have to run your business, perhaps for years, as if Erich Mannheim were about to walk back into our lives any moment.'

'But that is all I want,' she said involuntarily, surprised at how deeply the idea moved her. Her efforts on Leonie's behalf, and her fears for Erich, had recently freed her from the silken cocoon in which he had wrapped her since the war began. But the sense of freedom was in itself a kind of betrayal, if Erich had been killed.

'I can assure you, madame,' the lawyer said dryly, 'that if– when – we were in possession of proof of his death you would become one of the wealthiest women in Europe.'

CHAPTER TWENTY

Rumours of the Allied landings in Normandy the summer after Leonie was sent to Ravensbruck reached the camp through the complex web of information, gossip, and propaganda which was sifted by a committee of women prisoners intent on maintaining a link with the outside world. There were other committees, led by women who bore the stamp of survival, but did not always escape the beatings, or death, that were the reward of discovery. Leonie held back in the first weeks, her training in England standing her in good stead. She saw that life could profitably become an obsessive concern for detail, and that by eking out the day's small tasks she could make the time go by more quickly.

Watching her quiet, controlled behaviour from a distance, a Norwegian inmate approached her after a month and suggested that she join the group of women who made it their business to stay alive for just one purpose: to inform the outside world after the war what life at Ravensbruck had been. The Normandy landings came almost a year after Leonie's arrival, and gave the group the morale boost they needed. The knowledge that France had again become a battlefield both tore at her heart and gave her new hope.

She began to allow herself the luxury of memories, hugging them to herself at night as she lay between two other women on the narrow shelf that was their bed. The first days at Briteau, life with Sarah in Paris at the Collège Madeleine, seemed closer in her daydreams than the brutish reality of the camp. There was little sense of the seasons in concentration camp life apart from the intense heat and cold, and

Leonie found that she could evoke the shade of the trees at the edge of the terraces at Briteau, or the walk in the first snow through the Tuileries with Tony and Max, and then sleep refreshed, as if she had escaped her prison for a few hours.

When the Norwegian woman was executed among a group of prisoners chosen haphazardly in reprisal for some small offence by an inmate, Leonie's life entered a new phase. She made up her mind to survive, and to finish the work the dead woman had organized. She faced harsh reality every minute of every twenty-four hours, avoiding a guard in a bad mood, saving food on a good day to make more of the next, keeping her thin body and cracked skin free from lice, and at the same time she began to store a record in her mind of all that she had to witness.

Sometimes she thought of Erich Mannheim, without regrets. If he still lived with Zoe, he must live with the knowledge that her daughter despised him so deeply that she had chosen to lose her freedom rather than accept his patronage. When she thought of her mother, it was with a tenderness that had rarely existed between them.

On a Saturday in August, only days before the war went into its sixth year, Berthe de Byron took her walking stick from the hall cupboard and made her way down to the courtyard, where Jeannine and a group of neighbours who had lived all their lives in the rue Louis waited for her. In the morning sunlight the old people began to walk in the direction of the Champs Elysées. The narrow streets were busy with similar small bands of Parisians, the women arm in arm, the old men shoulder to shoulder. As they came to the Champs Elysées they were caught up in the larger crowds, and held on to each other tightly, fearful of separation. Then, as the parade that was the symbol of the liberation of Paris began, with Charles de Gaulle walking at its head, they pressed forward, men and women openly weeping.

There had been street fighting in the area as recently as the previous week; pockets of Resistance fighters taking reprisals from any Germans who had been left behind; Germans making a last stand against the American armoured cars; civilians letting fly at last against the army that had repressed their city for four years.

Now, from a rooftop somewhere above the dense summer green of the chestnut trees, a sniper opened fire. Instinctively, the crowds covered their heads, or fell flat, protecting each other with their bodies. Berthe de Byron was not in the habit of falling to her knees when she was afraid. Announcing to her friends from the rue Louis that she was not yet ready to be killed, she stood her ground, and was able to watch Charles de Gaulle continue his slow, unflinching march down the wide street as the sniping became spasmodic, and died away.

It was more than six months before the Americans crossed the Rhine and it became safe for Zoe to return to France. Leaving the details of the settlement of Erich's affairs to the lawyer in Zurich – who had at last initiated the procedures legalizing his death – she packed a single suitcase with essentials, and begged a lift in an American Red Cross car.

She arrived in Paris to find it in the grip of an ice-cold winter. The blue street lighting left over from the Occupation made the white faces of the people who walked hurriedly through the dark look like those of actors on a stage ill-lit for some old-fashioned melodrama. But through the windows of the many small cafés that had sprung back into life since the Germans left there were signs that the old Paris was still alive and well.

Zoe walked the last yards to the salon, and – as always – paused outside, remembering the time she had bought the silver hairband to wear on her first date with Paul. Then, taking a deep breath, she walked in – and found herself the centre of a clamorous welcome from the few staff who remained.

341

As she climbed the stairs to the first floor they clustered behind her, telling her how well things were going, how many old clients had returned – or disappeared.

A very thin, elegant figure in sables, the lines of tension and grief in her face concealed by a mask of perfection, she paused and looked back.

'I know it seems unfriendly,' she said, 'but just for the next few moments I have to go it alone.'

Closing the office door behind her, she walked to the centre of the room, put her suitcase down, and looked around. The offices were as beautifully furnished, as uncluttered, as when she had first designed them. Her desk was a pool of glass and chrome, the clean blotter exactly centred, the gold pen where she had left it in the crystal tray.

The walls were bare of pictures, but she had long since accepted that Erich would have sold the Picassos in the end if the price was right.

'But there's something else missing,' she said aloud, and went to sit at her desk, watching the room as if waiting for a clue to what had caused her mounting unease.

Then she remembered that from the day they had commissioned Tony Shaw to do the artwork for the Caresse campaign the room had been stacked with his paintings of Leonie. Now not a single canvas, not even a sketch of her daughter remained, the vanished portraits a symbol of Leonie's own disappearance.

Zoe picked up the telephone, at the same time reaching in her handbag for a scrap of paper on which the Red Cross driver who had brought her to Paris had scribbled an address. It was that of the old Gestapo offices in the avenue Foch, now a centre for the tracing and rehabilitation of prisoners of war, deportees, refugees, and the thousands of victims of the concentration camps who may or may not have survived.

Zoe gave her name, and her relationship to the person she wanted to find. She was put through to the young English girl who was assisting the head of the department which would help.

The dates of Leonie's probable imprisonment at Fresnes and her subsequent removal were noted. 'Give us an hour or two,' the girl said, 'and then perhaps you could call round? Lady Hume can see you early tomorrow.'

The two women met in the crowded offices of the rehabilitation centre, surrounded by anxious relatives who came there every day, huddled in their coats and scarves against the bitter cold. The SS had left the building without ceremony, and without heat. Lady Hume told Zoe that they had also left her club in a state of near-dereliction. But she had reclaimed it, and ran a centre there for women who had returned from camps to find that no one they cared about had survived the war.

'And Leonie,' she said quietly, returning to her desk. She ran her finger down a list of names. 'There was an old woman who came here every day for almost a month when we first opened. A Frenchwoman. De Byron. We had no news for her, I'm afraid. Then there was a gap, and after about a week the family lawyer came in her place.'

'Charles Vincent,' Zoe said automatically.

Lady Hume gave her a keen look. 'The old lady died, I'm afraid. This winter has been hell. Monsieur Vincent left his card. The address . . .' She flicked through a notebook.

'I know the address.'

'I think they'd like to see you. There is an apartment, on the rue Louis. The old lady left it to your daughter.'

'I see.'

Lady Hume walked with her down to the street. Looking up at the iron sky through the bare branches of the chestnut trees, Zoe felt that spring would never come.

'Don't give up hope. We do get the most incredible results. Come round to the club if you feel low – you'll see how many girls have survived, and all of them with much less waiting for them than Leonie.'

'Maybe she'll go straight to Briteau . . . if she's alive.

There's more for her there than I have ever been able to give her. Maybe I should look for her there.'

'I'll never forgive you if you do.' It was the voice of the formidable English aristocrat accustomed to getting her own way. 'There are still pockets of fighting on the west Atlantic coast. A patriot German will stick like a limpet. Anyone with the least bit of common sense will keep out for some time.'

As she walked away in the direction of the salon, other women eyeing her furs with hungry, suspicious looks, it occurred to Zoe that neither of them had mentioned the occasion of their first meeting. The first class staterooms, the parties, the designer clothes, had all been a glittering farewell, had they but known it, to the Humes' world of privilege and to Zoe's world of ambition pursued in style.

Now, as she walked quickly through the streets where she had strolled with Paul in the euphoric days after another war, she felt that there was nothing left but the ill-concealed envy in the stares of white-faced women whose brave attempts against all the odds to dress with the old Parisian flair made her heart ache. Nothing left, except to find their daughter. Strange, she told herself, that Paul – who had dishonoured them without knowing it – had taught her by all he had done for Leonie in the end, and by his death, what honour meant.

'It is a matter of honour,' she had said once to Erich in New York, when he was at the height of his campaign to persuade her to return to France. 'I made a pact.'

To her annoyance, at the word honour Erich threw back his head in one of his rare, deep laughs.

'My dear Zoe, you never cease to astound me. You are the most remarkable woman I have ever met. You cling to your own pain with such a degree of angst that I swear you were born out of the very heart of Europe. And at the same time you attribute honour to your motives. You are splendid. Now, please, can you bring yourself to tell the past to go to hell?'

Although the camp gates were open and the guards had disappeared, the women prisoners held back. Some of them clung to the high steel fencing, faces pressed close to it, as if doubting that they were at liberty to look through it from the other side – on a March day that froze the lines of prison huts black under a leaden sky, in a landscape peopled by women so thin that they were unsexed, eyes hugely radiant yet blank in emaciated faces, feet bound in rags.

The Americans had crossed the Rhine into Germany in March and the nightmare discovery of the camps had begun. Their armoured cars and transit vans turned into the Ravensbruck compound and bumped across the ridged, frozen mud. Some of the women turned away, covering their faces with their hands, others ran forward on legs that ten minutes before had barely carried them.

Leonie emerged from the hut she had shared with the Norwegians clutching the cloth folder in which they had stored the scraps of paper on which they had recorded their lives in the camp. They had kept it hidden, changing the hiding-place every few days, and as the first of the Allied staff cars drew into the compound Leonie went to retrieve it.

A square-shouldered US Army captain stepped from the passenger seat of the car as she appeared in the doorway of the hut. He moved cautiously, aware that the prisoners were akin to scared animals surprised in their lair. Then, as Leonie began to walk towards him he stopped, and waited for her.

'Do you have something for me there?' he asked as she came within a yard of him. He was struck by the fierce beauty of the wild, thin face, and the colour of the dark blue eyes against the white of the girl's short hair. The long legs moved awkwardly, yet the girl still had grace.

She held out the folder, the familiar American accent touching a nerve of memory, telling her she must trust someone.

But when she stepped back she said curtly, in her father's tongue: 'I am French.'

*

Charles Vincent looked down at the papers on his desk for a long moment as Leonie took the chair facing him, easing her legs stiffly, her thin hands grasping the straps of an old handbag given to her by Lady Hume as if she feared it would be taken from her. The girl was still beautiful, perhaps more lovely than when she had first called on him asking to meet her father. But the shock of the white hair against the olive skin went through him like a knife. It did not age her; the ageing was in the eyes, and it brought out a family likeness to the de Byrons that he had not seen in her before. It was as if he was meeting the young Berthe de Byron his father must have known, and the rightness of Berthe's legacy to the American girl was all that gave him the courage to meet the look in her eyes and tell her that the apartment in the rue Louis was hers.

'But I must go to Briteau, as soon as possible.' Leonie shook her head. 'There will be so much to do.'

'Your aunt – your father's aunt – will want you to use the Paris apartment. It has been in the family for generations.'

'Perhaps. If I visit here . . .' The life she had once led in Paris seemed grotesquely unreal since the months in Ravensbruck. She had been driven to the notary's offices in the boulevard de la Madeleine from the avenue Foch, and had sat well back watching the streets as if a German patrol might stop them at any minute. In the ancient cage of the lift she had felt sick, and as she stepped out at the *deuxième étage* she had fought a wave of faintness.

The attack had passed quickly, and she found that she could think clearly as Charles Vincent gave her the details of Tante Berthe's will.

'I just wish I'd seen her again,' she said at last. 'She'd know why I can't stay in Paris just now.'

'Of course. But your mother is here also – did Lady Hume tell you that?'

'Yes. I know I must see her. I – I want to. But first I am going back to the château. Will you tell her for me?'

346

Charles Vincent went on to say that Henri Massine had been murdered in Bordeaux during the war, by unknown assailants, and that Mireille and her grandmother would be on their way back from Canada as soon as a passage could be found for them.

'They too plan to go straight home,' Charles Vincent told her, 'to Bordeaux.'

'They may not want me to visit them . . .' Leonie's voice trailed into unhappy silence.

'Mademoiselle de Byron.' The notary got to his feet and came round the desk to put a hand gently on her shoulder. He sensed the automatic recoil of the thin body, and knew by it something of what the girl had been through since her arrest. But he did not move away. 'You must know that your sister has been asking for you. She is desperately afraid for you, and I have her strict instructions to find you and arrange for you to be together again.'

'Then you will call me?'

'At Briteau. As soon as I have the date of their arrival. You have my word.'

'And my mother?' She could not bring herself to admit that she was unable to face Zoe until she knew whether Erich was with her in Paris.

'I will tell her you have gone home.'

The brown Daimler trimmed with cream waited for her at the local station, Edith Darnand at the wheel. Marcel Darnand took her arm as she stepped down from the train, and held her tight as they went to the car. She had no luggage, and wore a plain shirtwaister she had found in her wardrobe at the rue Louis. It was very hot for the end of April, and the hands that still gripped the bag Lady Hume had given her were damp with sweat.

Edith kissed her, weeping openly. A man carrying a cardboard suitcase ragged at the edges followed her from the train and touched his beret, murmuring her name. As the car

347

eased its way though the narrow village street children whose faces were new to her stared, while their mothers waved from the doorways, welcoming her back.

'We leave you here, Leonie,' Edith said as they drew up in front of the château steps. 'It is best for you and Violette to be alone, to be quiet together. We are invited for another time. Pierre is here also, did you know?'

As they drove off, Violette's grandson appeared through the stable arch, a slim, wiry figure in the uniform of the army medical corps, and began to run towards her.

'Come, little American.' He drew her arm into his and led her round to the kitchen garden. 'It is my turn to lead you to freedom, eh? But not through the front door, not too grandly. Today it must be as if you had never left us.'

She took deep breaths of the mountain air as they walked, silently recalling how she had tried to remember the way the house was protected by the distant grey hills and the sentinel pines.

Pierre told her that she would find his grandmother quite unchanged. The Germans had requisitioned the house, and she had lived with the Fabris for some months, but once the Germans left the two women descended on the place in a frenzy of cleaning and reorganization, as if to exorcize the old enemy against the day of Leonie's return.

'Grandmère never doubted that you would survive,' he said. 'You are both survivors.'

The mention of Camille prompted Leonie to ask if all was well with Monsieur Fabri, and whether they had got through the harvest successfully the previous year. Pierre told her it had been mediocre, but they were due for a vintage year in '45. Fabri père had already begun to find labour for late summer.

'And Jacques?' She made it sound a casual enquiry.

Pierre shrugged, thin lips pursed in a line of disapproval. 'Nothing. We may never hear now.'

They walked side by side through Violette's garden, between neat rows of newly planted flowers and the pale green of young vegetables in the dark, freshly dug soil. At the kitchen door Leonie found that she was trembling, and knelt to take a sprig of rosemary from the bush that grew by the scrubbed stone step, crushing it between her fingers.

'For remembrance,' Pierre said softly, and she looked up into the yellow, sardonic eyes to find that they were filled with tears.

Leonie walked through the silent, sunlit rooms looking for Violette, and as she reached the first floor and the doors to her father's suite she was in time to see Violette appear at the far end of the gallery.

'*Mon dieu*, Mademoiselle Leonie!' Violette stood still, arms outstretched, as Leonie ran to her. 'I knew you would come back! Welcome! The house is ready for you, and those *sales Boches* have gone for good.'

'There are flowers everywhere – it's beautiful – thank you.' Leonie kissed her on both cheeks, noticing that in spite of what Pierre had told her Violette had a sad, pinched look, and her strong shoulders were slightly bowed.

'You are too thin – but you are well – I see that you are well.' Violette held her at arm's length.

'My hair –' It was the first time Leonie had felt the need to refer to the change in her appearance, and she brushed the short white hair back from her forehead with a nervous gesture that had recently become a habit.

'Very *chic* – and don't forget that plenty of women who did not fight for France have had their heads shaved! Yours is a banner of honour. Now –'

She looked over her shoulder towards the door at the end of the gallery which led to Leonie's old rooms.

'Is that where you were?' Leonie read her thoughts.

'They are clean, and they are empty. You need to forget what happened in those rooms, my child.'

'Perhaps.'

The dinner party which Violette prepared in celebration of

Leonie and Pierre's return was a formal affair. Leonie sat in her father's old place at the head of the table, the curé Yves Pascal at her right hand, Pierre on her left. The Darnands were the only other guests. It was a gathering of people who had endured the same hardships and held to the same loyalties.

Marcel Darnand was eloquent on the subject of the new threat from the Communists who had dominated certain sections of the local Resistance; Pierre was bitter about the massacres committed by the Germans as they retreated across France. The curé seemed content to let them talk, and occasionally gave Leonie a look of such understanding that she began to relax for the first time since her release from prison. She was with people who knew almost everything that had happened to her, with one man at least who knew that she had killed, and somehow after more than five years of a war for which they had paid with pain and loss they had reassembled at her father's table, and their lives had begun again. The thought that she was alone and might always be alone came and was suppressed. She would find her mother, go to Bordeaux and see Mireille, perhaps dare to wait for Tony in Paris.

Yves Pascal declared the meal a tribute to France and to woman's ingenuity. Food was still rationed, and would be for some time to come, but Violette had produced a regional culinary masterpiece, and they stood to toast her as she sat beaming at them all across the fine Sèvres porcelain and the heavy silver that was the de Byron family heritage.

'Tell me,' Marcel Darnand asked her, 'how did you manage to keep all these treasures from the Germans?'

'The night Mademoiselle Leonie was taken Camille Fabri and I moved everything into her house. For the rest of the war I slept with it under my bed!'

On the Monday morning Leonie shut herself in her father's study and telephoned Charles Vincent. He told her that he was waiting for an exact date of arrival, but Marguerite Massine and her granddaughter should reach Bordeaux at the end of May.

'Good,' Leonie said. 'Will you arrange for me to see them there? Then – perhaps I shall go to Paris in June, briefly. In July I must be back here, to work.'

'So shall I telephone you with the arrangements?'

'And –'

'Was there something else?'

'You have told my mother where I am, Monsieur Vincent?'

'She has known from the day I saw you here.'

'There has been no word from her.'

'Mademoiselle de Byron, if I may advise you? Your mother is deeply hurt by your silence. She does not want to widen the rift between you by making contact before you are ready. Perhaps it is you, now, who must make a move.'

She replaced the receiver, and asked for the number of the salon. As the phone rang she imagined Zoe in her office, where so much had happened. Tony had got his first commission from the company there, she had been launched on her modelling career and for a few, crazy months had found herself a celebrity. Erich had raped her there, and told her that he loved her.

Zoe's voice seemed a thousand miles away. At first Leonie could not speak, and Zoe asked, sharply, 'Who is this?'

'Mother.'

'At last! Oh, my God, at last. You're in Paris? Where are you? When can I see you?'

'I'm at Briteau. Are you alone? Is – is Erich with you?'

'Erich died, Leonie. Months ago, in a raid over France. His lawyers found a witness. I'm quite alone.'

'I see. I can get to Paris, Mother, but not until June, and not for long.'

'I'm leaving myself, as soon as the papers are signed. Erich left me everything – can you beat it?'

'I always thought maybe he had a wife and family hidden

away somewhere.' She regretted it the moment she had spoken, but it was out of reaction: relief that Erich's death meant she need not be afraid that Zoe would be hurt by what he had done. It freed her to meet her mother, to start again. And the fact that Erich had left everything to Zoe meant that there were no embarrassing, untidy traces of what had happened, of the love he claimed to feel for her.

'It will take a month, maybe more,' Zoe was saying. 'Then I must get back to Maddie. Don't leave it too long. I don't think I can wait much longer to see you, darling.'

'I have to wait for a date to see my sister.'

'Ah yes. Paul's marriage.'

'I'll be in Paris by the end of the month, I promise. We can talk about things then.'

'I love you, baby. Nothing's changed.' Zoe's voice was subdued, controlled.

'*Au revoir*, Mother.' Leonie put down the phone, and found herself wishing she had told her mother that she returned her love.

The Germans signed the final surrender, marking the end of the war in Europe, on 7 May. Violette celebrated by serving champagne with their breakfast, and an hour later Charles Vincent rang with the news that Mireille would be able to see Leonie in Bordeaux on the last day of the month. Making a note of the day she must travel, Leonie calculated that she could be in Paris with a whole week in which to settle things before the date on which she and Tony had once planned to meet, a month and a day after the end of the war. They had made the promise in the room where she sat, before Tony knew the truth. He had been silent ever since.

On the night before her departure for Bordeaux, she called at the Fabri house to make plans for her return to help with the summer work in the vineyards. She wanted to be back for

352

July, when they would have to begin to work hard. In her heart she needed to plan for it, believing that Tony would not keep their tryst in Paris, and that she would come straight back to Briteau and fling herself into the life she had chosen, without him.

She knocked twice on the white wooden door of the courtyard entrance to Camille's large kitchen, hearing voices inside as she waited. After a while Camille herself opened the door, smiling welcome. 'You have arrived "*au moment juste*", Mademoiselle Leonie!'

The lamps were already lit in the warm, low-ceilinged room, and a group of men in blue overalls and berets sat smoking at the centre table. As Leonie entered, Fabri père, in his place at the head of the assembly, paused in the act of filling a row of glasses from a giant carafe.

There was a silence. Then at the far end of the table a man got to his feet, his cadaver face still in the shadows.

'You see?' Camille led her forward into the lamplight with a shaking hand. 'He is back. He is safe.'

Jacques put out his cigarette and crossed the room to where Leonie stood. She thought that he had the look of a man pursued by demons.

He shook hands, a formal gesture for the others' eyes, then made her take the chair beside him, nodding to his father that she would drink with them. He lit another cigarette, eyeing her through the smoke, and she saw that the arrogance of the early days had been superseded by a piercing fanaticism. He drank quickly, Camille watching him with anxious eyes. Then he began to talk, the macho-silence she remembered now drowned in a torrent of excited speech.

His captive audience drank steadily as he asked them if they had not noticed that the returning government had already thrown out the people who had really saved France? The Resistance fighters had no say in local replanning in places where if it had not been for them there would be no communities left. The good socialists who had quickly got

353

down to putting some order back into the small towns had been ousted. De Gaulle had waited all these years, safe in England, for just this moment. A political soldier was a dangerous animal.

'France's only hope is Communism; you will see it sooner or later,' he said to the whole table, then turned to Leonie, 'and you, mademoiselle, who have given so much to France, must now give your land. It is the only way. We will work for the land – we will not work for you.'

'Enough!' Jacques's father thumped the table with a ferocity that made Camille cross herself, and the others began to shift uneasily in their chairs, preparing to leave.

'Please,' Leonie said. 'I understand. I know what it has been like for your son. I know very well.'

'They tell me –' Jacques looked at her keenly.

'It is over, Jacques, whatever you have been told. I am back where I belong. And I do not give my father's land away when it has been so dearly bought. We *all* need this place; we need to work.'

'My son does not plan to work with us this summer, Mademoiselle de Byron,' Fabri père growled.

'I will tell her myself, Father,' Jacques broke in. He got up, and stood waiting for Leonie to move.

'I came to tell you that I am going away for a few days. When I come back I shall be free for serious work – *le grand travail*, Monsieur Fabri. And I will have news of Mireille.'

'Ah, la petite.' Jacques smiled for the first time. 'I shall walk to the house with you, and you will tell me all that has happened to our little sister of so long ago.'

On the way back to the château he talked incessantly: of his plans to go to Moscow as soon as his orders came through, of his resolve to return to France and work for the Party as soon as he felt properly equipped to do so; the current factions in local and central government, the retributions Frenchmen were laying at each other's doors with total lack of discrimination, made a bad climate for reform. He would study, and bide his time.

'I think you studied a great deal while you were away,' she said.

'I worked, worked until I almost died, as did my comrades. We had no books. But we had our minds. And I learned from the Poles. You will see – one day they will invite in a new regime, and from within it they will find a welcome. France, too; our time will come.'

She felt exhausted by him, and yet they had spent less than an hour in each other's company. The energy and will he had put into their work for the Resistance, egging her on when she would have held back, were absorbed by his fanaticism into a self-consuming, destructive force. She had no answers for him, and knew it would have been useless to argue with him if she had.

'I will still be here, Jacques. I'll always be here, and my father's land will always be my concern; you know that.'

They turned into the drive, and she stopped, looking up into the drawn, half-crazed face.

'Do you remember when we went to find the eagle's nest?' Her need to reach him, to calm him, was so deep and yet so hopeless that she was unaware that she had placed her hands in his. *We were lovers*, she thought, then as Jacques's hands tightened on hers and he drew her to him she thought of Tony. Her body stiffened, an involuntary holding back, only to find as she stepped into Jacques's arms that she was in the embrace of a man who no longer felt sexual love.

'You always were a brave little American,' he said. 'When I and my kind return to France you will fight us bravely too, eh?'

They moved apart, and Jacques bent his head and kissed her on the forehead. She walked on towards the house, knowing that he had already turned away.

His pace quickened as he reached the road, remembering the girl who had walked towards him in the dawn in an absurd red hat, with the long, uncertain stride of a young thoroughbred.

*

Marguerite Massine put the finishing touches to her smooth ash-blonde page-boy hairdo and chose a lipstick from the array of make-up on her dressing-table. The face reflected in the mirror was that of a self-confident North American matron of uncertain years. The pallid languor that had been her trademark during the years of marriage to Henri Massine had gone, to be replaced by a cool poise. Life in Canada had saved her from herself, from her husband's domination and from her grief. Being responsible for Mireille, and answerable to no one but herself if she made mistakes, had given her a new lease of life. The news of her husband's murder had shaken her at first, but she had learned to see it as part of a war which he had denied her. By sending her and their grandchild to safety he had shown her he had no faith in her ability to stay and endure. Now, after a week at the house in Bordeaux, she had begun to realize that he had died because he deserved to. Why else would two different groups of patriots claim his assassination for their own?

She went down to the drawing-room, and told Mireille she was ready for the visit to their lawyers. Raymond brought the car round to the front of the house, and for the hundredth time since Madame Massine's return found himself astonished by the change in her. He watched her in the mirror as they drove into the city, and saw a serenity that made her as beautiful as he remembered her daughter had been.

That evening she sent for Raymond again, and told him that she was selling the house and returning to the south. She would buy a place in Provence, perhaps, close to her family. Her granddaughter was to go to Paris to complete her studies in medicine at the Sorbonne.

'You understand, Raymond? Since my husband's death, here in this house, nothing can be the same.'

'It is perfectly understandable, madame. And I can only thank you for keeping me in work even when Monsieur Massine had – had died.' He remembered the awkward way the knife had stuck in his employer's broad back, and the unexpected amount of blood.

'Someone had to look after the house. The Germans would have wrecked it before they left had you not been here, I'm sure. And you will be rewarded, Raymond. Tell me, what are your plans?'

He told her that he intended to marry. A widow who lived in the old quarter. He would always work with cars, of course, and had it in mind to open a small garage, for the sale and maintenance of only the most exclusive makes.

'Then I am sure I can help,' Marguerite said. 'My husband would have wished it, naturally. Now, before I forget, I want you to meet a young lady at the station tomorrow . . . she and my granddaughter will lunch together in town.'

The tall fair-haired girl in soft white angora sweater and long red tartan bobby-soxer skirt turned every male head at the station. Mireille waited for Leonie's train quite aware of the sensation her appearance caused. The years in Canada had not changed her inwardly, but the American image had been stamped, if only temporarily, on the way she dressed, danced, talked and, especially, dated.

Watching the two sisters walk back to the car together, arms round each other's waists, Raymond had his reward for the murder of Henri Massine. He had never been able to be sure that Leonie de Byron had survived all that his employer and the *Milicien* had tried to do to her, and he saw now that they had put her through hell between them, and that she had survived – with a strange, new beauty.

He left the sisters at the hotel where Leonie was to rest before the night train to Paris. They lunched in the restaurant, neither of them able to eat much, Mireille talking endlessly while Leonie listened. Finally the older girl broke in on a description of a surprise party given for Mireille before she left Canada. 'How about the boy from school that summer?'

357

Mireille coloured. 'He's at the Sorbonne – or will be. We're finishing our medical studies together.'

When Mireille told her that her grandmother was selling the house and moving to Provence, Leonie asked where she would live. 'I thought you'd want to be at Briteau. You know it's your home.'

'That's what I'd like, one day. But I want to finish my degree, and then I'll have to intern somewhere. It really ought to be Paris. I've lost so much time.'

Leonie told her about the apartment in the rue Louis. 'Please, it's yours. We can forget who owns what, you and I, can't we? Papa wanted it that way.'

'But a *whole* apartment?' Mireille's eyes shone. 'I thought I'd be living in a fifth-floor room on the Left Bank. That's where Michel is now . . .'

'Michel?'

'The boy from school.'

'Well, you'd better write to Michel and offer him a room. It'll all be quite proper. The concierge is a terror. And I'll stay from time to time, if that's OK.'

'But this summer . . .' Mireille hesitated. 'I had hoped that I'd get to Briteau for *le grand travail*. Grandpère never let me work with you all. Do you remember that English tutor? He was such fun, but he made me work so hard.'

'Yes, I remember him.' Leonie smiled. 'Maybe he'd like to come back too, for the harvest.'

'And do you remember the caged birds? And Papa? He was with us that day.' She swallowed hard, and Leonie touched her hand across the table.

'Let's go down to the river, after lunch,' she said. 'But I hear everything's badly damaged. Does it upset you?'

'The windows in St Michel were destroyed. The whole city's changed, Leonie, and my life with it. No, it doesn't upset me. Except that I wish I'd shared it all with you, and not run away.'

'I wanted to run myself, many times,' Leonie confessed. 'Some of us did – but not you. Have you heard anything of

Lise Verdier since you got back?'

Mireille pulled a face. 'Her father's lost everything, and she's going to have to work for a living. From what Grandmère tells me she's lucky she wasn't dragged through the streets and her head shaved.'

Leonie imagined that having to work would be the worst punishment Lise Verdier could be asked to endure. She was sure to find someone to keep her, when things had calmed down and the collaboratrices had all been rounded up. The Lise Verdiers of this world always did.

She telephoned Zoe the moment she arrived at the rue Louis. Jeannine had kept the apartment in perfect order since Berthe's death; the telephone was one of the few that still worked in Paris, and the rooms were a haven of cool shadows, blinds drawn against the early June sunshine.

She suggested that Zoe come to the apartment for their meeting, and began to give directions. She could never have faced her mother in the office at the salon.

'I know the place,' Zoe said. 'After lunch. You'll need to rest.'

Leonie spent the morning exploring the rooms, finding that nothing had changed since the two years she had spent at the Collège Madeleine. In her bedroom the pillows were plumped as they had always been, and the white lace coverlet smoothed tightly down.

As she unpacked her small suitcase she thought of the clothes she had worn when she worked for Caresse. Zoe would expect to find her in something to suit the occasion of their reunion. The only formal dress she had with her was the black Worth. She had packed it as if it were some kind of talisman against the black past.

She tried it on hurriedly, and saw at once in the cheval mirror that she was still far too thin – the dress hung loosely, but the exquisite cut could not be hidden. She found a wide silver belt and some high-heeled shoes in the depths of her

359

wardrobe, and was tightening the belt when the doorbell rang, giving her no time to change back into her day clothes.

Zoe did not see the dress, or her skeleton thinness, or the outmoded shoes. She saw only her daughter's fine eyes, and the white hair framing the strong face. They embraced for a long moment, both in tears, unable to speak.

'I've prepared some tea,' Leonie said at last, her voice trembling.

'That's so civilized, baby,' Zoe said. 'Just what we need. May I tidy up first? Do you mind?'

The door of Leonie's bedroom was still open, and she followed Zoe in, apologizing for the half-unpacked suitcase and the clothes strewn across the bed.

Zoe walked to the window and looked down into the courtyard. 'It's such a lovely day for us, isn't it?' She turned round. 'And you don't ever have to apologize for this room. It is here that your father and I began to love each other. Maybe that's why you feel you belong?'

'Tante Berthe told me you loved him, and he you. Other people – Papa – have told me it was real. I'm glad.'

'Glad enough to come back to the States with me? Maybe not.'

Leonie shook her head. 'I'm committed now, to Briteau. I don't think I could ever live in New York again.'

'Oh, it'll not be New York. I'll see Maddie, of course, and visit with her often. But I'm really going home this time.'

She explained that Erich, and the investment in Caresse, had left her an extremely wealthy woman, and she was interested in opening up new pastures. Airplane travel would mean that America became an oyster for anyone with the vision to start up outside New York. And she had a yen to go back to the midwest, now she could boast of a daughter who was practically a French aristocrat and owned a real château.

It was a brave speech, delivered with conviction. 'You see, there wasn't all that much to brag about last time I went home from Paris,' she finished wistfully. 'We weren't to know what a wonderful baby girl I was going to have.'

Leonie smiled, recognizing all the old Zoe's moods and postures and courage. 'Let's have tea.'

'The bitch of it is' – Zoe stood, touching the white lace coverlet with a gloved hand – 'that I'm already booked on a passage from Southampton. I have to get to England next week, and it means I'll miss your birthday.'

On 8 June, a week before her twenty-fifth birthday, Leonie ate a light lunch alone at the apartment, and walked through the Tuileries gardens, on her way to the Left Bank. It was a freak summer's day, with rain in the air, and she wore a light trenchcoat and low-heeled shoes. Her hair was partly concealed by a silk scarf tied under her chin, as the women wore their scarves at Briteau.

There were unusually few people in the gardens, and a woman walking her dog stared hard as Leonie passed, as if she knew her face. It was not the first time it had happened since her return to Paris, and the people who stared were all of a generation that would remember the face that was Caresse, not knowing that the girl whose photograph was on every magazine cover six years before had become the oddly beautiful, white-haired woman who did not bother with her clothes.

The concierge at the studio had left his three-legged stool out in the rain, and the door to his *loge* was locked. Thinking he must be taking a siesta, Leonie went next door, and found the street entrance open, the house deserted.

She climbed the five flights to Max Heller's room with an easy stride. Her health had improved rapidly in the few weeks at Briteau. But as she stood outside the room, her hand on the door, she began to shake. She leaned her head against the shabby plaster wall, thinking of Max as she had known him when they crossed the Atlantic, and later, as all that was happening in Europe took possession of him. She knocked on the door at last, and there was no answer.

Pushing it open, she stepped into the small room, and found it quite unchanged. Except that the piano was closed.

I did my mourning for you in Fresnes prison, Max, and in Ravensbruck. I fought your war in my own mountains.

She spoke out loud to him, then turned and fled.

As she reached the street she found that the rain had cleared, and the concierge next door had returned to his place in the sun. She made a pretence of wanting to talk, and stayed for a while, then as the sun warmed her she took off her headscarf and shook her hair free. It was at that moment that a tall, fair-haired man in an ex-USAF jacket turned the corner, carrying an artist's folder and a battered suitcase. As he saw Leonie he put down the suitcase and waited as she ran to him, dropping her gloves.

'Now that's what I call punctuality,' said Tony Shaw.